CELLULAR

More than anything else, however, she had to keep him staring directly into her eyes, keep him gloating while he enjoyed the sight of her terror, keep him enthralled and entertained by her helplessness in the face of his overwhelming power.

Until his arm was in exactly the right position—

He gave a small jump when he felt her cut him and then grabbed her wrist, roughly twisting her arm up to see what she had in her hand.

"Ooooh!" He laughed sarcastically and gave her wrist a hard shake to make her drop the shard of glass before he reached for her again.

But almost immediately, his hateful smile faded. She looked down and he followed her gaze to see that there was a river of blood gushing out of his arm onto the dusty floor, some of it splashing on his shoes and pants.

More New Line Novels from Black Flame

FREDDY vs JASON
Stephen Hand

THE BUTTERFLY EFFECT
James Swallow

THE TEXAS CHAINSAW MASSACRE
Stephen Hand

THE TWILIGHT ZONE #1
MEMPHIS • THE POOL GUY
Jay Russell

THE TWILIGHT ZONE #2
UPGRADE • SENSUOUS CINDY
Pat Cadigan

2000 AD Action from Black Flame

ABC Warriors

#1: THE MEDUSA WAR
Pat Mills & Alan Mitchell

Judge Dredd

#1: DREDD vs DEATH
Gordon Rennie

#2: BAD MOON RISING
David Bishop

#3: BLACK ATLANTIC
Simon Jowett & Peter J Evans

Strontium Dog

#1: BAD TIMING
Rebecca Levene

CELLULAR

Novelization by
Pat Cadigan

Story by Larry Cohen

Screenplay by Chris Morgan

A Black Flame Publication
www.blackflame.com

First published in 2004 by BL Publishing, Games Workshop Ltd.,
Willow Road, Nottingham NG7 2WS, UK

Distributed in the US by Simon & Schuster, 1230 Avenue of the
Americas, New York,. NY 10020, USA

10 9 8 7 6 5 4 3 2 1

Copyright © 2004 New Line Cinema. All rights reserved.

Cellular and all related characters, names and indicia are trademarks
and © of New Line Productions, Inc. 2004. All rights reserved.

Black Flame and the Black Flame logo are trademarks of Games
Workshop Ltd., variably registered in the UK and other countries
around the world. All rights reserved.

ISBN 1-84416-104-8

A CIP record for this book is available from the British Library.

Printed in the UK by Bookmarque, Surrey, UK.

No part of this publication may be reproduced, stored in a retrieval
system, or transmitted in any form or by any means, electronic,
mechanical, photocopying, recording or otherwise, without the prior
permission of the publishers.

This is a work of fiction. All the characters and events portrayed in
this book are fictional, and any resemblance to real people or
incidents is purely coincidental.

*This one is for Kim Newman:
talented, good-looking, indispensable
and permanently in my good books.*

PROLOG

Ah, the cellular telephone.

Where do *you* stand on this particular matter? Do you love it? Or do you loathe it? Gotta have it or gotta lose it? Never leave home without it, or leave it at home where it belongs? Sent by God or a tool of Satan?

No, now really, give it some thought: is the cellphone the single greatest development since the advent of green toothpaste, or is it just one more reason to hate technology?

The telephone itself has been generating controversy since its very inception back in the 1870s. Alexander Graham Bell and Elisha Gray were locked in a feverish and frantic race to perfect a mechanical instrument that would be able to transmit the human voice over long distances by means of electricity.

It is a matter of historical fact that the two men dashed to the patent office on the same day, and within mere hours of each other. There seems to be some historical uncertainty, however, as to which man actually got there first. Still, Bell won the race that counted—he completed his paperwork before Gray and so he obtained the patent.

Of course, that wasn't the end of the matter—this being the United States, the results were hotly contested in a major legal battle. Unfortunately for Elisha Gray, he fared no better in court than he had at the patent office and so it was Ma Bell and not Ma Gray that was unleashed on the hitherto-unsuspecting nation.

Bell's original intention had been to increase the efficiency of the telegraph, which was limited by the dot-and-dash of Morse code and the fact that it could only send or receive one message at a time. But the technology for the telegraph was already improving: thirteen years after the first transcontinental telegraph line had been laid, Thomas Edison and George Prescott developed the quadruplex system. Thanks to them, by 1874, two signals could be sent simultaneously on the same line in opposite directions.

British inventor Donald Murray came up with a multiplex system in 1903 that made use of a typewriter keyboard and a receiver. This meant that text could be printed out—a useful development, to be sure, but unfortunately it proved to be too little too late. The Bell, so to speak, had already tolled. The telegraph's days were numbered.

Naturally, Western Union was not best pleased with the continuing popularity of the telephone as the USA's communications device of choice, but there was absolutely nothing they could do about it. Squads of large, muscular men were dispatched to various hotels for the express purpose of persuading the management to rethink its decision to replace the longstanding, reliable telegraph system with the more efficient telephone. They took with them certain simple but effective devices like baseball bats, clubs and other heavy blunt objects for extra emphasis. But they could not succeed in delaying the inevitable. There was no halting the forward march of progress. When it was time for the telephone to take over, it did. That was the proverbial that.

And so it would seem to be with the cellular version of the instrument.

Starting out with roughly the same dimensions (and style) of a house brick, the cellphone quickly shrank to become the petite, stylish, sexy techno-toy owned and loved by just about everyone in the Western world today, from the dedicated gadget lover to the virtual Luddite.

But truth to tell, it's the sheer convenience of the cellphone that makes it far more than a twenty-first century status symbol. Of course, you don't have to take that statement on faith—just ask anyone who has ever tried to find a working payphone in a hurry!

Which is not to say that even the cellphone's strongest advocates enjoy hearing the latest popular ring-tone trill merrily in a darkened movie theater. And there are probably certain ring-tone melodies that even the most fervent champions of free speech with lifetime memberships in the American Civil Liberties Union secretly wish the Supreme Court would declare illegal.

And while we're on the subject, what's number one on your Top Ten List of Cellphone Ring Tones That You Never Want To Hear Again? "The William Tell Overture?" Every single Christmas-themed song ever written with absolutely no exceptions? But *most* especially "Jingle Bell Rock?" Or whatever happens to be number one on the Top Ten Most Downloaded Ring Tones Hit Parade this week?

Well, whether you love the cellular or hate it, most people will tell you that being without one these days is practically the equivalent of being without a phone at all. Even the cellphone's most dedicated opponents would concede that there is nothing worse than being stranded in uncomfortable or even dangerous conditions without the means to call for help.

Ask any parent how important it is to have a fast and reliable way for someone to get in touch with them in case of an emergency.

Admit it: it actually doesn't matter how many of the cellphone's less attractive features you can name. The obnoxious and/or badly timed ring tones, or the rude people who feel the need to bellow conversations no one else wants to hear; they are mere irritations. Mere annoyances. And even though we may find ourselves incensed, exasperated, infuriated and driven to the point of madness by them, the truth is, they all have to be listed under the heading of *nuisance* rather than *hazard*. Except under the most unusual and extreme circumstances.

It is no exaggeration to say that the single greatest advantage of the cellphone—being able to contact anyone, anytime, anywhere—is that it could actually save someone's life. Literally. It might even be the life of someone you know, someone who is very important to you.

Or it could quite possibly be your own.

ONE

Every clear morning, the lucky residents of a certain stretch of charming Craftsman bungalows on the outskirts of Brentwood (total population twenty-three thousand, three hundred, as of the first census of the twenty-first century) are treated to a spectacular view of the gorgeous San Gabriel Mountains, as well as the bright angles and shapes that make up the skyline of downtown Los Angeles.

The views weren't the only things that Jessica Martin loved about having a home there.

As the wife of a realtor, Jessica knew that most if not all of her husband's colleagues felt that those panoramas had more than a little to do with closing the sales on at least half the houses in the area. Personally, she felt that while the view couldn't be completely discounted as a contributing factor, there was a great deal more at work here than fabulous scenery.

After all, Southern California was full of great scenery and most of it was only a few minutes' drive from any given location. She knew that from firsthand color experience. For Jessica, it was having enough space for a decent-sized garden in a stable, quiet neighborhood. All the kids played outside routinely—that is, when their parents could pry them away from their video games. For Jessica that was the real attraction, and it was nowhere near as easy to find as pretty mountains. Feeling good and comfortable in her surroundings made her value her home in ways that had nothing to do with spreadsheets or property tax. That was the real deal.

These factors helped relieve the homesickness she still felt from time to time for the Deep South where she had grown up. Moving away from everything and everyone she had ever known and loved had been one of the hardest things she had ever had to do. Especially with so many of her friends and relatives telling her how much harder she was going to find living "Out There," and that practically all the people north of the Mason-Dixon Line weren't nearly as friendly.

According to the local down-home wisdom, the crime-ridden cities were unhappy, scary and dirty, filled with unhappy, scared and dirty people who drank too much and had to eat that Prozac stuff by the handful just so they could stand living in a place where, at any moment, a homicidal maniac might kill them and kidnap their children.

And things were no better in the supposedly less-dangerous suburbs. There was nothing in them except a whole lot of soulless cardboard, cookie-cutter houses inhabited by people who may not have been scared or dirty, but were still so unhappy that they watched too much television and had to eat that Prozac stuff by the handful just so they could stand living in a place with no sidewalks and hardly any trees.

California was the worst of all. It was full of all the flakes and nuts and downright psychos they didn't have room for in the other cities, and if that wasn't bad enough, the whole sorry lot of them were driving around those awful freeways in stolen cars, looking for innocent people to terrorize.

Well, all right, an awful lot of what she had been told was nothing more than friends teasing the bejesus out of her. Except for the stuff about California, which had come in all seriousness from her Great-Aunt Sue Della. Aunt Sudy was visiting Los Angeles when Charles Manson and his "family" were on trial for murder and she had never quite recovered from the experience. Jessica hadn't let any of it bother her for a moment.

Of course, she couldn't help feeling a certain amount of apprehension. After all, it was no small thing to uproot herself and start a new life with Craig in unfamiliar surroundings, far away from everything she was used to. Any nervousness she felt was only normal and she'd known it. At the same time, she had been eager to do something fresh and different, to have new experiences with new people in new places.

Her high school gymnastics teacher, Miz Peach, had encouraged Jessica's innate sense of adventure.

Get yourself goin', girl, and see what the big old wide world has to offer you, Miz Peach would tell her. Don't be afraid of the world—get right out there in the thick of things and get to know it.

To Jessica's mind, being a science teacher was a great way to do just that. Science was the way she could get to know the world—it always had been, which was why she loved the subject so much. And teaching helped her to get to know the people out there.

Since she and Craig had settled here with their son, Ricky, she knew many of the neighboring families, at least by sight, and if she didn't know them, Craig probably did. There was nothing like being married to an area realtor for being able to have your finger on the pulse of your own community. There were other advantages as well, not least the fact that Craig's job had made it possible for them to find their beautiful house in the first place.

Padding downstairs to the kitchen this morning, however, Jessica was still just a little too sleepy to contemplate the nature of her existence or think about how the garden she loved so much was flourishing. She was too groggy even to reach down and stroke the dense, comforting fur of the golden retriever that stuck close to her side at every step, bumping against her leg with unflagging doggy devotion and love.

She and Craig had bought the dog for Ricky, who had been overjoyed when the pup had arrived. But while boy and dog were inseparable companions, especially from Friday afternoon to Sunday evening, the dog had been quick to associate her with regular meals. By his canine reckoning that meant that every morning he was hers and hers alone.

She didn't mind at all. If anyone had actually asked Jessica Martin about her life, in whole or in part, she wouldn't have had to think about the answer. She would have said that she wouldn't have had things any other way; that she was exactly where she wanted to be with the people she wanted to be with. But since no one had ever asked, this wasn't something that crossed her conscious mind.

Nor did she ever give a thought to what she would do if things should ever change. Emergencies of just about every kind were covered—they had all the necessary insurance and the smoke detectors were all in place and working perfectly. Craig had even insisted on taking security to the max by installing a sophisticated burglar alarm system.

That had made her think of the way everyone had teased her back home, and she had told Craig that she felt an alarm system was taking this security thing just a little bit too far. Living in a place like Brentwood, she really couldn't see it as anything other than a completely unnecessary expense.

But Craig had been adamant and she had let him have his way. He wasn't one of those real bossy, chest-thumping husbands, and there weren't a whole lot of things he had ever gotten so insistent about. Jessica had decided that if he really felt they needed that extra security, she would oblige him.

The only condition she had insisted on was that the system remain off whenever there was someone at home—otherwise, they were bound to have alarm bells going off by accident all the time, which was something the police were none too happy about. They were starting to fine people for false alarms regardless of the circumstances, and they weren't little fines, either. Better just to activate the system when the house was empty and leave it off when any or all of them were at home. There was always the panic button on the front of the wall unit if they needed it.

At the moment, the only thing she needed was a cup of coffee and enough quiet time to drink it so she could wake up. Yawning, she grabbed a mug from the drainer on the sink and shuffled over to the coffeemaker to see what Craig had brewed up for her this morning.

Very good stuff, she thought, smiling at the cup and stroking the dog's head absently. It was something new from one of those gourmet stores her husband was so fond of. He loved trying new varieties and blends—the more exotic the better.

The only thing he absolutely refused to touch was chicory, which was really too bad, since she loved it. Miz Peach had introduced her to chicory coffee back in her competition days. Like most people in her family, Jessica had been a coffee drinker since junior high, something that would have scandalized most of her other teachers if they had known. But not Miz Peach, who believed in the benefits of indulging in what she called a little bit of sin. Sharing this particular secret vice had been only one of the many elements that had made up their special bond.

But for Craig, chicory just wasn't happening. Never had, and never would. There was something about the smell that put him off completely, which was a genuine mystery to Jessica. To her it simply smelled like coffee. Her husband's nose told him otherwise, however. So every time she craved a little taste of home, she had to wait till he was out of the house and then make sure everything was thoroughly washed up and clean, and the kitchen aired out before he got back.

Men, she thought. Even wonderful men like her husband could be such great big ole' babies.

"Buenos dias, Miss Jessica," said a friendly voice.

She looked up to see her housekeeper coming in with a basket of laundry. She toasted her with her coffee cup.

"Buenos dias, Rosario," she replied. "Como esta?"

As always, her Southern accent made Rosario break into a broad smile, which made Jessica smile in turn. She had been away from home for a long time now and to her own ear, her accent had diminished quite a bit. Unless she was highly emotional about something or attempting to speak a language other than English—then it seemed like her drawl would come back with twice the force. Buenos dias, y'all. Como estas, ya hear?

"Bien, bien," Rosario said, beaming at her to let her know that her Spanish was coming along nicely. "Miss Jessica, there was a telephone call while you were in the shower. I think they left a message." She made a small motion with one hand and Jessica turned to look at the answering machine at the other end of the counter, just under the wall-phone.

She raised her eyebrows in mild concern at the blinking message light. That was how sleepy she had been this morning, she thought. Dragging herself into the kitchen, she had been so out of it, she hadn't seen it. No one ever called this early. No one they knew, anyway; she would have staked her sleepy ole' life on that.

It certainly couldn't have been telemarketers, not at this hour—telemarketers usually didn't start dialing for at least another thirty minutes on average. Jessica liked to think that it was because they wanted to let people finish their first cup of coffee in peace before they started to bother them. It was the telemarketing industry's small concession to the needs of their target market. And besides, telemarketers weren't in the habit of leaving messages.

At least, she hoped telemarketers weren't leaving messages now.

Maybe it was Ricky's school, she thought suddenly. Instantly, a cold knot of apprehension began to gather in the pit of her stomach. Maybe there was something wrong with him; maybe the office was calling to tell her that her son had fallen ill or that he had been hurt in some way. Or what if he had somehow gone missing—

Steady now, Momma, she told herself in spite of the anxiety running through her like an electric current. Like your daddy always used to tell y'all when the lights went out during a thunderstorm. Let's us not go gettin' all worked up 'less'n we know for sure there's something real that we need to go gettin' all worked up about.

She put down her coffee and went over to the machine. But before she could even touch the play button, the bomb went off.

That was the only thing she thought could have happened: a bomb had exploded just outside the door, blowing fragments of glass and wood inward all over the kitchen. Except she couldn't see any smoke or fire.

Had it actually been an impact of some kind, then? Could a car have gone so wildly out of control that it had somehow driven into her backyard and ploughed into the house? Her brain worked to make sense of it and couldn't. Then she saw the men.

There were five of them, huge and dangerous in body armor and ski masks. They were carrying weapons—automatic weapons, vicious-looking and unmistakably lethal. They looked exactly like terrorists out of news footage or a movie.

But in Brentwood? In her kitchen?

No, that was patently impossible. Either she was dreaming or this had to be the world's most terrible mistake. If this was a dream, then she had to wake up right now, and if it wasn't, she had to make these men understand what a terrible mistake they were all making. Right now, before someone got hurt. But the kitchen was a whirlwind of noise and confusion. It was as if the house and everything in it were spinning rapidly in one direction while she was spinning just as rapidly in the other.

She caught sight of the dog leaping up with a vicious growl she had never heard come out of him before. His soft doggy devotion had suddenly been replaced by instinctive canine outrage at the threat and the violation of his territory. From goofy golden retriever to attack dog in a split second—Craig would never believe it unless he saw it on video, and maybe not even then, Jessica thought giddily. They'd have to put up a sign: This House Protected By Sophisticated Alarm System and Goofy Attack Dog.

And then all at once she heard a new noise, not quite as loud as the kitchen door exploding but loud enough to be scary, and she saw the retriever drop in mid-leap with a shocking suddenness, as if a switch inside him had flipped to off. It took her almost a full second of horrified staring at the furry, motionless heap lying on the floor in front of her before she finally understood that one of these big, dangerous men who didn't belong in her kitchen had actually shot Ricky's pet.

Even as her mind was telling her that this could not be happening, she was looking for Rosario so she could tell her to run, to get away and get help. But her housekeeper was already on the move. She was heading for the alarm system and the panic button as fast as she could go.

"Get away from there!" a man roared and Jessica froze, unable to make a sound. "Don't touch that!"

Jessica felt as if the voice were drilling right through her, penetrating all the way to her bones and rooting her to the spot. But it had no effect on Rosario, who gave no sign that she had even heard it, refusing to stop for any reason. Jessica could practically feel the strain of her effort as she propelled herself at the panic button.

No, she thought, trying to will her housekeeper to forget all about the stupid alarm on the wall and its stupid panic button, forget it all, forget everything and just go, burst out the front door screaming and run for her life, for both their lives, for all their lives—

Another blast shattered the air and filled it with a scorched, metallic odor (like fireworks, Jessica thought dazedly). This one was much louder than the shot that had taken down Ricky's dog and Jessica saw Rosario fall heavily to the floor several feet short of the alarm unit, spraying both the box and the wall around it with blood and small pieces of flesh.

Jessica felt her knees start to buckle as an intense wave of dizziness swept through her. The security unit Craig had said they couldn't live without seemed to float before her eyes like a cork on an ocean wave; some strange confluence of circumstance and natural law had caused the splatter of blood and gore to miss the panic button completely, leaving it untouched and unstained. It was almost as if the man who had shot Rosario had meant to do it that way, just to make absolutely sure Jessica got the exact, unambiguous message: Don't touch that.

Patches of darkness began to swim through Jessica's vision and she had the distinct and overwhelmingly physical sensation of everything inside of her beginning to shut down or go away. Her mind and body were parting company. Before she could even register this fully, however, a rough hand clamped on her arm, squeezing it like a vice, and spinning her around.

The black ski mask filled her vision so there was nothing else to see.

"Where is it?"

That voice. That was the voice that had killed her housekeeper Rosario. A gun had done the actual physical damage but what had really been the death of the woman had been that voice. And Jessica knew with no uncertainty whatsoever that that voice would be the death of her as well—no appeal and no reprieve.

Except that such a thing was impossible. This was her home and her home was not a place where anything even remotely like this could occur.

All at once, she felt as if she were caught in a strange, endless moment where she was straddling two different realities: in one, this man would kill her, and in the other, he would realize he was in the wrong house and leave.

"Where is what?" she said finally.

The answer came out as a low and lethal growl: "Wrong answer."

Jessica saw him raise his hand, saw the gun he was holding and knew which reality she had landed in. All feeling of her surroundings dropped away from her and she waited for the blast to end it.

But there was no blast to hear.

She heard nothing, nothing at all, neither the impact of metal on flesh when he hit her or his command to the men to search the house as she fell unconscious. And she also didn't hear the sound of them tearing her life to pieces as she was carried out of the house.

The era of recreational vehicles has brought about the more or less total eclipse of the humble van. Vans attract far less notice than most cars, and in the presence of the shiny SUVs that are favored by soccer moms, car poolers and weekend warriors everywhere, they go totally unnoticed.

Nowhere is this truer than on the many highways, routes and streets of the greater Los Angeles area, where driving is a sacrament and the vehicle is a testimony as to the driver's state of grace.

In that spirit, most people habitually avert their gaze at the sight of someone lacking in the latter—out of sight, out of mind. Consequently, a drab old black Ford van like the one traveling along a quiet back road in the hills might as well have been invisible. Jessica Martin's Porsche Cayenne would not have been following closely behind it if there had been even the slightest chance that anyone else would have been around to take notice of it.

But there was no one. Remote areas of the Hollywood Hills can be reached in a matter of minutes. It's an easy matter for people to disappear if they should happen to feel a burning desire to get away from it all.

Or if someone else has a burning desire to take them away from it all whether they want to go or not.

The Ford van and the Porsche Cayenne arrived at their destination without meeting any other vehicles in either direction. But even if there had been anyone else to see them as they turned off the road onto a dirt driveway, they would undoubtedly have passed unobserved.

There were lots of houses tucked away in the hills, none of them visible from the road. The people who lived in them liked their privacy, and privacy was the one thing that everyone would agree was becoming increasingly difficult to obtain and even harder to keep. Those who wanted to have their privacy respected knew that they had to respect their neighbors' privacy in turn. The sight of a workman's van or an owner's SUV coming in or going was not the kind of thing that anyone in the area would have thought of as remarkable, because doing so would have been rudely intrusive.

Jessica could smell the attic before they had even dumped her on the floor—it was reeking with dust, mildew and mold, signifying decades of uninterrupted neglect. The stench was worse than the heavy service-station odor in the van.

Almost choking, she clawed the blindfold away from her eyes with her bound hands. She found herself in a place that looked every bit as bad as it smelled.

In the semi-darkness she saw vague, shapeless shadows among roof beams and away in the corners. A storm of dust clots and cobwebs had been thrown into the stale air by her sudden arrival.

Blinking against the sting in her eyes, Jessica took another look around. She flinched when she saw him standing across the room by the open door. The man with *that* voice.

She knew that it could not have been anyone else. What little illumination there was in the room came from the window he was standing next to. The light spilled across his lower body and left his face mostly in darkness, so that the only thing she could discern about his features was that he was no longer wearing the ski mask.

But there was absolutely no doubt in her mind as to who he was. It was clear from the way he held himself.

"Wh..."

Her voice died in her throat. She wet her lips, swallowed against the dust and the smell and the fear and tried again.

"What do you want?" she asked him.

There was no answer, and no answer, and no answer, until Jessica thought she was going to scream. She waited; trying to brace herself for something she couldn't actually imagine and wondered if he could see how badly she was trembling.

Was that actually what he wanted: to see her trembling? And if it were, would he think she was trembling enough, or did he want to see her even more frightened?

Suddenly, for no reason, he turned and left.

Maybe he thought she was scared enough for the time being, she thought absurdly as her breath came out in a rush. It stirred up another indoor dust storm that did nothing to relieve the musty smell or the stinging in her eyes, but for the moment, she didn't care. She had lived through the last few minutes, and under the circumstances that equated with climbing Mount Everest.

But then, before she could even begin to wonder how she was going to survive the next few minutes, he came back.

This time he made a point of moving into the light so that she was able to see his stony face and soulless eyes with perfect clarity. She had thought that his voice was the worst thing about him and now she knew that she would never, ever forget those eyes. Somehow they were even more horrible now that he wasn't wearing the ski mask. And in his hands there was no longer a gun, but a sledgehammer.

It was a big sledgehammer, huge, the hugest thing she had ever seen. Even worse, it was actually getting bigger while she watched. It grew before her eyes as he came across the room toward her, his intentions clear.

Apparently she hadn't been frightened enough after all, she thought, and now he was going to punish her for it. There was no escape, nowhere to run and nothing she could do. But she heard herself pleading with him anyway, pleading and pleading in a very small voice, a voice that was as small as the sledgehammer was big.

"No, wait..."

He was hauling back now, getting ready to swing. Now her voice should have been too small to hear but she could still hear it.

"No! Please!"

The impact made the entire house shake. Well, perhaps not the entire house, but certainly the entire attic, Jessica thought dazedly. And somehow it went on shaking.

Then she wondered how she could possibly think at all. Hadn't the man just bashed her brains out with a sledgehammer?

The last thing she had seen before squeezing her eyes shut and covering her face with her hands was the sight of the metal head sweeping through the dirty air towards her skull.

Slowly, she took her hands away from her face. She raised her head and opened her eyes.

There were fragments on the floor all around her but amazingly, unbelievably, not of her skull.

She was looking at bits of plastic and wire and whatnot from the old-fashioned rotary dial telephone that had been hanging just slightly above her head on a wooden beam.

Jessica was still trying to come to terms with the fact that she was still alive when the man turned his back and stomped away across the attic. He didn't even bother to look back and see if she was suitably terrified. He simply left her there alone in the dust and the dark, slamming the door behind him with enough force to make the whole attic shake again. And just as before, it went on shaking.

After some time, Jessica realized that it was not the attic that continued to shake, it was her. She was trembling like mad as she sat on the floor in the musty darkness, and she was weeping as well. The feeling of tears running steadily down her dirty, bruised face suddenly became too much for her. There was a sensation of something giving way inside her and she broke down.

"What... the hell... is happening?" she sobbed into the darkness.

The darkness swallowed up her words.

TWO

There are a million and one things to do on the Santa Monica pier and all of them are designed to entertain those who want to do something but don't feel like doing anything in particular.

For almost a hundred years, the pier has been the perfect place for killing time rather than passing it. In fact, for those on the pier it often felt like time wasn't actually passing at all. It was more like this was where reality went on its summer vacation and the vacation had yet to come to an end.

It was an easy illusion to succumb to. More than one formerly young pier habitué had had the unfortunate and quite dismaying shock to discover that what had started out as a leisurely stroll in the sunshine had somehow turned into an extended period of inactivity. Meanwhile the rest of the world, unable to wait, had simply gone on without them.

Despite appearances to the contrary, Ryan Hewitt was well aware of how a person could get sucked into this sort of thing and he had absolutely no intention of letting it happen to him. Not if he had anything to do about it.

For some indefinite period of time now, he had gradually been losing his taste for just hanging out, on the pier or anywhere else. This was a feeling that had been particularly exacerbated by certain recent, less than encouraging developments in his life. They were not the kind of developments that he really wanted to dwell on but at the same time, he couldn't get them out of his mind.

Ryan could not bring himself to admit even to himself that he didn't actually *want* to get them out of his mind, no matter how painful they were to think about. Because if he actually did stop thinking about them, he would also have to stop thinking about Chloe. And the idea of not thinking about Chloe was just as painful as thinking about her all the time. Maybe even more so.

Of course, coming out to the pier with good old Chad certainly wasn't going to help, and Ryan knew it. He had known it when he'd let good old Chad talk him into it. He had known full well that he was only pretending that the fresh air, sunshine, the general carefree party atmosphere, the rides, crowds and the vendors and all that shit would cheer him up and let him forget, at least temporarily, everything that was bothering him.

As good an idea as it may have seemed on the surface, there had been a flaw in it. It was the only flaw, but it was a biggie: the pier was what was bothering him.

Well, it was not necessarily the pier itself but his having spent so much time hanging out there already. Most of the other people around him were no doubt there to enjoy a little break in routine. But for him and Chad, the pier *was* routine. And all along, Ryan had known deep down, even before things had blown up with Chloe that for him to spend most of his waking life roaming aimlessly up and down the pier really wasn't a good thing.

Chad being the good old Chad that he had always been would have given him a lengthy and vehement argument to the contrary, and every sentence would have been punctuated by the word "dude." As far as Ryan's good old best friend was concerned, the pier was complete and indisputable proof that human beings were party dudes and they had been put on this earth to party with all the other party dudes. Ergo (the only Latin word good old Chad knew, even though he didn't actually know it was Latin), there was no way that any roaming they did could possibly be called aimless. *Dude*.

Now, as he and good old Chad stood in the videogame arcade together, it occurred to Ryan not for the first time that life would be a lot simpler if he shared his friend's lighthearted, carefree perspective. But that just was not going to happen for a number of reasons. The biggest one concerned what good old Chad was doing right now.

It wasn't as if Ryan would have refused to admit that he himself had poured more time and money into the arcade videogame machines than he should have, or than he could reasonably afford. So he wasn't really trying to be critical of his friend on that score. But this was different.

Of course, good old Chad would have disagreed with him about this as well. Good old Chad would have insisted there was nothing wrong with watching other people playing a videogame, especially if the videogame was something as complex and demanding as Soul Surfer, which had defeated both of them more than once.

He would have gone on to point out that the only way to learn at all was to watch how other people did it. So, dude, like, ergo, who better than a couple of expert players? It was just a lucky break that they also happened to be hot babes. The fact that one of them had on a tight-fitting belly-shirt and the other was wearing a bikini just on the sunny side of legal was mega-wonderful not only on aesthetic grounds, but because the lack of extraneous clothing made it easier to study the moves. Dude.

Furthermore, it only made sense to make use of Ryan's Bluetooth cellphone to capture these expert, winning moves as a streaming video that they would be able to study at their leisure.

Or not, Ryan thought, as he looked at Chad and sighed. Judging from the madman grin on his friend's face, good old Chad had long ago forgotten all about making rationalizations and was now enjoying existence in an advanced and exalted state of pure and unabashed horn-dog.

Sensing Ryan's gaze, Chad turned to him and grinned more broadly.

"Dude, this is the single greatest videogame ever made," he said to Ryan in a goofball voice that somehow managed to sound both extremely jacked-up and deeply reverent.

"Okay, dude, you're really creeping me out now," Ryan told him firmly as he tugged on his arm. "You need help. Come on, let's split." As Chad pulled away and started to protest, Ryan plucked the cellphone neatly out of his hands and headed straight for the exit so that his friend had to follow.

The moment they were outside, however, Chad grabbed the phone back from him so he could drool over the playback of the Soul Surfer girls on the little LCD screen. Ryan thought about wresting it away from him again so he could just delete the whole sequence. He then decided that he simply didn't have the energy to put up with the grief Chad was sure to give him about it.

Besides, at the moment he couldn't see a goddamned thing. After the artificial light in the arcade, the sun was so bright it was blinding him. The noise level seemed to be a lot higher as well—it looked to him as if the number of people on the pier had doubled since he and Chad had gone into the arcade. There were definitely lots more beachgoers, pier bums and fishermen around today, and Ryan could have sworn that the tourists outnumbered them by a ratio of at least two to one. The sight of all those people suddenly gave him a strange sort of weary feeling that wasn't really physical.

A crowd of this size meant nothing but good news for the pier vendors, though. Business was booming. At every stall, stand, and pitch, people were buying and selling at top volume.

"Hey, you! Come! I draw you, five dollar! You, short lady—you come over here, I draw you taller!"

Through a break in the masses of people around them, Ryan caught sight of the Vietnamese caricature artist in his usual spot. He was standing on a stool so he could see over the crowd. He'd never paid much attention to the guy, except to admire his tenacity in a vague sort of way. On the pier, artists of all kinds—caricaturists, straight portrait painters, name-on-a-grain-of-rice carvers, even henna tattooists—were a dime a dozen (or a buck a gross, as Chloe would have put it), and the competition among them was actually a lot tougher than it was for other vendors. An awful lot of them came and went in a matter of weeks, or even days.

But this guy just kept on hanging on with industrial-strength stubbornness. It was like he considered outlasting the competition to be his special purpose in life. He never came late and never went home early; Ryan had never even seen him take a break for lunch.

Well, there were things worse than drawing caricatures of tourists that people could dedicate themselves to, Ryan supposed. If the guy was so crazy about turning people into cartoons that he would come to the Santa Monica pier every day for the express purpose of hustling total strangers into giving him money to do it, well, that was his business. And seeing as how his business usually seemed to be pretty damned good, it wasn't like anyone, least of all Ryan, could say the guy was wasting his time.

But late one night several weeks ago, in an effort to find some way to keep himself occupied while he lost sleep over Chloe, he had walked into a restaurant and seen the guy sitting in a booth drinking coffee by the gallon with two friends. While that had not been terribly remarkable, Ryan had been flabbergasted to hear him holding forth on the subject of the life and work of Immanuel Kant. And as if some cosmic force had decided that this alone wouldn't be amazing enough, the little artist had been speaking in an impeccable scholarly tone that Ryan instinctively knew could only have come from an education obtained exclusively in the English boarding-school system. He couldn't look at the man without thinking; I'm onto you, pal, right down to the phony accent.

"You, man in Speedos, I give you big package!" the artist called out. "Come to my booth down pier! Five dollar, draw you long time!"

Ryan watched him climb down from the stool as a tourist stopped in front of him and held up a wad of bills. As phony as it was, the accent was probably what pulled in so many customers.

By contrast, "Good day to you, ladies and gentlemen. If you'll come over here and let me draw an amusing caricature for the not unreasonable sum of five dollars, you'll be helping me to put myself through grad school" probably wouldn't do the job at all.

Of course, the offer of a big package, even in the setting of a cartoon rendering no doubt held a lot of appeal, especially for a tourist with a gym sock in his Speedos.

Ryan felt a sudden and powerful surge of restless irritation. He threw Chad an elbow forceful enough to get a startled yelp out of him. "Dude, give me back my cellphone," he said crossly.

"Wait a minute, okay? I'm right in the middle of emailing the video to my computer," said Chad, keeping his gaze fixed on the tiny LCD screen. "This is one I definitely want to add to my Girls Gone Wild collection."

He went on at some length about his famous and highly beloved Girls Gone Wild video collection, but Ryan wasn't listening. As far as he was concerned, Chad, the cellphone, Vietnamese Kantian philosophy scholars, tourists and everything else in the world had simply ceased to exist in any way, even theoretically.

Only the woman who had just walked by without seeing him was real to Ryan. Only her, and no one else. Only Chloe and that awful, irresistible, aching *pull* in his chest that made him incapable of doing anything except trailing helplessly after her.

All at once, a strong hand grabbed his arm and yanked him back several steps.

"Whoa, whoa! Hold on there, bro!" Chad spoke loudly, close to his ear, as if he needed to wake Ryan from a bad dream.

"But it's Chloe—" Ryan said, trying to pull away from him.

Unmoved, Chad yanked him back again. "I know it's Chloe—"

"I'm just gonna say hi—" Ryan insisted.

"And I'm just gonna stop you," Chad said, talking over him. Ryan continued to struggle but Chad exerted a surprising amount of strength, finally managing to turn him around so he could march him off in the opposite direction. "What the hell is your deal here, anyway? Have some dignity, dude. She dumped you."

Ryan made a painful face. "Right," he said with a low and reluctant edge in his voice. "You're right. And when you're right, you're right. Thanks, man."

"No worries," Chad told him expansively.

They went all of three steps before Chad finally let go of him. As soon as he did, Ryan was off and running to catch up with Chloe.

He had nothing against dignity, he told himself as he pounded down the pier. Dignity was a good thing and he was one hundred per cent in favor of it, no question. In fact, he was pretty sure that when it came to the subject of dignity, he knew a hell of a lot more about it than a guy who would borrow his cellphone to capture a video of a couple of girls playing Soul Surfer.

He would gladly tell Chad and anybody else who happened to ask that as far as he could tell, there was absolutely nothing wrong with dignity. But, like everything else in the world, it didn't mean dog shit without Chloe in his life.

Ryan dodged around an unwieldy family of tourists who couldn't seem to agree on a single direction to take and found that she had suddenly disappeared from sight. He called out, almost in a panic, "Chloe! Chloe!"

At first, he thought she was going to pretend she hadn't heard him and keep walking but finally she turned around. He noticed belatedly and without much interest that she had a friend with her, and that they were both carrying boxes.

As far as Ryan was concerned, it wouldn't have mattered if Chloe had had the *Creature from the Black Lagoon* with her as she carried a burlap sack full of rattlesnakes—she would have looked just as beautiful to him as she always did. He just wished that she had also looked glad to see him.

But at least she didn't look absolutely sickened and repelled by the sight of him, he thought. Maybe that should be some small consolation. Now he just had to make the most of the opportunity he had and not blow it.

For weeks, the only thing he could think about was trying to find some way to see her so he could tell her how wrong his life was without her: how empty the days had been since their break-up and how hard he would try to be a better person if she would just give their relationship another chance.

And now he had gotten his wish—here she was, right in front of him. Chloe was waiting for him to tell her of his sweet promises and dedication towards her, but instead of spitting it out, all he could do was just stand there and stare like the sad dork Chad kept telling him he was.

After an unmeasured period of time that might have been a hundred years or only a few seconds, Chloe gave him a small, awkward nod as if she didn't remember him very well. "Ryan." Her eyes flicked to his right. "Chad."

"Chloe," said Chad, mimicking her polite tone before turning to the woman standing next to her. "Friend with the nipples."

God, he just wasn't going to get a break today, Ryan thought, awash with despair. Why couldn't the earth just swallow him up right now so he wouldn't have to live through the aftermath of Chad's most recent social fart? Ryan thumped him hard on the chest as the women gave him two cold and very poisonous stares that were free of emotion; if looks could have killed... Chloe seemed to be making an extra effort to let Ryan know that her glare most definitely included him on her hit list.

He grimaced at her apologetically—hey, you know that's just good old Chad being good old Chad, and he's always like that, what can you do?

But her expression made it clear that she wasn't having any of his bullshit today, especially where his best friend was concerned.

Chloe had always regarded Chad as a waste of good space, valuable time and breathable air, and it was highly unlikely that her opinion would have changed even just very slightly in the weeks that she and Ryan had been apart. He had to think of something fast, or else she was going to walk out of his life, almost certainly for good. And that would be bad.

"Hey, I called you the other night," he blurted. God, that was brilliant, he thought. The only thing that would make it worse was if he could throw in something about what the weather was like when he called.

Chloe gave him another stiff little nod. "I know," she said. "My room mate told me."

"Oh, yeah?" Ryan winced at the familiar hard pang of loss in his chest. "So, uh, how come you didn't call back?"

He had a vague idea that he should have been embarrassed by the obvious desperation in his voice but he couldn't manage it.

For her part, Chloe didn't seem to notice his current state of deep humiliation. She wasn't even looking at him.

"Look, Ryan, we talked about this. You—" she sighed heavily. "You can't keep calling like nothing's changed—"

"I know—" he said quickly.

"'Cause everything's changed," she went on, raising her voice slightly to talk over him. "You've got to move on."

"Right," he put in, nodding. "I know all that—"

Chloe still kept talking, refusing to hear him. "Then what could you possibly have to say to me?"

"Well, I think—" Ryan hesitated, then took a deep breath. "I think we should get back together."

In the corner of his eye, he could see Chad looking at him as if he was the most hopeless dork that had ever used tools and walked upright. Hell, maybe it was true, but Ryan didn't care. If Chloe got back together with him, it wouldn't matter what anyone else thought.

Chloe gave a heavy sigh and nudged him with the box she was carrying, herding him a few steps away from her friend and the still disapproving Chad.

"Look, Ryan..." she started and then sighed again. "I really want you to hear this. Okay? Please?" She leaned in a little and, looking directly into his eyes, spoke slowly and carefully.

"We're. Not. Getting. Back. Together."

"Oh." Ryan gave a small, nervous laugh and shrugged. "What, you mean like, today?" he said with mock casualness. "'Cause, well, you know, that's cool—"

Chloe raised her eyes towards the sky and gave a loud groan of sheer exasperation. "Oh, of course," she said, her voice weary. "It's all a big joke for you, isn't it?"

"No—" he said quickly. He was desperate to get a word in. He had to explain to her that he had just been trying to defuse the tension with a little humor; that it was his way of coping and if that really bothered her, he'd never do it again. He'd find some other way to deal with it.

But he couldn't even find his voice and meanwhile Chloe kept on talking and talking and talking.

"You know, this is exactly why I broke up with you in the first place," she was saying. "You're irresponsible, self-centered, completely childish, and—and—" she shook her head. "And I need to move on."

She hefted the box and started to do just that. Gently, Ryan caught her arm before she passed him.

"Okay, wait, wait," he said, not caring that everyone could hear the way he was openly imploring her now. He could see that Chad was doing him the immense favor of recording this latest humiliation with his own phone. He was going to show him later what a pathetic shaved ape he was, but Ryan didn't care about that either.

"You're right, you're right," he said seriously. "I used to be that way. But not any more."

Chloe blew out a short, impatient breath and started to turn away. Ryan moved quickly to keep himself in front of her and put his hands gently on her shoulders.

"Chloe, I'm serious this time," he said, looking into her face and trying to capture her gaze with his own. "Ever since you left, I have thought about my life... and... well... I've *changed*."

She rolled her eyes. "Right," she said flatly. "You've changed. You've changed so much that the first thing you did when you got up this morning was race down here to screw around all day."

She glanced briefly to her left. "Tell me you weren't just playing games in the arcade with Chad."

"No, actually, we came down here to volunteer." The words were out of his mouth before he was even aware of what he was going to say.

"Volunteer?" She gave him a wary, sideways look. "For what?"

He glanced toward the end of the pier, where all the good causes usually set up their tables in an effort to do whatever it would take to save the world. Normally, there were at least a dozen good causes looking for money, manpower, or both, but today there was only one banner flapping in the breeze.

"Heal the Day," he told her.

Chloe's skeptical frown deepened. "You mean *Heal the Bay?*"

"Yeah, 'Heal the Bay'. That's what I said, right? Heal the Bay." He made a vague gesture toward the banner while his gaze finally fell on the box she was carrying. Heal the Bay. It was right there in front of him in big bright letters.

Chloe was shaking her head. "Don't bullshit me, Ryan," she sighed, her voice weary as she tried to push past him for the third time.

"I'm not bullshitting you," he insisted, stopping her again. "I swear I'm not. Test me. Give me something to do. You don't believe me? I'll prove it to you. Let me do that. It would be in a good cause, too," he added with a sudden burst of inspiration. "Right? There's that to think about, too, right? Right?"

He was half expecting her to use the box in her arms to shove him out of the way once and for all. He felt her push it at him hard. But she hadn't done it so she could walk away from him, he realized suddenly—she was handing the box over to him so that he could carry it.

He almost staggered, mostly with surprise, but also because the goddamned box was heavier than he had expected. Chloe must have been putting in extra time on her upper body since they'd broken up.

"Okay, then," she told him with a serious expression. "These flyers need to get handed out for the concert tonight."

"He can also pick up the T-shirts," her friend called over.

Ryan could hear the slight but definite edge in her suggestion. He forced himself to respond with an agreeable smile. He could smile at just about anyone for Chloe's sake.

"Right," Chloe said. Her gaze was even more serious and it seemed to be boring straight into him. "Four boxes of T-shirts need to be picked up at the Kinko's on Lincoln. You have your car here, right?" She didn't wait for him to nod his head. "So how about grabbing those, too?"

"Sure thing," he said. "I can do that. No problem."

She studied him for a long moment; then her serious expression deepened into a worried, speculative frown.

"You're really gonna do this, huh?" she asked softly.

Ryan knew that she was waiting to see if he was suddenly going to come out with some highly lame excuse and weasel out on her. Nope, no weasel moves happening around here, he promised her silently; not even the slightest weasel activity, not today, not tomorrow and not ever again.

"Yeah," he vowed. "I'm really gonna do this."

She refused to smile at him. "I'm serious, Ryan," she warned. "If you're not going to, just tell me right now—"

"Chloe, I'm gonna do it. Trust me, okay?" he said, unable to stop pleading with her again. "Trust me. You won't be sorry."

He kept his gaze locked on hers, willing her to see the truth of it in his eyes, willing her to believe that he really wasn't going to fail her, this time or ever again.

"Okay," she said finally. "Thank you." There was more than a trace of reluctance in her voice. Ryan could practically hear her telling herself that this was a bad idea. She was being foolish and she would end up regretting it. He wanted to tell her that this time he was going to prove to her that he was capable of being someone she could be proud of, but his voice had disappeared again.

Abruptly, Chloe took a step back and the moment was broken. The scorn with which she had greeted him made a sudden, unwelcome return and she gave him another stiff little nod before she walked off with her friend.

Barely aware of the box weighing down his arms, Ryan stared after her longingly. He wondered if she would be open to giving him another chance. Then he realized that even if it was hopeless, he had already gotten his hopes up, so damn the torpedoes and full steam ahead. He'd heal the bay, the day, good old LA and anything else she wanted. Single-handedly—

Chad materialized beside him. "Dude," he said mournfully. "That sucks."

Ryan turned and dumped the box into his arms.

"Aw, dude—that sucks even more!" Chad protested, holding the box at arm's length as if he were afraid it would contaminate him.

"Chad, do this for me." Ryan sidestepped him before his friend could give the box back to him. "Please. It'll only be ten minutes. Think about it. You get to hang out with Chloe's friends—hey, you know, I think that one dug you? Thanks, man, you're a god. I owe you," he added and ran like hell without waiting for Chad to reply.

He knew exactly what Chad would do next. It would take a second or two for Ryan's statement about Chloe's friend digging him to sink in. But then Chad's visual memory of her as the friend with the nipples would have him begging them to let him help. He'd spend the rest of the day running up and down the pier, handing out their flyers as if his life depended on it.

Of course, there was also a ninety-nine-point-nine per cent certainty that good old Chad would, as usual, do his good old Chad thing; he would run his good old mouth and come out with something that was either incredibly stupid, or offensive, or both. He just couldn't seem to get it through his head that staring fixedly at a woman's chest and asking, "Pretty chilly out, huh?" was not smooth or clever.

Ryan would have bet his rent money that the only reason Chad hadn't been killed was because most women paid absolutely no attention to a single word he said.

He had stopped at a light a few blocks away from Kinko's when he noticed that his cellphone was lying on the passenger seat. On the display was an image of Chloe.

"Hey, gorgeous," he said fondly and picked the phone up to have a closer look.

The image was actually the final frame of the brief video that good old Chad had courteously saved for him. Ever since Ryan had upgraded to the Bluetooth, Chad had found every possible opportunity to screw around with the video feature. Of course, this ran down the battery and left Ryan holding a dead phone at the most inconvenient times.

But this time he didn't mind. He didn't even mind that Chad's only intention had been to show him how pitifully dorky and sad his behavior was. He didn't mind making a fool of himself if it meant having Chloe to look at, on a few seconds of video. He might even have done it himself if he'd thought of it. Smiling at her image, he hit replay.

Immediately, his smile vanished as her beautiful face came to life with a sour expression.

"You know, this is exactly why I broke up with you in the first place," said her voice, tiny and filtered in the speaker. "You're irresponsible, self-centered, completely childish, and—and—" He watched her shake her head all over again thinking that she looked much more severe on video, even on low-res. "And I need to move on."

Ryan hit stop, feeling as if a large faceted object with a lot of sharp edges were rotating in his chest.

And I need to move on, she had said. Because he was irresponsible, self-centered and completely childish. Because the last thing that would ever occur to him was to think about what she needed. Throughout their entire relationship, he'd never given any indication that he cared about what she needed, so now she was telling him exactly what it was—

The phone rang in his hand, making him jump so hard that he bumped his thighs on the steering wheel. He felt a small pang when he saw that Chloe's image had been replaced by the "incoming call" graphic. He felt a wildly absurd hope that this incoming call might actually be from Chloe. She could be calling him to say thank you or maybe even to ask if he would like to get together later and talk after all.

It probably wasn't, but stranger things had happened.

"Hello?" he said cautiously.

There was a burst of static and something else under it that may or may not have been a human voice.

"Hello?" he repeated, a little louder.

There were several small scraping sounds, as if something was being dragged across a rough surface. And there was a tinny echoing, as if someone was using a speakerphone in an empty room.

Not that he cared. It wasn't Chloe, so he wasn't interested.

Jessica had been so intent on tapping the dialer wires together in just the right way that she almost missed the minuscule little voice that came out of the ruins of the phone.

She had to concentrate very hard to keep her hands from shaking too much. But then, she would have a hard time simulating a numeric pulse under any circumstances, even just for the hell of it: pulse dialing was about as current as ostrich quill pens and bustles.

And this was hardly the sort of thing she would do just for the hell of it.

Dear me, there's nothing on TV tonight and I'm so bored—what'll I do? I know: I'll pick through the pieces of a shattered telephone on a dusty floor in the attic of some derelict house out in God knows where, just to see if I can click two wires together and get a random number that somebody might just happen to answer! Oh, yeah, us science teachers sure know how to have fun. Are we a wild and crazy bunch or what?

"Hello...?"

The faint voice came out of a little tiny phone speaker; it was filtered and barely audible, but in the horrible dark prison of that dusty attic, that little tiny filtered voice was huge, it was immense, it was nothing less than world shaking.

For a moment, Jessica couldn't move. Then she dived for the ruined earpiece on the floor and pressed the side of her head to it. Desperate hope ran through her like an electric shock as she willed the voice to speak again.

It did. "Goodbye."

An unfamiliar voice but a familiar tone: bored, disinterested, and fading slightly on the last syllable.

Actually, it sounded a lot like she did when she got this sort of phone call, she thought—slightly irked at best, figuring it was nothing to get excited about, and putting the phone down again.

THREE

Ryan's thumb was almost on the end call button when he heard a frantic female voice begging, "Wait! Don't hang up!"

Well, it definitely wasn't Chloe's voice; in fact he didn't recognize it at all. Frowning, he put the phone back to his ear.

"Hello?" he said again.

"My name is Jessica Martin!" said the woman on the other end of the line in a hoarse half-whisper. "I've been kidnapped! I need your help! I need you to go to the police!"

Ryan gave a short, incredulous laugh, uncertain if he'd heard her correctly.

"Kidnapped, huh?" he said, going along with it.

This was definitely not your run-of-the-mill crank call; he had to give her a few points for originality and about a million more for her performance. If she kept up the scared breathing routine, however, she was going to hyperventilate and pass out. He couldn't imagine why the hell anyone would possibly want to work so hard.

But then again, he thought suddenly, maybe he could. "Who is this?" he asked. "Chloe? Is this some kind of a test?"

"No, please, I know what you're thinking but this is real!" The woman was sobbing. "I'm in an attic somewhere. I think they're going to kill me!"

Ryan rolled his eyes. The problem with stupid crank callers was that they always thought that you were just as stupid. "Nice kidnappers, to give you a phone," he pointed out conversationally.

"No!" the crank insisted, her voice trembling with hysteria. "You don't understand!"

He opened his mouth to tell her that he most certainly did understand, and if she thought he didn't, she must have spent most of her life locked in an attic. But his cellphone suddenly gave two electronic blips.

He checked the display on the faceplate.

Call Waiting. Accept?

Ryan's heart gave a hopeful jump. Maybe this call was from Chloe. In which case, so much for this bullshit; let the crank go play telephone games with someone else. He put the phone back to his ear.

"If you were really in trouble, you would've called the cops, not me," he said. "Later."

"Please, listen to me!" she pleaded, starting to sob even harder. "The phone I'm on—it's shattered. There's no dialer, I've been clicking wires together for I don't know how long, trying to get someone, anyone, and you're the only connection I was able to make."

"Clicking wires?" He laughed out loud. She must have really thought he was a genuine card carrying moron. "Phones don't work that way," he informed her. "So don't—"

"Rotary phones do!" She paused to do an authentic-sounding impression of a hysterical woman forcing herself to slow her breathing so she wouldn't lose control. "Please! I'm a science teacher. Just trust me that I'm telling you the truth!"

There was a small burst of loud static that cut off sharply. When the woman spoke again, the line was perfectly clear. "Just please, please— don't hang up! If you do, I may not get anyone else!"

Ryan wondered how many suckers the crank had talked into buying this science-teacher con. He could see how the average person might fall for it.

Then the call-waiting signal blipped again, reminding him he had a call on the other line that he was hoping might be Chloe. Definitely a more appealing prospect than a kidnapped science teacher.

"Right," he said, "that's a good one."

"Wait! Don't hang up! DON'T HANG U—"

He cut her off in mid-wail.

In the darkness of the attic, the click wasn't very loud at all.

Despite the fact that she was crouched on hands and knees with her ear practically touching the exposed speaker, Jessica was surprised that she had been able to hear such a tiny little noise over her own ragged breathing and the terrified pounding of her heart. But the precise clarity of the sound cut through everything so that it was impossible not to hear that he had hung up.

He had hung up and now it was all over. She had knelt in the musty darkness pawing through the fragments of the telephone until she had found the right wires, and then manipulated them with shaking hands that she couldn't steady even when she braced them against the floor.

Still, she had persisted in spite of her terror. She had refused to allow herself even to consider the possibility that the phone might be too antiquated for what she was trying to do. She had prayed to hear, against all odds, the familiar, mundane, miraculous sound of ringing interrupted by a live human voice. Hello?

But in the end, the whole thing had been for nothing. For nothing, nothing, nothing at all.

She was distantly aware of a pain in her legs from prolonged kneeling. The pain only went down as far as her ankles, though because her feet had gone numb. Since this, too, was all for nothing, there was no reason for her to care. For all the difference it would make, she might as well have been feeling someone else's pain from a long distance.

"Dude, I don't know what happened," said a familiar voice in Ryan's ear. "One minute I'm talking to

Nipples—" There was a rustle of papers. "The next I'm wearing a freakin' whale costume and I'm passing out flyers all over the place."

The mental image of Chad decked out in whale drag complete with fins and flippers came to Ryan so clearly that he had to clap his hand over his mouth so he wouldn't laugh out loud.

"Sorry, man," he said when he finally felt able to speak without losing it completely. "Sounds like she did quite a number on you."

"Well, yeah—" There were more rustling noises. "But, hey, I mean it's not like it doesn't have some benefits, too—"

Ryan heard a loud smack followed by an indignant female yell.

"Hey! What do you th—"

"Whales have mega-bad eyesight due to pollutants," came Chad's voice in an admonishing tone, some distance from the receiver. "Heal the bay!"

Good old Chad, Ryan thought, giving in to the urge to laugh. In the background, he could hear a lot of females giggling.

"Just get back here, will ya?" Chad asked him, slightly exasperated now.

"I'm on my way," Ryan said. He was tempted to make a sperm whale joke and then decided against it. "Hey, is Chloe around? Can I talk to her?"

"No, man," said Chad. There was a sudden, brief increase in the background noise as if Chad had held the phone out for a moment so he could listen to whatever was going on nearby. "Hear that? She's on her soapbox in save the world mode."

Ryan concentrated, trying to pick Chloe's voice out of the filtered din on the other end of the line; instead, he got another earful of Chad.

"A blue whale's penis is eleven feet long. Heal the bay!"

"Really?" asked an enthralled female voice.

Ryan was about to ask him the same question, along with how he had managed to come by this fascinating information but Chad mumbled something that sounded vaguely like "Gotta go," and broke the connection.

Good old Chad the eco-volunteer, Ryan thought, amused. Good old Moby Chad.

Look—up on the Santa Monica Pier! Is it a bird? Is it a plane?

No, dude, it's a representative of the world's most un-endangered species—a land-walking sperm whale with mega-bad eyesight and an eleven foot penis! Heal the bay and lock up the women! And hurry, before it's too late!

He was about to put the phone down on the seat next to him when he caught sight of the message on the display screen: Call on Hold.

Goddamn it, Ryan thought, making a face. He had forgotten about that stupid prank call. He turned to hang up, but hesitated.

He knew he ought dump the call. He didn't have time to waste if he wanted to convince Chloe that she should give him another chance. He couldn't give in to prank callers now; he had too much at stake here. His whole future with Chloe was riding on him not screwing things up this time. As far as he was concerned, that made it a matter of life and death.

Then, almost as if it had a will of its own, his thumb passed over the cut-off button and he was picking up the call again.

Jessica's first thought was that she was having an audio hallucination. Even as she cupped her hands around the phone speaker, she couldn't quite believe that he actually hadn't hung up on her, and he was still on the line after all.

"Can you hear me?" she asked.

"You still there?" He gave a short, cynical laugh.

Damn it, damn it, why did it have to be that kind of voice? Why couldn't it have been a compassionate, caring voice? What did she have to do? What miracle could she perform that would change it from hard and cynical voice to one that would respond to a cry for help?

She pressed her forehead against the floor, trying to think. What were the right words—if there were any words at all—that would make a voice like that really hear her?

"Okay, lady," said the voice in a final, no appeal tone. "Now you're creeping me out. Adios—"

"No, don't!" she pleaded. "They're going to kill me! Do you understand what I'm saying? They're going to kill me!"

The voice didn't answer. Please, she tried to say but her mouth just couldn't form the word. She had told the voice everything that she knew, everything exactly as it was, and the voice had simply refused to believe her. Then, when she had told the voice exactly what was going to happen to her, the voice had refused to answer. And she knew why.

The voice wouldn't answer because it was about to hang up on her once and for all. Any moment now, she would hear another click. It would be clear, sharp and precise, in spite of being barely audible; it would also be the last one ever.

"Please," she whispered, more to herself than to the voice. "You're my only hope. I just need help—"

She may as well have been talking to herself, Jessica thought as her voice died away altogether. She dropped her head into her trembling hands and broke down.

"I just need help—"

Followed by the uncontrollable sobs, of course. Like he couldn't even have guessed that one was coming. Ryan glowered at the cellphone in his hand. Oh, for Christ's sake. Certain things about women might be eternal mysteries but there was one thing that was true of all of them: when everything else failed, they turned on the waterworks. They all did it, from the very young to the very old. Even the ones who prided themselves on how tough and independent they were. The lip would start quivering, the voice would catch and the eyes would well up.

"No," he said firmly. "You need Prozac."

"Damn you!" she sobbed. "How can you be so—"

She cut off so abruptly that for a moment Ryan thought she had finally accepted defeat and hung up. Then he heard her ragged breathing again. She sure sounded like a woman trying to pull herself back from the brink of hysteria.

She had some serious, professional level talent going for her. Maybe what she really needed was an agent.

Hello, Hollywood? I've got a call here from a woman trapped in an attic and she needs a screen test and an Equity card as soon as possible. And a double latte, while you're at it. Except you probably better make that a decaf.

"How can you be so heartless?" she went on after a pause. "These men killed my housekeeper. You have to help me!"

Instantly, Ryan felt himself bristling. He *had* to help her? Boy, did she have the wrong number.

"What I have to do is pick up an order of T-shirts," he informed her fiercely. "Now, listen, lady, it's been real fun, but—"

"What's your name?" she asked suddenly.

The question startled the hell out of him. What was his name? He opened his mouth to tell her that getting personal with him wasn't going to do her the slightest bit of good.

"Your name," she insisted. "Please tell me your name."

"Uh…" He tried to think of a phony one but his mind was blank. "Ryan."

"Ryan," she echoed. "All right. What if it was your mother calling for help, Ryan? How would you feel?"

Amazing—yet another wrong angle she had chosen to try out on him. Man, this just wasn't her day, he thought. He was almost tempted to feel sorry for her now.

"Well, I'd be majorly impressed," he chuckled, but without much humor, "considering that she just happens to be dead."

"Just think about it logically, okay?" she snapped, her frustration boiling over. "Even if there's the slightest chance that I'm lying—"

"Yeah," he put in, laughing for real this time, "a ninety per cent chance."

"Fine," she said, snapping at him again. "But that still means there's a ten per cent chance you could be saving a life. What kind of person would walk away even at those odds? How selfish would you have to be? Is that the type of person you are, Ryan?"

Something in her voice caught him by surprise. He hesitated. In his mind's eye, he had a sudden shadowy image of an unknown woman crouching over a pile of phone parts on the floor in some dark, dirty attic room and shaking with fear.

Or maybe it was because she sounded so much like Chloe just then, he thought uncomfortably.

"Is it?" she prodded.

Ryan glared at the cellphone for a moment and then looked away. He was trying to think. Then he caught sight of himself in the sideview mirror.

To his dismay, he could detect the subtlest hint of wary expectation in his reflection. He was waiting with great interest for the answer to that age-old question: how selfish could Ryan Hewitt actually be?

Well, Ryan? We're all waiting to hear how this one breaks down. The whole world is waiting. Inquiring minds everywhere, including yours, are just dying to know. Come on, tell us: just how selfish are you?

Goddamn it, you knew it was a tough day when even your reflection is picking on you, Ryan thought.

Better not look in the rearview mirror, then, either, said a tiny voice in his mind. The reflection there probably isn't any better.

But he looked, of course. His gaze seemed to go on reproaching him even after he gave in and put on the Bronco's turn signal.

FOUR

There was any number of things that Sergeant Bob Mooney did not need on a day like today. He was so close to retirement he could taste it. One of them was to have the incredibly bad luck to be working the front desk while the West Side precinct house was full of gangbangers and drug dealers resisting arrest and threatening to murder each other.

Another was having to take a phone call from one of those industrial-strength jerks who thought they would have no trouble putting one over on him while he was trying to deal with this chaos.

The timing couldn't have been worse—you just did not want to be tied up on the phone when you were overrun with this many bad dogs, even if they were all handcuffed. He was just plain offended that anyone had the effrontery, the gall and absolute temerity to think that Bob Mooney was so goddamned stupid he would readily buy this bullshit. Some people, like the party on the other end of the phone, took extra convincing and that was far from easy in the current uproar.

And as if all of that wasn't anywhere nearly bad enough, some mega-idiot had decided to make things worse by turning up the sound on the TV. The maddening nasal bray of Mooney's least favorite news anchor added to the din.

"When a local workman stumbled across the grisly scene," blathered the hateful voice. "Two bodies shot execution-style to the head…"

Mooney winced as the anchor's detestably perky face was replaced by crime scene footage. Still holding the receiver, he stood up and scanned the room, looking for someone to turn the goddamned thing down, or better still, off.

"Now the police have identified the victims as members of a local gang involved heavily in narcotics trafficking," the anchor continued, her nasal bray turning solemn so viewers would know this was a very, very serious matter, "and are calling these murders yet another episode in the ongoing gang war over the illegal drug market…"

The noise level rose sharply as the bangers became more agitated, either in response to the story itself or because they couldn't stand the hideous voice. They now all seemed to have gone into Bruce Lee mode, throwing kung-fu style kicks at each other. Mooney could see only too well that it was not going to get any easier for the cops to keep the rival gangs apart. If things went all the way to critical mass, the whole precinct could blow up. In which case, no one was going to thank him for talking on the goddamned phone.

He sat down again and turned away, lowering his voice and speaking quickly in an attempt to bring the call to a fast, definitive end.

"Hold on a second, I said, hold. Shut up. Okay? Shut up!" Mooney snapped. "Now listen: I'm a cop, and I have been for twenty-two years. So let's cut the bullshit, pal, 'cause I've heard it all."

Several bodies slammed up against the front of his desk. Mooney switched the receiver to his other ear and bent over a little more in the chair, resting his elbows on his thighs.

"I know what I ordered," he said lowering his voice a little. "I ordered 'Rain Shower' with awapuhi. Don't even try to tell me jojoba is awapuhi, I wasn't born yesterday, you know." Mooney paused to take a quick look over his shoulder. "Now, here's how it breaks down: I'm sending back the two cases and you are going to refund all of my money. Or maybe I should drive down and discuss it in person—"

He suddenly became aware of someone looming over him and raised his head to see a uniformed police officer with one of those crew cuts that looked like it should have been trimmed back with hedge clippers. He was holding a box decorated with line drawings of mermaids smiling joyfully as they touched large puffy things to their gorgeous faces. The uniform's own face wasn't smiling joyfully nor was it gorgeous, but that was pretty much par for the course at West Side precinct.

Mooney held up his index finger, mouthing "One sec" at the guy.

"No," he said into the phone, turning away from him. "I said, no. I've got loofahs coming out of my ass. What I want is a refund. Okay? Thank you, I appreciate that. Yeah, uh huh." He put the receiver down a little harder than he needed to and turned back to take the box from the uniform.

"The lieutenant says he asked you not to have this shit sent here any more," the cop said, as he handed it over to him.

"I ordered this a long time ago, before he asked," Mooney told him with a flash of annoyance.

The cop didn't say anything; he was staring at the box with an expression of distaste mixed with suspicion, as if he were trying to make up his mind whether he should send for a sniffer dog or call out the bomb squad.

"It's sea sponge from the coast of France," Mooney added, hoping like hell that he didn't sound anywhere nearly as defensive as he felt.

"Sea sponge, huh?" The other man raised a dubious eyebrow, which made his crew cut surge forward. "Your husband likes that kind of stuff?"

A number of other uniforms nearby thought this was the height of wit, much to Mooney's increased annoyance. He was about to tell them all to get a life when Jack Tanner from the detective squad appeared seemingly out of nowhere in their midst and every single one of them gave ground in deference. Tanner's presence had always had that kind of effect on people, whether they were cops, crooks or none of the above, partly because he dressed like a man who had God's personal stylist on retainer. Today he was looking even more pressed, polished and dapper than usual. Because, Mooney realized, he had just been on the newscast that he had been trying to ignore. Jack Tanner, media star, always ready for his close-up, Mooney thought a bit sourly.

"Hey, lay off already," Tanner said, looking around at the uniforms with superior disdain. "At least Moon's got a plan for the future." He gave Mooney an approving nod, which made him want to squirm with discomfort over his own rather unkind feelings. "What do *you* have?" Tanner went on, slapping at the crew cut cop's fairly prominent paunch with a sheaf of papers he was carrying. "Bowling night and a beer belly?"

Tanner turned to Mooney with a satisfied grin as the cop, looking suitably chastised, decided he had to be somewhere else in a hurry, while the rest of the uniforms found they were suddenly very, very busy.

"Thanks, Jack," Mooney said as he grinned back, albeit a bit reluctantly. Tanner was a major showboat and grandstander, and it was hard not to see everything he did as some kind of personal display.

"Are you kidding?" Tanner clapped a hand on his shoulder, blasé and magnanimous all at once. "We went through the academy together— forget about it! You know I'll defend you to the ends of the earth." The detective paused and looked around as if to make sure no one else was listening before he leaned forward and lowered his voice confidentially. "But tell me the truth, Moon—are you sure about this beauty salon thing?"

"Day spa," Mooney corrected him, trying not to snap. Goddamn it, why did everyone have to keep referring to it as a beauty salon when he must have told them all about a gazillion times that it was a day spa? Just how hard was that to remember two little bitty words, for Christ's sake? "It's a day spa," he repeated. "And no, as a matter of fact, I'm not sure about shit."

Tanner looked wise. "Hey, if that's really the case, you know you could always come work for me," he said, still keeping his voice low. "I could use you on the task force. All your experience, really—"

Mooney put up a peremptory hand, feeling pleased in spite of his feelings. This wasn't the first time Tanner had brought the subject up and it probably wouldn't be the last. "I appreciate it, Jack, but like I told you, I made a deal with Mare. Besides—" Mooney jerked a thumb at the commotion of bangers and cops, which had actually begun to subside to the point where the room was clearing out and the cops were now able to herd their prisoners to the holding cells in back. "I'm bored. Twenty-two years—that's enough."

More than enough, he added silently.

"Hey, I think Marilyn's a great gal," Tanner said. "You know that, right? It's just..." he pressed his thin lips together and then shrugged. "Never mind. Forget it."

Mooney shoved the box out of sight underneath his desk and caught the other man's arm as he started to walk away. "It's just what?"

"Well—" Tanner shrugged again and gave him a pitying look. "She's got you whipped, Bob."

Whipped? Mooney's mouth dropped open. Had Tanner really just said whipped—with a straight face? The last time Mooney had heard anyone use that expression had been in high school.

"No, now look here, Jack, if this thing takes off, we could make a shit load of money," he told Tanner. "And then we'll just see who's laughing, huh?"

"Sarge?" interrupted a polite voice.

Mooney turned to see a young uniformed officer waiting in front of his desk with a file in one hand.

"Oh, sorry," said the cop, looking from Mooney to Tanner as he swiped a hand nervously over the top of his thick curly hair. "Am I, uh, should I—"

"Naw, kid, we're just talkin'," Tanner assured him, making a careless, go-ahead gesture.

"Well, I just wanted to ask the sarge—" the young guy made another, slightly more delicate swipe over his hair. "See, I was thinking of going more towards a tawny bronze? But Costello thinks it might be too harsh for my coloring. What do you think, Sarge?" His earnest young face broke into a broad grin.

Mooney rolled his eyes and groaned. "I think I have an excellent color for you, pal," he told the uniform. "It's called 'Kiss My Ass.'"

Several guys laughed as the young officer walked away, still making a show of patting his hair delicately.

But, of course, that wasn't going to be the end of it, not by a long shot. It never was. Every time one of them started, the rest had to rush to get their licks in, too. It was like they were all in some giant pissing contest for smart-asses. Mooney sighed. It was enough to make him wish for another influx of gangbangers just to keep them all too busy even to think about busting his balls.

"Hey, Mooney!" someone hollered.

Here we go, he thought, closing his eyes for a moment before he turned to see who was calling him. "Hey, what?"

A plainclothes guy across the room waved at him, and then turned around, lifting his shirt to display an exceptionally hairy back. "Think I should get this waxed?"

"Waxed? I think you should get it tested for rabies," Mooney retorted, getting a big laugh from everyone, including the plainclothes guy. "Now get outta my face already, will ya?"

The relative quiet that followed lasted all of three seconds. Then some more uniforms on the day shift arrived with a fresh batch of gangbangers and Mooney found himself back in the heart of desk sergeant hell.

Ryan brought the Bronco to a stop as close to the front door of the West Side precinct house as he could. "Okay, I'm here," he told the woman on the phone as he hopped out.

He actually had no idea whether the spot he had pulled into was reserved for police cars or handicapped drivers, or if it was actually a parking space at all. It was simply the first clear area he could find where he thought there was the least risk of his getting blocked in. It didn't seem likely that he would be getting a ticket, either—from the looks of things, the cops at the West Side precinct must have had close to half the city's gang population on the front steps in handcuffs and every last one of them was resisting arrest.

Ryan wondered briefly what was going on and then remembered the he had heard something on the news that morning about a gang war or a drug war. Or it could have been a gang-drug war or something.

Right, whatever. Gangbangers and drugs, so what else was new? None of that had anything to do with him; it wasn't his worry. He put it out of his mind as he darted up the steps two at a time, dodging elbows, over-priced running shoes and a couple of attempted head-butts.

He almost gave up at the front door, which was all but impassable. It was jammed up with even more bangers struggling with even more cops. Arms and legs were flailing wildly. Ryan barely managed to avoid being simultaneously clotheslined by a long, uniformed arm and kicked in a delicate area by a thick-soled basketball shoe. Someone's fist almost clipped his ear but he was more disconcerted by a slap on his ass, which felt neither accidental nor combative.

Holding the cellphone high over his head, Ryan worked his way around a husky cop who was reciting the Miranda warning in an absurdly calm voice to the equally husky banger he had pinned against the doorjamb. Then several people in the crowd behind him suddenly surged forward and he almost went sprawling on his belly as they pushed him over the threshold into the station.

Conditions were just as noisy and chaotic inside as they were outside, possibly more so. Lowering his tired arm and cradling the phone protectively against his chest, Ryan did a clumsy pirouette, trying to locate the front desk over the sea of bobbing heads all around him.

He was beginning to wonder if everything in the room had actually been trampled flat before he had gotten there. Maybe he'd be better to find another station. Then he spotted a uniformed figure that had to have been standing on a platform or a dais of some kind. Not only was he the only visible cop, he was also the only one in the entire room who didn't look utterly confused, irritated and overwhelmed.

That had to be the front-desk sergeant, Ryan decided and ploughed his way toward the man as fast as he could through the struggling, roiling bodies.

"Excuse me, officer—" he started. The sergeant held up a hand and mouthed something like "Wait a sec" at him. Someone large and heavy stumbled into Ryan from behind, shoving him into the front of the desk and then very nearly under it.

"Hey! Hey!" Ryan yelled breathlessly as he hung on to the desk for dear life. "I've got an emergency here—"

Two beefy cops used their shoulders and elbows to push him aside and then crowded in front of him as if he weren't even there. They stuck their clipboards under the desk sergeant's nose. The sergeant scanned them quickly, signed one, started to write on the other and then stopped. "Hang on a sec, this is the wrong form—"

"Is it?" said the cop, scratching his overly long crew cut with bewilderment, as if there weren't a near-riot going on all around him. "Well, crap. I could have sworn I grabbed an eighteen-nine."

Ryan could have sworn the guy was deliberately trying to make him crazy. He shoved the arm holding out the offending clipboard to one side. "Come on, no kidding, officer," he insisted. "I've got some lady on the phone here who says she's been kidnapped." He pushed the cell at him, willing him to take it.

The cop behind the desk frowned at Ryan's cellphone as if he had never seen anything quite so bizarre and outlandish in his entire life, before turning his suspicious gaze on Ryan as if he'd never seen anything quite like him before, either.

"Okay, kid, cut to the chase—is this some kinda joke?" he asked with a warning edge in his voice.

"'Cause if it is, believe me, you're not gonna be laughing when I toss you in a cell—"

"It's not a joke," Ryan said. "At least not one that I'm pulling."

He strained forward with the phone in his hand until it felt like his arm was going to pop out of its socket.

"Just talk to her, will ya? Please? Please?"

Please. Please. Please.

The word echoed in Jessica's head. She had said that word so many times today. She had probably said "please" more times in the last hour than she had in the last year. Please. Please. Please. She was beginning to wonder how long it would be until she stopped hearing it as a word.

"Please," she whispered, unaware that she was speaking aloud.

Instead of a keening sound, she heard a new voice now, annoyed, harassed and put-upon but still willing all the same.

"Okay, kid. Give it here."

"Oh, thank God! You've got to help me! My name's Jessica Kate Martin and I've been kidnapped!"

Mooney was barely able to hear the woman's tiny, frantic voice. He pressed the phone hard against his ear with one hand and groped around his desktop for something to write on with the other.

"This morning five men broke into my home in Brentwood and killed my housekeeper—"

His pen was flying over the scrap of paper he'd found as he automatically jotted down key words: *Jessica Kate Martin. Brentwood.* The idea was to get as much information as fast as possible without stopping to think about it—no mean feat when you were trying to listen to a hysterical caller on a cellphone in the middle of a gang war.

He was about to tell her to slow down and repeat the last thing she had said when the front doors banged open. A bunch of officers Mooney would have sworn knew better brought in a crowd of frenzied, struggling skinheads.

"Hey, yo, there's your shooters!" yelled one of the Hispanic bangers, twisting away from the cop who had been wrestling him toward the holding cells. "They's the ones who smoked Chuco!" He flung himself toward them, obviously not caring that his hands were cuffed behind his back.

"You got something to say to me, puto bitch?" replied one of the skinheads, thrusting himself forward to meet the banger's attack.

The last semblance of order disappeared with a furious roar as every banger and skinhead in the place lunged head first at each other, undeterred by their restraints.

"Oh, brother," Mooney groaned. Wearily, he turned back to the kid and held the phone out to him. "Here, take this thing upstairs to robbery/homicide on the fourth floor and ask for a detective. One of them can help you."

"No, wait," the guy kept saying. "You've got to help her!"

Of course the kid wanted to argue. Mooney sighed unhappily. Nobody was going to make anything easy today, so why would this guy be any different? He tried to make the kid take the phone back while he thought darkly about what he was going to do when he found out just who had thought it would be such a good idea to mix the skinheads with the homeboys.

But goddamn it, the kid wouldn't cooperate; he kept pushing Mooney's hands away, trying to get him to put the cell back up to his ear.

Finally Mooney gave up and put the cell on his desk. "Upstairs," he ordered the guy. "Now."

The kid would either leave the cellphone there on the desk or he would pick it up and do as he was told. Mooney just didn't have the time to wait around to find out; he waded into the melee.

Ryan stared at his cellphone on the cop's desk. He thought he could hear the woman on the other end saying "Hello, officer? Hello? Hello?" frantically over and over. But that must have been only his imagination, he told himself; there was so much yelling and screaming going on, he was barely capable of hearing himself think.

Finally, he reached over and picked the cellphone up again, looking around at the chaos while he tried to figure out how he was going to tell what's-her-name (Jessica, said a small voice in his mind; Jessica... Something... Martin. Right—Jessica Martin) that she could not have picked a worse day to need help if she had deliberately planned it.

Abruptly, he found himself face to face with a harassed-looking guy in rumpled plainclothes. The man didn't even glance at him as he started to push past; this had to be another detective, Ryan thought and grabbed the man's arm.

"Excuse me—" he started.

Still not looking at him, the guy tried to twist out of his grip.

"Excuse me!" Ryan shouted in his ear. "Are you a detective?"

The man turned to him with a look of pure disbelief. "Am I a detective?" he shouted back, directly into Ryan's face. "Am I a detective? I'm a victim! They dragged me down here."

Oh, Christ, Ryan thought. He let go of the guy and tried to shove through the teeming mass of struggling bodies surrounding them. But the guy had obviously been looking for someone to listen to his tale of woe and, having found Ryan, wasn't about to let him go that easily.

"They just dragged me down here like a common thug. No worse than that," the man babbled after him angrily. "They didn't even read me my... Hey! Are you even listening? Come back here!"

Ryan kept pushing his way through the chaos until the man's angry protests were dwarfed by the noise and chaos of the police station. Finally, he managed to make his way out of the crowd to a relatively quiet spot on the edge of the room and put the cellphone back to his ear.

"Oh my God..." Jessica said bleakly.

The hair on the back of Ryan's neck stood up. The only thing that had ever given him that sensation was being anywhere near deep water. Until now, that was.

"What?" he demanded. "What is it?"

No answer. Just the sound of her dropping the mouthpiece on the floor.

"Lady, what's going on?" Ryan shouted, terrified that she wouldn't answer, but even more terrified that she would.

Jessica had just enough time to shove the phone behind her before the attic door slammed open and he came in again, followed by one of his buddies.

No, those were henchmen. Kidnappers didn't have buddies, they had henchmen, she thought as she teetered giddily on the edge of hysteria.

Don't, she told herself firmly. No hysteria, not now. She couldn't get hysterical, she could not; she had to project self-possession, dignity and inner strength. Otherwise, these men would do anything they wanted to her.

Doing her best to keep her body in front of the phone wreckage, she drew herself up so that her shoulders were square rather than slumped. She refused to let herself cower as they came across the room.

The one in charge stood directly over her, appearing to study her with a detached expression.

"Where did he put it?" he asked her finally.

"What?" Jessica blinked up at him, unsure if she'd heard him right. Where did he put it? The question made absolutely no sense at all. "I don't—"

Her head snapped back as her brain exploded with light. Then she felt as if one half of her face had somehow collapsed in on itself. It was a full second before she understood that the man had slapped her as hard as he possibly could with his open hand.

Jessica felt a surge of dizziness. Her eyes seemed to roll around in their sockets like marbles, as much from emotional shock as from the physical blow itself. No one, man or woman, had ever intentionally hit her before.

Abruptly the man's stony features were bare inches in front of her.

"Where is your husband?"

"At work!" she blurted. The sound of him screaming into her face actually helped her steady herself. She had to get a grip, make sure they didn't discover the phone. "Why? What do you—"

This time when he hit her, she felt her head striking the beam behind her and realized in a strangely distant way that this had also happened the first time he'd slapped her. She had simply been too startled to notice. Her eyes felt as if they'd been shoved all the way through the sockets into the center of her skull. Another surge of dizziness, much more intense, swept through her and she felt herself wobbling on the verge of passing out.

"DON'T BULLSHIT ME!" he roared at her.

Again, the sound of his voice yanked her entire being back into focus. She swayed but managed to keep herself upright. The white-hot stinging in her face brought tears to her eyes, but she could stand it, especially since it was one more thing that kept her from passing out. Now if only she could stop trembling. If she couldn't hold herself steady they would see the phone cord and if that happened, she was dead. She could feel it in her heart.

Dead, her heart said by way of confirmation.

Dead.

Dead.

Dead.

Ryan stood frozen while the three-way brawl between the bangers, the skinheads and the cops escalated. He would not have been able to take the cellphone from his ear even if he'd wanted to. From time to time, one or another of the cops brushed roughly past him in the course of wrestling a gangbanger or a skinhead into submission. But Ryan was oblivious to everything except what he could hear on the other end of the phone.

There was a harsh male voice asking something about where somebody—he, whoever that might have been—had put it.

The woman's voice was saying something he couldn't quite make out. This was followed by an unpleasant noise.

The man again, harsher, meaner, nastier. "Where is your husband?"

"At work." Her answer was practically a bleat.

Then unbelievably, the sound of a hard slap and a wordless cry of pain. "DON'T BULLSHIT ME!"

No, Ryan told himself firmly, he hadn't just heard that. He couldn't have. This wasn't supposed to be a real kidnapping. It was supposed to be a crank call, some screwed-up kid playing a joke to get some attention or some nutcase's idea of a good time. It wasn't supposed to be real.

Except, obviously, he was wrong. It *was* real. "Shit," Ryan breathed, rooted to the spot. His mind replayed everything he had just heard on an endless loop. He had to do something, he told himself. He had to make himself move or else he was going to hear something even worse replaying itself in his head over and over for the rest of his life.

He looked around frantically, spotted the stairwell and sprinted for it, still clutching the phone to his ear.

"Please, he should be at the realty office!" Jessica sobbed. "Maybe he's showing a house! I don't know!"

There was a long, terrible period of time when the man just looked at her in silence. It might have been a second, an hour or most of a day for all she knew. For her part, she could do nothing at all except stare up into that hard, cruel face and beg silently for him to keep his eyes fixed only on her, to see nothing else, nothing at all.

Abruptly, he gave a short nod and began to turn away. Oh, God, thank you, God, thank you, she thought, feeling her breath came out in a rush. It was nothing short of a miracle, she had been spared, he hadn't seen the phone and there was still a chance for her to get out of this alive and protect her family—

All at once he whirled on her again. "You have a little boy, right?" he said, speaking in a very calm, matter-of-fact voice, as if he were merely conducting a survey. "Goes to the Wyman School in Westwood."

"No, no, no!" Jessica wailed, horror and despair spreading through her with a force that was physically painful. "What do you want with him? You have the wrong family, leave him alone!"

But the men had already left, slamming the door behind them.

"Ryan!"

He could hear a new terror in her voice. "I know," he told her quickly. "I'm trying to get help."

"My son—"

Grunting with effort, Ryan vaulted up the stairs three at a time, ignoring the immediate and excruciating burning in his thigh muscles. He had just reached the first landing when the cellphone in his hand emitted a burst of white noise.

"Oh my God, what's happening?" the woman asked.

"Nothing, it's just static," he said. "I'm running upstairs to the detectives. Hold on, I might lose you for a sec—"

"No, don't!" she begged, her voice rising with alarm. "Stop, you can't lose me—"

"Wait, we're almost there," he panted, using the railing in an attempt to pull himself up the stairs even faster.

"Stop! Ryan, goddamn it, stop, stop! If you lose me I'm dead!"

The raw-throated panic in her voice unnerved him so much that he came to a halt mid-stride three-quarters of the way up the flight.

"What the hell am I supposed to do?" he said, pulling the phone away from his ear to check the display. "Jesus, I'm almost there—" he broke off.

All of a sudden the signal strength indicator was down to one bar.

One bar—and he was going up? What the hell was that about? He could understand if he were going downstairs into the sub-basement level, but upstairs? It shouldn't have been happening this way.

Baffled, Ryan leaned over the railing so he could squint through the narrow gap that ran all the way up between the flights. He was trying to see what it was upstairs that would interfere with the signal. It just didn't make any sense.

For a long moment, he couldn't decide what to do. Then, mentally crossing his fingers, he took an experimental step up.

Immediately, the bar vanished.

Ryan put the phone to his ear; the connection was gone.

FIVE

Some people were incapable of learning to avoid doing things the hard way, Ethan Greer thought as he headed downstairs from the attic. That was just how some people were.

No matter how plainly he laid it out for them, some people just could not seem to get it through their heads the first time, or even the second, that there were two and only two kinds of people in the world: bullshitters and Ethan Greer. And that getting the two of them mixed up would be the absolute worst mistake they could make.

It was a mistake that would also usually turn out to be their last.

The thing that really mystified him, however, the one thing that he could never understand no matter how long he lived or how much he thought about it, was that none of these people could have been described as being exceptionally stupid. In fact, none of them was even a little stupid.

Like the bitch upstairs—she was a goddamned prime example. She was a goddamned teacher, for Christ's sake. That was supposed to mean she was an educated woman, someone with enough brains in her head that she had earned herself a college degree. She wasn't just a dumb suburban cooze whose toughest decision every day was trying to make up her mind whether she wanted to watch Jerry Springer or yack on the phone while she was doing her nails.

But what the hell—even if she had been just some insurance salesman's live-in cook, sex toy and brood mare, the woman was also a mother, for Christ's sake. Mothers had those maternal instincts that made them protect their young. Even dumb suburban cooze mothers. So that one upstairs should have done what she had to do just to make sure that her kid would be safe.

But wasn't that just the way it was with some women?

Greer felt his irritation building by the moment. This should have been a straightforward situation. Hell, for ninety-nine out of a hundred women, maybe it would have been.

But no—he'd had the shitty luck to draw this contrary bitch that was apparently of the lofty and exotic belief that she could just go ahead and jerk him around any old way she wanted to and get away with it. Well, she was about to learn otherwise and she would learn it the hard way, real hard and real fast. Real fast.

Even if he'd been inclined to put up with her trying to screw him around, he just didn't have time for it. And he was just going to have to teach her another fundamental rule of How The World

Actually Works. If he didn't have time for something, that meant she had run out of time as well.

He crossed the ground floor hallway to the living room, where the rest of the crew were hanging out, waiting for him to tell them what the next move would be. Some genius among them, probably Mad Dog, had actually managed to get the TV to work. He could hear that ex-model-turned-TV-reporter bitch he hated so much running down the latest on LA's latest gang war in what was easily the world's most annoying phony-sincere voice.

Not that any of the guys were actually paying close attention. He could hear Mad Dog telling some kind of long, involved story about some operation he'd been on in East LA once. And there was the rhythmic sound of somebody snoring. But the moment he reached the doorway though, every single one of them was alert and good to go.

He looked around at their expectant faces, sparing a meaningful glance at the table in the middle of the room where bricks of coke and cash sat in neat stacks around two oversized duffle bags. He knew that they understood his expression.

"We need to end this thing now," he said. "Dimitri. Deason."

The two men were on their feet before he finished speaking—best reflexes in the crew. They also looked like the mean-assed junkyard dogs they were. They were the perfect guys for this task.

"Go get the kid," he said and tossed them the keys to the Porsche Cayenne.

"Crap!"

Electrified with panic, Ryan jumped down several steps. Now what could he do? He was off the scale with frustration and terror. The mighty cellphone, miracle of technology—use it to make calls from anywhere aboveground, just as long as you were careful not to get too far above sea level. Maybe it had something to do with sunspots or the ozone layer or some other environmental thing. Somewhere out there were a lot of blue whales with mega-bad eyesight and lousy cellphone reception.

Ryan peered up through the gap again. "Hello?" he called. "I need a detective! Will someone get a detective for me? Please? I said, please?"

No answer.

He couldn't believe this. He was yelling for a cop in a police station and no one was answering him. No one was ever going to believe this when he told them about it. Even good old Chad would have accused him of making it up, for Christ's sake.

"You have gotta be shitting me," he fumed.

"Ryan! Ryan!"

He jumped, suddenly aware that the woman had been calling his name over and over for some time.

"Ryan, what time is it?" she asked. "Ryan!"

"It's 1:20," he told her. "Is anyone up there?" he added, calling up the stairwell again.

"Ryan, listen to me!" she begged. "My son's school lets out at 1:45. You've got to do something!"

"Look, I'm trying—"

"No, listen," she insisted. "They have my car. Do you understand what that means? My son will hop right in! You've got to do something!"

"Damn it." There she was again, telling him what he had to do. He stood wavering, unable to make a move one way or another. Her voice was echoing in his head; over and over, he could hear her sobbing and the sound she made when the guy was slapping her, laying into her for all he was worth. And then talking about where her son went to school.

"Damn it!" he howled and lashed out, slamming his fist against the wall. As soon as he did it, he felt like an idiot. Punching the nearest concrete wall was hardly the smartest thing to do under the circumstances and it certainly wasn't the most constructive—it would make a hell of a lot more difference to his hand than it ever would to the wall. At least, that was what his father had been fond of telling him back when he'd been younger and more prone to wall punching.

Just now, however, he was too upset to feel anything as inconsequential as pain. He ran back down the stairs.

Ryan burst through the door out of the stairwell to find that the number of people in the precinct seemed to have doubled and the chaos level had tripled. Dodging around two bangers who were throwing vicious kicks along with bilingual curses at each other, he grabbed the first uniformed person he saw.

"Officer, I've got an emergency—" he began.

The cop shook him off with an irritated grunt and turned to the gangsters, forcing himself between them. He used his entire body to pry them apart while two other cops dragged them away from each other.

"Ryan, listen, there's no time for this!" insisted the woman as he tried to snag another cop who evaded him and made a vague gesture at the front desk. "Just please get to the school, please!"

Ryan hesitated; caught between the urge to get one of the cops to pay attention to him and the urge to do as she was telling him and run back to his (possibly) illegally parked Bronco. The best way, and the only way he could really help this woman was to get the cops working on her case—the cops could do a hell of a lot more for her than he ever could.

The problem was he had managed to find the one police station in the whole of the Los Angeles area where the cops were too swamped to hear him. If he ever got any of these guys to take him seriously it would almost certainly be too late to save this woman and her son. And driving around looking for another police station might take even more time.

The situation might not be any better at any of the other police stations in the immediate vicinity. Or even in the not-so-immediate vicinity. With a gang war or a drug war, or whatever kind of war this was, things might be just as crazy everywhere, maybe even crazier. It wasn't like Los Angeles hadn't ever gone crazy before. In the so-called City of Angels, anything was possible. All told, Ryan thought unhappily, this was a remarkably shitty day for anyone to have to dial 911.

You have a little boy, right? Goes to the Wyman School in Westwood.

He ran for the front door.

"Where are you now?"

She must have asked him that a thousand times in the last thirty seconds, Ryan thought, and it was really starting to make him crazy.

"I just got off Sunset," he told her, controlling his impatience.

"Then it'll be on your left, two miles up the road. Hurry! You've *got* to hurry!"

No shit! he wanted to yell back at her. He barely managed to restrain himself. "Will you relax?" As the words were coming out of his mouth, he knew what an absurd thing it was to say and he winced. "Where the hell is a cop when you really, really need one? That's what I'd like to know," he muttered, looking around for the speed trap that should have been lying in wait for him and that on any other day would have caught him.

He took a hard right, knowing he was pushing the Bronco a lot harder than he should have been. Even the shrill, piercing way the tires were squealing sounded like a protest. "Just what do these guys want from you anyway?" he asked the woman.

"I don't know," she wailed helplessly. "I teach fifth grade science and biology. What would anyone want from me?"

Good point, Ryan thought. "What about your husband? Is he, like, uber-rich?"

"What? No, he's a realtor," the woman told him, her voice trembling. "None of this makes any sense."

To Ryan's dismay, she started weeping uncontrollably again. Directly into the phone, of course, which took it directly into his ear and straight into his brain. Damn it, if he were forced to listen to much more of this seemingly endless crying, he was going to break down himself.

Never in his life had he heard anyone cry with so much intensity for such an extended period of time. He would not have believed it possible for a single human being to go on crying as hard and as long as this woman had and still have even the tiniest drop of moisture left in her body.

Of course, it wasn't like she didn't have something to cry about. But Jesus, she was crying and crying and crying and crying and then she was crying some more. And it just wasn't doing anyone any good at all. If anything, it was actually making things worse—he was trying to help her out, but he was barely able to function with her constantly bawling and sobbing in his ear.

He was trying to ask her about something important, something that could end up saving both her kid's life and her own. What he kept getting from her instead, however, were variations of "I don't know," followed by a fresh bout of hysterics and waterworks.

Goddamn it, did this woman have any idea what it was like to drive in LA traffic, let alone having to do it with someone alternately sobbing like mad in your ear and nagging the hell out of you to go faster? He was driving like a maniac, weaving in and out of traffic. He was seriously lucky that he hadn't had an accident by now.

No, screw that, he was double seriously lucky that he hadn't had a dozen accidents—

He realized just in time that the car in front of him labeled Tagert Driving School was not, in fact, going to move over so he could pass it. And the driver would not be exceeding the thirty-five mile per hour speed limit now or at any time in the foreseeable future.

Great, he thought, pounding the steering wheel in frustration. This was all he needed.

"Yo, grandma!" he yelled, leaning his head out of the window as far as he was able to. "Come on, will ya?"

He might as well have been telling the car to sprout wings and fly for all the good that did. Fuming and swearing under his breath, he switched to the right lane just as a Mercedes slid into the space ahead of him. Then the driver settled in at a sedate thirty-five while he enjoyed a nice leisurely chat on his own cellphone.

The term "road rage" didn't even begin to describe how he felt, Ryan thought. If his head exploded, this guy and the Tagert Driving School's star student would be to blame.

On the extremely lengthy list of Things That Should Not Have Been Allowed, being boxed in on a multi-lane highway was way up there for Ryan—beyond squalling infants in movie theaters, bad service in restaurants, the indiscriminate use of the smiley face, or even stores that used the crappy take-a-number-and-wait system.

He was in an emergency and stuck behind two slow-asses in the fast lane. They were both so frickin' dim they didn't know someone was trying to go around them. This kind of stuff seriously lowered the quality of life. Even *his* life, which was currently without Chloe.

Oh? And how about other stuff like being kidnapped and locked in an attic and beaten up, asked a small voice in his mind? Think that might be equally crappy? Or maybe even crappier?

Ryan pounded on the horn with his fist even though it was all too obvious that the guy in the Mercedes couldn't hear him. The guy didn't *want* to hear him, or anyone else. That was what made a Mercedes such a desirable car in the first place—the total driving pleasure of having such a nice quiet ride, with very little in the way of road noise. So there wouldn't be a freakin' uproar in the background to get on your nerves, just peace and quiet while you were crawling along the highway and having a friendly chat on your cellphone.

"Fuck this shit," Ryan growled under his breath as he swerved into the breakdown lane and stomped on the accelerator. He pushed the Bronco hard until he was even with the Mercedes. Either he'd get past these two idiots or he'd finally get a cop's attention.

"Hang up your goddamned phone, you douchebag!" he screamed at the guy in the Mercedes.

The guy threw back his head and laughed soundlessly in response to whatever he'd just heard on the cellphone. Yeah, that was a Mercedes for you—one real nice quiet ride for sure, like a living room on wheels.

"Goddamn it!" Ryan screamed, more for his own gratification. "Concentrate on the r—"

It was actually the sight of the lifting crane on the other side of the highway that caught Ryan's eye and finally made him look away from the jerk in the Mercedes. Otherwise, he almost certainly would not have seen the work crew on the sidewalk, much less the gigantic potted palm tree sitting squarely in front of him in the breakdown lane.

The palm was attached to the crane by several long cables and Ryan could see that at any moment it was going to be lifted into the air so it could be transported to a spot that had been determined by municipal landscapers to be absolutely perfect for it.

Then all the good people of Los Angeles would be able to drive past it every day and admire it. The palm would appeal to their sense of aesthetics and as a result it would make them feel better about the surroundings they lived and worked in, suggesting to them that this was indeed a beautiful world. This in turn would raise their flagging spirits, bring a spontaneous smile to their lips and, in the long run, make them far less prone to blasting away at each other on the freeway in fits of road rage.

As imminent as the moment of the palm's lift-off and transport might have been, however, the problem for Ryan was that all of it was still in the future. For now, the gigantic pot was sitting in the emergency lane as if it had been waiting for Ryan to show up, while for his part, Ryan was hurtling toward it in the Bronco with the unchecked momentum of a man who knows he has a date with destiny and doesn't want to be late for it.

He jumped on the brake pedal with both feet, distantly aware that although he was screaming in terror, the screech of the Bronco's tires was a hell of a lot louder, easily drowning him and everything else out. He had never done a power-skid this major in his life—hell, even the guy in the soundproof Mercedes might hear something, provided there was a lull in the conversation.

And then without fanfare or warning, the gigantic pot levitated.

Before Ryan's wide, terrified eyes, the thing simply went up in one smooth, graceful motion which allowed the Bronco to continue its power-skid unimpeded through the spot where the palm had been scant moments before. Ryan was unable to do anything except stare up at the words PROPERTY OF THE CITY OF LOS ANGELES on the bottom of the pot in utter astonishment as it sailed over his head with mere inches of clearance.

All at once, he felt his mind unfreeze and begin to work again. Ease off the brake pedal, his brain instructed him with a quiet confidence he was surprised to find in himself. Steer into the skid and straighten out, and live to drive another day.

Then he realized he had, in fact, already done everything right. The Bronco was back under his control and had been for some time. Damn— suddenly and without warning, he had turned into Mr Competent.

This was a good thing, his brain informed him, still in calm lecture mode. Now that he knew he didn't always screw everything up, he could give his attention to more important matters. Like the fact that the Wyman School was coming up fast on his right.

He skidded to a stop at the curb, right in front of a sign advising him of when the Wyman Private School For Boys had been established and by whom, along with a lot of other information that was actually impossible to read from a moving vehicle.

"How much time do we have?" the woman asked him as he hopped out of the Bronco and jogged toward the main building.

Ryan glanced at his watch: 1:44. It was probably too much to hope that it was running fast. "One minute," he told her.

"Run to the main building," she told him. Her voice, still tense, had become steady now, even composed, which Ryan had always thought was the way a teacher was supposed to sound. "His classroom is on the left."

Ryan made a noise of assent. For the very first time, he was getting the feeling that all this frantic activity was actually going to accomplish something. He was also starting to get a much better idea of this woman on the cellphone, a more complete mental picture of who she was and what she was like.

He could tell that the woman he had been listening to all this time was a regular person, someone with a normal life that included family and friends and people she worked with. She had things she liked to do, like eat ice cream or watch Humphrey Bogart movies or—what the hell—maybe even go to the Santa Monica Pier.

Maybe she liked to go to the pier a whole lot. Maybe it was a place where she liked to go with her kid on the weekends—after all, it wasn't just the tourists who loved the carousel. For all he knew, he'd passed them so often when he was on the pier that when he did find her son, the kid would actually look familiar.

Okay, so that idea was probably a bit on the fantastic side. But it was no more ridiculous than the notion that a Vietnamese caricature artist could be studying for an advanced degree in philosophy.

"Okay," Ryan said to the cellphone. He trotted down a long hallway and hoped that he was at least getting close to the right place. "What's your kid's name?"

"Ricky," she answered.

"Ricky what?" he snapped impatiently.

"Martin."

In spite of everything, Ryan almost stumbled. "Ricky Martin? You named your kid Ricky Martin?"

The defensive tone in her voice gave Ryan the idea that he probably wasn't the first person to have that reaction. "Hey, it was before the singer ever—"

"Forget it," he told her quickly. "What does he look like?"

Damn, there was nothing to see but lockers and bulletin boards with flyers for the chess club stapled to them. Where the hell were they hiding this famous classroom anyway? In an underground bunker?

"He's eleven years-old, blond hair, green eyes. He's small for his age," she told him briskly as he reached the end of the hallway. He started down another and was dispirited to see that it was nearly identical to the other one. "He's wearing a light blue shirt, khaki pants—"

As if summoned by her description, a group of boys came out of a classroom several feet ahead of him and milled around in the hall, chattering to each other in slightly hushed voices. Ryan stopped short and stared at them. "They're all wearing blue shirts and khaki pants!"

Even worse, they all seemed to be about the same general height and coloring. Ryan spotted another classroom door and ran over to look through the window. Still more identically-dressed little boys. God, nothing about this was easy in the slightest. He was trying to think of some other distinguishing characteristic he might be able to ask her about when the group of boys came up the hall towards him, watching him with wary eyes.

Ryan stopped one of them immediately, grabbing the kid by the arm to spin him around.

"Ricky Martin?" he asked the kid, looking into his face intently.

The kid shrank back from him, his large eyes getting even larger. "No."

Ryan dropped his hold and turned to another boy. "How about you? Are you Ricky Martin?"

All the boys shook their heads and walked away quickly. He looked around, frustrated.

"Ryan, go to the administration office!" Jessica said suddenly. "Give them the phone and I'll tell them what's going on. Then they'll call his class so they won't release him to anybody!"

But before Ryan could do anything at all, a heavy hand landed firmly on his shoulder and pulled him around.

"What do you think you're doing, sir?"

Ryan realized the man confronting him was a rent-a-cop. It was all he could do to keep himself from throwing his arms around the guy in an enormous joyful bear hug. "Oh, great!" he said cheerfully. "Do you know where we can find the administration office?"

As if in direct response to his question, the air was filled with the painfully shrill clanging of the bell for dismissal. Instantly, the corridor was flooded with little boys, all of them in uniform, all of them laughing, talking, yelling as they stampeded toward the exit as fast as their little legs could carry them. He tore away from the security guard and followed them. Goddamn, he just wasn't going to catch a break, Ryan thought, completely forgetting about his close call with the giant potted palm on the highway.

"You can't go there right now, sir," the rent-a-cop informed him, his tone no less stiff and cold despite the fact that he had to shout.

Ryan ignored him. "Ricky Martin!" he hollered as loudly as he possibly could. He began running down the hall with the streaming mob of children and hoping he would be able to stay in the middle of the torrent without getting knocked down and trampled. "Does anyone here know where Ricky Martin is?"

It was impossible to tell whether anyone had actually heard him in the after-school clamor. In fact, the only person paying any attention to him at all was the rent-a-cop, who was plowing after him waist-deep in bobbing heads and looking about as friendly as a thundercloud.

This was definitely not a good development. It finally dawned on Ryan that the man had made certain assumptions as to why he was wandering around in the hallway looking for a little boy. None of those assumptions was especially savory.

He'd better keep moving, he told himself. Keep moving and keep his eyes open, try to get a good look at as many of these kids as he could, in spite of the fact that he absolutely no idea what Ricky Martin actually looked like. After a time he became aware of another sound underneath all the kids screaming and yelling. A small filtered but piercing woman's voice was in his ear asking, "Was that the bell, Ryan? Was that the bell?"

"Yes!" He looked around, raised his voice. "Ricky Martin! RICKY MARTIN!"

"He'll go to the parents' pick-up area!" the woman told him. She was speaking quickly and she sounded as breathless as if she were running alongside him. "Hurry, oh, God, Ryan, they're going to get him!"

Ryan let the current of noisy, energetic children pouring toward the exit carry him along with them. As soon as they were outdoors, the kids scattered in all directions and he sprinted away from the rent-a-cop who was still hot on his heels. He followed the signs that directed him to the pick-up area at the front of the school.

He hadn't actually noticed the pick-up area when he had first pulled up, but now it was impossible to miss, thanks to all the cars and SUVs lined up at the curb. There was a loose crowd of kids wandering all over the place, pausing now and then to stand on tiptoe as they looked for their rides. They would wave their arms overhead to let their parents or carpool drivers know where they were. It may have been organized but it looked like a mess to Ryan. Jesus, none of this was going to get any easier for him, no matter what he did.

"All right, parent pick-up, I got it, he'll definitely go there," Ryan said, combing his fingers through his hair. "What kind of car do you have?"

"It's a black SUV," she told him.

A black SUV. Jesus, this just got better and better. How could he not have seen that one coming? "Of course you do," Ryan groaned, closing his eyes for a long, world-weary moment and then opened them again. "There's like fifty of them!"

Had he actually said fifty? That was a laugh. More like a hundred and fifty, God help him. All makes, all models and quite a range of years, but one and only one color. Of course. What the hell was going on with these SUV people, he wondered, that they were all so crazy about black? Was it because they actually thought that black wouldn't show the dirt or something?

"It's a Porsche Cayenne!" the woman added desperately.

He started to tell her he wasn't so sure that detail would actually be of any help to him when the security guard from the hallway suddenly materialized next to him as if by magic and took a firm hold on his arm.

"Excuse me, sir," the man said, pulling him away from the pick-up area, "but you'll have to wait down there with the other parents."

Ryan tried to twist free of him. "Listen, I'm looking for a kid named Ricky Martin," he said, scanning the multitude of children and vehicles.

"He'll have his *Lord of the Rings* backpack on," Jessica was saying.

As if on cue, a blond-haired green-eyed boy wearing a *Lord of the Rings* backpack rushed past him toward a Porsche Cayenne.

"Ricky Martin!" Ryan bellowed the name with enough force to make his own head pound, more in desperation than in any real hope that the kid could possibly hear him over the cacophony in the lot. But somehow, the boy did hear him and, although he had already opened the back door of the SUV, he paused before climbing in, turned around, and by some fluke looked directly at Ryan.

For a long moment, he and the boy were staring directly at each other and Ryan dared to think it was actually going to work. Ricky Martin was going to step away from the Porsche Cayenne and come over to him.

Then Ryan would hand the phone to him and that would be that. The kid would hear his mother on the other end of the line, she would explain what was going on and then the kid would explain to the rent-a-cop, who would finally understand that Ryan wasn't there to stalk little boys but to avert a kidnapping and worse.

The security guard would then call the real cops, the real cops would ride to the rescue and everyone would be saved. He then could get back in the Bronco, go pick up Chloe's T-shirts at Kinko's. She would believe he was the new improved Ryan Hewitt after all, they would get back together and everyone else would be saved, himself included.

He could actually see the whole scenario unfold in his mind in an orderly and perfectly detailed sequence. It wasn't out of the question, it could have happened. It could have happened just the way he had seen it. All it took to kick it off was for Ricky Martin to move away from that black SUV and come over to him.

The boy took a tentative step toward him. Okay, kid, Ryan thought at him, now another one, faster this time. But the kid hesitated, his round face puckering with uncertainty. Ryan could practically hear him recalling his parents' instructions: *Never go with anyone you don't know, no matter what they tell you. If a stranger comes up to you after school and tells you there's some kind of emergency with Mommy and Daddy, you tell one of the teachers and go right to the admin office.*

Ryan had a sudden vision of himself, as he must have looked to the boy—a strange man calling out to him, trying to distract him while he was being dragged away by one of the school security guards. Yeah, Ricky Martin was definitely going to run right over to him so he could find out what was going on!

Then a hand reached out of the darkness of the Porsche Cayenne, snagged the kid by his backpack, and yanked him inside.

Ryan's jaw dropped as the door slammed shut. The whole thing had taken all of a second, if that. He turned back to the rent-a-cop who still had his arm in what was a surprisingly strong grip. The guy was as clueless as hell. "Shit, did you just see that? That little kid was just kidnapped!"

"Ryan, please, don't let them get away!" Jessica begged. "Go after them! You've got to go after them!"

"Jessica, I can't! My car's on the other side of the freaking school!" he said, struggling furiously with the cop while he watched the SUV nosing its way into the driveway traffic looking for all the world like it was just one more tank from the suburbs come to cart junior's pampered behind back home or to soccer practice or piano lessons the way it did on every other ordinary, unremarkable, same old shit day. There was nothing about the SUV either to suggest that today was any different. But this happened to be a day when there were actually a couple of thugs behind that expensive tinted safety glass and they had just kidnapped an unsuspecting eleven year-old boy named Ricky Martin, who was small for his age and had no idea that his mom was locked in an attic somewhere and the housekeeper who took him to school in the mornings had been murdered—

Ryan had a sudden vision of the terrified boy in the backseat of the SUV, trying to get his mind around what had just happened. Meanwhile some thug would be trussing him up like a turkey or hog-tying him like a rodeo calf, maybe even holding a weapon on him.

And this goddamned guard didn't want to know about it. He ignored Ryan except to tighten his grip on him.

The image of the kid's terrified face filled Ryan's mind until there was nothing else that he could see. This wasn't a joke or a game or a reality show with hidden cameras—an eleven year-old boy had just been kidnapped in broad daylight from in front of his school by real thugs. Ryan knew for a fact that they weren't bluffing.

There was no turning back for Ricky and his mother.

Ryan's adrenalin surged; he twisted and flailed like a mad thing, not caring if he hurt himself or this stupid security guard who refused to listen to him. "Goddamn it, listen to me! That little kid over there was just kidnapped! Do something!"

The rent-a-cop just kept on doing what he was already doing, which was trying to get some kind of judo-style grip on his arms as he wrestled him roughly down a grassy slope toward a car idling at a nearby curb. It was a standard rent-a-cop-mobile, Ryan saw, a tin can with a sewing machine under the hood and those stupid rent-a-cop flashing lights that never impressed anybody bolted onto the roof. It also had nobody behind the wheel.

"Hey, man," Ryan said, turning to the guard with a deeply apologetic expression on his face.

"You know, I'm really, really sorry about this—" The cop was so startled he loosened his grip on Ryan's arm. Immediately Ryan jerked free of him. "But I have to borrow your car!"

Ryan was already down the slope before the rent-a-cop could even yell "Hey!" after him. He reached the car and automatically vaulted over the hood before he even realized what he was doing, flung himself into the driver's seat and stamped on the gas pedal with both feet.

The engine on the rent-a-cop mobile sounded like a cross between a rabid chipmunk and a rabid chipmunk's equally rabid sewing machine, but to Ryan's surprise it had slightly more zip to it than he had imagined.

Maybe that would make up for the fact that the tires seemed to be practically bald, he thought, as he slalomed through the sedate, residential streets of Westwood in pursuit of the Cayenne. It had a head start on him of at least a quarter-mile.

"Please tell me they didn't get him!" begged the woman's tearful voice in his ear.

"It's gonna be okay," Ryan told her. "I can see them ahead!"

His first instinct was to get right up on the Cayenne's bumper, except he didn't want them to realize that someone might be following them. He was uneasily aware of how conspicuous the security car was in a neighborhood like this. If one of the kidnappers just happened to look back and see it chattering along behind them, would he become suspicious?

There were two cars between him and the Cayenne now. Maybe if he was careful to maintain that distance, Ryan thought, he might actually be able to follow them all over the state without them suspecting they had a tail.

"Look, don't worry," he said to the kid's mother reassuringly. "This is actually a good thing. Now I can follow them back to wherever they're holding you and then call the cops."

She didn't compliment him on his plan but he thought her breathing sounded a little calmer, which was just fine with him. She could save all her compliments for later, when the cops swarmed in and rescued her. Ryan didn't mind waiting.

On the other hand, he thought suddenly, why wait any longer than he had to? Maybe he was being a little too cautious following them this way; he gave it a little more gas and sped up so he could pass one of the cars in front of him. The guys in the Cayenne had no reason to think anything was wrong; it was more likely that they figured they'd gotten away with it and didn't give a shit about what was behind them.

In which case, it might as well be him in the car traveling directly behind them, he thought, and moved out into the left lane to prepare to pass the next car. This was definitely going to work out, he thought, provided the sewing machine under the hood didn't give up the ghost.

He could feel how the little car was approaching the top limit of its zip capacity. Getting the tin can past the next car meant having to all but stand on the accelerator, and he had to stand on it pretty hard, for a pretty long time before he could finally position himself directly behind the Cayenne.

So far, so good, but he decided that he would do better if he kept the rent-a-cop car just close enough to them to make sure no one else got between them. He started to close the distance.

He was doing pretty well with this tailing thing, even coping with a stick shift, Ryan said to himself. But then it didn't seem to him like it was really terribly hard in the first place. It wasn't like this was frickin' brain surgery, for God's sake, it was driving, almost anybody would have been able to do it. Hell, even a frickin' child could—

The enormous, grimy silver shape that surged into the space directly in front of him didn't register right away as a city bus. It took him a moment to realize what it was even with the familiar logo—Public Transportation: We're Going YOUR Way—ALL The Way!—taking up the entire view through his windshield.

For crying out loud—he would have sworn a bus would never have been able to fit into the relatively miniscule space between him and the Cayenne. He had thought that all the buses in LA were extinct anyway. The last time he could even remember seeing a bus had been in a movie about poor people.

He didn't actually give a shit one way or the other about buses and would not have shed any bitter tears if he had lived the rest of his life without a single reminder that any buses existed. Least of all this one, which was belching ecologically-sound, lead-free poison gas in his face at twenty-five miles per hour. Ryan could only splutter incoherently.

"What's the matter?" the woman on the phone kept saying over and over. "Ryan? What's the matter now? Talk to me!"

"This stupid bus just cut me off!" he said when he was finally able to speak.

He swerved to one side and then the other in an attempt to see around its grimy silver bulk. To his relief, the Cayenne was still up ahead but there was no way to tell how much longer that would last.

And just when the hell was that goddamned bus going to pull over for another stop? He thought that it would have already pulled over another two or three times by now so he could go around it. Weren't these goddamned things supposed to stop every hundred feet or something?

He punched the horn but it was highly unlikely that the bus driver could hear the pathetic noise this car made in lieu of a real horn. Or if he had, he probably wouldn't think for one moment that it could have been anyone honking at him. Anyway he probably wouldn't have cared. Why would anyone honk at a goddamned bus? There was no point.

Abruptly, Ryan caught sight of a set of controls for the bubble lights on the roof and flipped them on. Maybe the bus driver would see the flashing and think that some city official wanted him to pull over.

Yeah, right. No such luck; all he got for his trouble were a lot of very funny looks from people in the cars going the other way. He should have known better, Ryan thought. If it had been him, he wouldn't have pulled over, either.

"Don't lose them!" begged the voice in his ear.

"All right, this ain't working," Ryan muttered, more to himself than to her. "Hang on—"

"Wait, Ryan—"

He tossed the cellphone into the passenger seat and edged the car as far over to the left as he could safely. The traffic going the other way kept on coming in a steady, continuous stream but he held his position and waited until finally, finally, finally, there was a break in the flow.

Immediately, Ryan stamped on the accelerator and the sewing machine engine chatter raised an octave in pitch to an all-time sewing machine high as he slam-shifted it into the next gear. As he pushed the clattering, shaking car even faster, the sewing machine pistons began to ping a clear warning as to the state of things under the hood. It was as if they were admonishing him about his recklessness.

"Come on," he muttered, keeping the gas pedal mashed to the floorboards. Now he could see he was gaining on the bus; he was already past the rear wheels and almost to the midpoint. All he needed was two more seconds—

The reappearance of oncoming traffic was nowhere near as surprising to him as it was frightening. In some small part of his mind, far down in the area reserved for contemplation of absurd ideas and bad timing, a small voice was giving him an I-told-you-so about how it would be impossible for him to drop back behind the bus again, and he should have thought of that. Ryan shook the thought away; if he were going to survive the next few moments, he had no choice but to jet across the oncoming lanes and hope for the best. Whatever the best turned out to be.

To his amazement, the oncoming cars streamed to the left and right, veering around and away from him. Like Moses parting the waters, Ryan marveled, watching as the traffic rushed toward him and then divided.

He then found himself roaring up the farthest lane, still going the wrong way but with traffic dodging him on only *one* side. That was progress of a sort, he supposed.

Now, if he could just bring the still-shaking and chattering car to a stop gradually enough to keep from losing control—

The taxi facing him at the curb did not jerk a cry of terror out of Ryan because it had appeared in front of him out of nowhere. He had had a clear and relatively unobstructed view of its approach in the oncoming traffic; but he didn't actually start screaming until it swerved directly into his lane and came to a complete stop not even twenty feet ahead of him to let out a passenger.

Fortunately, Ryan's disbelief didn't interfere with his reflexes. He cleared the taxi's outside headlight with inches to spare and slid past close enough to read the total fare on the oblivious driver's meter. Now he just had to re-enter the oncoming traffic.

He wasn't getting much in the way of the previous Moses-parting-the-waters effect this time. There were a hell of a lot more cars and they all seemed to be coming at him a hell of a lot more quickly. He might as well have been trying to steer the tin can between raindrops in a thunderstorm.

He had to get his ass back to the right side of the road now or he was going to end up smeared over half the front bumpers in LA. While the kid in the back of that Porsche Cayenne was going to be—

Car horns were blaring long and hard in an off-key chorus. There was a hideously shrill squeal of tires laying down streaks of rubber on asphalt as Ryan yanked the steering wheel to the right and plunged across several lanes of traffic. Cars and trucks and SUVs were skidding sideways all over the place, their drivers and passengers looking terrified, enraged, confused, all at once. Their enthusiastic hand gestures were unambiguous.

Ryan paid no attention to any of them as he swerved around a Honda that had slewed crazily across two lanes; he managed to miss the car by a hair along with the less-fortunate VW Beetle that hadn't and was now hopelessly entangled in the Honda's crumpled bumper. He told himself he would be able to panic about all this shit later. He kept his gaze fixed firmly on the other side of the road, refusing to be distracted by any of the other extremely close near misses he was having with larger vehicles. He had to keep his concentration focused on just living through this; once he had accomplished that part, he could allow himself to panic about anything he wanted later on, even the shit that wasn't scary.

Right now, however, he was now finding it extremely difficult to shut out the terrible sounds of impact all around him coming one after another in quick succession as cars and vans and SUVs piled into each other. Not the most pleasant noises to listen to but nothing dramatic enough to be heart stopping, or so he kept telling himself. Besides, he had almost made it; he was almost there. In two seconds, all of this would be in the past—he would be on the right side of the road again, finished with stunt driving and back on the (comparatively) straight and (more-or-less) narrow.

Then all at once he found that he was back in the right lane and traveling with the flow of traffic instead of against it. He had perhaps two seconds to feel the intensely joyful relief of still being alive.

Then he was treated to the sight of the driver of a tractor-trailer who was losing his struggle to stop without jack-knifing in the nearest oncoming lane.

The truck-driver's pale, panicky face was clearly visible to Ryan as the forty-foot trailer he was pulling skated around to the side, looking almost weightless as it displayed its cargo of lawnmowers. The machines were stacked on the trailer's open framework in a rather ingenious assembly of interlocking pieces.

For a fraction of a second, Ryan hoped that the lawnmowers might actually be wedged together too securely to be dislodged. Then they all flew apart, spilling out of the framework and across the road in an avalanche that was both unwieldy and graceful at the same time.

Ryan managed to dodge one of the mowers and barely grazed another. But he had no choice except to plow the rent-a-cop car directly into a third, obliterating it in a spectacular explosion of parts. To his great relief and even greater surprise, however, this had no effect on the tin can sewing machine he was driving. It continued to chatter along more or less as if nothing had happened.

Even better than that, Ryan realized with a fierce surge of triumph, he had left the bus behind. The big stupid thing was absolutely nowhere in sight.

Then he took another look around and the feeling of triumph halted. It wasn't only the bus that was nowhere in sight.

There wasn't a single black SUV to be seen anywhere on the street around him, least of all a Porsche Cayenne with a terrified, kidnapped eleven year-old boy in the back seat.

SIX

The utter pandemonium Ryan had just survived on the highway was nothing compared to the tumult that was going on in his ear and in his head now.

The woman on the cellphone was in all-out panic mode, begging him over and over to tell her what was happening. Please, please tell her what was going on, please, please tell her that he hadn't lost them, not that, please, anything but please not that. Please don't tell her that he'd lost them.

And more than anything else in the world he wanted to say he wouldn't tell her that. No, ma'am, this was the one thing he wouldn't ever tell her. Except right now, that just happened to be the only thing he was certain of. Not to mention it being the only thing he couldn't stop telling himself.

The Cayenne was gone as if it had never been. And there was nothing on the mundane LA streets to give him the slightest hint as to where it might be. Gas stations, convenience stores and parking lots went by one after another on either side of him, sailing through his vision and out of sight. There were so many of them, all of a sudden—gas stations and convenience stores, bearing the names of every chain and every franchise he had ever heard of including a few he had thought were defunct. There were some he wasn't familiar with at all.

How many of these goddamned places did LA have, anyway? And why were there so goddamned many of them? Was it some kind of hot new trend, to open franchise businesses on every available plot of land or were these places actually breeding on their own in some way, untouched by human hands? Was it like this all over town or was it just something about this stretch of road?

But the real question was: why, when he knew with absolute certainty that a Porsche Cayenne with a scared little boy in the backseat would *not* stop at any one of these places, why, why, why didn't that make it easier to find out where the goddamned thing was going?

Because, Ryan thought, as he peered down a side street to his right, when you took away all those gas stations and convenience stores, the only things you had left were tacky car dealerships with plastic pennants, day-glo banners and chain restaurants with color schemes even more lurid, that served breakfast all day or all-you-can-eat buffets till three. And, let us not forget, ye olde drive-through banks which, of course, were also no good because they were all just more places where the Cayenne wouldn't be.

How the hell was he supposed to reassure the hysterical woman on his cellphone that he hadn't lost the Cayenne with her son in it, when everywhere he looked all he saw were a hell of a lot of places where her son could not possibly be?

"Just give me a second," he said, slowing down at another cross street and looking both ways. No black SUVs in either direction, either on the road or parked.

Christ, what had happened to all the traffic? Where the hell had it gone all of a sudden?

Something started to bubble in the back of his mind, a vague memory of something he'd heard on a cop show once. Something about how people who were actively trying to lose someone tailing them would be far more likely to turn right than left because a right turn was easier and faster.

That theory did make a great deal of sense, Ryan thought, except for one small detail: the guys in the Cayenne with Ricky Martin wouldn't have known that they had anyone following them. On the other hand, they might have been the kind of professional thugs who always drove as if they had someone tailing them, just to be on the safe side.

Oh, right—as if Ryan Hewitt possessed special expert knowledge in the area of thug behavior and tactics! He didn't know shit about this sort of thing—he was so far out of his depth that even real thugs probably wouldn't think it was funny. His frustration mixed with uneasiness.

But then, where was a person supposed to go to learn about that stuff in the first place—Thug U?

Yeah, right—try prison, you dork, he told himself bitterly. How freakin' clueless was he? Even good old Chad would have gotten that one on the first try.

"Jesus," he groaned, forcing his attention back to the road ahead of him and scanning it desperately. "Where the freakin' hell could they possibly have gone?"

Ryan pressed harder on the accelerator, ignoring the chattering complaint from the sewing machine under the hood. The damned rent-a-cop tin can was beginning to lose its pick-up. He had to prod the goddamned gas pedal several times to keep the car moving ahead and on course as the road made a hard bend to the right.

Finally, just as he straightened out the steering wheel, the engine woke up again and surged forward—or tried to. The pick-up was still lagging, which turned out to be a good thing. It meant he had just enough time to stand on the brakes before he drove squarely into the rear end of the car that had stopped in front of him.

Hearing Ryan squeal to an extremely short stop behind him, the driver of the car in front casually twisted around in his seat and looked back with a mixture of boredom and disdain. He seemed to make a point of staring at Ryan long and hard as if to make sure he understood that anyone in a hurry right now was, by general consensus, a major asshole. Ryan looked past him at all the other unmoving vehicles sitting bumper to bumper in every lane ahead of him.

Well, now he knew where all the traffic had gone. Nothing special, just one more instance of traffic achieving critical mass and turning a highway into a multi-lane parking lot. Just business as usual on the streets of LA. There would be no easy way to get himself out of it, either, Ryan saw. More cars were pouring in behind him and around him, quickly filling every available gap until he was locked firmly in place.

Ryan leaned forward and banged his forehead against the top of the steering wheel several times. "I don't believe this," he groaned.

The woman on the phone was speaking again; she almost sounded calm now but her tone was still urgent. "Ryan, listen to me," she said. "You've got to go back to the police—"

He lifted his head with a shout of incredulous laughter. "Are you, like, high?" he asked her. "The only way to follow them was to take this car! You don't go to the cops after you ta—uh, borrow a car!"

All at once, he realized how loudly he'd been speaking. Alarmed, he looked around to see if anyone in any of the other cars sitting close by had happened to catch him. But as far as he could tell, they were all too bored and fed-up to pay any attention to him or just about anything else, for that matter. At least, he didn't see anyone staring directly at him with an openly suspicious expression.

Which was one more enormous relief in a too short series. Being stuck in goddamned gridlock was bad enough—the last thing he needed was to have some citizen gifted with better than average hearing and an overdeveloped sense of civic duty decide that this would be a good opportunity to take a bite out of crime with their freakin' WAP phone. Nothing in the world could have been worse than that right now. Absolutely nothing.

As if on cue, his cellphone began beeping.

"Oh, great," Ryan moaned.

He didn't have to look at the faceplate to see what *that* sound was all about. God knew he'd heard it often enough before, especially after Chad had been playing with the video function. But naturally he looked anyway.

LOW BATT. LOW BATT.

The words flashed on and off while Jessica Martin asked him what happened, what was going on, please, please, he had to tell her, what was wrong now?

"Now the battery's dying," he said, his voice flat with misery.

All told, it was actually some kind of minor miracle that the phone hadn't started beeping ages ago. That would be another minor miracle, he supposed, in today's series of minor miracles, none of which had been of much real help to him. Was he ever going to get a frickin' break?

"Don't you have a charger?" Jessica Martin asked him. He could have sworn that he was hearing a faint tone of admonition in her voice.

"Oh, sure," he said grandly. "Sure I've got a charger. At my house."

The beeping became faster and more urgent. He checked the faceplate again to see that a power bar had disappeared from the battery icon and another was already starting to fade. Shit. The next time good old Chad tried to use the video function, Ryan was going to jam it so far up his—

Or maybe not, Ryan thought suddenly. Maybe rent-a-cops carried phone chargers.

"Hang on, I'm checking," he told Jessica and rooted around in the armrest with one frantic hand, unfortunately coming up with nothing more than dozens of receipts from fast food joints. Oh, yuck, he thought, tossing aside tiny slips of paper by the fistful; this guy had one very major Gigunda Burger habit. Man, that was pretty bad—even good old Chad knew better than to put a Gigunda Burger in his mouth. How could any human being survive on a steady diet of meat byproducts covered with artificial cheese byproducts? Smoking crack was probably healthier.

Disgusted, Ryan reached for the glove box, grateful that the car was so small he barely had to lean over. As soon as he touched the button, the door flew open and a .38 Special tumbled out.

"Jesus!" Ryan yelped, snatching his hand back as if it had been burned.

"Did you find one?" Jessica asked him anxiously.

Ryan hesitated before answering. "Uh, no. Not exactly."

He glanced at the .38 nervously, almost expecting it to do something dangerous all by itself. Jesus Christ, he thought with a genuine chill of fear. He had stolen a car from a guy who ate Gigunda Burgers and carried guns—and not just some plain old guy but a rent-a-cop. Who knew what a guy like that was capable of? Damn, but it was a freaky and dangerous world filled with freaky and dangerous people.

The phone beeped again, more insistently this time.

"Ryan, don't lose me," Jessica begged. "Ryan? Ryan?"

"I know, Jessica," he said feelingly. "I know."

He knew; God, did he ever know. He knew a hell of a lot more than he'd ever wanted to and God, did he wish that he didn't. Maybe he should tell her about the gun, he thought, and then decided that he wouldn't, at least for the moment. For some reason, he felt it would be a lot easier on both his nerves and hers if he kept that bit of information to himself for the time being.

The phone erupted in a steady flow of beeps then, by way of announcing its imminent death.

Damn, but he was really starting to hate this fucking cellphone, Ryan thought blackly. If he ever got through this, he would never touch another one of the goddamned things, never. Not ever. For any reason. The next time good old Chad wanted to use the video function on his Bluetooth, he wouldn't shove it all the way up to his tonsils, after all—he'd just hand the goddamned thing to him and run for the hills.

And while he was on the subject of things he was losing his taste for, Ryan added to himself, he could definitely put driving on the list. He looked around for any indication of imminent forward motion, a sign that something might open up near him on the road, a gap that he might be able to inch through and escape the jam.

Nothing. Damn, this gridlock wasn't just bad. It wasn't even just unbelievably bad. This was genuine stuff-of-legends bad. No, worse than that, Ryan decided. This was nothing less than a preview of what the driving in the Ninth Circle of Hell would be like.

It was so bad, in fact, that he would have been no better off if he had been riding a motorcycle. The cars were crammed together so closely that there wouldn't have been enough room for a famine victim on a bicycle to slip between them.

There wasn't even an emergency lane, the shoulder was all crowded up with enormous yellow and black construction vehicles. And there was no guardrail between the road and a long drop down a hill to the ample parking lot of another of those classic blights of western civilization, a freaking strip mall—

The sign seemed to materialize out of thin air, even though Ryan knew he'd been looking directly at the goddamned thing without seeing it while he'd been sitting there in the jam.

457 COMMUNICATIONS.

He must have seen a million of these signs about a million times before, but now that he had really had a chance to look at it, particularly in the context of the strip mall where the store was actually located, the implications were rapidly becoming clear to him.

And how about that—three cheers for Ryan Hewitt! He congratulated himself as new hope surged in his chest with an intensity that came close to pain. All at once he felt as if he really understood what people meant when they used the expression "thinking outside the box."

He wiggled out from behind the steering wheel and pushed himself up to have a look out the window. Hello, world, this is Ryan Hewitt and I'm not just thinking outside the box, I'm also thinking outside this tin can I'm driving. He could feel himself grinning madly as he scanned the road-turned-parking-lot.

Then, as if on cue, the traffic began to inch forward with excruciating slowness. He could see now that there was an exit ramp only a quarter of a mile ahead of him but at his current rate of speed, he wouldn't get there before his next birthday.

Beep-beep-beep-beep-beep, the phone said by way of agreement.

Ryan was still staring at the off-ramp when a large danger-yellow-and-black tractor crawled up and over the crest of the hill, in the process of grading a dirt access road on it.

Was that really an access road, Ryan wondered? Or was it just the tractor making its own access?

It was impossible to see anything beyond the edge of the hill. If the tractor had been able to manage it, then the drop could not have been too sheer.

He hoped.

On the other hand, the rent-a-cop car he was driving was not even remotely like a four-wheel-drive vehicle (or a black SUV, a nagging voice in his mind added), let alone a tractor. Sure, the thing had front-wheel drive but that wouldn't do him a whole lot of good in light of how bald the goddamned tires were.

Beep-beep-beep-beep-beep-beep, the phone reminded him.

He was just going to have to hope for the best yet again.

"You are gonna owe me soooo big for this one," he said to Jessica Martin as he dropped himself back into the driver's seat.

"Ryan?" she asked, obviously puzzled.

But there was no time for him to explain. He stamped on the gas pedal and hauled the steering wheel hard to the right. He was thinking almost absently that he would have to talk to her at the first available opportunity about how it was asking too much of him to provide her with a running color commentary on events as they happened. Some things he could explain but with others you just had to be there.

Like now, he thought, catching a glimpse of the tractor operator's startled face as he floored the sewing machine. He couldn't even begin to explain what he was doing to the people who were right there in front of him.

A second later he found himself airborne as the car flew off the side of the hill.

This, Ryan reflected with a strange, surreal feeling of detachment, was *another* perfect example of a situation that was impossible to describe as it happened. He had just discovered that he had driven a car over the edge of a cliff and he had achieved the same state of weightlessness he'd have felt if he were a trainee astronaut in the cabin of a jet in a steep dive.

It felt a hell of a lot more like floating than falling. But how was he supposed to explain that to Jessica when he couldn't even begin to explain it to himself?

Then he saw the ground rushing up at him. Before he even had time to be scared of the impact, he found himself bouncing down the slope and his butt felt as if it were being imprinted with every spring and wire in the crappy driver's seat all the way down to the brackets on the floorboards.

Damn, this thinking-outside-the-box thing could be really hard on the ass. But at least he was going to live long enough to have the satisfaction of knowing that he'd been right about the hill not being a completely sheer drop.

What it really was, as it turned out, was a sudden-death obstacle course of tractors and graders and all kinds of other big danger-yellow-and-black machines with the biggest freakin' metal teeth he'd ever seen. Not to mention the shovels and half-tracks like tanks. If a tiny little piece of crap like the tin can he were currently bouncing around in happened to hit any of these monsters, it would bounce off without leaving a dent.

Ryan clamped the cellphone antenna between his teeth so he could use both hands to fight for control of the car. He was barely managing to maneuver it around one mechanical monster after another. If there was any bounce left in the tin can's shocks after this, he thought madly, he would gladly kiss them.

And then in the middle of all the noise and the frenzied bouncing and bucking and jouncing up and down in front of him, he could hear the familiar female voice coming from the cellphone speaker. It was asking an all-too-familiar question.

"What's going on? Ryan? What's going on?"

Purely out of habit, he actually tried to answer but the antenna in his mouth rendered it as "*mmmrrrmph mrm mrmph.*" It was just as well; the ride was getting rougher and rougher. Never mind the shocks, which had to be a lost cause by now—he was bouncing up and down so vigorously he would be lucky if he could even stay behind the wheel.

And then there was the problem of getting the car back under control, which was beginning to seem more and more unlikely by the second. When a barrel went over Niagara Falls with a marble in it, Ryan thought giddily, it did not mean that the marble was doing the driving.

The phone went flying out of his mouth just before he saw the fence ahead of him. He had a fraction of a second to hope that the thing was as flimsy as it looked before he crashed through it and zoomed across the busy boulevard on the other side.

The sound of cars screeching to a halt around him had become so mundane that he didn't hear any of it. The only thing he did care about was that the very dented, bashed and scratched nose of the rent-a-cop tin can was pointed directly at the entrance to the strip mall parking lot right in front of him. And it was the actual entrance, which meant he would not have to crash through a fence or go over a cliff to get to it—he could just drive in. What a break!

He skidded to a stop directly in the front of the phone store and began to search the car for the cellphone. He found it on the floor in front of the passenger seat, right next to the handgun.

Ryan froze. Christ, he had forgotten about that thing. Man, if there was one thing he really didn't need right now it was to have some cop finally pay attention to him only to bust him with a goddamned handgun. He shoved the .38 out of sight under the seat and pounced on the cell.

"Are you still there? Can you hear me?" he shouted at the phone, almost forgetting he had to put it to his ear.

"I'm here!" said the tiny voice.

Okay, they were still in business. There—that was yet another break. Maybe that was a sign that everything was going to start getting easier; not that he could think of any way things could get any harder. He jumped out of the car and raced into the store.

Exactly which major shopping holiday was this, Ryan wondered in horror as he surveyed the horde pushing and shoving and jostling each other in front of him. And why was he the last person in the world to know about it?

He was starting to feel the familiar beginnings of panic as he waded into the mass of people who had crowded into the ridiculously small store. This was as bad as what he had seen at the police station.

No, it was worse than that, because none of these people were gangbangers fighting a drug war with each other. This was something a lot scarier than that, more terrifying than a drug war, far more harrowing than driving on a freeway in the Ninth Circle of Hell.

!SALE!

The word leaped out at him from high up on the walls and dangled over his head from the ceiling.

!Half-Price SALE!
!Special Purchase SALE!
!Mid-Week SALE!
!Treat Yourself SALE!
!Upgrade SALE!
!SALE SALE SALE SALE SALE!

The effect was beyond nightmarish. People were reacting like sharks in a feeding frenzy. Every salesperson was surrounded by a near-hysterical babbling mob of customers, all of them desperately jockeying for the front-and-center position. It was as if their lives depended on their being able to spend money. Ryan hadn't seen anything quite so extreme outside of a toy store on Christmas Eve. What could these people possibly be thinking, any of them?

Beep-beep-beep-beep-beep! suggested the phone in his hand.

"Hey, what do you think you're doing?" someone yelled in his ear as he squeezed forward, trying to see over the heads around him. "There's a line, you know!"

Yeah, and I crossed it a long time ago, Ryan answered silently.

"It starts back there!" the person shouted at him and then began complaining loudly to the world in general about inexcusably rude morons who couldn't wait their turn because they had no respect for people who had gotten there ahead of them and had been waiting longer—was that unbelievable or what? Ryan ignored him, along with all the other customers who were giving him dirty looks, and kept squeezing himself forward as best he could—if he stopped moving in this mob, he might never get started again.

Finally he managed to elbow his way over to a salesman giving cellphone chapter and verse to a customer who obviously thought that mobile telecommunication was the best thing that could ever happen to anyone in the entire history of the universe.

"...and if you get the new Nokia 6600, you can switch out faceplates to match your mood!" the salesman burbled, sounding both perky and lascivious at once. "Today we're having a special on tiger stripes! Are you feeling fierce?" He punctuated the question by pawing the air playfully, causing his customer to respond with a noise that seemed to be a cross between a fierce yodel and the call of a lovesick moose. "Oh, how fun is that!"

Ryan took advantage of the customer's momentary swoon to edge himself into the space just in front of the salesman. "Excuse me—"

"Sorry, sir, I'm with a customer now," the salesman said smoothly, "but if you take a number, someone will be with you shortly." He made a vague gesture at something over Ryan's right shoulder.

With some difficulty, Ryan turned around without falling over and found himself facing the stuff of nightmares: a big yellow smiley face offering tickets from its mouth.

No, Ryan thought in horrified disbelief. It couldn't be. Not that. One or the other by itself would have been bad enough, but not both. Not take-a-number and a smiley face together.

Beep-beep-beep-beep, confirmed his dying cellphone, just to let him know that in no way could this possibly be a dream.

Ryan watched as a passing customer tore off one of the tickets. There was a cheery sort of click and another ticket appeared immediately, marked *Number Ninety-Seven*. He looked around and spotted a large display box high on a far wall.

Damn—exactly how could he possibly have failed to notice something that big on his way in, he wondered? For that matter, how could he have failed to notice the travesty of a smiley-face machine, no matter how crowded this place was?

NOW SERVING: NUMBER SEVENTY-ONE.

Nope, this was definitely not going to work for him.

Ryan reached out and caught hold of a busy salesman with a sheaf of contracts in one hand. "I've got a life and death call on this phone and my battery's dying!" he said quickly as he shoved his cellphone in the man's face. "Do you have a charger?"

The man blinked, looking as nonplussed as if Ryan had just asked him if he sold cellphones. "Sure," he said, flip and cheerful. He smiled gently as Ryan sighed with relief before adding, "Just take a number and one of the sales associates will grab you one when your turn comes up."

Before Ryan could even start to protest, he pulled free and disappeared into the crowd.

Beep-beep-beep-beep-beep! the dying cellphone in his hand reminded him urgently.

Ryan felt his physical state change from the mere discomfort of cold sweat to a more unnerving sensation of something squeezing his chest and throat in way that was making it increasingly difficult for him to breathe. Jesus, it couldn't end like this, it just couldn't, he thought; he had not stolen a car and driven it off a cliff only to have everything fall apart because his goddamned cellphone battery had to go and die while he was standing in the middle of a fucking cellphone store!

"Please!" Ryan wailed. No one even looked at him.

He turned around and grabbed the first person he saw wearing a nametag: a plump, motherly-looking saleswoman who seemed completely unfazed by the frenzy around her. "Please, I have an emergency!"

"Sorry, sweetie." She actually patted his cheek. "I'm on break. Take a number."

Take a number.

Ryan felt the room start to spin as she walked away. The words were echoing madly in his brain.

Take a number.

"—switch out faceplates to match your mood! And we have a special today on—"

"Oh, how fun!"

Take... a... number...

"Would you text my aunt in Sheboygan? She—"

"I don't think I really need eight million colors. Is it cheaper if I only go for four million?"

Click!

NOW SERVING: NUMBER SEVENTY-TWO.

"Can I give each of my friends a different ringtone?"

He was going to go crazy, Ryan thought hopelessly. He was going to go crazy right here in the middle of a cellphone store. They would have to take him away. They would carry him out in a straitjacket and put him in a padded cell and if any of his friends wanted to call him, they would have to do it on his padded cellular.

Beep-beep-beep-beep-beep-BEEP! the cellphone declared as the last power bar on the display began to flicker out of existence.

Unbidden, a new and different image appeared in his mind's eye blinding him to everything else around him. It was a terrifying image—something awful, hideous, and not just seriously illegal but criminal—and if he actually resorted to it, he knew he would be committing himself to something gravely irrevocable. This was something that would set him on a course of action from which there would be no going back, not for him and not for anyone else, either.

He also knew that it was the only chance he had. Which meant it was the only chance Jessica and her son had, too.

Ryan shoved his way out of the store as quickly as he could, which turned out to be pretty quickly—the crowd was far more willing to let people out than they were to let them in. He raced back to the car, grabbed the thing he needed, and then marched back in, elbowing his way roughly through the crush until he was standing directly in front of the take-a-number smiley face.

The thought occurred to him as he put the barrel of the rent-a-cop's .38 against the bright yellow plastic of the grinning yellow minimalist travesty that if Jessica Martin were to ask him what was going on right at this moment, the only thing he could have told her was that he was acting out a lifelong fantasy.

He then blew the freaking thing into dust particles.

Instantly, he was the only person in the room standing; everyone else had dropped to the floor. Even better, they had all shut up. Ryan looked around with a feeling of satisfaction so great that it was almost religious.

"Oh, look!" he announced. "Now serving number *thirty-eight special!*"

None of the people cowering on the floor seemed inclined to give him an argument. How about that? he thought as his ears rang; he had just gotten yet another break. Well, it was a sort of a break and he could settle for that. It was a hell of a lot better than standing around with a dead cellphone in his hand for sure. So what the hell, yee-haw, let's fire things up and get this show on the road.

"Okay. Now that I have everyone's attention," he said, looking around quickly until his gaze fell on the nearest cowering salesman, "who's gonna get me that goddamned charger?"

SEVEN

There were some days when he got to the end of his shift, Bob Mooney reflected as he changed into his street clothes in the nearly empty locker room, and all he could think was how very much he was going to miss being on the job at the West Side precinct after he pulled the pin.

Today, he could say with complete and utter honesty, was definitely not one of them. Any day where you had to deal with a mob of gangbangers and skinheads all packed into the same room and trying to murder each other could in no way be considered anything like a good day.

Christ, they had been mixing it up with each other like rabid football widows in Loehman's back room at a sale on Super Bowl Sunday. Not that he had actually seen such a spectacle himself, but the stories Marilyn had told him had been lurid enough to make his hair stand on end.

And, goddamn it, he still had no idea which genius in the precinct had decided that putting gangers and bigots together under one roof at the exact same freakin' time wasn't the worst idea in the world. But he would find out—he was the front desk sergeant and nobody could keep any secrets from him. He could find out anything about anyone, any time, anywhere and by any means and when he found out who this idiot was, heads would roll and asses would be kicked. At least one, anyway.

The whole friggin' mess had been on top of everything else the West Side precinct was expected to take care of. As if all the usual shit that came at them in the course of a regular day wasn't enough—the people calling up to make complaints or the self-styled good citizens calling in to report crimes. Or coming in with emergencies, like the guy earlier who had had the incredibly bad timing to show up just a few seconds before the skinhead invasion.

Mooney paused as he started to button his shirt, and frowned a little as he tried to remember exactly what the kid's deal had been. Something about a woman and somebody's cellphone. Okay, now whose cellphone had it been? This woman's, whoever she was? Or had it belonged to the guy?

It had been his phone. Yeah, that was it—he remembered now. The kid had told him that a woman in some kind of trouble had called him on *his* cellphone. Mooney had even talked to the woman himself. Her name was—

Okay, he had taken her name down. Hadn't he?

Mooney winced. Christ, what kind of dumb-ass question was he asking himself? Of course he had taken her name. He must have; nobody who had ridden the front desk for as long as he had would actually forget to take a goddamned name. But after the day he'd just lived through, he was simply unable to remember, just off the top of his head, a single thing she had told him.

Just like everybody else. Mooney sighed and tucked his shirt in. He took a moment to feel pleased with himself for not having developed one of those classic paunches so common to veteran police officers—unlike certain fellow officers he could name. Sometimes when he was on the front desk, he was filled with an almost uncontrollable urge to tell every single person that demanded his immediate, uninterrupted and undivided attention, whether they were gangbangers, skinheads, Russian Mafia or plain old good citizens, to just take a freakin' number, sit their asses down, and shut the hell up till he got back from his coffee break.

It had just been one goddamned thing after another without let-up, all goddamned day long. And while he was on the subject of it being a long goddamned day, his shift had been officially over for half an hour before he had actually been able to knock off and hit the locker room. Mare would already be wondering what the hell was keeping him.

She would also be worrying about him. She never told him in so many words how much she worried about him, but she didn't have to. They were the kind of married couple whose successful relationship was due in no small part to the fact that they understood a great deal about each other on a non-verbal level. She had never had to tell him she worried; he knew how she felt, the same way that she knew how sorry he was that there was no real way for him to allay her fears.

All cops' wives worried (there were worried husbands, too, of course, though not as many as there were wives). Worrying came with the territory. A lot of cops' wives went into their marriages thinking they would be able to handle it. But then something would happen—not necessarily to their husbands or even to someone they knew personally, but it would be something so awful and so devastating that they could not help being affected by it.

That was when they found out that there was a big difference between knowing that they were going to be worried and actually having something to be worried about. Intellectual knowledge was no match for the experience of real life. What happened after that didn't usually involve any kind of a happy ending.

Mooney had always counted himself among the extraordinarily lucky ones because Marilyn had been strong enough to hang in there with him. She had hung tough and kept the faith, as they used to say. Back when Bob Mooney had been a little more fresh-faced and a lot less bored. A hell of a lot less bored.

When the chief had tapped him to man the front desk, he had actually been able to see the decrease in Marilyn's worrying. Not that she stopped worrying altogether—there was no area of police work that was guaranteed one hundred per cent safe, and desk sergeants could and did get shot right in their chairs.

Or they were knifed by suspects who had somehow managed to conceal a blade from the officer who had taken them into custody. Or they got bitten by junkies or prostitutes of any and all sexes who were living out their last months with AIDS and suddenly got the urge to share the love. No, Marilyn wasn't going to stop worrying about him until the day he was off the job for good.

Well, that day was no longer somewhere ahead of them in a vaguely conceived idea of the future; now it was actually in sight. Twenty-two years was more than enough time on the job. When he had told Tanner that he was bored, he hadn't been kidding. He was bored out of his mind and Marilyn was tired of worrying—'nuff said.

Only now as the big day of his retirement was looming closer and closer, he knew that Marilyn's anxiety was rising again. He knew why that was, of course—she was worried about him coming out of the job in one piece, afraid that at the very last moment, when they thought they were home free, something bad would happen to him.

It wasn't impossible. The one and only guarantee anybody ever got in police work was that there *were* no guarantees for anybody. Everyone on the job had heard at least one story about some poor guy who had been just weeks or even days away from his retirement when he'd gotten his head blown up by some scumbag who'd managed to get off a lucky shot.

Of course, that didn't happen to *all* the guys on the home stretch. No guarantees also meant that there were no guarantees that such a thing would happen to him. Thank Christ. If anyone had pressed him on the matter, Mooney would not have denied that from time to time he did feel something in the way of a little superstitious dread. But he also knew better than to fixate on that kind of thing. Stuff like that could drive you crazy if you let it, which was all too easy to do. Some of the cops he'd seen it happen to had been guys that he never would have thought for one moment would end up that way, either.

Well, if the bear could eat them, it could eat him, too, as Mooney's training officer had said, his first day on the job. The circumstances had been completely different but over the ensuing years, Mooney had discovered this bit of wisdom applied equally well to a wide variety of situations, both on and off the job. In this case, he knew he was better off concentrating on the extraordinary good fortune that had never deserted him even for a moment throughout his entire career—twenty-two years on the job and he had never had cause to draw his gun.

Not that he would have hesitated if circumstances had called for it. In fact, it was one of that funny little twists of irony that he was actually an excellent marksman—one of the best shooters West Side Precinct had ever had and that was no exaggeration. He had never failed to qualify on the shooting range, a claim that not a whole lot of other cops could make.

And of those who were able to boast a perfect pass rate, not a single one of them was on the detective squad. Tanner for one wasn't even close, a fact that Mooney often found himself taking comfort in more and more often lately, especially when Tanner started busting his balls about the day spa he was going to open with Marilyn.

Thinking of Tanner brought his mind back to the kid with the cellphone. Mooney had lost track of the kid after he'd told him to go upstairs but he was almost certain that Tanner would have been the only available detective up there to take his report. If so, he was really curious as to what Tanner had made of him. But he couldn't remember seeing Tanner after he had been so kind as to hand-deliver the box of sea sponges to him at the front desk. With a side order of ball busting.

Yeah, that was when he used that quaint old expression, *pussy-whipped*. Which had been only a minute or two before the kid had come in. Very likely the two of them had even caught a glimpse of each other. Like proverbial ships that pass in the night, Mooney thought. Or, in this case, the fight.

He finished changing his clothes, picked up a folder of paperwork and headed out. A few of the guys nodded at him as he walked through the precinct and he nodded back on automatic pilot, not really seeing anyone. Most of them probably wouldn't understand why today was one of those days that made him really glad he was about to pull the pin and leave all the madness behind. Especially the young guys, who craved danger and excitement.

Of course, fifteen years ago, he probably wouldn't have understood, either. Maybe not even ten years ago.

And he'd certainly never imagined that when he did leave, he would have been throwing all this wonderfulness in so he could run a day spa with his wife. Well, sometimes you just had to say what the hell, Mooney thought, and if some of the guys took the day spa business to mean he was the world's biggest pussy, then they could just kiss his rosy pink ass, which he had been busting on this job for over twenty years and which was still, as a matter of fact, rock-hard.

Come to that, not a whole lot of them could do this job any better than he had. God knew that if they had been able, Mooney wouldn't have had to give the guy with the cellphone the brush-off because the house was full of badass bangers and rabid skinheads.

He paused for a split second at the front door, tempted to go back and check on who had ended up taking the kid's report and how it had been handled.

Nah. It wasn't his problem and Mare was waiting for him. Each and every day, good or bad, had to come to an end and the best thing a cop could do was let it. He headed out of the precinct house and into the parking lot, his resolve making him feel a little bit lighter in spite of his fatigue.

Spotting the familiar old gold of his Crown Vic, Mooney started to search his pockets for his keys when he saw Jack Tanner emerging from what was obviously his latest hot new acquisition. It was the sort of thing that Mare referred to, with no little disdain, as a hard-on-mobile. Good old Mare. Privately, Mooney wished her attitude could have rubbed off on him so he would stop wishing he had one himself instead of a decommissioned cop car repainted and bought on the cheap.

Abruptly, he thought of the kid with the cellphone and forgot all about letting the day come to an end. "Hey, Jack!" he called.

Tanner turned around and Mooney saw he was holding a cellphone to one ear. He muttered something to it as Mooney came over to him. "What's up, Moon?" he asked, his friendly tone sounding just slightly forced.

"I sent some kid up to see you guys this morning. Had a phone with him and some woman on the other end. Said it was an abduction or something like that." Mooney glanced at the car, hoping he didn't look half as envious as he felt. "Did you do anything with it?"

Tanner made a non-committal gesture as he disconnected his call. "You know, I've been stuck all morning down at City Hall doing a press conference on the gang killings. But I'll ask around for you."

"Okay," Mooney said, sneaking another glance at the car. "Sure. Thanks, Jack." He made himself turn away and head for the Crown Vic before he started drooling.

"Oh, and hey, Bob?" Tanner called out suddenly.

Mooney paused to turn back to him. "Yeah?"

"I was just thinking about it," the detective said with a broad, sunny grin, "and you and Mare will do great with that beauty parlor."

"Actually, it's a day spa," Mooney told Tanner's retreating back, wondering why he was even bothering. As if Tanner the exalted detective would actually trouble himself to remember something as inconsequential as a question from a uniformed police officer.

Mooney wasn't fooled by Tanner's camaraderie bullshit. Although they had gone through the academy together, he knew Tanner looked down on him, just like all the detectives on his elite task force looked down on cops in uniform—or, for that matter, anyone else who wasn't in their exclusive club, including other detectives. The only reason Tanner kept bringing up the possibility of him joining up was Mooney's skill as a shooter. Being able to claim he had the best shot in the department on his team would hold a lot of appeal for him. Not that it would keep Tanner from lording it over him every chance he got and Mooney knew it.

Sighing a little, Mooney put the paperwork he was carrying down on the trunk of the Crown Vic and began patting himself down in his usual search for his car keys. This time, it only took him fifteen seconds to discover he had hidden his keys from himself in his shirt pocket. Not a new world's record, but not bad. Some days he had to stand around frisking himself for close to a minute, or even longer.

Okay, so maybe his memory was going to hell, but he could still shoot like a bad ass and he could still move as fast as he ever did. And what the hell—his memory couldn't be all that terribly bad. After all, he could still remember to pick up the papers on the trunk of his car before he drove away. Unlike a few others in the department he could think of—

He was in the act of reaching for them when his gaze fell on an invoice for beauty supplies paperclipped to the top of the pile. There was something besides the details of the order scribbled on it.

Martin. Brentwood. Right—the woman on the kid's cellphone. Jennifer or Jessica Martin.

Mooney unclipped it and took a quick look at the total amount due and wondered if it wasn't just slightly excessive for sea sponges. After all, it wasn't like they had to be dug out of mines or something. They were just laying around in the ocean, for Christ's sake; all anybody had to do was pick them up and put them on a shelf somewhere to dry out. He folded the paper in half and stuck it in his shirt pocket.

He then immediately took it out again and unfolded it to have a closer look at the notes he had written on it.

Jessica Kate Martin
327 Bonhill Rd
Brentwood

The whole situation came back to Mooney at once. A woman on the kid's cellphone told him she had been kidnapped. She was now being held prisoner in some unknown location by people who were threatening to kill her.

Frowning at the woman's name and address, Mooney gave it some thought. He could wait for Tanner to run down the information and get back to him. Unless of course he wanted to know anything this year. All of a sudden he had the strongest feeling that he did. Not just this year, but this afternoon, as soon and as much as possible.

Mooney's frown deepened as he pulled out the nifty UCLA-themed cellphone Marilyn had given him for his birthday. She was definitely not going to be very happy about this, he thought as he punched for the phone book. But he knew that she would understand and cut him a little slack about it. At least, he hoped that was what he knew. He hit the second number on the list, which was the number for the day spa.

"Hi, honey," he said when he heard his wife's voice on the line. "Listen, there's something I gotta—well, it's a—well, I'm just gonna be a few minutes late…"

Man, in the course of his very busy lifetime, he had had occasion to toss more than a few people's homes, especially since he had been tapped to run with Greer's crew. Some of them had been very odd places indeed. There were some he could remember just on account of how incredibly freakin' filthy they were, while others were memorable for the sheer stupidity the occupants had shown in their choice of hiding places for their valuables.

But this was like nothing he'd ever seen, anywhere, any time—a real first. Without a doubt, the Martin house had to be the most boring crib he had ever had the bad luck to get stuck with having to toss. Bayback had given him a song and dance about how the place wasn't really all that bad and he was just being a fucking drama queen about it. But then, Bayback would feel that way.

How the frigging hell anyone could possibly stand to live like this was something he would never be able to understand. The furniture was nothing, pure middle class crap that they must have bought right off the display. When they got it home, they probably made sure they got it all set up so it was exactly the way it had been in the store, before they ordered an extra case of Scotch-guard so it was easier for the maid to clean up the dog puke.

Kind of a shame about the dog, though. That was the one thing he actually felt bad about. If it were up to him, no animal would ever have to take a bullet when there was a human to shoot instead. But those were the breaks.

And if all the middle-class, white bread shit in this dump wasn't boring enough, there was the goddamned video collection. Jesus H Christ, it was a goddamned good thing boredom couldn't actually kill you, although after going through all their shit, he started to wonder if maybe he wouldn't end up being the first.

It was bad enough being forced to go through dozens of videocassettes of fairytale this and animated that. But to add insult to injury, this Martin broad had also recorded every single episode of *ER* with George goddamned Clooney. At least, he was assuming it was the broad who had done that.

Then there had been the sheer, unbelievable torture of having to look at junior's first birthday. Junior plays with the puppy, Junior sings Christmas carols with mommy, Junior learns to ride his bike, Junior washes the car with daddy, etc, etc, etc.

And that was friggin' all. No porn, not a single cassette, homemade or otherwise, just hours of nothing and all of it so boring that it wasn't even funny to watch speeded up. What kind of people were they that they didn't have any porn in the house? Bunch of weirdoes.

No, they were beyond weirdoes. Seriously abnormal was the only way to describe what these people were. Thank Christ he didn't have to touch any of their DVDs except to pull them off the shelves and see if there was anything hidden behind them.

There had been nothing in any of the bedrooms, of course. Bayback was going through them again to make sure but he was pretty certain that there would still be nothing in the closets but clothes—very boring clothes—and nothing in the drawers except socks and underwear, which would be even more boring. Nothing under the beds except boring bedroom slippers, boring dust and just plain boring nothing, nada, not a frigging thing to be found anywhere, not under the mattresses, not in the mattresses.

It was like these people had dedicated their lives to being the most boring nobodies that ever walked the earth and all three of them spent every day working their boring asses off to stay that way. And what the friggin' hell, he thought as he surveyed the array of incredibly boring family photos on the wall, it turned out that they actually hadn't worked hard enough. Not that he would have guessed from looking at these.

Mom and Dad and Junior go to Disney-Whatever; Junior meets Donald Duck; Mom and Junior down on the farm with a cow; Junior and Dad wash the SUV. Mom on the beach; she had a pretty nice body for a schoolteacher. How the holy fuck middle class white bread like the Martins had managed to get themselves on Greer's radar was something he would never understand.

Christ, why was he torturing himself looking at this crap? It should be fucking illegal for anyone to be this boring, it should be a felony. With mandatory jail time.

He headed back to the kitchen and, for the fourth or fifth time, started to sort through the mess of boring dishes and other boring junk on the counter. His attention began to wander almost immediately—not a good thing, but Christ, on a job this boring he was doing pretty good not to be in a goddamn coma.

Truth be told, he was starting to wonder if maybe the Martin woman wasn't lying when she claimed she didn't know what was going on. Maybe they really did have the wrong house. If that was the case, then they were really in the fucking shit now.

Just as he was doing his best to re-focus his concentration, he noticed a tiny movement at the edge of his vision: something under a pile of papers. He shifted them to find that it was just the light blinking on the answering machine.

He started to go back to the papers and then hesitated. If the light was still blinking, then it meant that nobody had listened to the message yet. It probably wasn't anything worth listening to, just some boring shit from one of the Martins' boring friends—Hi, there, this is Jane Boring from down the street calling to invite you guys over to our boring house for a boring dinner on Saturday. Nothing fancy, just my special boring meatloaf and even more boring tapioca.

But he had to check it out anyway. Shit. He pushed the play button.

"Jessica? Honey, listen to me!" said a man's voice, frightened and breathless. "You have to get out of the house! Something's happened! There's no time to explain, just get Ricky and meet me at our place at Left Field as fast as you can! Please, honey, hurry!" Pause. "I love you," the man added, almost choking a little. "Now go!"

Beep.

Well, holy shit, he thought. How about that—at last he had found something in the house that actually wasn't boring.

There were no more messages after that one, which was just fine by him. He couldn't really say that this made up for the hours of unspeakably crushing boredom that he had been forced to suffer through. But thank Christ he wouldn't have to look at any more of the Martins' incredibly boring middle class white bread shit again.

He headed down the hallway to the bedrooms so he could inform Bayback of this new and interesting development.

"There we go," Ryan said matter-of-factly.

"Oh, thank God," said Jessica, feeling an overwhelming wave of relief. The voice that had been getting fainter and more muffled to her ears was finally coming back in strong and clear again. In fact, the connection was so good now that she could even hear him fiddling with some of the phone gear he'd gotten from the store.

Stolen from the store, she corrected herself. He had stolen all of that phone gear from the store and he had done so at gunpoint. Because he'd had no other choice for her sake, and only for her sake. For no other reason than because she needed his help and it was the only way he could give it to her.

The enormity of everything that this young man—not simply a disembodied voice but a real person, someone whose existence she had been completely unaware of only hours earlier, this total stranger—had put himself through for the sake of helping her, was only just beginning to dawn on her.

And as it did, she was fast coming to the conclusion that this was a realization that was every bit as scary as being kidnapped, locked in an attic and threatened with death.

In fact, if she was going to be perfectly honest about the whole situation, it was as if she had actually kidnapped him.

That idea made her feel very unsteady and very queasy and very, very close to breaking down again. But she couldn't do that, she just couldn't. There wasn't time for her to go all emotional again, not right now. She had to keep herself focused. Staying focused was the only way she would be able to help him help her.

That was important not only for her and Ricky but for Ryan himself. Because after he was done helping her, then she would be able to help him. And he was really going to need a lot of help from her when this was over.

She just hoped that she actually could help him when all of this finally came to an end. What if things turned out all right for her and Ricky and Craig, but not for Ryan? What if he ended up behind bars like he was just one more of the bad guys?

What really frightened her was the knowledge that there was really no way at all for her to be sure that such a thing wouldn't happen. There was no possible guarantee whatsoever that after she told the police everything that had happened to her, they would not just throw this poor guy in jail anyway, saying: Gosh, that's all really awful and too bad, but it doesn't change the fact that armed robbery is armed robbery and we gotta lock him up no matter what. Now just move along, ma'am, the show's over. Take your son and your husband and go home, lady, there's nothing more to see here.

God, Jessica thought miserably. She needed to work as hard as she could to keep it together, she had to concentrate on getting through, taking one thing at a time, one minute at a time if that was how it had to be.

She had to make Ryan see that she was more than just a hysterical, scared woman locked in an attic, a whole lot more. And she had to let him know that she understood how much she was asking of him.

"Look... Ryan," she said hesitantly. 'I... I just want to say... thank you. Thank you for... for doing all this."

Jessica squeezed her eyes shut. God, how lame did that sound? Thank you for doing all this. Like he'd just cooked dinner for her or loaned her his jumper cables because her car wouldn't start.

Thank you for doing all this. Was that the epitome of eloquence or what? Jessica Martin, fifth-grade science teacher and freelance silver-tongued devil.

Thank you for doing all this.

Hallmark Cards would have paid her a million dollars for six words that extraordinary. Thank you for doing all this was exactly the right thing to say when you wanted to thank someone for doing something special for you, whether it was remembering your birthday, helping you carry your groceries or committing armed robbery as a personal favor before you had even actually met face to face.

Thank you for doing all this.

Yeah, that certainly did say it all. The fact that the poor guy hadn't said anything in response was probably just the kind of answer she deserved.

"You still there?" she asked nervously after a moment.

"Yeah," he said. "Yeah, I..." She heard him take a shaky, emotional breath and her heart gave a small jump. Any person who was not only resourceful enough but also willing to do all the things that he had done for her would also have to be a lot more insightful than the average person and would be likely to understand what she was really trying to say. "You're welcome, Jessica."

The familiar voice suddenly sounded different. It wasn't unfamiliar or distorted, it was still recognizable but... As if something had happened, not just to him but to her as well. She felt a mild almost-spinning sensation in her head. Then light dawned—or as Craig would have put it, the penny dropped.

For the very first time ever, he had addressed her as Jessica.

She had told him what her name was almost immediately, and after insisting that he tell her his, she had been calling him Ryan ever since. But for his part, he had only called her "lady" if he called her anything at all. And despite the fact that he now knew that she wasn't trying to put some kind of sick joke over on him, that all of this was real, to hear him actually call her by her name didn't just tell her that he took her seriously. She had become real to him.

But it was more than that, much more. In some strange way, his calling her by her name somehow made him feel more real to her. It was as if he wanted her to understand beyond a shadow of a doubt that she would be able to believe in him, that he knew she had put her life literally in his hands and nothing would keep him from doing whatever she needed him to do.

Tears threatened again but she refused to let them come. Angry with herself, she squelched the feeling. With one word, Ryan had reminded her of who and what she was—Jessica Kate Martin, wife and mother, former Olympic-level athlete and the only three-time winner of the Contra Costa County Teacher of the Year Award. She was resourceful enough to jerry-rig a broken phone so she would be able to call someone for help and clever enough to make the person who answered the phone believe her and go out of his way to help her.

Jessica Kate Martin was not just some hysterical damsel in distress whose sole ability was marathon bouts of uncontrollable weeping. From now on, she decided, whenever she felt as if she was going to cry she would put it off until later, when there was time to indulge in that kind of acting out. Right now—

Right now, she realized suddenly, there were heavy steps on the stairs and they were coming up fast.

Oh God, she thought, feeling a wave of terror intense enough to induce vertigo. She had to hide the telephone—

Even as she was turning toward the phone parts lying on the floor, intending to shove them out of sight behind the wooden beam with her foot, the door had already banged open and he was striding across the room, like a human freight train.

Jessica froze, trying to will the world to freeze with her but he just kept coming. It would take a lot more than the world freezing over to even slow this son of a bitch down, she thought. Fear made her giddy again.

He came to a stop and loomed over her in silence. Jessica stared up at his expressionless face, waiting for something to happen—another backhand slap followed by a threat. Or perhaps this time he would hit her with his closed fist. And of course, things would definitely go downhill from there.

God. Despair was a sinking sensation in her stomach. She had been so busy telling herself how brave and clever and resourceful she was that she had actually forgotten to be brave and clever and resourceful.

She should have remembered not to let her kidnapper walk in on her before she had time to hide the phone. And now there it was, lying on the floor in plain sight and everything she had done, everything Ryan had put himself through for her sake—all that was for nothing now. She had blown it.

This thug standing over her probably wasn't a rocket scientist but he certainly wasn't so stupid that he wouldn't be able to figure out what she had been doing if he got a good enough look at the telephone wreckage.

Abruptly, he sat down on the box next to her, keeping his cold, steely gaze locked on her face. This was going to be it. This was it, and there was nothing she could do. He would be able to see the phone; he would be able to see that she had been working with the parts. So why couldn't he just get it over with? What could he possibly be waiting for? Just say it: tell her he had caught her and now he was going to have to kill her?

As if he had somehow picked up the flavor of what she was thinking, he tilted his head slightly to one side and asked in an eerily calm, grotesquely conversational tone of voice, "Do you want to die here?"

"Do you want to die here?"

EIGHT

Jesus! The question was like a fist in Ryan's stomach. He stomped on the brakes and the rent-a-cop car came to a long, skidding stop that ended in a hard jolt as it hit the curb. He didn't notice. He could only sit as still as a statue in the driver's seat of the rent-a-cop car, one hand on the steering wheel, the other holding the cellphone and a newly acquired ear-bud mic. All awareness of his immediate surroundings had vanished. Ryan Hewitt was actually in the attic with Jessica Martin and whatever happened to her now was going to happen to him.

Do you want to die here?

The question seemed to hang like the dust in the stale attic air while he waited for her answer. He didn't take his gaze from her face.

"N-no," she said finally in a choked half-whisper. Her throat was tightening as the tears rose, welling up in her eyes and then spilling down her cheeks. "Please... My family's done nothing to you..."

He kept on staring at her, his face in the sort of authoritative repose she had previously associated with certain male assistant principals under five feet, four inches tall on cafeteria duty.

Except he was looking only at her, Jessica realized. Only at her. Because as far as he knew, she was the most important thing to look at.

Careful to keep her suddenly rekindled hope from showing, she shifted position, moving herself away from the phone. The man's stare followed her and she knew then that as long as she could keep his gaze fixed on her, there was little chance that he would take notice of any detritus lying around on the floor.

He stared at her a little bit longer and then said, "Your husband left a message asking you to meet him in 'left field.' Where's that?"

Oh God, she thought, drawing back from him. "What? I don't understand what—"

He gave her a brief nod and stood up, to look at the window behind him. It was only the briefest of glances, lasting barely a second but it was just enough time for her to nudge the phone behind a nearby wooden beam with her toe.

"Go to the window, Jessica," he told her, his tone practically conversational. "There's something I want you to see."

Her heart was pounding as if it was a fist in her chest. She had actually gotten away with it. She hadn't blown it after all. Relief steadied her and gave her the strength she needed to push herself to her feet so she could do as she was told. She might still be his prisoner and she was certainly a long, long way from actually escaping, but at least she had managed to keep him from finding out about the telephone after all. That meant he really wasn't as much in charge as he thought he was; he didn't have complete control over the situation—or her—after all.

The sight of her Cayenne parked in the cracked driveway hit her with a renewed feeling of dread. No, she thought, fear building in her as she looked down at the scrubby, neglected yard.

Behind her, she heard her kidnapper mutter into a walkie-talkie. "Dimitri, bring him out."

That must have been Dimitri climbing out of the Cayenne's back seat, Jessica thought. He was big, really big. He must have felt cramped even in the roomier-than-average back seat of the Cayenne. It must have been even more uncomfortable for him to have to share the space with another person, even if it was a small person.

Like Ricky, who was getting out after him.

Jessica felt her knees start to buckle and caught herself on the sides of the window. Patches of darkness swam through her vision but she commanded herself to stay on her feet. The last thing she could do right now was to let herself pass out. She had to hang on now no matter what, because they had Ricky.

Ricky, she thought, or said, or whispered or mouthed. She was trying to will him to look up at her. The big man, Dimitri, led him toward a run-down guesthouse on the other side of the property. But her son never raised his head, never even glanced over his shoulder. Instead, it was Dimitri who looked up at her.

"You've got three seconds," said the low, menacing voice close to her ear. He was close enough for her not only to feel his breath but to smell him. The mix of oil, cordite, grease and sweat turned her stomach. "Three seconds to tell me where this 'left field' is. Or you're never going to see your son again."

Three seconds. She couldn't move, couldn't speak and couldn't think. Ricky was walking ahead of the man now, his head bent and his shoulders slightly hunched, as if he were expecting to be hit from behind at any moment. As if he knew for a fact that he had good reason to expect such a thing, even though neither she nor Craig had ever laid a hand on him.

But of course, that didn't mean someone else wouldn't. Or hadn't.

Oh my God, she tried to say, but no sound came out.

She went on watching as Ricky reached the front door of the guesthouse and then, obviously in response to a command from Dimitri, simply stopped. Dimitri carefully positioned himself behind her son, at an angle that kept him out of Ricky's sight but allowed Jessica a clear and unobstructed view of his shoulder holster when he opened his coat.

"One," said the man beside her at the window. His breath fell on her cheek and stirred her hair.

"Please," Jessica said, almost choking on the word, both hands pressed against the dirty glass. "Please believe me, I don't know!"

The big man slipped the gun out of the shoulder holster. He was handling it with a show of casual expertise, displaying for her benefit how easily he used a gun. Just like other people used more mundane objects. Like, say, telephones.

Ricky still didn't turn around, didn't look over his shoulder; he didn't move at all. Jessica's hands slid down on the filthy window until she had her son and the big man framed between them. But it made no difference—the man still had the gun in his easy, expert hand and her son was in danger.

And the man standing next to her in the attic said, "Two."

"He's just a child!" she wailed, clenching her hands into helpless fists. "How can you do this? He's just a child!"

Dimitri was staring up at her expectantly while he held the gun on Ricky. The barrel was so close to the boy that it was almost touching his hair. She could see now that this man had felt nothing one way or another for her or for Ricky. There was just nothing there inside him, nothing at all, not hate, not contempt, not even the slightest bit of interest and there never would be. It was just the way that he was. Whatever came next would just be something that happened and it would bother her a hell of a lot more than it could ever bother him.

"Three," said the voice in her ear.

Everything came to a dead stop, including her breathing. Had she really heard him say it, she wondered, or had she just imagined it?

"Did I say 'three'?" he asked lightly as if he had been reading her mind, feigning a mildly absent-minded tone as if he really weren't sure himself. The kidnapper in a playful mood, having a bit of a laugh for himself in the course of a day's work.

Then she felt him move, felt him raising the walkie-talkie to his mouth and heard him taking a breath so he could give the order to kill her son.

"Wait! Wait!"

The words came out in a howl. Her knees were buckling again but she still wouldn't let herself fall. Not yet, not until she was absolutely certain that her son was all right.

"I'll tell you!" she sobbed. "Don't kill him, I'll tell you! I'll tell you!"

Standing next to her in the attic, he waited and down in the yard standing behind her son, Dimitri waited, looking vaguely curious but otherwise unperturbed.

And still, she had to swallow twice before she was able to make her voice work and the words came out.

"LAX. Left Field is a bar at LAX," she managed, almost choking on the words. "We met there in college on our way home for Christmas."

Very, very slowly, the world began to tilt sideways but Jessica kept her hands pressed to the glass, still refusing to weaken and give in to the dizziness pulling at her vision and her balance.

The man standing next to her in the attic spoke again, saying something about "Got it" and "Put the kid inside." All the while, the world continued its slow tilt until the angle became quite dramatic, more difficult for her to counter.

Down in the yard, Dimitri was demonstrating that putting his gun away was just as easy for him as taking it out, whether her world was tilting sideways or steady as a rock. She was mildly amazed to see that this equilibrium somehow extended to Ricky, who turned around half a second too late to see either the gun or the shoulder holster. Only when the big man opened the guesthouse door and pushed him inside did her son seem even slightly unsteady. But only just very slightly.

Dimitri closed the door in a way that reminded her of Craig letting the dog in. Then he locked it from the outside and walked off without even the briefest glance up at her in the window, as if he had forgotten she was there.

The last shred of will keeping her upright finally gave out and she collapsed in a loose heap on the floor. The thug stood over her silently and she could feel his gaze on her as he waited for her to break down. He wanted her to break down.

Don't, she commanded herself fiercely. Don't cry. Don't you dare cry. Don't give him that.

After a long moment, he stepped past her, heading for the door. She raised her head and looked up at him sharply.

"They'll catch you bastards," she promised him.

He stopped and turned around, looking at her with an odd, unreadable expression on his face.

"When I didn't show up at work," she went on after a deep breath, "someone called the police—"

"I'd be hoping they didn't, if I were you," he said quietly.

Jessica watched him pull a black box that was obviously some kind of electronic device out of a pocket in his jacket and she was horrified to see that he was smiling.

"Police scanner," he said, holding it up as if it were a trophy. "We get one hit on this—just one—and we bury you and your kid and just disappear."

He was sliding the scanner back into his jacket when she heard it. Not the one hit he had just been talking about but something else entirely, the only thing that could have been worse.

But worst of all, she could tell that he had heard it too.

For the last several minutes, Ryan had been unable to do anything except sit and listen to the way things were playing out in the attic. Thoughts and emotions were pin-wheeling crazily in his already over-stressed mind to the point that he was starting to have trouble keeping track of what had happened. What hadn't happened yet but still might and where he himself was in all of it.

These guys who had Jessica had her son now, too. Because in spite of his best efforts to follow the Porsche Cayenne after they picked up her son at his school, he had got stuck behind a bus and lost the SUV. If he had just been able to find the boy before they had actually been able to grab him. If the stupid rent-a-cop security guard at the school had paid attention to what he was trying to tell him instead of manhandling him like he was some kind of dangerous pervert.

But instead, everything that could have gone wrong did go wrong in the biggest possible way, and—

And Jessica Martin had been lying to the men who had kidnapped her, and she had kept on lying while she watched them put a gun to her son's head.

At some point while all of this was speeding through his head like a runaway car on a roller coaster, he had begun shaking and he couldn't seem to stop. But at the same time, he found that he couldn't actually move. Hell, he was barely able to think.

The only coherent thing in his mind was the voice of that guy, the way he sounded as he told Jessica that he would count to three. And her making no sound at all. She let him do it, she let him actually say "three" out loud before she told him what he wanted to know.

And that was all wrong. It was all so wrong he didn't understand why everything didn't just come to a screeching halt. How was it that the rest of the world could simply go on as if nothing bad were happening to these people? Why couldn't every person within a hundred-mile radius feel there was something extremely, hideously, unspeakably wrong?

A Mercedes sedan, pimped out so ludicrously that no real pimp would have been caught dead even in the trunk, pulled up next to him. The rap music blasting from the super-sound system practically had the crappy little rent-a-cop car bouncing on its wounded shock absorbers. Ryan felt a surge of white-hot outrage that made him want to fling himself right through the open window and punch the guy's head in before ripping out his badass speakers so he could smash them on the pavement and stamp on the pieces. Listening to that beat, that *boom-chikka-boom-BOOM* was like listening to the guy mock Jessica while she pleaded for her kid's life.

Which was what she was doing right now, he realized, heart sick and horrified all at once.

"Look, all that matters to me is the safety of my child," she was saying, and the terrified desperation in her voice was more intense than ever before.

That was because she knew, Ryan thought. She realized what a close call it had been for her son and now she felt guilty about it.

"You want me to cooperate? I will," she said, her voice rising. "I hear you. I hear you."

"Shut up," the man snapped. He was standing in the middle of the attic, turning around slowly, trying to listen properly. Jessica pushed herself up on her elbows, hoping the incidental noise of her moving around would cover the noise coming from the phone.

"I'll do whatever you want," she said, raising her voice even louder, so that she was almost shouting, trying to make herself sob. Maddeningly, the tears wouldn't flow; her eyes were so dry they hurt. "I want you to understand that. I hear you loud and clear!"

"I hear you loud and clear!"

The words finally penetrated. Ryan punched for the menu screen on his cellphone and scrolled through it as quickly as he could, searching for the mute command. The beat from the Mercedes seemed to be getting louder. He waved at the driver frantically, signaling him to turn the music down. The driver nodded at him, winked smugly, and turned the volume up. Jesus, what was wrong with this asshole?

He had to page through one more menu before he found the command he was looking for and even then he almost missed it. The up/down toggle on the phone was too small to operate easily.

Just as his thumb hit the right button, he heard the explosion.

Then there was no sound at all, nothing except a long and terrible silence.

Jessica's sob of terror was all too real as she scrambled across the floor, trying to get his attention. She opened her mouth to say something, anything, yell, beg, cry, whatever. She saw him turn toward her holding something in his hand. Before it could even register on her as a gun, an area of the wall next to her head exploded.

She let out a cry of raw terror as she covered her head with both arms and braced herself for the next shot. Perhaps she wouldn't actually hear the explosion, only feel the pain of impact; maybe it traveled faster than the speed of sound.

But an eternity passed and nothing happened. There was no second explosion, no impact, no pain. Too frightened to look up but even more frightened not to, she cautiously raised her head.

The heavy stood motionless with the gun still in his hand and his head cocked to one side, listening. She had no idea whether she was hearing nothing or the sound of her blood ringing in her ears. After a pause, he put the gun away and walked out without even looking at her.

Jessica stared at the closed door. His voice came to her, faint and muffled, as he spoke to someone in the hallway.

"LAX. Let's go."

That was all. There was still nothing to hear in the attic, nothing at all, not even her own breathing. All sound was somehow swallowed up or smothered. Jessica kept one hand pressed hard against her chest, thinking that was the only way she would know when her heart started beating again.

NINE

"Jessica? Answer me, goddamn it!" Over and over. That tiny voice, Ryan's voice, filtered but still clear and sharp. It came from somewhere in the musty gloom pressing down on her. So many years of accumulated dust had turned to simple dirt; Jessica could feel it scraping her cheek at even the slightest move.

Eventually, she lifted her head from the floor and sometime after that, she made herself crawl across the filthy floor to where the telephone was still concealed behind the thick wooden beam.

"Jessica!" Ryan pleaded in a voice close to a sob. "Jessica, answer me, goddamn it!"

"I'm here," she said, her voice little more than a dry croak. She swallowed, wet her lips and tried again. "I'm here, Ryan. I'm here."

"I'm here."

Ryan let his head fall back against the headrest as his entire body sagged with relief. He had been straining his ears, listening as closely as he could to the silence that had followed the gunshot, waiting in near-painful desperation for some sound that would tell him she was still alive, the sound of her moving around, weeping with reaction, anything.

But there had been nothing and more nothing, and still more nothing, until he was too scared not to risk taking the phone off mute and calling out to her. If the guy heard him this time, Jessica was dead for sure.

Unless she was already dead. He had no way to know, but he had to find out.

I'm here.

He hadn't realized how terrified he was of not hearing her voice again until she answered. His heart had not yet been able to unscramble the message that Jessica was still alive—it was still pounding too hard and too fast in his chest. But she was still alive and that meant he would be able to pull himself together.

He wouldn't fall apart, and neither would this hopeless piece of crap he was driving. The pimped-out Mercedes had thumped and boogied its way on down the road. But good God, if there was any more shit like that, he would crumble, no matter how desperately she needed him.

"What the hell did you think you were doing?" he asked when he finally found it becoming a bit easier for him to breathe. "Why'd you lie to them?"

"God, don't you get it yet, Ryan?" She made a noise that was a cross between a humorless laugh and a sob. "Once they get Craig, we're all going to die."

"You don't know that," he began stubbornly, but she paid no attention.

"Think about it," she went on, talking over him as if he weren't speaking. "We've seen their faces, they can't let us live. The only chance Craig's got—the only chance we've got—is if you can get to the airport and find him before they do."

He straightened up in the driver's seat, wincing absently at the feel of the lumpy cushion under him. "No," he told her, firmly. "No, Jessica, you gotta wait a minute now, just hold on here—"

"Ryan, please, there's no time!" she wailed. "Just get to the airport, please, just get to the airport and—"

"But I can't!" he said. "They'll recognize me!"

"They won't!" Jessica insisted. "You're invisible to them, they don't know who you are. Please!" Now she had begun to sob again. "Please, Ryan, you've got to try, you've just got to!"

Ryan felt a sharp surge of completely irrational anger. "Lady, I've stolen a car, driven off a cliff and shot up a phone store!" he shouted, knowing full well he wasn't making any sense but unable to help himself. "Don't tell me I'm not trying!"

He heard her take several ragged breaths in an effort to get herself back under control. "Okay," she said after a bit, hoarse and breathless. "Okay." Pause. "Look, I know I have no right to ask you this, Ryan, but you're my family's only chance... and I am asking."

He let out a long, noisy breath and put the car into gear. Yeah, she was asking, all right, and as always, he was answering and the answer was yes.

He stamped on the gas pedal, flooring it before he could be even slightly tempted to have second thoughts.

Talk about your hardcore 'burbs. Mooney found himself actually marveling as he guided the Crown Vic along Bonhill, looking at each of the house numbers. This was beyond 'burbs—the only place he had ever seen so utterly suburban was in a movie. Compared to West Side, this was a different planet altogether.

No gangs or colors here, just lawns and gardens; a perfect suburbia. The only posses they had in this 'hood were little kids on those plastic Big Wheel tricycles and the closest thing to gang rivalry would be face-offs at the garden club and rose-growers going mano à mano with shrubbery purists. All followed by a barbecue—everyone invited and bring-your-own.

And more power to them, Mooney thought as he pulled into the driveway at 327. The people who traveled these not-very-mean streets were more than simply hardcore 'burb dwellers. They also just happened to make up a substantial percentage of those conscientiously well-groomed people who kept day spas in business.

That was what Mare had told him, anyway, and Mooney had no reason to doubt her expertise, which extended to every area of the day spa business. She was especially good at identifying all the characteristics of their target market, everything from the range of their annual income to the most common skin type.

Mooney, on the other hand, was having a much harder time getting the hang of all that stuff, and in particular anything to do with determining skin type, which he found more difficult than police work by several magnitudes. When in doubt—and that was always—he tended to fall back on combination skin, figuring that at the very least, he'd be half-right.

He had to knock twice before he finally got an answer. The woman who opened the door to him had perfect skin, or so it seemed to his inexpert eyes. Mare had told him in no uncertain terms that there was no such thing as perfect skin, of course, and if they were going to make a living, he was going to have to accept her pronouncement on this as an incontrovertible and universal truth.

While Mooney was more than happy to accept all of Marilyn's day spa pronouncements as incontrovertible and universal truths, he still wasn't at all confident that would be able to sell the combination-skin thing to any woman with a complexion as beautiful as this woman's.

The polite smile on her (not really) perfect face took on a hint of puzzlement and he realized he'd been staring at her like a dork. He had a feeling that this might be something she was used to, however. He looked down quickly at the paper in his hand.

"Ms Martin?" he asked.

Her smile widened a bit as she raised her perfectly shaped eyebrows. "Yes?"

"Jessica Kate Martin?" he asked, hoping he didn't look as disappointed as he felt.

"Yes," she said again and her smooth forehead puckered very slightly with concern. "Can I help you, Mr...?"

Damn, Mooney thought as his disappointment intensified. He should have known better. He had bought into the whole story the kid with the cellphone had given him. It had been sitting in the back of his mind all day, mainly because it was the only serious call that had come in that was not related to gang activity. Or at least he'd thought it was serious—

Abruptly he became aware that the woman was still waiting for him to answer her. "Sorry, sorry," he said quickly, and showed her his badge. "Officer Mooney. Sergeant Mooney, West Side precinct. And no, I guess you can't help me. Unless, uh—" he laughed nervously. "Well, unless you've been kidnapped today."

Now the woman looked somewhat alarmed as well as curious.

"Sorry," he added sheepishly, wishing he could sink into the concrete steps and vanish. "That was just a joke. I'm really sorry to have bothered you, Ms Martin." He gave another nervous laugh. "Have a nice day."

Mooney wasted no time getting back into his car and getting the hell out of there. Boy, there was nothing like making an ass of yourself to put the perfect stupid cap on an overly-long, Grade-A rotten day, he thought as he crumpled the invoice with Jessica Martin's name and address on it.

But at least he could console himself with the knowledge that he would almost certainly never have to suffer the embarrassment of ever seeing Jessica Martin again. The way she looked, it had probably never occurred to her to go to a day spa and probably never would, for the simple reason that no one had ever told this woman she didn't have perfect skin. Mooney would have bet his life on that.

The woman with the beautiful complexion had continued to do her Jessica Martin impersonation by standing in the half-open door and watching with a pleasant, if slightly puzzled, smile pasted on her all-but-perfect face until she knew for certain that Mooney, West Side precinct, good cop and boy scout, positively and absolutely would not be back, either to ask another question or just to double-check the situation with a casual drive-by.

Only then did she step back inside, closed the door and put down the handgun she had been holding behind her back.

What an ordeal. Thank God he had been so easy to get rid of. The only thing that could have been worse than being stuck in this house with a dead body to get rid of, she thought, busily dialing her cellphone as she walked past the housekeeper's corpse, was if she had been stuck here with two dead bodies to get rid of. Especially if one of them happened to be a cop.

Well, there was no danger of that now since he hadn't insisted on playing detective. According to his ID, he was a uniformed officer, so it was probably safe for her to assume, from the street clothes and the dog-tired look on his face, that this was just a matter he had decided to look into on his way home after his shift. Which meant it was unofficial, off the record, nobody knew, and since it didn't pan out, nobody would ever know.

Still, she had better give the guys a heads-up, she thought, listening to number ring. So much better to be safe than sorry.

"It's Bayback," she said when the call connected. "We had a visitor. No, no shit. For real. But everything's okay. It's taken care of. Yeah, I'm sure."

In spite of her best intentions, Jessica had started crying again. She wasn't sobbing hysterically, at least. It was just continuous, soundless weeping. Tears were pouring down her face in two steady streams and she simply could not stop, no matter how much she wanted to.

Ultimately, it didn't matter one way or another. There was no point in her even thinking about whether or not she could stop crying. The only thing that mattered was Ryan getting to the airport and finding Craig before they did.

"Where are you now?" she asked him, smearing the back of her hand across one side of her face and then the other.

"It's okay, really," he told her. "I'll be at the airport in twenty min—"

"Twenty minutes is too long!" she said frantically. "You've got to go faster!"

"Jessica, this car has a sewing machine for an engine!" he shouted over the chattering of the motor and the traffic sounds. "I can't go any faster!"

"I'm sorry." She pressed the heels of her hands against her eyes for a long moment and then smeared away even more of her endless tears. "I just—"

Her voice died in her throat as her gaze suddenly fell on a mirror leaning against the wall in the far corner. For some reason, she hadn't noticed it before. It was old, dirty, fly specked and cracked but it reflected without distortion. She found that a great deal more surprising than the sight of her bruised, dirty face, her hair hanging in strings and her torn clothing.

An old, broken mirror that still reflected this well—that was amazing. Her reflection was what they would see when her body was found.

Assuming, of course, that her body would ever actually be found.

"Jessica?" Ryan asked in a high, tense voice. "Jessica, are you there? Jessica? Jessica?"

"Ryan? Do you think…" She paused for a moment and then the words came rushing out before she was even really aware of what she was going to say. "Do you think God will forgive me?"

Of everything she had said to him in the course of the day, this was truly the last thing Ryan had expected her to come out with. Not to mention the most unsettling.

Do you think God will forgive me?

No one had ever asked him anything remotely like that. What could he possibly say in response? Did a question like that even have an answer?

"Uh… What do you mean?" he said finally.

"For what I've done," she said. The misery in her voice was so explicit that it was actually painful. "For giving up Craig."

"Jessica, they have your kid," Ryan said, desperately trying to find the right words to comfort her while he kept a careful eye out for the turn-off to the airport. "You had no choice."

"I don't know." She took a shaky breath. "I don't kn—"

"I know," Ryan told her in his best no-nonsense tone. He ran another red light, responding to all the angry one-finger salutes he was getting from the drivers he had cut off with a sheepish look and an apologetic wave. "I know. I heard what they were doing to you. You held out for as long as you could."

He heard her take another shaky breath. Please, please, listen to me, Jessica, he begged her silently as he accelerated around a car going only ten miles per hour faster than the posted speed limit.

This earned himself yet another one-finger salute from the driver. Please listen to me, Jessica, please hear me and please believe me.

"But they already have us," she said. "Me and Ricky. Maybe I could've saved Craig."

The hopelessness in her voice spooked him to the point where he could feel each individual hair on the back of his neck stand straight up on the chilled flesh. "No—" he started.

"My son and I are going to die here, Ryan."

"No, Jessica, listen to me!" he said, trying to overrule his own sick feeling of horror as well as her despair. "I'm not gonna let that happen. Do you hear me? I promise you. I promise you that I will not let that happen."

She didn't reply but he could tell by the way her breathing began to lose its shakiness that he had gotten through to her. He swerved around a few more cars, noting with a small part of his mind that the traffic was becoming an awful lot heavier.

Hang in with me, Jessica, he thought at her, maneuvering back and forth between lanes. Hang in with me, Jessica. Please. Please. Just hang in and hold on.

The words began to echo in his mind like a mantra. Hang in and hold on. Hang in and hold on. Hang in and—

"...and the partners wanted me so bad they bought me a new Carrera," said a male voice suddenly. Ryan jumped, thinking that the one of Jessica's kidnappers had gone back to her in the attic and found the telephone after all. Then the words registered on him and he realized this was a new voice prattling complete and utter bullshit. "Yeah, it's sweet. Convertible, Arctic blue, zero to sixty in five-point-two seconds and gets the ladies' panties off in three—"

Crosstalk—oh, God, no, Ryan thought, horrified. This was just as bad as the kidnappers finding out about the telephone—maybe even worse.

"Jessica! Jessica!" he yelled. "Are you still there? Jessica, answer me!"

"Hey! This is a private call!" blustered the new voice, highly offended.

This lofty pronouncement was immediately followed by several short bursts of static. Underneath them, Ryan could hear Jessica's voice very faintly, cutting in and out.

"I'm... ere, but... y.... aking up!"

"Get off my line!" the strange man commanded. Then, in a gentler tone: "Mom, you still there? Mom?"

Goddamned crosstalk. Ryan wanted to bang his head on the steering wheel. Crosstalk was number one on the list of things he didn't need right now, like running out of gas or driving into a tunnel or wrecking this piece of shit vehicle beyond all hope of recovery. Ryan clutched his forehead.

"Listen, whoever you are," he said, "this woman needs help—"

"Is that so? Well, you know who's gonna need help?" the new voice brayed, drowning him out. "You, to pull my subpoena out of your ass if you don't hang up right now!"

There was another long burst of loud static.

"Jessica, don't hang up!" Ryan yelled, not knowing if she could even still hear him, let alone whether they were even still connected. "Whatever happens, Jessica, don't hang up—"

"Yadda, yadda, yadda!" taunted the cross-talker nastily. "Get off the phone now!"

"Jessica!" Ryan tried blocking his other ear but he still couldn't hear anything except static and this asshole lawyer in his asshole Porsche. He was probably stopped at the same goddamned light he was—

Not just any asshole Porsche, Ryan corrected himself as his gaze happened to fall on one of the cars ahead of him: an asshole Porsche Carrera convertible in arctic blue, which an asshole lawyer might conceivably describe to his mother as sweet.

He jumped out of the rent-a-cop car and hurried up to where the Porsche was stopped, ignoring the frantic honking from the drivers behind him.

The license plate on the Arctic blue Porsche read, WL SUE U 2. Ryan decided to laugh later when he had more time to do it properly. The guy behind the wheel was ranting and raving to the empty climate-controlled air around him.

Well, of course—along with all the other sweet features on that sweet car, he would have the convenience of a hands-free speakerphone. How nice for him.

Jessica's voice broke through the static in his ear. "Listen to me for just a second, please!" she was saying. "You don't understand, I've been kidnapped! I don't know where I am, they murdered my housekeeper—"

"Murdered your housekeeper?" the asshole brayed over her in that stupid, bullying tone. "Okay, you know what? Don't waste my precious time, lady. I'm a lawyer. I get paid six hundred dollars an hour to listen to drivel like this. One more word and so help me I'm gonna start billing you—"

I'm gonna start billing you. Ryan could see that the man's lips were moving in a perfect match to the brutish asshole voice coming from his cellphone. All right—I've got you, you bastard. Ryan bared his teeth in a grim smile and raced back to the rent-a-cop car. He hopped in just as the light changed and hit the accelerator hard enough to let him bypass first gear entirely and go directly into second.

He made a screeching swerve around all the cars in front of him and got to the intersection well ahead of the Porsche. The asshole lawyer was still ranting and raving when Ryan yanked the steering wheel hard to one side, veering sharply into his lane to cut him off, and then braked hard.

The expression on the asshole lawyer's red face went from pissed off to totally terrorized as he slammed on his expensive anti-lock brakes, almost kissing the rent-a-cop car's passenger side door with his perfect bumper. Ryan's grim smile widened; someone should call the ABS people and tell them they had another satisfied customer, he thought as he grabbed the .38 Special and hopped out of the car.

The asshole lawyer now looked like he was going to wet his asshole pants at the sight of Ryan banging on his windshield with the gun. His eyes were almost popping out of his head as he began to fumble around for his cellphone.

"Gimme that phone!" Ryan screamed at him, holding up the .38. He turned and aimed the handgun at the Porsche's hood. "Gimme that phone right now or I shoot your car!"

"Ryan?" came Jessica's voice from inside the car, trembling with disbelief.

"I'm here, Jessica!" he called back loudly as the asshole lawyer handed the cellphone over to him with shaking hands.

"No, no, be cool!" the guy begged in a voice so high that he was almost squealing. "Here, here, man, it's all yours—"

Ryan snatched it away from him. He was just turning away when he looked up to see a cement truck barreling toward the intersection, bearing down on him—or more precisely, on the rent-a-cop car. He could hear the truck-driver make a token stab at braking even though there wasn't the slightest chance that he would actually be able to stop in time. Nor was there any way the truck could swerve around the car. There was only enough time for Ryan to think that he really could not believe his incredibly shitty luck today before the irresistible force of the cement truck met the in-no-way-immovable object that was the rent-a-cop car and demolished it with utter thoroughness and what might as well have been extreme prejudice.

Both Ryan and the asshole lawyer watched in open-mouthed awe as flaming rent-a-cop car debris rained down all around them. As far as Ryan could tell, the largest of the pieces were only slightly smaller than a softball. Which, he supposed, was only to be expected for sewing machine wreckage. At least none of it was large enough to do any real damage to anything it landed on, although this new development did leave him with a very serious problem.

He turned back to the asshole lawyer, who met his gaze with a rabbit-in-the-headlights expression, still too startled to speak.

"I'm gonna need your car, too," Ryan told him.

He wouldn't have thought the asshole lawyer could actually look any more terrorized, but somehow he did. "No, no, no!" the guy begged. "Wait, wait—"

But Ryan had absolutely no intention to wait for the man to recover his asshole wits. "Sorry, man," he said, yanked the car door open, dragged his ass forcibly out from behind the steering wheel and hurled him to the pavement with a strength he had never even suspected he possessed.

"Ryan?" As he jumped in behind the wheel of the Porsche, Ryan noticed Jessica's voice was coming out of the radio and he turned it up. "I thought I lost you. I thought I was dead—"

"I'm here, it's okay!" Ryan told her. "It's okay now." Jesus Christ, the guy had already filled the passenger seat with a pile of fast-food trash. Ryan tossed his cellphone into the passenger seat thinking that the guy was an even bigger asshole than he had thought. He deserved a sewing machine, not a sweet machine like this.

"Hey, now, wait a minute," the asshole whined, getting to his feet and sidling toward the car. "Can't we just talk about—"

Ryan shot him a dirty look as he stomped on the accelerator. The Porsche sprang forward with a roar that sounded both powerful and refined and in no way suitable for an asshole lawyer who would willingly stuff his face with the classic trash cuisine of Chez Gigunda Burger. The glorious growl of that engine was almost enough to drown out the sound of the asshole standing in the middle of the street and calling *him* an asshole.

"I thought I lost you," Jessica said again. "I thought for sure I was dead—"

"You're okay," he repeated. "Be sure of that, everything's okay now." Well, everything was mostly okay, if he could keep this Porsche reined in; the wheel was so responsive that he kept oversteering. Every time he passed a car, he was practically all over the road.

He was only half aware of the hum coming from the radio speakers until Jessica started to say something else. Then the hum suddenly became static which swelled to drown her out in barely a moment.

Then the static itself began to fade away along with Ryan's phone connection and, in an extremely strange development, the daylight.

"...yan? Are you there?" Jessica's voice was cutting in and out. "...at's appening..."

"We're okay," Ryan told her emphatically. "We just got our lines crossed with some lawyer but I've got his phone and car and—"

Realization came just before he would have lost Jessica altogether.

Tunnel!

"Ryan? What is it?" she asked.

"A tunnel about a mile long," Ryan said grimly. "I have to stop or I *will* lose you."

God bless the Antilock Braking System again, Ryan thought, wincing at the discordant chorus of angry car horns all around him as he brought the Porsche to a neat and stunningly short halt. He just hoped that enough of the cars in his immediate vicinity also enjoyed the benefits of ABS, and that all the cars without it would slide into anybody else but him.

"Can you back up?" Jessica asked in a high, anxious voice.

"Yeah, right," he said, looking around while trying to avoid making eye contact with any of the furious drivers still honking their horns. "There's traffic everywhere." Thanks to his own brilliant maneuver, there was no possible way he was going to be able to turn the Porsche around. He had only one option and he knew that he had better take it in a hurry. He shoved the stick shift into reverse and twisted around to look over his shoulder. "Backing!" he announced and hit the gas.

He still wasn't used to how quickly the Porsche would respond. He felt as if he had been squirted out of the tunnel like a melon seed while all around him, the rest of the drivers were going crazy at the sight of him zipping past them in reverse. He couldn't blame them. "I am in deep shit!" he wailed as the car reached the mouth of the tunnel and swung itself around smoothly in a one hundred and eighty degree turn.

"What? You're what?" Jessica asked, completely baffled.

Ryan didn't answer; he couldn't. The way the car jumped forward the moment his foot touched the gas pedal was startling to the point of scary.

Scant moments later, he found himself looking at the car's original asshole owner through the windshield. The asshole lawyer gaped at the Porsche bearing down on him in disbelief, then threw back his head and looked up at the sky with open arms, thanking the Almighty or the equivalent for bringing his sweet, brand new, four-wheeled panty-remover back.

"Yeah, man, I see why you drive a Porsche," Ryan muttered. "Asshole." He didn't quite aim directly at the asshole. Not really. At least, he was pretty sure that he wouldn't have hit the man even if he hadn't jumped out of the way. And even if he had hit the asshole lawyer, it probably wouldn't have been much more than the very slightest graze, something so minor as to be unworthy even of a Band-Aid.

So the guy really had no call to yell "Asshole!" at him again. Really. No call at all, none whatsoever.

TEN

By the time Ryan got to LAX, he had stopped thinking of the car as the asshole Porsche and started thinking of himself as royally spoiled. He had ridden in one or two fairly high-end cars but never one quite as high up as this one. And for damned sure, he had never gotten behind the wheel of a machine even remotely comparable to this.

If he had never understood the appeal of a car like this before, he certainly did now. And anyone who thought Americans, particularly Angelenos, drove too much had never had the pleasure of driving something like this. If the Porsche had actually been his, he'd have happily driven to LAX at least once a day.

If he were to be perfectly honest even just with himself, however, he would have to admit that, under the circumstances, he really had no business enjoying the Porsche this much, or for that matter, at all. Even leaving aside the consideration that the lives of a woman and her family were at stake, there was also the small matter of this being his second act of Grand Theft Auto today.

No matter how all of this played out, there was going to be some very serious fallout for him to deal with. Even if he ended up getting a medal from the President along with a signed affidavit pronouncing him a genuine hero, he would still have to face the consequences of having stolen a Porsche from a lawyer—an asshole lawyer with a vanity plate that read WL SUE U 2. One way or another, his ass was grass.

Until that time, however, he had to keep his mind on the task at hand, which was saving Jessica's life, and the lives of her son and her husband. He cruised along the upper level of the service road looking for a decent temporary parking place when he suddenly spotted the one thing he really hadn't wanted to see at all.

"Shit," he said, slowing down as the Porsche sailed past a very familiar SUV that was just pulling into the curbside spot he had been eyeing for himself.

"What?" Jessica asked him, immediately on the alert.

"Your car's here," he told her grimly. He circled the roundabout as quickly as he could and pulled over at the red curb. As he watched, two guys got out of the Cayenne, one fairly big and one closer to his own size.

Jesus, but they were a bunch of mean-looking bastards, Ryan thought, fear tightening his stomach. No wonder Jessica Martin was practically scared out of her mind. If he ever looked up and saw even just one of these bruisers coming to get up close and personal with him, he would probably wet his pants.

"Ryan, please! You've got to hurry and find Craig!" her voice begged from the radio. "Just find him now!"

He grabbed the phone and hopped out of the Porsche, keeping his gaze fixed on the two heavies as he hurried into the terminal after them.

"Okay, Jessica, what does your husband look like?" he asked, trotting a little to keep up with the men striding ahead of him. At first he'd been concerned about staying a safe distance behind them; now he was just trying not to lose them. These guys were like Olympic race-walkers. Great big ugly violent Olympic race-walkers, with guns.

"He's forty-eight years-old," Jessica was telling him. "Six feet tall. Trim build. He's got thinning hair."

Great! That description got things narrowed down to maybe every second or third guy he had seen since he had walked in. Ryan stifled a groan of impatience. "What else? What's he wearing?"

"I'm not sure," she answered. "We have completely different schedules. I was fast asleep—"

He listened with half an ear while she gave him a pointless summary of a day in the life of the Martin family. Ahead of him was a roped-off area with three points of entry, each one supervised by uniformed airport staff. Passengers were lining up in front of them, waiting to be admitted one by one.

PERSONS MUST HAVE TICKET BEYOND THIS POINT.

Ryan stopped short, staring at the sign. Dead-end; there was nowhere else to go unless you turned around and went back the way you'd come. This meant the bastards holding Jessica and her son had been able to get through the ticket checkpoint.

Only they couldn't have, Ryan thought frantically. They couldn't have already had airline tickets—they hadn't even known they would have to go out to the airport in the first place, so how the hell had they gotten through? They sure hadn't stopped at a ticket counter after they got here. Did they just keep airplane tickets lying around the hideout, just in case they had to make a last minute run out to the airport and kidnap somebody? Or did they have some friendly criminal travel agent, maybe, someone who specialized in last-minute refundable E-tickets for kidnappers?

It didn't matter, he thought, looking around even more frantically. He didn't have a ticket and he didn't have any tricks up his sleeve and if he didn't find a way to get through, he was going to lose them and they were going to find Jessica's husband—

The Eurotrash woman who bumped into him almost hard enough to knock him over was too busy shouting a fractured mix of French and English into her cellphone to notice Ryan at all, let alone to say either "Excuse me" or "Watch it, buddy." Ryan glowered at her tacky, garishly-dressed back as she ambled away, too distracted to notice the dirty looks she was getting from a number of other people who objected either to the bodily contact or just the sound of her voice. The woman had no manners, crap taste—damn, Ryan thought, she could actually give Eurotrash a bad name.

On the other hand, she wasn't really a total loss. There was one thing she did have going for her after all, Ryan saw with a burst of inspiration, and it was the lovely and quite stylish plane ticket, which just happened to be sticking jauntily out of a pocket in the Louis Vuitton bag slung over her shoulder. With everyone else around the Eurotrasher working as hard as they could to ignore her existence, it was ridiculously easy for Ryan to amble up next to her and relieve her of it.

The Eurotrasher was still all wrapped up in her loud, accented conversation, working as hard as she could to offend the world at large as Ryan stepped up to one of the airport staff at the checkpoint and handed her the ticket.

She flipped open the jacket, scanned the contents briefly, and handed it back to him with a professional smile. "Have a wonderful flight, Mr D'Aubigne."

Ryan blinked at her. "Oh. Yeah. Uh... Oui. Oui."

"Blue jeans," he heard Jessica saying thoughtfully as he spotted the heavies just ahead of him. He shoved his way through a knot of confused travelers who kept asking each other where their gate was. He had to run to keep from losing them among the multitude of travelers milling around on the concourse. "Blue jeans, I think. Craig almost always wears blue jeans—oh, and a Lakers jacket!" she added. "Yes, his Lakers jacket! I remember him grabbing it off the chair this morning!"

Ryan didn't answer. He had stopped short and was trying not to groan so loudly that he attracted attention. The two mean bastards had separated and were standing in two different lines of people waiting to go through the metal detectors. So what had he been expecting them to do, join hands like a couple of big ugly first-graders on a field trip? Oh, sure. Remember, boys, stay with your buddy and don't go off to kidnap anyone all by yourself.

"...and Left Field should be just past security," Jessica was telling him. "On the left."

Of course it would be on the left. That was probably what had inspired them to call it Left Field, Ryan thought sourly. And sure enough, there it was. He could see it from where he was standing with no trouble at all. He could also see that the mean bastards were going to get to it long before he did, which would mean among many other things that Jessica and her little boy and her husband were dead and he had committed a hell of a lot of felonies today for nothing.

No—not in this lifetime, he promised himself vehemently and started pushing his way past a lot of very annoyed travelers to reach the front of the line. "Sorry... Excuse me... Pardon, I mean, pardonnez-moi. I'm sorry, but my plane's about to leave... La plane de ma tante, s'il vous plait... Zee plane, zee plane... Oh, really, really sorry about that..."

He just had to remember that it wasn't actually him doing any of this, Ryan kept telling himself all the while, wincing at his own actions; it was really that Eurotrasher, D'Aubergine or whatever his name was. He just had to remember to keep on using a French accent.

He finally managed to reach the front of the line just as the bigger of the two mean-looking bastards was about to step forward into the metal detector. This had to work, Ryan thought grimly, it just had to. Because if it did, they were all home free big time. But if it didn't, no one would be going home for a very, very, very long time. Like, ever.

He had only meant to brush up against the guy in a way that wouldn't attract a lot of attention from anyone, especially the guy himself. Instead, he found himself practically bouncing off what felt like a brick wall wearing a motorcycle jacket. It was an impact that most definitely failed to go unnoticed.

The heavy turned around immediately with a look that suggested he was in favor of the death penalty for any loser stupid enough to breathe his air. All Ryan could do was hope to God that the brute had not identified him as the felony breather in question; there was no safe way that he would be able to check to see whether he had or not. From where he was now standing in the next line over, he could only see the guy in his peripheral vision. Maybe making eye contact with the guy wouldn't give him away, but there was no reason to take any chances now that they were all so close to being home free. The urge to look directly at the mean bastard was almost overwhelming but he kept his gaze fixed on a vague point just over the left shoulder of the woman in front of him.

At last, before Ryan could break down and look or die of suspense, a security guard was motioning for the guy to come forward. Ryan watched intently as the man took off his jacket and put it on the scanner conveyor belt. It disappeared into the scanner as he emptied his trouser pockets into a small tray and then walked through the metal detector.

All right—I really got you now, you mean frickin' bastard, Ryan thought as he watched for the reaction from the security guard on the scanner. I really, really got you. I got you like nobody ever got you before, and I got you bigger and badder than you could ever get anybody else, now or ever again, suckah!

His heart gave a triumphant leap as he saw the security guard's eyes widen. He muttered something into a radio and then motioned for a nearby guard to intercept the mean bastard.

"Excuse me, sir, would you step this way, please?"

Greer watched as a tense security guard looked Deason over with extreme suspicion. Christ, if there was anything they didn't need right now it was an overeager soldier in the war against terror who was convinced he had some kind of sixth sense about who might be dangerous. Frigging airport security guards; some of these guys could be major clowns, worse than rent-a-cops.

"Is there some problem?" Deason asked, flicking a glance at Greer and frowning.

"It will just be a sec," said the tense guard, looking even tenser.

Deason glanced at Greer again. Masking his growing exasperation, Greer made his way around the end of the conveyor belt. He reached the spot where Deason was standing just as another, much younger security guard held up the jacket that had just come out the other side of the scanner. "Is this your jacket?" he asked Deason.

"Yeah," Deason said matter-of-factly. Greer wasn't sure whether Deason actually started to reach for it or whether he only turned toward it. All he knew for sure was that in the next moment, all hell broke loose.

"He's got a gun!" hollered the young guard in a high, panicky voice.

As far as Greer could tell, the armed regiment surrounding him and Deason had simply materialized out of thin air, possibly as a by-product of the ear and brain piercing alarms going off everywhere.

"GET DOWN!" one of the armed men bawled at him. "GET ON THE GROUND NOW!"

Greer held up a finger, intending to tell him to wait, just hold on, he could explain.

"HANDS! HANDS! Do as you're told NOW, gentlemen, or we WILL hurt you!"

It might have been the same guy yelling at them or it might have been somebody different; Greer didn't have time to figure it out before a human tidal wave surged over him and Deason and buried them.

Ryan suspected that if he kept standing there grinning like some kind of jacked-up whack job, he might end up attracting some very unwelcome attention to himself from the already hyper-alert security squad, but he simply couldn't help it. Whole battalions of great, big, armed men, a lot of them bigger than both the mean bastards put together, were literally coming out of the woodwork—out of the freakin' walls, even. They were bursting out of doors Ryan hadn't even known existed because they had been painted to be indistinguishable from the walls around them.

This was what he called one hell of an armed response: one hell of a very seriously bad assed, life-and-death armed response. In his opinion, it was even better than having an Anti-Lock Braking System because it didn't involve him actually having to do anything other than stand around and watch the fun. Exciting yet completely safe fun, at that. This had to be the safest fun he'd ever had in his life. Even if those two mean bastards had been able to dig their way out from under the super-bad dog-pile currently mashing their mean bastard faces into the gray carpeting, they were totally surrounded by a frigging army of meaner bastards, all of whom had automatic weapons and itchy trigger fingers. This was just too great, it really was. These two mean bastards probably weren't going to see daylight again until Jessica's first twelve grandchildren graduated from college. At the very earliest.

Now if only he could get through the security check fast enough to find Jessica's husband and give him the cellphone before the mean bastard out in the Cayenne got the idea something was wrong and decided to alert the rest of the mean bastard crew. Ryan edged a little closer to the metal detector.

Just then, the terminal killed the ear-splitting alarms and everyone in the area gave a collective and highly audible sigh of relief. Ryan included. Now he could hear a familiar mean bastard voice coming from the bottom of the dog-pile of security guards. Of course, it was more than a bit muffled so it didn't have the same cruel and dangerous edge that it had had when Ryan had heard it making threats to Jessica in the attic, asking her if she wanted to die there and giving her to the count of three to save her son's life. But there was no doubt in his mind that it was the same voice. There was a tremendous amount of satisfaction to hear this bastard have to plead with someone for a change.

"Just listen to me for a second!" the voice was all but whining. "Look in the tray! For God's sake, someone, look in the goddamned tray! Now!"

Ryan very nearly laughed out loud as one of the regular security guards picked up the tray holding the items that the big guy had put in it. Damn, this was already the best show in town and it was about to get even better. What were the security guards supposed to find in there—a note from the mayor?

"Look at my ID!" the guy was yelling. "Check it! Just check it, will ya?"

"Hey," said the young security guard, taking something out of the tray and holding it up so everyone could see it clearly. "He's a cop."

Ryan's mouth fell open.

"That's what I'm trying to tell you!" roared the mean bastard. Instantly, all the uniformed men who were piled on top of him sprang back as if they had been burned, letting both him and the bigger mean bastard get to their feet. "We're cops."

No, Ryan insisted silently as a senior guard stepped forward to examine it. That had to be a fake badge, not a real one. There was no way it could have been real. No way, no way in hell.

"Run it," the senior officer told someone and turned to the bigger mean bastard with a look that warned him not to make any sudden movements till the results came back. "You're supposed to declare your weapons."

"I know," said the big one. "I just—"

"Badge matches his ID," someone broke in.

The senior officer hesitated, looking as if he really would have preferred to get a second opinion on the matter. "All right, all right," he grumbled finally and motioned at the guards holding them in custody. "Unhook 'em. Stand down, security."

No, Ryan thought again. There was a sensation in his chest as if his torso were slowly filling up with cold swamp water. He watched the two mean bastards quickly collecting their stuff from the trays.

Stop! Ryan yelled silently. Everything must stop NOW!

But nothing stopped. The mean bastards went on putting everything back in their pockets; the battalion of security guards left as quickly as they had come and the lines of people waiting to put their bags through the X-ray machines and go through the metal detectors began to move forward again. Everything was moving except him, and if he didn't snap out of this waking coma, he might as well stand there till doomsday.

With a superhuman effort, Ryan forced himself to turn around and march through the metal detector, ignoring the offended noises coming from the older woman who had been just about to step into it herself. Then he sprinted down the concourse toward the Left Field sign.

"Holy shit, Jessica, these guys are cops!" he said, dodging around all the curious people standing in the middle of the concourse watching the security guys clear out and asking each other if they knew what the fuss was all about.

"They're what?" she asked, mystified. Then: "Never mind that—do you see Craig?"

He skidded to a stop in front of the bar and scanned the people milling around. Craig Martin—forty-whatever, thinning hair, wearing blue jeans. What the hell else had she told him? Something important—

Right—Lakers jacket!

And there it was, practically right in front of him! A Lakers jacket worn (with pride, no doubt) by a guy looking very forty-something-ish in vaguely hippie-style blue jeans, not to mention his thinning hair and his slight build. Like everyone else in the immediate vicinity, he was staring down the concourse to where the metal detectors were, wondering what had had just happened.

Unlike all the other rubberneckers around him, however, he was going to find out and boy, was he going to be surprised when he did.

ELEVEN

Ryan swooped in on the unsuspecting Craig Martin so quickly that he managed to hustle him fifty feet further down the concourse before the guy could even start to give him a hard time.

"Hey, what the hell?" he said fussily, trying to push Ryan away with no success. He was definitely n ot much of a physical guy, Ryan thought; it was a goddamned good thing he had managed to get to him before the mean bastards found him. The big one would have just crumpled him up like a piece of paper and stuffed him in the same pocket as the .38. "Get your hands off me—"

"Shut the hell up and keep walking," Ryan told him, his voice low and serious. He risked looking over his shoulder to see if the mean bastards had followed them and discovered that it was impossible to see anything that way when you had to walk and struggle with someone. Even if it was someone as non-physical as this guy. "If they see us, they'll kill us both. Your wife sent me."

"She did?" Craig Martin's mouth was a perfect round oval in surprise. He tried to stop but Ryan yanked him forward and quickened the pace.

"Would you hurry your ass already?" he hissed. "You need to hide. They're here and they're looking for you. They already have your family."

"I don't understand," said Jessica's husband, practically whimpering as he trotted along beside Ryan with quick, jumpy little steps.

"It's okay," Ryan told him and held up the cellphone. "She'll explain it to you." He put the phone to his ear. "Okay, I'm handing you over now. Here he is."

"God, thank you," Jessica said, relief large in her voice. "Thank you so much, Ryan."

"You're welcome. Now, here you go—" he shoved the phone at Craig Martin, pushed him forcefully into a nearby men's room, and strode away. Now he would be able to relax, he told himself, because his part in this was over. Even though his gut was still churning with paranoia and he still had no idea how he was going to get himself out of all the trouble he'd gotten himself into, if that was even possible. He no longer had to tear around southern California with a cellphone clamped to his ear, listening to a kidnapped woman being terrorized while he was stealing cars. No more of that for Ryan Hewitt, no way, no how—at last it was over for him.

He would now be able to go straight. Which was to say, straight down the terminal concourse and straight out of the first exit he came to. And after he was outside, he would just keep on going straight ahead as fast as he could, not stopping until the statute of limitations on Grand Theft Auto expired. Or until he was forty, whichever came first.

In reality, he managed four determined strides before he felt his legs turning to rubber and he had to grab a piece of the nearest wall or fall on his ass. That was okay, though, Ryan told himself. Intense relief was just like that. Intense relief would really take it out of you. And that was assuming there was anything left to take out of you after you'd had a full day of stealing cars and saving lives.

Man, he'd better not overdo this superhero stuff, he thought, or he'd die of old age by the time he was thirty. Tomorrow, he'd just finish getting back together with Chloe and then take the rest of the week off.

Ethan Greer had not been able to trust himself to speak until they had nearly reached the bar. He still had not completely ruled out the possibility of killing Deason with his bare hands; that option was going to look very attractive to him for quite some time. He had simply had to make certain that he wouldn't lose control and put Deason out of his misery right now.

"Just tell me," he said to the other man in a low voice. "What made you decide to be an idiot and bring a fucking gun?"

"I didn't," Deason said, sounding extremely uneasy. "It's not mine."

Greer brought them both to a stop several feet from the bar entrance so he could take a careful look at that ugly-as-sin face. Deason was not one of those clueless fucks who was given to stumbling around wondering why so much weird shit happened to them. In fact, one of the reasons he had put Deason on the crew was that his weird shit quotient always came up as a nice solid zero.

Which meant that there was something extremely and dangerously rotten in the state of Craig and Jessica Martin.

"Ryan?" someone called out. "Hey, Ryan?"

Sorry, sweetie, I'm on break, he thought, still leaning against the wall with his eyes closed. Take a number and I'll get back to you.

"Ryan!"

On break? Excuse me, a better way to put it was, he was out on his feet and dreaming that there was someone nearby calling his name. He knew he had to be dreaming because no one had any reason to call his name any more. His work here was done.

"Ryan?" said the voice, closer now. "Hey, Ryan!"

Damn it, the goddamned dream was actually going to wake him up. Couldn't a hero get even two little tiny minutes to himself? Sighing in resignation, he opened his eyes and saw Jessica's husband coming toward him with the cellphone and looking scared out of his mind.

"This isn't my wife," he said.

Ryan felt a sensation in his middle as if his stomach had suddenly dropped ten stories. No, he tried to say, but the guy kept on pushing the phone at him along with the bad news that Ryan really didn't want to hear.

"My wife's name is Patty," the man was saying to him. "And I'm Ed. Ed Phillips."

The guy wasn't kidding, Ryan thought, bleakly incredulous. He really wasn't Jessica's husband and there was nothing he could do about it. It wasn't over. He wasn't free, he wasn't done and he wasn't dreaming. He was back in the nightmare no matter how hard he wished otherwise.

Ryan snatched the phone out of the guy's hand and raced back to Left Field as fast as he could. There weren't as many people milling around in front of it at the moment, so he had a clear, unobstructed view of the two mean bastards going up to someone just outside the entrance, a tall, slender man just starting to get a little thin on top but otherwise in fairly good shape for forty-something-or-other. He looked like an intellectual but he was also definitely a big fan of the Lakers; you could tell by the neatly folded jacket on his arm.

The mean bastard who had asked Jessica if she wanted to die in the attic was smiling like a freakin' ape. He threw one arm around Craig Martin's shoulders while the other one moved in close on the other side, boxing him in. Even if anyone other than Ryan had been paying attention, they would never have thought there was really anything out of the ordinary going on. Just three guys meeting up outside a bar.

Hiya, pal, howya doin'? Meet my other pal, big mean bastard. Hey, big, this is Craig Martin, the guy whose wife and kid we're gonna kill. Whaddaya say we go do that right now? No time like the present, right? Then afterwards we can all go have a beer and talk about the good old days.

The concourse was filling with people again as the two men hustled Jessica's husband away, keeping him between them and moving quickly but without actually appearing to hurry. Ryan kept his eyes locked on them as he struggled through the sudden rush of travelers who were streaming in and waving at each other, hugging, asking where they were supposed to claim their baggage or catch the shuttle or find the restroom. Christ, Ryan thought as a grandmotherly type with a fistful of shopping bags and a straw hat tried to walk directly through him to hug someone called (apparently) Bitsy Girl. Was it a federal law that all the flights had to land at exactly the same moment?

Ryan fought his way back to the security area with the metal detectors just in time to see the mean bastards walking Jessica's husband back through the ticket checkpoint.

He followed them at a run, barely pausing when he spotted the Eurotrasher. She was no longer talking too loud on her cellphone but frantically searching through the contents of her Vuitton bag, most of which were scattered all over the floor in front of an airport employee who was deeply and obviously unsympathetic.

Ryan altered course for a moment so he could pass close to her.

"Here I think you dropped this," he said, tossing the ticket in her general direction like a Frisbee.

The Eurotrasher called something after him that might have been either Merci or Bite me; Ryan waved to her without looking back. The heavies were already outside. He could see through the glass that Craig Martin was starting to give them a little trouble now as they tried to load him into the Cayenne at the curb. Martin drew back from the big bastard who was holding his arm none too gently now and tried to start arguing with the other guy.

The big mean bastard responded by slamming his head against the side of the door and shoving his limp body into the backseat.

"No!" Ryan yelled, sprinting for the automatic door. He hit the sidewalk just in time to see the Cayenne pulling away.

He looked for the spot at the red curb where he'd left the Carrera but there was some kind of big truck in the way, right in front of it. Hope it didn't ding that expensive bumper, Ryan thought, feeling more than a bit surreal; the asshole lawyer would do more than merely complain about any scratches and dents when he got his precious panty-remover back—

Then the truck rolled away from the curb and Ryan saw the words QUICKSILVER TOWING go by just before he saw the Porsche Carrera chained to the truck's flatbed. It was sporting a large sticker with an LAPD insignia on the passenger side window; that definitely didn't go with the arctic blue color scheme.

Ryan stared after it in disbelief, his mind a complete blank until he heard a burst of static and the sound of a radio behind him. He turned to look.

"We just recovered the stolen vehicle. It's heading back to impound now," a detective said to the radio in his hand. "Gonna have to look around for the suspect, though—"

The detective's partner was already in the process of looking around and his gaze happened to fall on Ryan. Without looking away from him, he elbowed his partner and pointed.

"Oh, great," Ryan muttered to him, wondering if the neon sign that read CAR THIEF floating just over his head was visible to everyone in the world or just to experienced detectives. He took several fast steps backwards and suddenly found himself engulfed in a crowd of people boarding an airport transit bus.

Definitely a good opportunity to find out if this bus was going his way all the way, he thought.

Even though Jessica knew they had taken him at the airport, it was a shock when the door of the attic finally banged open and the men dumped Craig on the floor. They hadn't been any gentler with him than they had with her—there was dried blood in his hair and on his forehead. But at least he was still alive. And so was she. As long as they were still alive together, they had a chance of getting out of this. Or, at the very least, Ricky would.

The men stood over him watching as he sat up and shook his head groggily. Jessica supposed it was too much to hope for that they'd just go away now and leave the two of them locked in the attic alone together.

Or maybe they would, she thought suddenly. If they thought Craig was too out of it to be of any use to them, maybe they'd just go away for a while and let him come to. Even if it was just a little while, that might be enough—

"Jess?" he asked, one hand to his obviously aching head as he squinted through the semidarkness at her.

Instantly, she ran to him, compelled as much by the instinct to protect as she was by the need for his protection. Still groggy, Craig had only started to reach for her when she felt a fist dig into her hair and yank her back hard, making her cry out.

"Hey!" Craig pushed himself to his feet and took a step toward her. She tried to cry out again, this time to warn him that the big guy on his left was already swinging on him, but there was another hard yank on her hair and she could only cry out in pain as the man drove his fist into her husband's stomach.

The sound was ghastly, sickening enough to make her grab her own stomach as if she had been punched. "Don't! Please, don't hurt him!" she begged as Craig lay curled up on his side, gasping and choking. The guy still holding onto her hair made a disgusted noise and let go of her, giving her a hard shove that sent her down on top of Craig.

She wrapped her arms around her husband, willing him to breathe, trying to breathe for him somehow until he was able to catch his breath. The thug who had punched him watched with a contemptuous grin on his ugly face for a few moments. Then he turned to the head kidnapper and rolled his eyes as if to say, "Do you believe this act? I barely touched him."

Jessica ignored them and concentrated on trying to pour comfort from herself into Craig. After a bit, his breathing became less labored and the spasms wracking his body diminished. When she was sure he was able to move again, she helped him sit up, keeping one arm around him and her face close to his.

He gazed at her questioningly. "Ricky?" Their son's name came out as a hoarse croak.

She nodded and his eyes filled with tears. "Oh, God, Jess." He touched a careful finger to her cheek and she could see that he was only now realizing that her face was actually more bruised than dirty. "What have they done to you?"

She grabbed his hand and pulled it away from her swollen cheek. This moment was not going to be about pity; she wouldn't let it. She raised herself up so that she was kneeling at attention before him.

"Now, tell them, Craig," she said firmly. "Tell them they have the wrong family. Tell them they've made a mistake."

He looked from her to the two thugs that were watching them with boredom and contempt on their brute features. Then he looked back to her.

Tell them, Jessica willed silently, staring into his eyes while she waited for him to do it.

She had willed so much already—willed a broken telephone to work, willed a total stranger to help her, willed the man threatening her not to notice the phone even though it was lying on the floor in plain sight, willed the man with the gun not to kill Ricky and willed Craig's pain away.

Now she just had to will this one last thing and they'd be home free. And this one would be easy, easy-peasy-take-it-easy, because unlike everything else she'd willed, this one wouldn't take a miracle.

"This isn't a mistake, Jess."

Wrong answer.

The words came to her unbidden, along with the sense-memory of falling into darkness. Then she realized that she really was falling, because the head kidnapper had pushed her aside. As she hit the floor, he stepped over her and backhanded Craig with the butt of his gun.

"Where is it?"

Jessica looked up at him desperately but Craig wouldn't meet her gaze. Instead, he kept his gaze fixed on the kidnapper and when he finally spoke, he didn't bother to wipe the blood trickling from his mouth.

"I'll have to take you to it. But—" he added quickly, raising his voice, "But. You have to let them go, first."

The man in charge gave his head a brief, incredulous shake. "I... what?"

"You heard me. I've made arrangements," Craig said with the calm solemnity of a man used to dictating terms. "I locked it in our safe deposit box where you can't get to it. There are instructions that if anything happens to us, anything at all—"

The head kidnapper had punched Craig rapidly several times before Jessica could understand what she was seeing. She had never seen anyone punch another person, let alone punch hard with the intent to hurt. It was ugly and horrifying and worst of all, it was fast, way too fast for her comprehension to keep up.

And yet, she could see what was going on, she could even hear what he was saying to Craig as he knocked him down, kicked him, hauled him to his feet and began to punch him again.

"Who do you think you are?" he bellowed, shaking Craig like a rag doll. "You don't tell us what to do! You don't tell us shit!"

Jessica reached out, thinking irrationally that she could pull her husband away from the man but the man had already slammed Craig against the wall, away from her. She was struggling to stand up as he took hold of Craig's shirt and smashed him against the wall again and again.

"If you do die, who do you think will be the detective assigned to investigate your killing?" he bawled into her husband's bloody face. "I will, you idiot! I'll make sure of it! And I'll be given access to all of your property, including your deposit box!"

"Stop it!" she screamed as he let Craig slide down the wall to the floor. "You're killing him, stop it, please..." She crawled toward her husband, expecting one of the men to hit her at any moment.

"So, you wanna deal?" the guy was saying. "Fine, here's a deal. Either you get us what we want," he pulled out his gun and pointed it directly at Jessica's head. "Or I blow her brains all over you right now."

Craig turned his battered face to look at her.

"Your call, Craig," the man added. "It's an eighty-five cent bullet to me."

The sound of the gun cocking produced no reaction in her. She had no thoughts, no feelings, and no memory.

Then Craig clenched his eyes shut and he nodded. "Okay," he said brokenly. "Okay. Just don't hurt her."

The head kidnapper's voice was very faint in Jessica's ears, as if it were coming from far, far away now. "Where is it?"

"Our bank," Craig said. Suddenly he sounded virtually normal, as if he were having a discussion about mortgage options with a first time buyer. Century City.

The other man stepped forward and dragged Craig to his feet.

"Hold on a minute," Craig said, looking from one man to the other. "How will I know she's okay?"

The man gave him a mighty shove toward the door. "Move!"

"Wait!" Jessica cried suddenly. "Wait!" She rushed past the man holding onto her husband and threw her arms around Craig, buried her face in his neck and let the sobs come. The big man started to pull her away but the lead kidnapper motioned for him to let her be.

How nice of him, letting us have a last kiss, she thought bitterly, imagining the look on his cruel and ugly face.

"I love you," Craig whispered into her hair.

She pulled his head down so she could put her lips right against his ear and spoke very quickly. "You'll-have-help-at-the-bank-don't-give-it-to-them-or-they'll-kill-us."

In the lumpy back seat of the cab, Ryan leaned forward and tapped the driver on the shoulder.

"Change of plans," he said. "I need to get to Century City. Fast."

The cabbie gave him a breezy, agreeable nod and put on his turn signal. Ryan sat back again, making sure that the cellphone was still on mute before he put it back up to his ear to listen for anything else that might be useful.

Before Craig could show how surprised he was by jerking his head back, Jessica jammed her mouth hard against his and held it there until she felt the muscles in his face and upper body relax. Her husband still looked surprised and confused when she finally drew back but not so obviously that he would rouse anyone's suspicions.

"Let's go," said the head kidnapper contemptuously and gave him a hard shove.

Jessica forced herself to wait until the sound of their footsteps on the stairs began to fade before she allowed herself to rush for the telephone.

"Ryan?" she said breathlessly. "They're going to the Brener Building on Century Park and Olympic!" She started to sob again and Ryan didn't blame her. After what he had just heard, he felt like sobbing himself.

"Already on my way," he told her.

TWELVE

Marilyn Mooney didn't just love the mural of the rising sun and the crescent moon on the day spa storefront. She embraced it as the symbol of her life. She identified with it. She could not have lived without it. And she loved it, too, of course.

And it was a goddamned good thing she felt that way, Mooney said when he saw the bill. For what that goddamned mural had cost, it should have been painted by goddamned Monet in a formal dinner jacket and not by a couple of goddamned sign-painters in stained overalls.

Both Marilyn and the Signz O' The Tymez company had given him a long explanation about the challenge of weatherproofing and the problem of general outdoor durability in an age of growing environmental damage. What it all boiled down to as Mooney understood it was that it wouldn't have cost him any more to put all that fancy environmental sealant and weatherproofing shit on an original Monet. In fact, he was starting to wonder if environmental sealant wasn't the sign painter equivalent of the automotive undercoating baloney that car salesmen were always trying to sell you.

But what the hell—Marilyn loved it, and he loved Marilyn.

More than that, he was crazy about Marilyn because as well as being able to hang tough for so many years, she was actually still crazy about him—no mean feat for a cop's wife.

But Mooney knew for a fact that she was still crazy about him because he knew Marilyn. His wife would never have gone into business with someone she wasn't crazy about, even if the someone in question was a man she happened to be married to.

The mural she loved so much went along with the name she had chosen for the business: The Sun & Mooney Day Spa. It may have been closer to corny than it was witty but Mooney knew that it was further evidence of her feelings. And it was right up in the front window in large gold and silver letters, too, something that made the secret romantic in him feel all warm and fuzzy.

Or, rather, the large letters on the front window would be gold and silver when the painter finally finished filling in the stencil. The guy had been dabbing and gilding and lacquering for two days now and he'd only been able to get as far as the second "O" in Mooney. God only knew how long he was going to take to finish the whole thing, which included a second line underneath: Escape to Tranquility.

To Mooney, the fact that the second line doubled the price eliminated all possibility of an escape to tranquility where he was concerned. But Marilyn had carefully explained that it wasn't enough to have just the name on the window, even if the name was as easy to remember as this one. You had to take it all one step further—the really clever marketing strategist knew that you had to tell people what to do, use the power of suggestion to tap into their tendency to obey signs they saw on the street: walk, don't walk, no parking, stop, yield, escape to tranquility.

Privately, Mooney thought that if it were really that easy, they could have replaced a lot of cops with street signs: Don't Walk Or Steal and Keep Right And Your Hands To Yourself and No Parking Or Murder Any Time. But this was what Marilyn wanted. Marilyn loved the sign and he loved Marilyn, so all he said was, "All right, hon," and "What the hell."

Right now, however, what he really wanted to say was, "All right, hon, what the hell did you put on my face and is it supposed to burn like battery acid?"

Since Marilyn was the skincare expert, it was only natural that it would fall to him to be her test subject, a job he had automatically assumed would not involve either long hours of study about collagen or physical danger. In terms of the former, he'd been correct. Usually, the routine was fairly undemanding, at least where he was concerned: Marilyn would sit him down in one of the expensive but incredibly comfortable salon chairs, cover him with a vinyl poncho, and slather something all over his face. Then she would step back and stare at it for some period of time that might be as long as twenty minutes or as short as three minutes, after which she would either wrinkle her nose and shake her head or beam with pleasure and tell him to order a case.

Mooney had no idea what criteria she based her decisions on but he suspected that a major part of it was whether she still liked the smell after the allotted time was up. To Mooney's self-admittedly uneducated nose, most of it smelled an awful lot like Johnson's baby lotion, but he didn't tell her that.

He was also careful never to ask what was in any of the goop she tested on him. If Marilyn was anointing his face with a thick mixture of cow placenta, witch hazel, and goat musk, Mooney figured he was better off not knowing.

Fortunately, Marilyn never seemed to be inclined to volunteer any information concerning the ingredients, for what he suspected was the same reason.

In any case, the only thing he could really say that he knew about the green stuff she had put on him barely a minute ago was that it now seemed to be burning his face off. Maybe that was what it was supposed to do. If so, it was Mooney's less-than-expert but highly logical opinion that this was a product that really didn't fit in with the escape-to-tranquility thing they were trying to promote.

The burning sensation was bad enough to make him forget how much he enjoyed sitting in the ergonomically correct salon reclining chairs. The price tag on those had taken Mooney to a whole new level of sticker shock. But now that he had discovered what the term ergonomically correct really meant in terms of physical experience, he knew this would not be an expense that he would ever come to regret.

Still, the sublime pleasure of perfect support in his well-worn lumbar region just could not compensate for the discomfort of having his face eaten away by acid. Even if it happened to be fruit acid, which, as Marilyn had finally informed him, was scientifically proven to make skin of any age look younger in seven days.

Apparently, there was no fruit acid whatsoever in the concoction she was testing on herself. Same company, slightly different product—the stuff on her face was a lovely ice blue.

Ice blue was one of those colors that, according to Mooney's observations, usually meant the product was guaranteed to do little more than smell exceptionally wonderful, but at twice the price of any and all equivalents offered by competing companies.

"This definitely has a more soothing quality," Marilyn said. She was sitting in the recliner next to his but she still had to raise her voice over the sound of the work crew hammering and thumping and power-sawing. Given how close the spa was to being finished, Mooney was surprised at how much hammering and thumping and power-sawing was still necessary. Maybe tranquility was like air conditioning; great once you got it running but noisy as hell to install. "Is the fruit acid still—"

"It's burning the shit out of me," Mooney said, unable to keep himself from snapping a little. His watering eyes had now begun to sting as well.

Marilyn's ice blue face was sympathetic as she held up the fancy package she had been studying so carefully. "Then I think this blue one is the way we have to go."

"Yeah, but Jesus, Mare—" he looked down at the invoice on his lap, which was bringing tears of a slightly different sort to his eyes. "It's highway robbery. What about that other blue one?"

"I didn't like the way it dried," she told him firmly and he knew the discussion was supposed to end right there. Because that was the Marilyn Mooney Absolutely Final Thumbs-Down for any and all products under consideration; no matter what it was, if Marilyn didn't like the way it dried, it was history, even if it smelled good. "It's the live algae in this one that makes the difference."

Mooney sighed, looking at the invoice again. "Hon, I'm not being negative, okay?" he said. "But it just sounds like bullshit to me. I mean, these guys are probably laughing at us. They scoop it out of their fish tank and you rub it on your face."

"Well," Marilyn said, bristling a little, "it works."

And that was the Marilyn Mooney Absolutely Final Thumbs-Up for any and all products under consideration. No matter how disgusting, expensive, or ridiculous something might be, if it worked, it was in.

The phone in the office started ringing and Mooney caught his wife's arm as she got up to answer it. "But maybe it's the, you know, the whaddaya-call-it," he said with a faint pleading note in his voice. "The collagen."

"They both have collagen," she assured him and patted his knee fondly. "I'd better get that, it could be the painter."

The painter? And where the hell could he have been calling from—the front door? Mooney was bewildered. He had thought that except for filling in the letters for the sign in the window, all the painting was done.

Unless the other painters had had to come back because all the goddamned hammering and thumping and power sawing was spoiling the rest of the spa's expensive paint-job. What with all that and having his face burned off, Mooney was really starting to wonder about the business they were going into—

Abruptly, his gaze fell on the television, which had been playing silently in the corner for some reason—so the guys could hammer and thump and power saw without having to miss their soaps, maybe—and what he saw there made him forget about anything and everything else, including the fact that his face was still on fire.

The image of the man on the screen had been captured from a surveillance camera. As fuzzy and low resolution as the face was, it was absolutely recognizable as the kid who had come into the precinct with the cellphone. Apparently, he didn't confine his activities just to reporting bogus emergencies—it looked like he had branched out into armed robbery as well. Mooney pounced on the TV and turned up the volume.

"...and authorities are now asking your help in identifying this man, believed to be responsible for today's bizarre string of crimes, most notably the theft of an eighty thousand dollar Porsche Carrera and the robbery of a 457 Communications Store, both at gunpoint."

A cellphone store? Mooney blinked as the report cut to a reporter interviewing a cellphone salesman with a thousand-yard stare.

"Well, he was very rude. He kept demanding to be waited on and constantly trying to cut in line." The salesman's eyes suddenly swiveled to look directly into the camera as he attempted a weak smile. "But here at 457, no customer is more important than the one we're helping."

"And what did he do?" asked the reporter, pulling him around toward the microphone again.

"He... he shot Mr Smiley." The salesman had to stop and take a breath after reliving this horror. "We were all afraid that he was going to rob the cash registers but all he ended up doing was buying a charger."

This admission seemed to be troubling to him for some reason; his gaze was slightly fearful as it drifted back to the camera.

"Bought?" the reporter said with some surprise. "He *paid* for it?"

"Oh, yes. Overpaid, actually," replied the salesman, looking happier now. "You see, we're having a sale on all 9600 accessories, and..."

The report cut back to the studio where the news anchor launched into more detail about the kid's wild crime spree, which apparently included a rather bizarre visit to a private boys' elementary school where he'd been asking for a boy whose name was either Kenneth or Ricky Martin.

In his minds eye, Mooney could see the name and address he had jotted down on the back of the invoice as clearly as if he were looking at the actual paper: Jessica Kate Martin, 327 Bonhill, deep in Brentwood, the hardest of hard-core 'burbs.

That was the lady with the beautiful complexion who had answered his knock looking cordial and a little bit puzzled and not at all kidnapped. Which meant he could take it for granted that the case was closed and the show was over, move along, nothing more to see, no matter how sure he might have been to the contrary.

And damn, but he really had been sure there was something to the story that the kid had told him. If he hadn't been facing a precinct full of gangbangers in a full-blown drug war, he never would have put that phone down. Or, rather, given it back to the kid, who couldn't have looked less like a one-man crime wave if he'd tried. But even if he'd been the meanest gangbanger in the place, the woman on the cellphone had sounded real enough. Her voice had been—

The thought came to him unbidden. Mooney grabbed his cellphone and punched for information.

"Thank you for using PacBell, this is Claire," said a musical female voice. "How may I help you?"

"Yeah, I need the number for a residence," Mooney said, hoping the green goop on his face wouldn't eat through phone receiver and cut him off before he was finished. "Jessica Martin in Brentwood."

"That number is 555-990-6763," sang the operator. "For an extra seventy-five cents—"

Mooney hung up on her without answering and dialed the number himself. The line rang half a dozen times and then he heard the mechanical click of an answering machine.

"Hi," said a young boy, "you've reached the home of Ricky—"

"—and Craig," a man put in as the boy giggled.

"—and Jessica Martin," added a woman, while the other two giggled some more. "We can't get to the phone right now, but if y'all leave a message, we'll call back real soon now, ya hear?"

"She has an accent," Mooney said, unaware he was speaking aloud as he stared at the phone in his hand, horrified. He knew that voice; he'd heard it before, not at the front door of the Martin house but on the kid's cellphone. A Southern accent was one of those things that you couldn't help noticing, even if the accent was no longer all that heavy.

And no matter how faint the accent might become, no one ever lost it completely. There was always just a little bit of a drawl, like he could hear on the answering machine.

Her accent had been a lot more pronounced when she'd been talking to him on the cellphone—a high level of emotional excitement would do that. But no matter how calm she was or how long she lived in Brentwood, there was no way that she would ever sound like the woman who had answered her front door.

Mooney grabbed a towel and scrubbed the green off his face as fast as he could. "Hey, Mare, I've got to run," he yelled, dropping the towel on the receptionist desk as he raced out the door.

The awful part, Ryan thought, was that he could see the Brener Building from the back seat of the cab. The damned building was right there, barely a mile away. Unfortunately, he happened to be right here, in the middle of a highway that was fast becoming another multi-lane parking lot.

"You gotta be kidding me," Ryan complained as more cars accumulated around the cab. Frustrated, he undid his seatbelt so he could lean forward and tap the driver on the shoulder. "Can't you back it up?"

The expression on the driver's face said that he thought *Ryan* had to be kidding. Ryan made a furious noise of disgust and sat back, grimacing at the way the cab was solidly locked into place. This time, there really was nowhere to go; even if he'd decided to throw caution to the winds and go for his third Grand Theft Auto, forcing the cabbie out of the car so he could take the wheel, he wouldn't have been able to do anything except wait it out.

Of course, that was if he decided to stay in the cab. That was the only thing the cabbie could do—stay there and wait for the jam to break. Ryan, on the other hand, had no such constraint; he could just jump out and run like a rabbit. It wasn't a very nice thing to do to the poor cabbie, bailing out and stiffing him like that. Unfortunately, he would have been forced to do that anyway when they finally did get to the Brener Building. The amount on the meter had exceeded his entire bank balance several miles back. If he waited till they finally got to the Brener Building, the fare would be even greater.

Which meant that technically, his skipping out on the cabbie now rather than later would actually be kinder. Or, well, not as cruel, at least.

His new life of crime must be twisting his mind, Ryan thought ruefully. Either that or LA traffic had driven him completely out of his mind.

"Aw, screw this," he muttered. He threw open the door, jumped out and took off running as fast as he could.

He didn't hear the cabbie yelling after him as he hopped the guardrail, but then it wasn't as if he was trying to listen for it. He had to get down the side of this hill without killing himself and then reach the Brener Building before the mean bastards showed up with Jessica's husband.

Christ, but this slope was a lot steeper than he'd thought. Since when did LA have so many goddamned cliffs? Where had they all come from and why hadn't he noticed them before?

He managed to reach the bottom with only minor bruising and all his bones unbroken and intact. The Brener Building was almost right in front of him. All he had to do was sprint flat out for a couple of blocks, dodge a little more traffic—damn it, why was it that the streets he needed to cross on foot were never grid locked?—and hope that he had had enough of a head-start to beat the thugs holding Craig Martin to the bank.

Sweat was pouring off him as he ran toward the front entrance. He was thirty feet away from the revolving door when a van sped past him and pulled up at the curb directly in front of it. Ryan skidded to a stop immediately, hoping he wasn't about to see some mean bastards escorting Craig Martin into the lobby. But he knew that this was exactly what he was going to see.

Jesus, but they had sure worked the poor guy over, Ryan thought as he followed them in. He had heard the whole thing on the phone but the poor guy looked really, really bad. And poor Jessica had had to watch while they had put the beat-down on him. Jeez, it was a miracle the poor woman was keeping it together as well as she was—

There was an explosion of static in his ear from the phone. "Wait a minute, Ry—" Jessica's voice was barely audible. "What are you going to do now—"

"Now?" he said, dashing across the lobby to the nearest window, hoping that would reduce the amount of interference. All the goddamned steel and concrete in the goddamned Brener Building added up to cellphone hell. "Jessica, I haven't had a clue what I was doing all day."

Staying close to the window, Ryan watched as the mean bastards marched Jessica's husband through the lobby towards the bank. There were only a few more windows between where he was now and the entrance to the bank. The best he could do was to rush from one large pane to another, hoping each burst of static didn't mean he lost the line for good.

But at least the heavies hadn't taken any notice of him. He was doing his best to look simply like any other guy trying to keep from losing a call on his cellphone and not like he was skulking around after them. As far as he could tell, however, he had managed to escape their notice entirely.

They reached the entrance to the bank just as Ryan ran out of windows. He could see that there were plenty of windows in the bank, though. Not that this would necessarily make any difference in terms of helping or hindering—Ryan simply had to follow them in and be ready to go into action at the earliest opportunity. He tried not to dwell on the fact that he had no idea what he should be watching for, or that he had no idea what he would do or how to do it. He was just going to have to improvise.

Ryan squared his shoulders and strode toward the bank. The thing to do now was look like a man who had a whole lot of very serious banking business on his mind. As he approached the entrance, he saw the bigger mean bastard usher Craig Martin in ahead of him.

Instead of following him in, however, the other mean bastard, the meaner one who had threatened Jessica and beat the crap out of her husband, suddenly took a casual step to one side and gave way to a woman coming in behind him. She smiled her thanks as she went past and returned her gesture with a polite nod. Ryan paled, feeling his stomach roll over with queasy nervousness. Jesus, lady, if you only knew he'd just as soon punch you as hold the door for you. It just went to show you the truth of the old cliché, he thought; the one about how you never knew who, or what might be standing in line with you at the bank.

Except nobody was going to be standing in line at the bank with this mean bastard, Ryan realized with a sick, dropping sensation in his stomach. The guy was moving a few steps further away from the front door and then simply stayed where he was, in a formal sort of posture.

This hard-hearted bruiser was going to stand out here by himself and keep an eye on everybody who went in or out. But especially the people going in.

"Shit," Ryan muttered. But it only figured, of course—he was a cop. Naturally he would be watching for anything that didn't look right. With his experience, he would know if something wasn't right the minute he looked at it.

All right, then, Ryan decided—that meant the only thing he could do was to keep walking straight toward the entrance without hesitating. He would have to go right inside just as if this was his bank and he belonged there. And when he walked past the guy, he had to avoid giving him any sort of funny or wary look. If he did anything else, if he hesitated or stopped or showed any sign and body language that he wasn't just one more guy who was walking in off the street, he would raise the bastard's suspicions immediately, and if that happened, he was screwed. The guy would be all over Ryan in two seconds and no one would stop him. Because all he would have to do was flash his badge and everyone would just stand back and watch as he beat Ryan up, or dragged him away, or even killed him in cold blood.

Ryan was relieved to see that the dickhead didn't seem to be paying any more attention to Ryan than he was to the other people who walked past him on their way in or out. He had a small flash of inspiration and switched hands with the cellphone, so that he was holding it on the side facing the guy and obscuring part of his face. As he drew nearer to the entrance, he turned away slightly in the classic posture of someone trying to keep his conversation private in spite of the public venue.

Ryan reached the door just as a woman, also holding a cell to her ear and not watching where she was going, reached the other side. She almost walked into him on her way out and he had to step back in a hurry to avoid bumping into her. Still not seeing Ryan, the woman stopped half in and half out of the building, still listening intently to her phone while she dug clumsily in her purse for something with her free hand.

So much for his plan to pass unnoticed, Ryan thought miserably. The asshole was probably looking right at this little tableau. So don't look at him, he commanded himself, just before he did.

The cruel bastard's gaze bored straight into him. Blew it, Ryan thought, pinned to the spot; he knows. He knows there's something funny about the way I'm looking at him.

Then the moment passed and the mean bastard's gaze shifted away from him to someone else coming across the lobby. The woman in the doorway brushed past him and Ryan found himself standing inside the bank.

THIRTEEN

Ryan crumpled the deposit slip he had just scribbled on and took another one, while his mind replayed what had happened on his way into the bank for the thousandth time. The guy had looked through him, not at him. Biggest non-event of the day. Now he had to stop thinking about it and try to figure out some kind of plan to help Jessica's husband, who was waiting in line only ten feet away from him.

He could tell that Jessica had managed to tip him off by the way he kept looking around. The bigger heavy who had come in with him watched steadily from where he was sitting in the waiting area, but apparently he didn't notice Craig Martin darting glances all over the place.

Or maybe Craig Martin wasn't behaving any differently from any other person that the hard-hearted bruisers beat up in the course of an average day. Ryan didn't care; if the bigger mean bastard actually didn't feel inspired to look around for anything suspicious that was perfectly all right with him.

Now if he could only decide how to go about catching Craig Martin's eye without giving them both away. Should he pretend to be an old friend, call him by name?

Hey, Craig, you old son of a bitch! What a coincidence running into you here! How long has it been? How's Jess? How's that kid of yours? What's-His-Name?

Yeah. Right. That was so freakin' brilliant. Even if the bastard watching from the chair bought the act, the one outside wouldn't fall for it. As soon as he saw Ryan approach Martin, he'd know something was up and he'd be on the horn to the other guys holding Jessica and her son, and the two of them would be dead.

Ryan shifted nervously from one foot to the other, trying to keep one eye on Craig Martin and the other on the watchdog in the waiting area. If the bastard would just look away from Martin for two seconds. One second. Half a freakin' second, even. Then he might be able to signal Craig Martin.

Or maybe if Craig Martin himself would just goddamned look at him for longer than a fraction of a freaking second. Each time the man turned his head in Ryan's direction, he tried to do something that would get his attention—nothing showy, just a casual bit of movement, a little something that he thought might draw the eye of a casual observer, especially somebody who knew that he ought to be watching for something in the first place.

It should have worked, Ryan told himself as he stretched one arm over his head in what he hoped was an easy casual way before he bent his elbow and lowered his hand to scratch his upper back. Damn it, if Craig Martin really knew to watch for someone—and Jessica had assured him that she had tipped her husband off—then there was no way it couldn't work.

Unless, of course, the last person Jessica's husband would have thought to watch for was someone like him, Ryan thought gloomily. He was starting to get the very definite idea that this was, in fact, the case. Craig Martin was just not going to see him.

It was like the man was incapable of seeing him. He would have to do cartwheels before the man would notice him, Ryan thought unhappily, and even then Craig Martin was more likely to figure Ryan was just some whack-job who had forgotten to take his medication today. The idea that he might actually be Jessica's secret helper would probably be the last thing that would occur to him.

Ryan scowled and reached for another deposit slip. He wrote a few random numbers without looking down at the paper. He watched with increasing anxiety as Jessica's husband finally reached the teller's window.

The young woman behind the counter looked up and started to give him a standard cheerful yet businesslike greeting. Then she cut off sharply, her friendly, professional smile changing to unguarded surprise and dismay.

"Mr Martin—oh, my!" she blurted, her eyes wide. "Are... are you all right?"

No, he's not! Ryan screamed at her silently. Nobody who looks like that is even on the same planet as us! Go get your supervisor!

"Just a car accident, I'm fine, really," Craig Martin said with a smooth sincerity that Ryan found positively astounding. "I need to get back into my safe deposit box, please."

Instantly reassured, the woman smiled at him again. She nodded and beckoned to a security guard. And it was an elderly security guard, of course.

Ryan almost groaned aloud as Craig Martin followed the old man into the vault. What the hell was this thing that banks had about hiring elderly security guards? Was there actually some kind of federal banking statute that specified all bank security guards had to be past retirement age? Had it really not occurred to anyone that this policy might have a few drawbacks in the event of a real emergency?

He looked over at the evil bastard in the chair. From this angle, Ryan couldn't see his face very well but he figured that it was safe to assume the guy wasn't too worried that Jessica's husband might pass the security guard a note asking for help. There was a very good reason for that.

Abruptly, the guy stood up and Ryan saw that Craig Martin was already coming out of the vault, carrying a bag. The big guy stepped up to him smoothly, relieved him of the bag and began to escort him to the front door before he could pause for another look around.

This was it, Ryan thought, moving quickly after them. He was going to have to do something now because he just wasn't going to get another chance.

He cut through another waiting area full of empty chairs, picking up a heavy potted palm as he went and managed to position himself slightly ahead of the two men.

"Hey, excuse me, sir?" he heard himself saying as he hurried toward the big guy. The man was just starting to turn toward him with a faintly curious expression. Without waiting for him to say anything, Ryan swung the pot up in one continuous motion, noting in a sudden micro-burst of surprise that the thing was almost an exact replica in miniature of the gigantic potted palm that he and the Bronco had very nearly become one with on the highway. He slammed it full force into the mean bastard's face.

Soundlessly, without so much as a grunt, the big man simply dropped to the floor.

For a moment, Ryan could only stand over his motionless form and stare, shocked by the suddenness of the result. Had he really done that? With a potted palm? He looked down at the plant lying on the carpet in a mess of dirt and broken ceramics and remembered the gargantuan version from the highway. Christ, these goddamned things were lethal at any size.

No, this couldn't be, he told himself. This just could not be. Nothing could possibly be that easy, especially something like this—the guy had to be faking it or something, trying to fool him.

Then a woman screamed and the sound galvanized Ryan into motion again. He turned to Craig Martin, who looked a hell of a lot more surprised. An alarm went off.

"Come on!" Ryan shouted at him over the racket. Without hesitation, Jessica's husband scooped up the bag and they ran for the exit. The other bastard was already coming straight at them. Won't be so easy trying to catch two guys by yourself, you dickhead, Ryan thought as he dodged around him.

Apparently, he must have been thinking along the same lines, because he ignored Ryan and tackled Craig Martin, slamming him to the floor with a noise that turned Ryan's stomach. He reached for the bag but Craig had just enough energy to whip it away. The bag slid across the floor and stopped at Ryan's feet.

"Run," Jessica's husband told him. The mean bastard gave him a vicious kick to the head and turned to Ryan.

"Don't you fucking move!"

The bag was in his hand before Ryan was even aware that he'd picked it up. He tore out of the bank and into the lobby of the Brener Building, looking for a way out other than the front door. The alarm was still ringing in the bank but over it, he could hear a different man's voice holler,

"Drop your weapon!"

Every fiber of his being was crying out for him to turn around so he could see the mean bastard pointing a gun at him through the glass. But Ryan knew if he did, the man would shoot him dead. And as soon as that happened, there'd be no stopping him. He'd flash his badge at all the people in the bank and tell them to call 911 and they'd all do as they were told.

But the son of a bitch wouldn't dare shoot him in the back, not in front of all those witnesses. With any luck, they'd keep him busy long enough to let him get away, Ryan thought. He looked around desperately as he got closer to the front entrance.

Abruptly, he caught sight of big, stenciled letters on a door off to one side: FIRE DOOR.

"Drop your weapon!"

Greer couldn't believe it. They had actually gotten the goddamned thing. Dimitri had been holding it in his hands and they were all home free. Then all of a sudden he was watching a punk-ass kid take off with it while some old coot who should have been out gumming an Early Bird Special had the drop on him. Taking a breath, he slowly turned his head to look at the security guard.

"I'm a cop," he said firmly.

"Drop it now!" the guard said, keeping his gun on him. Shit—Greer could see that the guy actually had a goddamned steady aim for an old coot.

If he pulled the trigger, he might actually hit something serious.

Still moving slowly, Greer put up his hands and turned toward the guard so he could see the badge clipped to his belt. "LAPD," he said slowly, pointing to it on each letter. "I'm. A. Cop."

The guard looked suitably chastised as he reholstered his weapon. For all the good that did him—he turned back to see that the kid had vanished. Then a small movement to one side caught his eye and he looked just in time to see the door to the fire stairs slamming shut.

He turned back to the security guard. "Lock the building down!" He went over to where Dimitri was slowly pushing himself up to his feet, one hand cupped over his badly broken nose. Both eyes were already black and getting blacker. Shit. They just didn't fucking need this.

"Deason, get in here!" he said into his walkie-talkie and then looked questioningly at Dimitri.

Dimitri gave him a small nod to let him know that in spite of his gushing nose, he was still on the clock and on the case.

"Get him out of here," he said, gesturing at Craig Martin who was lying motionless on the floor. Then he took off after the kid.

Ryan had barely reached the third floor before he heard the ground level fire door bang open, followed by footsteps echoing as someone pounded up the steps behind him. Goddamn, it sure hadn't taken him long, Ryan thought, panting. Now what was he supposed to do?

As if on cue, the fire alarm appeared on the wall just before he got to the next landing. Couldn't hurt, might help—he gave it a hard yank and he jumped for the next flight.

The clanging shattered the air and hit his ears like a physical blow, making him stumble. He recovered quickly and kept going, forcing his legs to stretch three steps at a time. Just as he reached the next level, the door flew open and panicky people streamed into the stairwell, heading for the ground floor in a hurry.

Hugging the rail, Ryan managed to slip around them without having to slow down. But there were more people coming down from the upper floors in an even greater hurry. He had to hang onto the rail and haul himself upward with both hands to keep from being swept along with them.

Judging from the cursing he could hear above the sound of the frightened mass exodus, however, the asshole was having a harder time than he was. Guess it's not that easy to wave a badge and a gun around and fight a current this strong, Ryan thought with black humor. He supposed it was too much to hope that the bastard would miss a step, fall on his face, and get thoroughly trampled.

Two more flights and the stream of people suddenly thinned out to nothing. Ryan pushed himself to go faster, using the rail as an impromptu vault. He refused to give in to the burning in his chest or his legs, telling himself to climb, damn it, climb, climb, until there was nothing more to climb and the only thing in front of him was a sign that read ROOF EXIT.

His legs tried to give out under him as he barreled through the door but he wouldn't let himself go down. He staggered into a huge roll of tarpaper, rebounded and almost tripped over a wooden pallet. If they were doing construction up here, then they had to have some way of getting up and down on the outside of the building, Ryan thought, looking around desperately.

The aluminum trash chute in front of him seemed to materialize out of thin air. He ran over to it. No help there—just a straight drop down to a dumpster on the ground, a one-way ticket to the morgue. Just what he didn't need Ryan thought, his heart sinking. Then he noticed the speed rail scaffolding supporting the chute.

His heart immediately stopped sinking and jumped painfully in his chest with an absurd mixture of blind panic and renewed hope. Panicky hope, he thought, forcibly suppressing the giddiness that threatened to sweep through him. Without knowing exactly what he was doing, he leaned out over the drop, gripped one of the rails and swung his body out, carefully aiming his foot at the nearest pipe.

He reached it on the first try. That had to be a good sign he thought, and put his weight on it. The moment he did, however, the pipe rotated like a well-oiled ball bearing and suddenly there was nothing under him but the air and a very long drop to the ground.

Without thinking, he grabbed at the first thing he saw with both hands, which happened to be another pipe. His shoulders protested mightily at having to bear the sudden burden of his full weight; Ryan ignored them, along with the sound of his own terrified screams. The only thing he paid any attention to was the sight of the cellphone tumbling end over end to the pavement below.

"No!" he wailed, even as he saw it shatter into a million useless pieces.

It was all over now, he thought as he stared down at the wreckage; it was all over for Jessica, for her little boy, and for her husband. That wasn't just a broken cellphone down there, it was an entire family wiped out by a bunch of thugs, a gang of murderers hiding behind police badges.

He then became aware of the intense burning sensation in his shoulders and knew that if he didn't do something right now, he was going to be in roughly the same condition as the cellphone and just about as useful. While these mean bastards would get away with murder.

Ryan managed to swing himself onto another part of the scaffolding and clambered back up to the top of the chute. God, the pain in his shoulders was actually getting worse, as if his body was deliberately punishing him for what he had just put it through. He was going to be more than a little stiff tomorrow, Ryan thought. Of course, that was assuming there would be a tomorrow.

Suddenly, the door to the roof flew open with a deafening bang and Ryan found himself staring at the wrong end of the mean bastard's gun. In the next moment, there were three sharp blasts and sparks exploded out from the scaffolding around him in three different places, all of them unnervingly close.

Okay. Now he's going to kill me, Ryan thought. But there was no panic in him now. Instead, his mind filled with an eerie calm as it yielded all control to his instincts.

His instincts took charge by hurling him feet first down the trash chute.

It was probably the most immediate thing that had ever happened to him; it was actually closer to instantaneous, happening so fast that there was no time for so much as the faint beginning of either a second thought or fear. He just went, straight into the chute and straight down to the dumpster six stories below.

FOURTEEN

Jessica knelt on the floor in the attic, trying to make sense of everything she had just heard. At first, she thought both Ryan and Craig had escaped from the heavies in the bank, but Ryan's was the only voice she could hear. Had something happened to Craig or had they just split up?

She told herself that it had to be the latter because she wouldn't be able to function if it wasn't and she had to keep functioning, not only for Ricky's sake and her own, but for Ryan. She could tell that they were chasing Ryan, which meant that *he* must now have whatever it was these thugs were after.

She then had heard the sound of a fire alarm followed by the excited voices of a mob of frightened people who were in a very big hurry to be anywhere other than where they were at the moment. But Ryan seemed to be going in the opposite direction, away from everybody else—the voices as well as the alarm became distant and faint until all she heard were ragged, rushing noises like hard gusts of wind. She listened closely, baffled.

Where could Ryan possibly have gone now, what kind of place had noises like that in the background?

She had been calling out to him, asking him to tell her what was going on when she had heard a long howl of despair that faded away as the ragged, rushing sound returned, growing louder and louder—

And then only the hiss of static.

She took her hands away from her mouth and bent down close to the speaker.

"Ryan?" she asked. "Oh my God, Ryan? Ryan?"

The hissing went on unabated, impassive and impersonal. Something had happened to the phone, she realized. Something irreversible, irreparable, and quite, quite final.

Unless he counted the time his stepmother had tossed him into the twelve-foot deep end of a swimming pool in a playful attempt to teach him how to swim, the greatest height Ryan had ever fallen from was roughly eight feet. That particular drop had been a completely voluntary act, undertaken in the wee hours at the end of a most entertaining and pleasurable evening. And he had landed on a bed, with someone else.

That had been the first night he and Chloe had spent together and he had known that it was going to change his life, which in his opinion was a pretty neat way to end a really fun night. The landing, along with everything else that followed, had felt great. In fact, it had felt better than great. This landing didn't.

This landing felt as if a giant had sneaked up behind him and given him a strong and overly enthusiastic slap on the back with a hand that had covered the full length and width of his body. All the air rushed out of him but for some reason, his lungs didn't seem to know that they were empty. They went on compressing, flattening, squeezing until he thought they were going to turn themselves completely inside out.

Automatically, he began fighting to breathe in but it now felt as if the giant who had slapped him on the back had decided to step on his chest.

So that's what happens when you fall off a building, he thought as patches of darkness began to shimmer and undulate through his vision; it's not really so much that every bone in your body breaks, your lungs just go flat like a couple of bad tires and you suffocate.

And then all at once air was rushing back into him so hard and so fast that he thought his lungs were going to burst like balloons. Just as he put one hand on his sternum in an unconscious effort to contain himself, something exploded.

Not his chest, thank God, he realized with great relief that he was alive and in one piece with no broken bones. But something in the dumpster had blown up dangerously close to his head.

His vision cleared and he found himself staring straight up the trash chute at the silhouette of a man on the roof. He was leaning over the opening and pointing something at him with both hands.

Terror was a pale word for what Ryan could feel charging through his entire being like chain lightning, hitting him over and over and over again. That son of a bitch, that cocksucker was pointing a fucking gun at him. The mean bastard was going to shoot him while he was lying flat on his back in a fucking trashcan.

Without hesitation, Ryan flung himself sideways out of the dumpster and did a hard belly flop on a lumpy section of broken, dirty pavement. Before he could move, he heard another blast and grit flew into his face as a bullet hit the ground only inches away.

"Goddamn it," he grunted as he flattened himself against the side of the dumpster.

Another bullet clanged off the metal rim over his head and he heard the guy yelling at someone named Deason to go to the north side of the building right now. North side, and make it fast, goddamn it.

Okay, great—whatever side that was, he would avoid it, Ryan thought bitterly, something that would be incredibly easy if he was pinned down here for the rest of his too-short life. He looked around for anything else that might provide shelter but the only thing he saw was his ruined cellphone on the ground several feet away.

"Goddamn it," he muttered, surveying it miserably.

All at once, an entirely new sound burst in on his awareness. It was the noisy rumble of an approaching truck.

Instincts, don't fail me now, he thought and peered around the corner of the dumpster.

The delivery truck was moving slowly enough along the narrow alleyway and Ryan knew that he would be able to run fast enough to cross its path and get around to the other side of it, even as shaky as he still felt after his six-story express flight down. He was sure that the tiny rocks and chunks of pavement that were spraying his legs as bullets hit the ground behind him were also spurring him on.

He was trotting along the alley with the truck between him and the asshole on the roof with the gun and that was the end of target practice for the time being, Ryan thought giddily. He patted himself all over with both hands as he kept pace with the truck, just to make sure there really weren't any bullet holes in him. But he really was fine, he discovered; he had fallen six stories into a dumpster and then shot at but he had survived it all. He was still alive and now he was also out of there, man, he was gone, he was history. But he was history of the very best kind—ie, living history. Suddenly, in spite of the few lingering physical aches in his back and his shoulders, especially the left one, he had never felt so God mothering damn good in his entire life.

Because this was the God mothering damned best day of his entire life, he thought. Triumph surged through him with the force of a flash fire. A little shoulder pain and a few bruised ribs couldn't do anything to take the shine off this day. If anything, a few little pains actually made the day even sweeter for him.

Because this wasn't just the God mothering damned best day of his entire life, it was the best God mothering damned day that anyone, any person...

No, make that the best God mothering damned day that any creature—any animal, vegetable, mineral—had ever had since the dawn of time. Because he, Ryan Hewitt, was by God going to mothering damn live through it.

The overwhelming sense of triumph burning inside him intensified as he and the truck came to a corner and parted company. Ryan sprinted down the side street to the main road and freedom. Not until he reached the sidewalk did he finally allow himself to stop for a moment and orient himself. He then looked down and discovered that the strange aching he felt in his left shoulder was due to the fact that he was squeezing Craig Martin's bag so tightly against his body under his arm that his muscles were cramping.

Before he could decide whether to try straightening his arm out or just start running again now and take an aspirin later, there was a sudden flash in the corner of his vision and he jumped, thinking he was being shot at again already.

He then saw the words printed on the side of the tow truck, large and shiny on a silver background—QUICKSILVER TOWING. Fancy meeting them here, Ryan thought; small world.

Correction—make that a really, really small world. He also recognized the distinctive, delicately cool blue car enthroned on the flatbed like a queen riding a float in the Rose Bowl Parade.

A broad grin spread over Ryan's face as he stepped into the middle of the street and flagged down a cab.

"I need to follow that tow truck," he said as he threw himself into the back seat. The cabbie grunted and started the meter. Ryan sincerely hoped this trip would be short enough that he could afford it. The way he saw it, stiffing two cabbies in a single afternoon was a crime of much greater magnitude than stealing some asshole lawyer's Porsche, and far less excusable.

His gaze fell on the bag beside him and he realized that he had no idea what was in it. That was absolutely ridiculous, he thought as he opened it up. Because of the contents of this bag, a woman and her entire family had been kidnapped, intimidated, beaten and threatened with death. Whatever this bag contained, it had caused him to blow off the only woman he had ever really loved so that he could spend the day stealing cars, shooting up cellphone stores, ambushing thugs in a Century City bank, jumping off a tall building into a dumpster, and, lest anyone forget, getting shot at. If anybody had a right to open this bag and see what the incredibly freaking hell all the excitement was about, it was him and nobody else.

Ryan frowned as he lifted the video camera out of the bag. It was a very nice video camera, still fairly new, not seriously top of the line but light and compact, and not too complicated-looking, but not exactly what he had been expecting.

He turned it over carefully in his hands, inspecting it for damage. There was none that he could see, which was pretty good for something dropped off the top of a six-story building; but after all, he had broken the fall with his own body. He found the power button and the video camera came to life immediately—nice to see that the battery was still in good working order. He wondered how video camera batteries compared to cellphone batteries in that area, whether they were better or worse or about the same.

All right then, he thought as he opened the LCD screen and thumbed the play button. Let's see what's on the early show.

"Oh my God," said Craig Martin's voice as the interior of a car appeared on the screen. He was the one who had recorded this, Ryan realized as the point-of-view swung around clumsily and finally settled on the corner of a warehouse as seen through a car window.

"My God," Jessica's husband said under his breath, "I can't believe this." The scene began going in and out of focus and Ryan could see he was having trouble with the zoom. Then he apparently hit the right button; all at once the image snapped into perfect clarity.

The Chevy Impala blocked in by the two police cars, unmarked except for the detachable bubbles on their roofs, was obviously a gang mobile. Ryan had seen enough of them to know, although he wasn't knowledgeable enough to identify which gang in particular, just that a lot of the customizations on it were obviously gang specific. Like the nice shiny custom wheels that it sat so low on, as well as the custom paint-job, which Ryan could tell had once been nice and shiny.

At the time the video had been recorded however, the paintjob was very much the worse for wear, marred by dents from things like blunt objects, bullets, probably even other cars, not quite as flashy but also heavily customized, as well as spatters and splashes of blood.

But the car was nowhere near as damaged as the two young Hispanic guys on the receiving end of the beating that was still very much in progress. But the heavies looked like they were getting a little tired. Ryan could see that it was really getting to be an effort for the big son of a bitch he had clobbered earlier with the potted plant to haul the skinny gangbanger he had been waling on up to his full height and give him another punch in the head. One of the other two cocksuckers had stopped altogether and was just watching now, except for an occasional well-placed kick.

"Why are they doing this?" said Jessica's husband.

Jesus. You're asking me? Ryan answered silently.

Then someone new appeared, a woman who was apparently the only mean bastard he hadn't met yet. The woman opened the Impala's trunk and began transferring the contents to the police cars. Ryan watched her moving busily back and forth with her arms full, looking for the entire world as if she were simply taking delivery on some groceries. Except each load was a combination of cash in thick, tight little bundles and brick-shaped packages that must have been drugs.

The woman paid absolutely no attention to the beating, which was still going on in spite of the fact that the Hispanic guys were little more than boneless bloody rags now. Even the big bully was starting to run out of steam; the way he was panting, anyone would have thought that someone had just chased him up six flights of stairs.

Your tax dollars at work, Ryan thought bleakly.

On her last trip between the Impala and the police cars, the woman was finally forced to demonstrate she was actually aware of what was going on around her since she had to step carefully over the Hispanic guys now lying bloody and motionless on the ground. As soon as she had finished, she turned and said something Ryan couldn't hear to someone off-screen.

Ryan wasn't really surprised when the last mean bastard finally appeared. He had been waiting for him to show up, since he was obviously the mean bastard in charge, the big mean bastard on campus as it were.

Or was he? Suddenly Ryan wasn't so sure about that after all. There was another man with him, someone he hadn't seen before. At least, he didn't think he had seen this guy before, but there was something vaguely familiar about him. Ryan could not help thinking that maybe he had seen the guy somewhere before. But where would that have been?

Oh, probably at the police station, he thought suddenly with a terrible sinking feeling.

Well, of course he was a cop. There was no "probably" about it. Standing there with the rest of those corrupt killers, with the gang members lying on the ground in pools of their own blood. What else would he be? But was this the guy who was actually in charge, Ryan wondered? Or was it the mean bastard who had shot at him? The original and meanest bastard of them all?

Would his knowing one way or the other make the slightest bit of difference?

The original mean bastard began gesturing at the other guys, obviously giving orders. As the cops began dragging the Hispanic guys up to their knees, the picture suddenly shifted crazily all over the place. It took Craig Martin a few seconds to get it settled down again. Or at least he did his best to try to hold it steady. His hands must have been shaking pretty badly and Ryan could hear the faint sound of his scared breathing in the background.

The Hispanic guys had finally been arranged kneeling upright on the ground and Craig Martin managed to get the camera to zoom in on their faces. Jesus, these kids had been disfigured,

Ryan thought, sickened now as well as horrified; they were going to need some very serious plastic surgery and plenty of it, maybe years and years of it, before they looked anything like human again.

His horror deepened, as he suddenly understood that the Hispanic guys were begging for their lives.

The camera perspective pulled back just enough to include the original mean bastard along with them. The gangbangers were pleading so hysterically that Ryan could have sworn that he could actually hear them faintly. He wanted to look away now, this was too hard to watch, too awful, but his gaze was locked on the screen and he was going to have to see everything, all the way through to the end.

That's the same gun he tried to shoot me with, Ryan thought, watching as the original mean bastard pulled it out. He didn't know where that idea could have come from or exactly why he felt so sure about it. He actually knew next to nothing about guns except for a couple of minor things he'd picked up just today: a .38 popped like a firecracker while the weapons carried by mean bastards roared like hand cannons.

But he was still willing to bet that it was the same gun, for no other reason than it seemed to be the murderous bastard's favorite and he really liked to use it. A lot.

No, the fact was, he loved to use it. Ryan could tell from the way he used it first on one Hispanic kid and then on the other. Up close and very personal.

A large, abstract red flower blossomed on the car behind each kid's head a fraction of a second before they fell to the ground. Ryan felt the temperature deep inside of himself plummet rapidly from cold down to icy and then finally to absolute zero.

This is the so-called gang drug war, a small inner voice told him matter-of-factly; not gangbangers killing each other but dirty cops executing drug dealers for cash and product.

Ryan nodded to himself. All right, so now he knew. But we've seen enough now, so please turn this fucking thing off, he thought at Craig Martin who was still holding the video camera in his shaking hands, before something else happens.

But Jessica's husband didn't shut it off, of course. He had to keep it trained on the original cocksucker as he bent down to collect the shell casings from his gun.

No littering, Ryan thought, feeling surreal. Shut off the fucking camera, damn it. Before something else happens—

And then the original mean bastard raised his head and looked directly into the lens.

"Shit!" yelled Craig Martin in an obvious panic.

The screen careened around crazily, coming to rest in a sideways view of a car door at seat level. There was the sound of a motor and then nothing. No sound at all and nothing on the screen but snow.

Ryan stared blindly at the cab's colorless ceiling. His head felt as if it was filled with mounds of fluffy cotton.

"I'm a dead man," he told the ceiling.

It was nothing less than the truth. He was a dead man; he really was.

FIFTEEN

The Martin house looked just as peaceful and unremarkable as it had on Mooney's earlier visit. But this time, he thought as he got out of the car and went up to the front door, he wasn't going to be quite so easy to get rid of. There was no answer when he knocked. He gave it twenty seconds before knocking again, much louder and then waited with his ear close to the door. Still no answer, and no indication there would be one. He now tried the bell; five more seconds of nothing. Impatient, he decided to check things out in the backyard.

He took a quick look through the bay windows as he walked along the side of the house but all he could make out through the diaphanous white net curtains were some vague, lumpy shadows and nothing else. Nor could he see any signs that there was anyone moving around inside.

"Hello?" he called out. "Mrs Martin? Are you home? Is anyone here?"

Still no response. Mooney paused at the rear corner of the house and surveyed the back yard with an experienced eye. The Martins had a very nice spot, he thought; it was very well planned, allowing adequate amounts of space for a garden and for kids to play in, and all of it was nicely maintained.

Then his gaze fell on the splintered hole where the kitchen door had been and he froze.

All right, he said to himself, that was definitely not a case of renovating gone wrong. Even the first work crew they'd had at the spa whom Marilyn had fired after only four hours would not have been this bad. This could not have been anything other than a classic home invasion, and not a real quiet one, either.

Mooney took a brief glance over his shoulder at the nearby houses as he drew his gun. How the hell could something like this happen in such a nice, quiet neighborhood without any of the neighbors hearing it?

He moved carefully up to the splintered doorframe and stuck his head into the kitchen. Blood smear on the kitchen floor, he noted; someone had only wiped up the worst of it.

"LAPD!" he shouted. "Anybody home?"

Silence. He took a cautious step inside and looked around the kitchen. Now he could see that the room had been tossed with the utter relentlessness of people who knew what they were looking for and weren't leaving without it. Like burglars or gangbangers.

Or narcs.

Mooney stepped over a saucepan on the floor and then paused to have a look at the scatter of papers on the counter. Nothing useful there. No messages showing on the answering machine at the end of the counter but he would have to get back to it later, listen to the old messages and find out if there was anything useful in any of them.

As he moved slowly and carefully into the hallway, he saw the alarm system unit on the wall. A fat lot of good that had done, he thought sadly. And given the bullet hole in the wall just underneath it, he could safely assume that the dark smear on the plastic casing was more blood that someone hadn't bothered cleaning up thoroughly.

He would secure the scene, Mooney decided, and then call for backup. Normally, he'd have done it the other way round but he didn't have his radio with him. This hadn't been an official call in the first place and still wasn't, and though he could see in hindsight what a mistake that was, he had to deal with the situation as it was right now. Ergo, his course of action was clear. First, secure the scene.

Holding his gun up and ready in a two-handed grip, Mooney began to inch his way down a narrow hall lined with several open doorways on either side. There was no shortage of places to hide around here, but he was just as likely to find an injured victim as a perpetrator, a victim who might have been able to get hold of a weapon by now and might take him for another one of the bad guys since he was out of uniform. He remembered one of his training officers saying years ago that the only thing deadlier than an armed perp with nothing to lose was an armed victim with everything to lose.

Just as he drew even with the first doorway on the right, he heard a noise. He pivoted sharply, knees slightly bent and saw that he had the drop on an antique rocking chair.

Had it moved? Was that what he had heard? Cat in the house? Or something a bit larger?

He held his position, studying what he could see of the room and its furnishings, and listening for anything else.

Abruptly, he caught a flicker of movement at the extreme limit of his peripheral vision. He was automatically turning towards it when he heard the blast and something hard, sharp and extremely hot bit a chunk out of his neck.

The impact spun him further around to his left and he fell backwards into the room, one hand clamped on his bleeding flesh.

"Damn it, this is the police!" he yelled hoarsely. "Put your gun down! Now!"

No answer. Still holding his neck, he managed to push himself up on his right elbow and look around. Classy décor, someone's updated version of an old-fashioned sitting room. Sure hope the bloodstains come out, he thought, feeling slightly sick from the pain as well as dizzy. Wanting more than anything to lie down, he forced himself to get up and stagger across the room with the voice of every CPR instructor he'd ever had alternating in his head: whatever you do, make sure you keep the wound higher than the heart. Apply steady, direct pressure, and never use a tourniquet except as a last resort.

Yeah, no shit, especially around the neck.

And which wise guy had come out with that one? Might have been anybody. Might even have been himself. Jesus Christ, but this mother hurt. Getting shot really fucking hurt. This was agony. The pain was killing him.

The wound, however, was not killing him, he realized suddenly. He might have been a bloody mess but apparently the bullet had missed all the important blood vessels—otherwise, he would have passed out by now. That didn't help the pain any and he still felt dizzy and nauseated, but at least he knew he wasn't going to bleed out in the next few seconds, no way. A wound like this wouldn't kill him for another half an hour at the very least. About time he had some good news, he thought, lightheaded, listening as the soft pad of approaching footsteps in the hallway came to a stop outside the sitting room.

Dumb ass uniformed flatfoot pain in the ass, Bayback thought, eyeing the sitting room doorway. Why the hell had he come back? What in God's name was he thinking? Goddamn it, the last thing she wanted to do right now was pop someone else. They had more than enough bodies to take care of already. Goddamn. Maybe after she got rid of this guy she would put a cap in Ethan Greer's ignorant ass, too. You don't have to worry about that guy. Tanner told me about him. He's just an overgrown boy scout. Now that he's checked out the situation and seen for himself that everything's all right, he'll forget all about it. From what I hear, he's too busy fussing over color schemes for some beauty parlor he and his wife are gonna open to suspect you're not the real deal.

Yeah, right. What a good call that had been. Maybe she ought to let this guy live and kill Tanner along with Greer instead, just on general principle.

The sound of movement in the sitting room brought her mind sharply back into focus. Goddamn it, now she was actually trembling. She tried to steady herself against the doorjamb for a moment before she stepped into the room with her gun up and ready in a two-handed grip.

There was nothing there except a lot of quaint, cutesy shit like what you could see in those stupid decorate-your-home magazines. And another open doorway that bypassed the hallway and led directly to the living room. Great. Now she had to stalk him.

Or she could just follow the trail of blood, she corrected herself, looking down at the carpeting and smiling grimly. About time she got a break. Now she would be able to wrap this up and have enough time to rip Tanner a new one—no, make that two new ones.

She moved silently to the doorway.

Behind the couch, Mooney remained completely still with one hand clamped on his neck, not even breathing.

He then heard the floor squeak ever so faintly and knew that she was in the living room. She didn't have to be Sherlock Holmes to figure out where he'd gone and finding him behind the couch was even more of a no-brainer. He was going to have to come up with a move that was nothing short of brilliant or he was going to die the ignominious death of a sitting duck.

He looked up then and noticed, for the first time, that there was a pedestal with a goldfish bowl on top of it at the other end of the couch. From where he was lying, his leg was just long enough to reach it. Sorry about this, my fishy friend, he thought and gave the pedestal a hard kick.

There was barely time to register the shockingly loud smash of glass before the shooter began blasting away. The whole room seemed to rattle with each shot and the heavy smell of cordite mixed with the odor of scorched paper and wood from the bookcases. Mooney scurried around the other side of the couch and put himself behind her.

"Drop the gun!" he yelled, bracing himself on the arm of the couch.

The woman stood motionless with her back to him. She was still aiming her weapon at the now devastated bookcase, almost as if she really thought there was a chance that it would somehow return fire.

"I said, drop it!" he bellowed, watching her shoulders with a careful, experienced eye. He saw them come down an inch or two as she lowered her arms. Her bowed head should have come up then but it didn't. Mooney felt his heart sink. Don't, he begged her silently, but it was already too late. She whirled on him.

The gun in Mooney's hand roared twice in quick succession. For a split second, the woman actually looked surprised before she slammed into the bullet-peppered bookcase behind her and collapsed to the floor. Mooney stared at her, feeling an overwhelming urge to scream but when he opened his mouth, no sound came out. Nearby, he caught sight of the goldfish twitching on the carpet. Shit.

He started to look around but turning his head sent a fresh wave of agony through his neck. "Goddamn it," Mooney said, wincing, trying to feel the extent of the damage without causing himself even more pain and failing utterly. "Twenty-two years. Twenty-two years without this shit!"

He realized then that he was actually yelling at the woman on the floor. Going over to her, he kicked her gun away and knelt down beside her.

"A-ambulance," she rasped, looking up at him with tears pouring from her eyes.

"Where's Jessica Martin?" he said.

"P-please," the woman said. "Call..."

"First things first," Mooney insisted, gritting his teeth against the pain. "Tell me where Jessica Martin is or you bleed to death right here."

"Please... I'm..." the woman coughed, fought for air. He felt like a monster but Goddamn it to hell, she'd had to go and shoot him, and then try to finish him off. "I'm... a..."

"Where is she?" Mooney barked at her.

The woman tried to reach for him. "I'm... a... cop."

Oh, God, no, Mooney thought, patting her down until he found the wallet. The sight of her badge sent a new wave of dizziness through him. Reeling, he grabbed his phone and punched in 911.

"Request emergency back up and medical units! Officers down! Repeat, officers down!"

He turned back to the woman to demand what the fuck all this was about. First she had lied about who she was and then she tried to fucking kill him even though she knew he was a cop, too. For God's sake, what was all that about? What had she thought she was doing? How could she do this to him when he had been twenty-two years on the force without this shit? He wanted answers, goddamn it—

Then he saw that she had died on the floor, and the words died in his throat.

SIXTEEN

"Just give me my goddamned car!"

Watching from his hiding place on the other side of the Quicksilver tow truck, Ryan had to suppress a laugh. Into each crisis, he thought, a little comic relief must fall and today, fate had chosen to present Ryan Hewitt with the asshole lawyer to laugh at.

The impound yard cashier at the payment window, on the other hand, didn't seem to think the asshole lawyer was even mildly humorous.

"Don't take that tone of voice with me, sir," she said, world-weary and bored. "I've already told you we do not release vehicles until: All. Impound. Fees. Are. Paid."

"But I didn't cause it to get impounded—can't you understand that?" hollered the asshole lawyer. "It was stolen from me!"

There was no expression at all on the cashier's bland, plain face. "Sir, do you want the car back or not?"

The car in question was idling at a gate under the patient supervision of another impound yard employee. This employee was smiling broadly—apparently, he did find the asshole lawyer entertaining. He also happened to be wearing the grungiest jumpsuit Ryan had ever seen. A lot of the grease stains had a shiny, still-wet look to them and Ryan suddenly got the very definite feeling that the outfit was the standard employee uniform for anyone chosen to drive particularly expensive, brand new cars belonging to assholes of a particularly rude and unpleasant nature who tended to take the frustrations of a bad day out on innocent bystanders—for example, people who worked at police impound lots.

"Yes, I want it back!" snapped the lawyer, ignoring the man's friendly wave. "But I'm not paying for it!"

The cashier shrugged and gestured at her coworker. "Never mind, Howie, take 'er back."

Howie made an OK sign as he ambled around to the driver's side, opened the door and started to get into the Carrera.

"Wait! Wait!" Suddenly the asshole lawyer's voice was two octaves higher and close to hysteria at the idea of all that shiny fresh grease on his arctic blue upholstery. "All right, you bloody fascist, I'll pay! I'll pay!"

He slammed his checkbook down on the small ledge outside the window and fumbled in his jacket for a pen, ignoring the one the cashier held out to him. "But if there's so much as a scratch on it, even just one little scratch."

He went on grumbling as the cashier signaled Howie, who ambled away with his hands in his pockets looking pleased with the world. The cashier then reached for something on her right. The gate in front of the still-idling Carrera began to swing open slowly.

That's my cue, Ryan thought, and ran for it. No one paid any attention to him, least of all the asshole lawyer, who went on ranting at the cashier without a pause until Ryan put the Porsche in gear.

"Hey, that's my car!" Ryan heard him yell.

"And that ain't Howie," added the cashier, sounding intrigued rather than upset or even surprised. Ryan resisted the urge to wave as he floored it.

The last thing he heard was the asshole lawyer wailing in horror and outrage as Ryan took the speed bump way too fast. It wasn't something he had really intended to do, but by the time he'd seen it, it had been too late to slow down. Lousy way to treat the chassis, but he had needed the extra bit of time. If he had cut across the lanes of traffic even one second later, that truckload of junk pallets would have spilled right on top of the Carrera instead of scattering all over the street. Not that the asshole lawyer would appreciate how much effort it had taken him to avoid scratching the finish on his high-performance panty-remover.

The guy was such an asshole that he probably wouldn't even notice the undamaged paint job because he'd be too busy bitching to high heaven about the black grease stains on the upholstery.

Silent nervous laughter bubbled up inside Ryan and he suppressed it. When this was over, he could laugh, cry, scream and go nuts all he wanted, but right now, he had to keep his grip. And while he was on the subject of grips—

He felt his hand close around when he reached under the passenger seat. At least, that was what it felt like. He was almost afraid to pull it out and look at it. If the thing in his hand turned out to be the asshole lawyer's asshole garage-door opener, his head might explode for real.

Chloe's face stared up at him from the screen of his Bluetooth cellphone. "God, thank you!" he said, his breath coming out in a rush. His relief vanished with the very next breath as his stomach began to twist into a cold knot of unhappiness.

He had been so completely focused on helping Jessica that there had been no room in his mind for Chloe. He hadn't even given a passing thought as to how she'd react when he told her why he hadn't picked up the T-shirts for her. But then what she would say when she found out that he was a genuine hero who actually saved people's lives?

He'd tell Chloe that he hadn't picked up her T-shirts from Kinko's because he'd been trying to rescue this woman and her family from kidnappers but it didn't work out because while he was jumping off the roof of a six-story building to escape the bad guys, he dropped the cellphone and it broke. And things didn't go so good after that. So how was your day? You give any more thought to us getting back together?

But he still had the bag with the video camera. His mind lit up with a sudden and wonderful inspiration.

Of all the goddamned people who could fuck things up for them, it would have to be Bob Fucking Mooney, Tanner thought irritably as he pulled up in front of the house on Bonhill. A combination of anger and apprehension was stirring up a fairly potent case of heartburn.

The way Tanner saw it, heartburn alone was grounds enough for homicide, regardless of who you happened to kill. And if his heartburn got any worse, someone would be very lucky not to die this afternoon, because this was Greer's case. He, Tanner, wasn't supposed to be here.

Hell, he wasn't even supposed to have to think about this. When Greer was on the case, you were guaran-damn-teed that he was covering every goddamned step, every goddamned angle, every goddamned thing. Greer and his team were supposed to take care of the whole package. And that included any shit that went wrong.

That was the biggest reason as to why Tanner had decided to work with him in the first place, because when he did the job, he did the whole job. That way everybody else would be allowed to get on with theirs. At this very moment, Tanner's job was supposed to be holding down the fort at the precinct and making sure that no one had any reason to believe that every person in residence at 327 Bonhill Road in Brentwood wasn't having a very ordinary and uneventful day.

That hadn't been real hard, what with all the non-stop gang action going on. Just to make sure everyone kept busy, he'd arranged for the skinheads to be brought in at a time when they had a houseful of gangbangers.

And what a fucking glorious mess that had been. Tanner had been really pleased with himself for coming up with that one. That really had been inspired. He could have spent the entire day congratulating himself on the sheer genius-level perfection of the plan. The rest of LA could have gone up in flames, or disappeared under a tidal wave, or even have been abducted lock, stock, and freeways by a giant UFO under the command of *ET*, *Alien* and Darth Vader, and it would have been at least three more shift changes before any of the guys at the West Side Precinct would have noticed that anything was different. The only thing that had happened in the West Side precinct today was, it had been raining gangbangers, hallelujah, and they had all gotten absolutely soaking wet, thank you, Los Angeles, and good night.

So if everything was so fucking great, why the fucking fuck did he have to come here? And, even more important, what the fuck was that big fucking pansy Bob Fucking No-Balls Mooney doing here?

There was nothing in the log about an emergency call from this address. But even if there had been, Bob Mooney would have been the last person at West Side to answer it. Mooney rode the fucking front desk, for Christ's sake.

And since he had been riding said fucking front desk earlier in the day when World War Three had broken out between the gangbangers and the skinheads, he shouldn't be on duty now. Mooney's shift was long over and done with.

In fact, Tanner had been surprised to find the big pansy still at the precinct when he ran into him at the front door. On his merry, big pansy way to the beauty salon that his precious ball-buster of a wife Marilyn had pussy-whipped him into running with her. Mooney kept insisting that it was something called a day spa, whatever that was supposed to mean.

Tanner didn't give a fuck if every other guy at West Side was buying all that bullshit the big pansy was selling about the kind of place he was going to be running. They could all believe whatever they wanted about Mooney's big business opportunity but Tanner wasn't fooled for a New York minute. Not even a New York second. He had no idea what the hell a day spa was, but he sure knew what a beauty salon was and that was what Mooney would be running, whether he wanted to admit it or not.

Well, according to the man himself this big fucking deal beauty salon was supposed to open any day now and the moment it did, Mooney said he was going to pull the pin and spend his retirement shrinking pores or whatever. The big pussy-whipped pansy had spent every single day on the job in uniform, and after a crap career like that, Tanner thought, the best thing he could do with himself was shrink pores all day. Shrinking pores was probably the one thing in the entire world that a schlub like Mooney had been born to do.

Of course, Tanner knew that cops like Mooney could suddenly come down with a case of late-blooming ambition. It was this weird kind of mid-life crisis thing cops were especially prone to, where they suddenly decided to try capping an otherwise undistinguished career with a big heroic bang. It didn't happen all the time but it happened often enough that it wasn't completely out of the question.

Tanner did not for one moment consider himself an expert on guys like that but he probably should have guessed it was Mooney's turn. All those awards for marksmanship on the target range just weren't enough for him after all. The schlub probably thought a Medal of Honor would look real nice framed and hanging on the wall of his beauty salon.

Still, Tanner couldn't help thinking that this really didn't seem a whole lot like something Mooney would do. In fact, he'd have bet real money against it. That would teach him. He was now he was betting heavier stakes than just a little real money. And on that big pansy Bob Mooney, of all people. Bob Fucking Mooney. What kind of a miserable, fucked-up world was it, he wondered, when a guy like him ended up virtually betting his life on a big pansy like Bob

Fucking Mooney? A really miserable, fucked up beyond all hope of redemption kind.

Grimacing painfully, he heaved himself out from behind the wheel of his car. The whole situation had given him a raging fucker of a case of indigestion and the burning in his chest was getting worse by the aforementioned New York second.

His mood, already dark, got even darker. Oh, yeah, someone was going to be very, very lucky not to die this afternoon.

He then noticed that the car he had pulled up behind belonged to the medical examiner and he realized with a small chill that it was too late. Somebody else's luck had already run out.

Compared to the little fellow's previous residence, something this cramped could only be a comedown. But limited water had to be a hell of a lot better than no water at all, Mooney thought as he watched the shimmering goldfish exploring the limited area in the glass, its fins waving like graceful, diaphanous banners.

At the time, it had seemed extremely important to Mooney that he not let the goldfish die on the carpet. He seemed to remember once hearing something about how the maximum amount of time a goldfish's memory could cover was a mere three seconds.

By that reckoning, this little guy lived out his days, however many of those there might be, solidly and irrevocably in the present. Or, as all the self-help-actualization-pop-psychology aficionados put it, the Now. And what all that amounted to was, a goldfish only knew what was happening to it at any given moment—it had no memory of things being any different for it and no notion of conditions ever changing. So when it was twitching and flopping on the carpet working its gills in a futile effort to breathe, it had no idea that there had ever been a time when it had not been dying.

Talk about getting a shitty deal! As Mooney held still under the expert ministrations of a paramedic who was tending to his neck wound, he watched the goldfish swimming around in one of the Martin family's water tumblers, living out its life three seconds at a time and decided that he had been right. It had been extremely important not to let the poor little guy die on the carpet. And he was willing to bet that the fish would have agreed, even if that limited fish brain could have remembered nicer accommodations than a water glass.

"Well, the bullet missed all of your major pipes," the paramedic told him solemnly, "but it's a pretty deep graze. I still want to take you in and... what the hell?"

"What is it?" Mooney asked, wishing she would just slap a Band-Aid on him and let him get out of there. He wanted to go back to the spa and let Marilyn finish burning his face off with fruit acid; it was probably the only thing that was going to distract him from the pain of the gunshot wound.

The paramedic lowered his voice anxiously. "Some of this tissue looks... er, gangrenous." He dabbed at his neck some more, wiping something off the edge of the wound. Mooney pulled away and twisted around to see him looking closely at a slimy green blob on a piece of gauze. Before the paramedic could stop him, he swiped the blob onto his fingertip and held it up to his nose for a sniff.

"Avocado mud mask," he said, meeting his shocked expression with a shrug. "For combination skin."

The paramedic looked appalled. Mooney shrugged, moving only the shoulder on his unhurt side. It wasn't his problem if he wasn't acquainted with the concept of combination skin. He helped himself to a fresh gauze pad and wiped his finger. The paramedic moved Mooney's head back to its previous position and resumed working on him without comment.

Mooney considered asking him if it could have been the avocado that had produced the burning sensation on his face. Even if he didn't know anything about skin types, he would still be able to tell him what could burn skin and what couldn't. But before he could say anything, he found himself staring at a familiar pair of expensive shoes.

"For Christ's sake, Mooney," Dick Tanner said, his tone dripping with the fatigue of a cop who felt put out and fed up with the folly of the human animal. "What the hell happened here?"

Much to the displeasure of the paramedic who was working his neck, Mooney raised his head to look up at the detective. "I don't know," he said honestly. "I'm trying to make sense of it."

He paused, suddenly feeling ashamed of himself. What the hell kind of a thing was that to say: I don't know. A woman had died here; a fellow officer had been killed and he was the one who had pulled the trigger.

"I came in," he went on after a moment. "I identified myself as a cop, and... and, well, she opened fire on me. She didn't say anything, she just—" he had to pause again and take another breath. "I checked her ID. Her name's Dana Bayback out of Centinela Division."

"Bayback." Tanner's voice was flat and expressionless. "Never heard of her."

"She was pretending to be Jessica Martin—"

"Whoa, whoa, hold on," Tanner interrupted. "Who's Jessica Martin?"

"The owner of the house—" Mooney winced as the paramedic did something that pinched his skin. "Jack, I think the real Jessica Martin might be in trouble."

Tanner seemed to think it over for a moment and then nodded. "Did Bayback say anything to you?" he asked.

Mooney shook his head, ignoring the tsk of complaint from the paramedic. "She never got the chance," he said sadly.

Having to admit that made him feel even more despondent. The one time he fired his weapon anywhere but on the target range and he ended up shooting a fellow police officer. A woman from the detective squad, no less. And he'd killed her before she could say anything to him.

Maybe if she had been able to get a few words out, he might have found out what the hell had been going on. Maybe he would have found out that it was all some kind of stupid mistake, a misunderstanding of some kind and she hadn't really been trying to shoot him after all. And the poor woman would still be alive.

It crossed Mooney's mind then that what had happened in the Martin house today was the sort of thing that was going to be extremely difficult for him to come to terms with.

If he ever did. Mooney didn't think it was possible, even if he lived to the ripe old age of a hundred.

Fuck this, thought the gentleman known to both friends and enemies as Mad Dog. I hereby fucking pronounce and declare that this fucking bar is fucking open for fucking business.

He moved around to the other side of the dusty wooden counter so he could help himself to a likely-looking bottle, then paused at the sight of the neat pyramid of shot glasses stacked upside-down next to it. He had never been the kind of pussy who went around insisting on formality.

But hey, what the fucking hell. Today he'd get fancy, frills, the whole nine yards. It wasn't like he was going to have to wash the dishes. He picked up the top glass and took a close look at it in the light.

Seemed pretty clean, he thought. He ran a fingertip around the inside, and inspected the results. He then caught himself and burst out laughing. What the fuck did he think that was supposed to tell him? His fucking finger was probably a hell of a lot dirtier than the goddamned glass. And what the fuck, a little dirt just might make it taste better.

He poured himself a generous shot and tossed it back. Yeah, this was definitely VSOP—very shitty and overpriced. Especially for a free drink. Fuck free, someone should have been paying him to drink this. And since he was only getting paid to provide Greer with some of his good old quality Mad Dog muscle which at this particular moment meant guarding the bitch up there in the attic, his drinking this shit meant that technically, he was violating his sacred personal rule about throwing in extra services for free.

Mad Dog laughed again. Ah, fuck it. He tossed back another shot. He was so fucking bored. He no longer gave a shit about anything except when they were all getting the fuck out of this dump so he could just get in the fucking wind.

What the fuck did Greer think he was doing by fucking around like this? He should have called in already to let him know they had taken possession of it, they had it right in hand and he could now go ahead and dispose of both the bitch and her kid. Nothing could have been simpler, so what was the fucking hold up? Something wrong with Greer's phone? Like he forgot to charge the fucking battery or something?

Or maybe it was something else. What if there was something wrong with the fucking phone here? He thought it over as he poured his third shot. goddamned place was a fucking dump, after all. Every phone was the old-fashioned kind with the dial, including the one in the attic that Greer had smashed up.

Man, that was so fucking weird, a phone in a fucking attic. Who'd have bothered to make a phone call from the fucking attic? There were phones in every goddamned room in the place except the crapper; he knew because he'd personally ripped out every single one of them. But he'd replaced the one in here with a new cordless deal and a fax. Greer's orders.

But what if all the new modern shit couldn't make a connection on the old lines or something?

Goddamn it. It hadn't occurred to fucking Greer to check on that, Mad Dog thought, tossing back his sixth shot. So maybe he'd better do it himself.

He went down to the phone at the other end of the bar. Shit, he thought as he picked it up, he couldn't remember if it had rung since they'd arrived here. Maybe he'd better call Greer, just in case—

At first, the red light on the base unit made no sense to him. There were actually four lights, to show you that you could use up to four separate lines on the one phone. If one line was in use, you had three others free. But the only time any of the lights would actually light up was if one of the lines—

He dropped the bottle and ran for the attic.

SEVENTEEN

"Ryan? Are you there? Please, answer me! I can't hear you!"

It didn't matter if it was hopeless, Jessica told herself as she went on tapping the wires together, she had to keep trying. Hopeless didn't enter into any of this. The whole issue of hopeless was irrelevant, beside the point, utterly moot. If Ryan's phone had somehow been destroyed, then she just had to work at making another connection and that was all she would allow herself to think about. Empirical evidence proved that such a thing was possible; therefore, she would proceed on the basis that it was still possible. That was the scientific method that she'd taught to a thousand kids if she'd taught it to one. No point in crying about it.

Tears continued to pour down her face anyway. Science was unemotional, but scientists hardly ever were and that went double or even triple for science teachers, she supposed. It was just normal human nature. It was all part of the human condition to invest quantitative things with qualitative features. Being a science teacher, therefore, she was the most human of humans. The best she could manage under the circumstances was to act as if she weren't crying. She had to just keep on tapping those wires together and ignore the tears and maybe after a while they would go away.

Only when the attic door crashed open did she realize that she had also been ignoring the footsteps pounding up the stairs in the hope that they would go away, too.

Which one was this, her mind babbled as the man stomped across the floor and loomed over her. He couldn't be the big one; well, not exactly, not the only big one, because all of them were big. Except for the one in charge—he wasn't quite as big as the rest of them, but that didn't matter. He was the most dangerous one.

Except he wasn't here right now and this one was, which made him the most dangerous in every way, especially to her. She had no idea why he had charged up here, but he smelled like bad, cheap booze so it wasn't going to be for anything good.

"You stupid BITCH!" he roared and she realized that he was looking at the jerry-rigged phone on the floor.

Jessica scuttled away from it quickly as he scattered the pieces and found the phone wire. He wrapped it around his hand, and ripped it out of the wall with a bellow of outrage.

"Who were you talking to?" he yelled, advancing on her. "You fucking bitch! Who was on the phone? Answer me!"

She put up one arm to shield herself as he reached for her. "No, don't hurt me, don't—"

His hand was not so big that it could completely encircle her neck, but it was big enough that he was capable of actually picking her up, lifting her right off the floor just with that one hand and hurling her across the room.

Jessica didn't feel the impact so much as she heard it. There was a furious shattering of glass, a terrible, nerve-jangling scary sound that made her think of danger and disaster and pain. Then there was the dull thump of her body landing on the filthy attic floor.

For a moment there was complete silence. Slightly dazed, she raised herself up on one elbow, and found that she was lying sprawled among the fragments of the old mirror.

Well, that's seven years bad luck for somebody around here, a voice in her mind babbled. Her hand seemed to move with a will of its own, palming a tiny shard of glass as she pushed herself to her feet.

"You and your kid are DEAD!" the man bellowed. His voice seemed to reverberate in every beam and board around them.

Then he was right on top of her; his big hand closed around her neck again and began to squeeze. This was it, she realized, this was That's all, folks, thank you, Los Angeles and good night, right here at this very moment before her very eyes with her very own throat. And after he was through with her, Ricky—

"Please," she gasped. "Please don't hurt me. I'll do anything. *Anything.*"

She stared into his eyes, willing him to read exactly what she meant by anything, willing him to hear it, to see it in her face and feel it in her flesh.

The man's mouth stretched in a slow, nasty smile and the big hand around her neck began to loosen. Oh, yeah, he understood, all right; he understood exactly what she meant by anything.

The depraved smile on his ugly, malevolent face also told her that he understood she was such a stupid bitch that she really didn't know he was going to kill her and Ricky anyway. Nothing had changed for either of them, except that now she was going to do something—anything—before they both died.

We'll see who's stupid, Jessica told him silently.

It took an extreme effort to keep herself from trying to pull away from him as his hand moved down and began to explore her body. She had to hold perfectly still no matter what he did, she told herself and remain silent no matter how it felt.

More than anything else, however, she had to keep him staring directly into her eyes, keep him gloating while he enjoyed the sight of her terror, keep him enthralled and entertained by her helplessness in the face of his overwhelming power. She had to hold his gaze, make him believe that he could watch her utter humiliation and subjugation in them.

Until his arm was in exactly the right position—

He gave a small jump when he felt her cut him and then grabbed her wrist, roughly twisting her arm up to see what she had in her hand.

"Ooooh!" He laughed sarcastically and gave her wrist a hard shake to make her drop the shard of glass before he reached for her again.

But almost immediately, his hateful smile faded. It was replaced by a puzzled expression. That would be the first very slight wave of dizziness hitting him, Jessica knew. Possibly he was also confused by the strange sound of liquid half-splashing, half-spilling somewhere nearby.

She looked down and he followed her gaze to see that there was a river of blood gushing out of his arm onto the dusty floor, some of it splashing on his shoes and pants. He let go of her and took an unsteady step back. He then raised his head to look at her in complete bafflement. His face had suddenly turned a ghastly shade of paper white and his lips were gray. The sight filled her with a sickening mixture of pity, guilt, and spiteful relief.

"Fifth grade biology," Jessica told him sadly. She began to edge away from him as she spoke. "The brachial artery pumps up to thirty liters of blood per minute. But there are only five in the human body."

The man looked no less puzzled as his legs gave way and he sank to his knees in a pool of warm, sticky blood.

"I'm sorry," she added, wondering if he understood she had never meant those words more than she did right now.

Perhaps he had already lost too much blood to understand anything she had said. Perhaps he wasn't even capable of understanding what was happening. And even if he did understand that he was dying, he had lost far too much blood to be frightened or upset in any way. A little bitter comfort from Mother Nature for those facing the final extremity.

He toppled over on his side and thumped heavily down on the floor. The flow from his arm was becoming more sluggish. It wouldn't be long now before it was all over for him. Game over. No replay.

Oh my God, what did I do? Jessica thought suddenly, feeling a surge of horrified panic. What did I do, my God, what did—

She slammed a mental door on the thought, even as she was thinking it.

That wasn't the right question to be asking, not in this place, and not at this moment. There wasn't any right question she could ask in these circumstances, there was no room for the luxury of questions here. But if she really couldn't help herself, what she should have been asking was, what had she just prevented that man from doing, not just to her but to her flesh and blood, to her son. To Ricky.

Since she already knew the answer to that one, standing over a corpse in this filthy hole while she thought it over was just a goddamned waste of time.

She tore out of the attic and raced down the stairs.

It wasn't until she was sprinting across the dead brown lawn to the garage where Ricky was that she realized she had simply assumed there would be no one else in the house. Lucky for her she'd been right, but oh, God, what if she had been wrong.

She squelched that thought firmly out of existence, too. If she really had to ponder the what-ifs of the day, she could do it later, when there was more time to have hysterics over all her close calls and near misses. Right now, she had to find Ricky and get them both as far away from here as possible.

The padlock on the side door was about the same size as her fist. The door itself was thick and solid and didn't budge even when she threw all her weight against it. Jessica could feel her breath beginning to come in frantic gasps as she ran around to the front, looking for another entrance.

She knew even as she tugged on the handle of the wide, rolling door that it would be locked as well—otherwise, Ricky would have raised it and escaped already. But she had to try, just in case the door had simply just been too heavy for a frightened eleven year-old boy to manage.

It only rattled as she yanked on the handle. No luck. What else? There had to be something, she thought, looking around desperately.

Windows!

She could see two of them high up on the door itself. They were very small and just out of her reach but if she could get to them, they might help her get in so she could get her son out. She searched for something tall enough that she could use to stand on and then spotted a large, rusty pail off to one side of the building. Quickly, she grabbed it and turned it over, rapping the bottom with her knuckles to make sure it wasn't so rusted that it wouldn't bear her weight.

To her relief, it seemed to be as solid as the door she couldn't budge; she jumped up on it and pounded on the windows with both fists. "Ricky!" she yelled. "Ricky, it's me, it's Mommy! I'm here!"

Her son appeared in the shadows, looking up at her with a fearful desperation that broke her heart. He was pale and dirty but he seemed to be unhurt.

"Mom!" he said, on the verge of tears. "I didn't know where you were!"

"I'm here now," she told him. "Baby, are you okay?"

"I want to go home!"

Me, too, baby, Jessica added silently. All she had to do was get him out of there, which would be no mean feat. Even if her son had been able to find something tall enough that he could stand on to reach the windows, they were still far too small even for him to squeeze through.

Her mind raced as it searched for alternatives, anything at all. Then her heart gave an enormous leap as her gaze fell on the Cayenne sitting in the driveway. But before she could even start to think about what to do next, she heard the crunch of gravel and the sound of the van's mistimed motor.

Oh God, they're back! her mind screamed. They're already back!

Without a word of explanation to Ricky, Jessica dived off the bucket and scrambled out of sight around the corner of the garage just as the van pulled up and stopped in front of the house.

Shaking, she hardly dared to breathe as she watched the three guys who had taken Craig away climb out of the van. But there were only three of them. She could see no sign of her husband at all.

Her husband wasn't with them.

For a long, frozen moment, she could not imagine what this meant, especially in terms of what she had just done in the attic. Had they? Was Craig... Was her husband—

But she couldn't even think it. Her mind kept blanking it out, refusing to let her go there.

Then all at once, new hope flared with a near painful intensity in her chest. Maybe Craig wasn't with them because he had managed to escape from the fuckers and ran away. Maybe he was safe, maybe right now he was telling the whole story to the cops—the good cops. There had to be some good ones, somewhere. There just had to be.

Had to be! Had to be! Had to be! Had to be! Her mind chanted the words like absurd mantra as she watched the men go into the house. All right.

Once they were all inside, that would give her just enough time to jump into the Cayenne and—

But to her horror, the third one stopped on the porch, lit a cigarette, and leaned against the wall as he settled in to smoke it.

No, she thought, desperation taking her to the thin edge of hysteria. He *couldn't*. He just couldn't stay out here and do that, he had to go in the house with the other two and smoke his cigarettes in there.

The only movement he made was to shift position so that he was more comfortable as he went on smoking.

Jessica watched him in disbelief. The son of a bitch was a dirty cop, for crying out loud—he kidnapped women and children, he beat people up and he killed them. He had no respect for the law, for personal property or for human life. Why in God's name would someone like that refrain from smoking inside of his own goddamned hideout?

What was wrong with these bastards? Just what kind of evil men were these people?

Greer was about to head up to the attic when he heard the fax machine go off in the living room.

"Yo! Bank photos of the kid are coming in!" Deason called.

That was fast, Greer thought as he went into the living room to have a look. But what satisfaction he felt vanished as soon as he saw them.

"Shit, they've got to have better ones than this," he complained, ripping one page after another out of the fax machine. "Look at that. You can't even see his face. What good is that?"

Greer crumpled the pages angrily and threw them aside, wondering where the hell Mad Dog was. He had expected to find the man lying around on the couch, watching TV while he pretended that he hadn't helped himself to some of the shitty booze in the house. The TV was off but there was an open bottle sitting on the bar. The guy was getting careless in his old age, Greer thought, leaving the evidence right out in plain sight like that. Must have been in the can, now.

He could bust the Dog's balls about it later. At the moment, he was a hell of a lot more interested in seeing the look on the Martin bitch's face when he told her what was coming up next for her and Junior. He considered having another look at the faxed photos again and then decided to do that later, too. He gestured for Deason to follow him up to the attic.

Just as they reached the first landing, the phone began to ring. Greer felt a flash of renewed anger. Interruptions; always goddamned interruptions. And why the hell hadn't Mad Dog picked it up already? What was the stupid dickhead waiting for, an engraved invitation? He jerked his chin at Deason, who hurried back down to the living room to pick it up.

He reappeared almost instantly, holding the telephone with a very disturbed expression on his ugly face. "E? You better take this," he said in an ominous tone, and tossed the receiver up to him.

He didn't like the sound of that, Greer thought as he put the handset to his ear. "What?"

"I've got what you're looking for," Ryan growled into his cellphone, doing his best to sound vicious. I've got you now, you bastard, he added silently; I've got you now, courtesy of the good old Last Incoming Call feature.

"Oh?" said a male voice.

"Yeah," Ryan said and braced himself for a storm of abuse.

Jessica could hear the phone inside faintly from where she was and realized that as far as she knew, this was the first time it had ever rung. Of course—maybe that was the only line they had, in which case she had kept it tied up for most of the day. So who could possibly have been calling on it now?

What if it was Ryan?

"Okay," said the voice on Ryan's cellphone, sounding agreeable. "What I do for it?"

Ryan was so startled that he hit the brakes on the Carrera harder than he should have and almost lost control of the wheel in spite of the anti-lock brakes. "What?"

"What I do for it?" asked the voice on the other end of the line. "You tell me now!"

He knew that voice. But it couldn't be, it was impossible. He hadn't called *him*. For God's sake, he didn't even know the guy's number. He didn't even know the guy had a phone—

"Wait, who did I call?" Ryan asked fearfully.

"I no call you! You call me on pay phone, I run all the way down here!" shouted the Vietnamese caricature artist on the pier. "You waste my time, I have picture to draw!"

Jesus Christ, Ryan thought, stunned; just how bat shit was this guy that he couldn't drop the me-so-artistic-draw-you-long-time act even just to answer a goddamned payphone? He heard the rumble of skateboards in the background and a voice said, "Dude, that looks like shit."

"That no like shit, you like shit!" yelled the caricature artist angrily. "You like shit, smell like shit—"

Well, that answered the how-bat-shit-was-he question, Ryan thought as the man began ranting in rapid-fire Vietnamese. He then stopped listening altogether as a new thought occurred to him.

Chad, he realized, overwhelmed with dismay; it had been Chad.

Good old Chad had made the last incoming call, and he had made it from a payphone on the Santa Monica Pier.

Chad. Not Jessica, but good old Chad.

EIGHTEEN

"You told me the situation was under control!" Greer made a face at the sound of Jack Tanner's voice in the phone receiver. For Christ's sake, the guy sounded like some whiny punk having a tantrum in the holding cell. "It is," he said.

"Oh, really?" Tanner snapped. "Maybe we should ask Bayback about that!"

Greer clenched his eyes shut for a second. Leave it to Jack fucking Tanner to call him over nothing. When this was over, he was going to twist his motherfucking head off and jam it so far up his old dirt road that it popped out of his neck again. "I heard about the cop. She handled it already."

"Oh, yeah? Did she tell you that before or after he killed her?"

Greer had to replay that twice in his brain before he was sure he'd heard Tanner correctly. "What?!"

"She's dead," Tanner snarled.

Shit! Greer squeezed his eyes shut again, unable to say anything in response.

"The cop was investigating Jessica Martin's disappearance," Tanner went on. "Said something about a kid who tipped him off."

A kid. With no conscious effort on Greer's part, his mind began to put it all together. A kid. Which was to say, the kid at the bank. And before that, the mystery gun that had materialized in Deason's pocket out of nowhere at the airport. The kid must have had something to do with that, too. Jesus Christ, how long had this kid been on their tail?

"I think we should get rid of him," Greer said. "He knows too much."

"Mooney doesn't know shit!" Tanner bellowed. "And from now on, you leave the goddamned thinking to me!" There was a sharp click as he hung up.

Well, that was just fucking peachy, Greer thought as he slipped the telephone into his pocket. His gaze fell on Deason whose startled expression made it clear that he had caught both sides of the conversation. That was just peachy, too. But at least Deason had enough sense not to open his big fat ugly yap about it. Motioning for him to follow, Greer headed upstairs to the attic.

Jessica's heart leaped with a combination of terror and hope. Before she could even start to get her mind around what it would mean if it really were Ryan calling, the guy on the porch stubbed out his cigarette and went inside.

Immediately, she jumped up on the pail again and tapped on one of the tiny windows in the garage door.

"Baby, listen to me. I want you to stand way back." She cupped her hands around her head and squinted into the shadowy garage, looking for something that might afford him some protection. "Go to that big cabinet in the far corner over there. Get behind it—"

"No, don't leave me!" Ricky wailed tearfully. "Don't leave me!"

The terror in his voice hit her harder than any of the physical blows she had taken.

"Honey, I'm not leaving," she said, struggling to keep her voice from breaking, "I'm getting you out of there!"

Her son didn't find this reassuring. "Where are you going?"

"I'm only gonna be gone a second and then we're gonna go home," she told him. "But you have to do this first. Now go. Go!"

For a moment, she wasn't sure she could get him to do it. Then he nodded and ran to the cabinet.

Good boy, she thought fiercely, racing for the Cayenne. They might get out of this yet.

"Go back to the bank and get the video of the kid," Greer told Deason as they went up the steps. "Check every frame until you find one we can use to ID that son of a bitch."

Deason gave a grunt of assent and started to say something about possibly getting hold of surveillance footage from the lobby of the building just as they opened the door and stepped into the attic.

As soon as she had jumped into the Cayenne, Jessica had reached for the ignition only to find they hadn't left the keys in it. Frantically, she searched the visors, the dash, yanked open the glove box and tore everything out of it, pawed through all the small items and papers in the console next to her seat, scattering them all over with shaking, panicky hands. No keys, no keys anywhere! Oh, God, she thought, one of the men must have been carrying them!

For a moment, Greer could only stand next to Deason and gape.

The heavy smell of blood was strong and oppressive in the confines of the attic; it hit him in the face hard enough to make his knees buckle slightly. Then the body on the floor finally registered on him as Mad Dog's and immediately he looked around for Jessica Martin. Her body had to be lying around somewhere, too, because all that blood could not have come out of Mad Dog alone. There was way too much of it, way, way too much even for a big bastard like him. It had to be from more than one person. The two of them, Mad Dog and the Martin bitch, they must have killed each other because there was no way some pampered little bitch from Brentwood could slice up the Dog and leave him lying in his own blood.

But the only other thing he could see was the wreckage of the telephone lying on the floor trailing a cord that ended in a wiry fray. Recently ripped out of the wall. Which was what he should have done after he had used the sledgehammer, Greer realized. What Mad Dog had done, only he had done it too fucking late.

The coin tray seemed to materialize before Jessica's eyes as if by magic, holding the keys in a nonchalant little heap. Ho-hum, here they are, of course. Where else would they be?

With a cry of startled relief, she scooped them up, picked out the right one and slammed it into the ignition.

"Motherfu—"

Deason cut off sharply at the sound of the Porsche Cayenne roaring into life outside. Greer was already pounding down the stairs again.

Seatbelt, don't fail me now, Jessica thought, barely aware of her own nervous laughter as she drove the Cayenne straight at the garage door. No ketchup, hold the airbags. Just before impact, her laughter cut off sharply as a new thought flitted through her mind: Ricky, baby, please stay behind the cabinet.

She then heard the smash of wood and glass and the scrape of metal and she slammed hard against the back of the seat, crying out as she brought one arm up protectively.

But nothing came smashing through the windshield at her; the glass didn't even crack. The garage door on the other hand was only good for toothpicks now. She released her seatbelt and tried to open her door, only to find herself jammed in by debris. At least the driver's side window still worked; she lowered it and stuck her head out as far as she could.

"Come on, baby!" she yelled.

Ricky ran to her—directly to her, not to the passenger side of the Cayenne, but that was all right. She simply reached down and hauled him in through the window, practically throwing him into the seat next to her. In spite of the rougher-than-usual handling, the boy never made a sound, immediately reaching for his seatbelt without her having to tell him to.

Habit made her check the sideview mirror just as she threw the Cayenne into reverse and she saw that the two big ugly guys were practically right on top of the rear bumper.

Beep, beep, boys, she thought spitefully. She could feel herself grinning with vicious triumph as she stamped on the accelerator.

She had a quick glimpse of them diving out of the way as the Cayenne shot backwards out of the garage. Steve McQueen and *Bullit* got nothing on me, Jessica thought, her grin widening as the Cayenne came to a shuddering, skidding stop. She hauled as hard as she could on the steering wheel, and slammed the shift into drive.

"We did it! We did it!" Ricky was shrieking as they hurtled down the driveway toward freedom.

We sure did, baby, Jessica thought. She opened her mouth to say so, to celebrate being able to get herself and her son to safety, and to roar like a mother grizzly bear.

But he then stepped into the driveway in front of her from behind that goddamned van, and she could see all too clearly that the man he was dragging along with him was Craig. Her husband looked even worse than before and he could barely stand but the guy only needed one arm to keep him upright. He didn't even look at Craig. Instead, he looked directly at her while with his free hand; he held a gun to her husband's head.

Jessica felt as if her heart had slammed to a stop at the same moment she slammed on the brakes. Barely five feet in front of the SUV, Craig look directly into her eyes and mouthed, Go, Jess.

But she couldn't move, not even to shake her head no at him. There was no way she would ever be able to do such a thing, not even to save Ricky and herself.

All at once, Craig came to life, throwing himself bodily into the man with the gun and knocking him aside. "Go!" he screamed at her. "Go, go, go!"

Even her tears were frozen in place, she thought, still sitting motionless behind the wheel of the Cayenne. How could he imagine that she would ever be able to leave him there to die? She was no more capable of driving off and abandoning him than she was of sprouting gossamer wings and flying away.

Then the man with the gun was all over him, beating him down again, pistol-whipping him relentlessly into a bloody heap on the ground. Now the tears came and she found she could move again. Instinctively, she tore off her seatbelt and tried to wrap her body protectively around her son but the man was already flinging her door open. His fingers dug hard into her hair and she thought she could feel her scalp actually stretch as he hauled her out of the Cayenne.

"Who did you tell?" he bellowed as he shoved her to the ground.

"Nobody!" she screamed.

Jessica automatically grabbed for the hand in her hair and he gave her a vicious shake as he forced her down on her knees.

"Lying bitch!" he roared into her face. "Who was that kid at the bank?"

He shook her again even more roughly and she screamed in pain and terror, dimly aware that Ricky was screaming as well, begging the man not to hurt his mommy.

This only enraged him even more and he continued to shake her by her hair as if she was a rag doll. When he stopped, she felt the gun against her head, the metal pressing so hard that she thought he intended to stab her with the gun, to drive the barrel all the way through her skull with sheer brute force.

She squeezed her eyes shut, thinking "I'm sorry, Ricky, I'm so, so sorry for this," and waited for the last thing she would ever hear.

Instead, the phone began to ring again.

Everything in the world stopped.

All movement ceased and all sound cut off. Except for the ringing of that stupid fucking cordless phone which he had absentmindedly stuck in his pocket before finding Mad Dog's body on the attic floor.

That stupid fucking lying murderous bitch. She must have thought she was one clever little suburban cooze, not only to be able to make contact with somebody on the outside and get herself some help, but killing Mad Dog too. She had probably lured the dumb son of a bitch up to the attic for the express purpose of seeing if she might be able to work a little trade with him, offering some of her special suburban cooze action if he would let her and the brat go. Greer could just see her turning it on for him.

And old Mad Dog had gone for it—the cooze, that was, not the trade. There was no way he would have let her and the brat get away just because the bitch waxed his board a little. The Dog would have been all ready to bury her pitiful bones after he jumped them.

But he had probably poured most of a bottle down his throat before he went up there and the poor bastard had let his guard down along with his zipper. There wasn't any other way the bitch could have managed to get on his blind side and that was the end of that story.

And now, just as he was about to show her exactly what a bitchy little suburban cooze would get when she tried to fuck Ethan Greer over, just as he was about to blow her treacherous bitch brains all over the yard-—

The motherfucking goddamned son of a bitch bastard phone rang.

Interruptions; always these motherfucking interruptions. Except when some fucking bitch decided to kill one of his crew and take off with her fucking brat kid, of course. The goddamned phone never rang then.

No, the son of a bitching thing had to ring now, and Jesus Jumped-Up Christ, the fucker was still ringing, getting louder each time. And it was probably just dickhead fucking Tanner calling back to piss and moan about something else.

Greer was fuming audibly as he pulled the handset out of his pocket. What the fucking hell did that ass wipe think they were running here anyway, a fucking frat party?

"Bad timing, Tanner," he snapped.

"Feel like a trade?" someone asked him. Someone who was not Dick Tanner.

The voice Greer heard belonged to someone else entirely, someone who sounded like he might be very young, very full of himself and very much a major pain in the ass.

For a moment, Greer couldn't even move, let alone speak. Then he stuck the gun in his waistband and snapped his fingers at Deason, making him pay attention.

"How did you get this number?" he asked the kid in a low, dangerous voice.

The kid actually had the huevos to give a nasty little laugh. "Gotta love this modern technology, dontcha?" he said. "My phone knows the numbers of the last fifty incoming calls."

He had to cut this little fucker's bullshit off now, Greer thought, before he got the mistaken idea that he was a goddamned hero. "What do you want?"

"Oh, just the woman and her family," said the kid offhandedly.

"Okay, now let me tell you what I want," Greer said, glaring at the Martin woman. Her gaze was riveted on the phone as if it were the Holy Grail and she thought Jesus Christ himself was going to pop out of the receiver at any minute. "I want you to tell me where you are, right now, or some bad, bad things are gonna happen to this little family."

The prick actually chuckled again. "Sor-ree, pal," he sang. "It doesn't work that way."

"Really?" Greer put the handset close to his mouth that the jerk couldn't miss a thing he said. Then he turned to Deason and jerked his head toward the Martin brat. "Go cut the kid's throat."

To his complete astonishment, the goddamned smartass on the other end of the phone didn't even hesitate. "Fine. Your loss. Nice talking to you," he said.

And hung up.

Ryan sat in the Carrera rocking back and forth with both hands over his eyes, almost unable to believe he had actually had the stones to do what he had just done. Only... what in God's name had he just done? What had he done?

He lowered his hands and looked over at the cellphone lying on the passenger seat.

"Ring," he begged, his voice bleak. "C'mon, you son of a bitch, ring, damn it, ring! RING!"

NINETEEN

Immediately, as if in direct response to his plea, the cellphone trilled.

Ryan all but jumped out of his skin at the sound. Then he let it ring a second time, mostly because he had no choice—it took him a couple of seconds to get his motor functions back under control. Although he told himself that it was also to make the mean bastard sweat a little.

He cleared his throat before pressing the answer button. "Get the point?" he said carelessly.

"You're playing with fire, kid," the mean bastard growled at him.

No shit, Sherlock? "And you're lucky I'm still talking to you," Ryan said, forcing an even more blasé tone into his voice. "From here on, you do as I say—exactly as I say—or I slap this bitch on Nightline and we all call it a day."

Silence.

Ryan hardly dared to breathe while he listened. He was, trying to hear something, anything that might tell him what was happening on the other end, whether Jessica and her family were still alive. The background noise sounded weird, like they had the phone outside or something.

He heard the mean bastard take a fed-up breath. "Okay, so how do you want to do this?"

Ryan hoped he didn't sound like someone grinning so broadly that his face hurt. "The Santa Monica Pier," he replied.

"No," said the mean bastard immediately. "Too busy."

"That's kind of the point, genius," Ryan snapped at him.

Another fed-up breath. "How will I recognize you?"

"You let me worry about that," Ryan told him airily and punched the air with a triumphant fist. "Just give me a number I can reach you at."

Things happened very quickly after that, so quickly that Jessica wasn't sure that she had the energy to keep up.

For a certain amount of time, the only thing she really knew was that she was still alive and Ricky had not been forced to watch a crooked cop blow his mother's brains out all over a gravel driveway. Because someone had stopped it from happening by calling on the telephone and it was someone he didn't like at all. It was someone he hated so much that Ricky had almost gotten his throat cut.

Except... had it really been a matter of almost? For some reason, she couldn't help thinking that it hadn't been such a near thing after all, that whoever had been on the phone had successfully called his bluff.

Her mind seemed to be whirling in one direction while the world was spinning in the other and she was having trouble keeping her feet. She was off balance anyway because they had cuffed her hands behind her back, like a criminal, and it was hard for her to walk at all, let alone walk as fast as they wanted her to.

There was a flurry of activity and then they were shoving her into that van of theirs, the one they had brought her here in. When she had arrived in this shabby, broken-down place, she had been unconscious and alone. They were now taking her away wide-awake, in the company of her husband and son. They had cuffed Craig to a bar on the inside of the back door and shoved Ricky in right next to her.

Jessica was relieved to have her son close to her; she just wished that her hands weren't cuffed so she could put her arms around him. The poor kid couldn't even hang onto her—his hands were cuffed behind his back, too—but at least all three of them were together. They were all together and they were all still alive because somebody had called at exactly the right moment on the telephone. Somebody who could only have been Ryan.

Please, let it have been Ryan, she prayed. Please, please, please let it have been Ryan.

Of course it had been Ryan, she told herself fiercely. It had to have been Ryan. It couldn't have been anyone but Ryan.

The van hurtled down the twisting mountain road, sending her and Ricky sliding back and forth on the seat while her mind cycled from certainty to desperate prayer and back again, over and over and over.

As soon as he heard Greer's voice on his cellphone, Tanner moved away from where the goddamned paramedic was working on goddamned Bob Mooney, who was still holding that goddamned water glass with the goddamned goldfish in it and staring at it like he was goddamned Hamlet contemplating the goddamned skull of What's-his-face.

Goddamned Mooney; the guy was such a goddamned, fucking schlub.

"Where's your cop friend?" Greer wanted to know.

"About to go to the hospital," Tanner told him.

"No, we need him," said Greer. "We're making a trade with the kid at the Santa Monica Pier and your guy's the only one who can ID him for sure. Get your ass down here and bring him with you."

"On it." Tanner snapped his phone shut, frowning, and then ambled back over to Mooney.

"So how's he looking?" he asked the paramedic offhandedly.

"He needs to go to the hospital," he said in a firm, non-negotiable tone.

Tanner nodded, grimacing as he made a small, disappointed noise.

"Why? "What's up?" Mooney asked, turning his head to look up at him. The paramedic pushed it back to its previous position.

"Hm? Oh, nothing." Tanner moved so Mooney had a good view of him shrugging hugely. "We just caught a break with the kid who robbed the cellphone store, is all."

Mooney pounced on the bait and swallowed it whole without batting an eye. "That's the same kid who came into the station!" he said eagerly.

"They know he's at the pier," Tanner went on sadly, "but they're having a helluva time ID'ing him. No one knows what he looks like."

"I do," Mooney said, even more eagerly. "I saw him this morning." He started to get up but the paramedic pushed him back down with one hand.

"Absolutely not," he said, more firmly and non-negotiable than ever. "You need to get looked at."

"I could point him out to you," Mooney said to Tanner, ignoring him.

Damn, this was almost too easy, Tanner thought and motioned at Mooney's wounded neck. "But your—"

Mooney surprised him by managing to get to his feet in spite of the paramedic's best efforts to force him to sit down again.

"I really don't think this is a good idea—" he scolded him.

Abruptly, Mooney shoved the glass with the goldfish into his hands. "Here, take care of this guy," he said and pulled his shirt back on. "I can wait twenty minutes."

The paramedic looked from the goldfish to Mooney in frank disbelief; then he sighed and stepped back.

"Hey, now, you sure you feel up to this, buddy?" Tanner asked as they headed for the door together.

Mooney hesitated and for a moment, Tanner thought he was going to change his mind or maybe go weak in the knees and keel over in a faint like the big pansy he was. Then he straightened up, squared his shoulders, and nodded.

"Let's solve this goddamned thing," he said.

Tanner gave a convincing impression of an approving nod. Jesus, what a goddamned, fucking schlub.

The carousel on the Santa Monica pier is not actually part of the Pacific Park amusement park, nor is it even located nearby. It's one of the first things that tourists encounter as they step off the path that passes the UCLA Ocean Discovery Center and step onto the pier itself.

Every year, millions of people come from around the world to do just that. During the high season, there is an almost constant bottleneck near the entrance to the pier because most of them can't help stopping to stare, transfixed, at the sight of it.

The original carousel was built in 1916 by an imaginative man named Charles ID Looff (the Looff Hippodrome housing it is a genuine, no-kidding National Historic Landmark). The City of Santa Monica took it over in 1977 and devoted most of the early 1980s to its careful restoration. A favorite spot for birthday parties, weddings, and fashion shoots, it is famous among movie fans around the world for its appearance in *The Sting*, where in the opinion of many, the three-second shot of the carousel and its graceful passengers upstaged both Paul Newman and Robert Redford.

The most Ryan knew about it was that it was a pretty cool-looking merry-go-round which had been in a lot of movies. Right now, he was barely aware of its existence. He had parked the twice-stolen Carrera in the nearby lot facing away from the carousel so he could sit behind the wheel and keep an eye out for a certain van.

The only activity at the moment, however, was a seven-year-old rapper with a cheap sound box who was entertaining a small audience with some pint-sized phat beats. As he watched the boy, it occurred to Ryan that he probably had no more idea of what he was about to do than a second-grade gangsta had of ASCAP's position on sampling. Or quite possibly less.

That kind of thinking wouldn't do him any good at all, he told himself, and it sure wasn't going to help Jessica and her to family stay alive. He started to get out of the car and then paused, spotting what looked like a jacket folded up and stashed behind the passenger seat. Curious, he pulled it out to have a closer look.

It was a jacket, all right, a big waterproof thing with a hood, and exactly what he needed under the circumstances. Very handy for a situation that called for a little something in the way of camouflage.

Smiling grimly to himself, Ryan slipped the jacket on and headed quickly toward the end of the pier, melting into the crowd and the general mayhem of the Heal The Bay charity concert.

"I'm in position," said Deason's voice in the walkie-talkie.

"Copy," Greer replied. "Dimitri?"

"I'm here," came the reply.

Greer gave him a grunt of acknowledgement. With Deason in the van in the pier parking lot and Dimitri posing as a tourist and keeping watch from a coin-op telescope, he was free to roam the pier looking for the smart-ass prick that had spent the day fucking their shit up so royally.

But Jesus Christ, did he hate the fucking Santa Monica Pier and every motherfucking loser asshole roaming around and getting in his way. He couldn't decide which of the asshole losers he hated more—the clueless fucking tourists stumbling around with their goddamned video cameras or the resident garbage walking around upright and passing itself off as local color. Every single one of them was a fucking waste of space and he'd spent too many goddamned years busting his ass as a fucking public servant.

"Servant?" Shit, that was a good one. More like a fucking public slave. And for what? To protect the losers. And what was he protecting them from? Usually themselves, as it turned out, something they did not fucking like one fucking bit. They would all just as soon kiss the ass of some gang-banger with a Glock and spit on the cops who were trying to make sure they didn't get their clueless fucking heads blown up in a drive-by while they were scoring.

So fuck that, and fuck it big-time. If the clueless fucks of LA wanted to make drug dealers rich, then so be it—this was a democracy, so give the people what they wanted, let them have it their way. If drug dealers were the fucking top of the fucking heap, Ethan Greer was more than happy to help himself to some of that.

Or, what the fuck. All of it.

The only thing he really would have liked to know, he thought as he passed a dumb-ass tourist pointing a very expensive video camera at his equally dumb-ass, giggling family, was why none of those self-appointed good citizens and guardians of the public morals ever managed to turn up, video camera in hand, when the gang-bangers were kicking somebody's head in.

Greer thought it was a reasonable question. Just where the hell were any of them when a car full of horny bangers decided to pull a few girls off the street for a party whether the girls wanted to go or not? Or when some crack-head put a beat-down on an old lady for her pension, or when some toddler on a tricycle got caught in the line of fire and took a round in the throat?

That fucking jerk-off kid dared to dictate terms to him—who the hell was he anyway? Just an asshole that wanted to send a tape of him doing a little much-needed clean up, taking care of human litter, to fucking Nightline in a heartbeat.

But if it had been a tape of gangbangers doing the exact same thing, no one would ever have even known he was alive. Hell, he wouldn't have known about it to begin with, because Craig Martin would already have taped reruns of the *The X-Files* over it.

So fuck him, Greer thought, gritting his teeth. Fuck him, fuck the Martins, fuck the entire city of LA starting with these fucking idiots all around him on the pier. Fuck 'em all, the long and the short and the tall. Fuck the tree-huggers and granola queens and their Heal the Bay charity concert, and fuck the idiots who showed up for it.

And especially fuck the moron wearing a fucking whale costume who was body-surfing the audience. Greer winced at the sight and shook his head. Yeah—now there was a prime example of the goddamned public he was supposed to bust his ass for. Probably a twin to the fucking kid who had run off with that goddamned video camera.

Greer heard his phone ring then and put it up to his ear immediately. He was barely able to make out the kid's voice over the music and noise around him.

"You here?" he said, holding his walkie-talkie in his other hand.

"Yeah," said the kid.

Greer pressed the phone against himself to muffle it. "Showtime," he said into the walkie-talkie.

"He's on." He turned back to the phone. "So now what?"

"First you show me that the Martins are okay," came the answer in that smartass belligerent tone.

"There's a black van in the parking lot," Greer told him, moving in that general direction. "In the northwest corner, next to the SPY Sunglass truck."

"Hang on—"

Greer listened hard, trying to hear something in the background noise on the other end that might give him some clue where the kid might be.

"Okay," said the kid after a moment. "I can see it."

Greer muffled the phone and put the walkie-talkie close to his mouth. "He's within visual of the van." To the cellphone: "Now look at the passenger side window." Careful to muffle the phone again, he spoke to Deason: "Show him the woman and her kid. Lower the passenger side window only."

Just as Greer had told him to, Deason kept the walkie-talkie link open so he would be able to hear the sound of the van window going down. This was followed by the woman and her brat crying out as Deason grabbed hold of them, shoved them into view, and then yanked them back before either of them had the bright idea of calling out for help. Not until Greer heard the window go up again did he turn back to the phone.

"Did you see that?" he asked.

Ryan wished he had chosen to stand in a spot where there was something nearby for him to lean on. He was extremely relieved to see that Jessica and her son were still alive but he could tell even just from a split-second glimpse that this rough ride they were all on was getting even rougher, not only from the way the guy in the van handled them but also from the bruises on Jessica's face. It looked like her kid had a few himself now, too.

"Yeah," he told the mean bastard, adjusting the hood so he was sure that it completely covered the ear-bud mike he was using. It was easy to see why so many people liked this hands-free mobile thing but it also felt kind of funny to be talking on a phone that was actually in his pocket.

"He's around the passenger side," Greer said to Dimitri on the walkie-talkie as he pushed his way through the milling crowds. "Have you found him yet?"

"No," Dimitri snapped, "I don't know what the hell he looks like!"

Jesus Christ, just how incredibly fucking stupid was Dimitri? Greer fumed and began shoving people out of his way with increasing force. "He's the one on the cellphone, you idiot!"

"Is that so, boss man? Well, guess what, Albert Einstein—everyone's on a goddamned cellphone!" Dimitri shouted.

Greer felt himself sag as he realized that Deason was telling him the truth. Now that he bothered to look, at least half the people right there all around him were on cellphones. Sweet mothering Jesus.

Why the hell couldn't he get a fucking break today?

An enormous screaming roar went up from the crowd behind him then, followed by a deafening blast of music as Incubus kicked off the Heal The Bay concert in high gear.

Mooney felt as if the music had hit him with all the force of a physical blow from a heavy object. He stumbled, wincing in pain and put his hand to his neck, although at the moment that wasn't quite as painful as it had been—the paramedic had numbed him up pretty good and it still hadn't worn off.

But man, he was really starting to regret agreeing to go along to the pier with Tanner after all. He had been fine in the car on the way over but after struggling through the crowds of people and trying to keep up with Tanner, who was practically race-walking, he was starting to feel drained and slightly dizzy and, on the whole, impaired in a very substantial way.

It was probably shock. Mooney tried to remember what he knew about shock but his brain wouldn't cooperate—it was too busy operating his body so he wouldn't lose Tanner in the masses of people milling around on the pier.

What the hell was this sudden big concern Tanner had about the kid, anyway, Mooney wondered crossly. This morning, the guy had refused to be bothered and tonight he was acting like the fate of the nation was at stake.

Detectives, thought Mooney. Bunch of loons, every single one of them.

"Your turn," said the mean bastard. "Now you show me something."

From where he was standing by the payphones, Ryan had a good view of the van in the parking lot without having to make himself too conspicuous.

"No," he replied evenly, "now you let them go."

"I don't think so," the mean bastard told him. "Not until after you give me the camera."

"Yeah, well, I've been thinking about that," Ryan said, keeping his gaze locked on the van. "And I decided that it does me no good to hand over the videotape only to have you guys turn around and take us all out."

The heavy made a put upon noise. "I swore I wouldn't do that."

"Like you swore to protect and serve?" Ryan asked. No answer to that; judging from the silence, he figured he must have hit a sore spot. "Look, it's your choice, man," he went on after a bit. "The Martins or the videotape. Either way, I'm not hanging around any longer."

"Wait," said the mean bastard quickly. "I'm thinking."

He was thinking about it. That was pretty freakin' rich, Ryan thought. He took a quick look around while he waited for the guy's next pronouncement, just in case the mean bastard or anyone else from the mean bastard crew happened to be lurking in his vicinity. But there was no sign of anyone who looked familiar.

Except—Ryan did a double take. While Incubus were kicking it hard, Chloe's friends from Heal the Bay were shaking their tanned, Pilates-trained, aerobicized booties and waving to the appreciative crowd.

But most surprising of all was the figure actually edging out one of the Incubus guys for a spot in the middle of the babe line, a guy bouncing up and down to the funk-metal beat in a rubber whale suit. Ryan knew immediately it couldn't have been anyone else in the world except good old Chad.

As he watched, good old Chad threw himself off the stage and into the mosh pit, which sent the audience into screaming ecstasy. Moby Chad, the ocean activist.

"Okay, I've thought about it," said the mean bastard suddenly. "No."

Panic surged in Ryan's chest. "What?!"

Nasty little chuckle. "I said, no."

"Do you really want to have a standoff?" Ryan demanded, doing his best to sound angry even though he was practically shitting pears.

"No," said the mean bastard with another nasty little chuckle. "Which is why I want you to think about something. You've only got one tape. I've got three hostages, and I don't mind evening the numbers a little bit."

"Six feet tall," Mooney was saying breathlessly as he and Tanner worked their way through the edge of the concert crowd. "Light brown hair, early twenties..." he paused, wishing that Tanner would show him some consideration and slow down, even a little. "Damn, I wish I could remember what he was wearing."

Finally, he grabbed Tanner's sleeve and signaled that he had to stop for a minute and catch his breath. Impatience flashed across the detective's face; then he covered it with a neutral expression and obliged him, looking around while he waited for Mooney to get his breath back.

Holding his neck, Mooney looked around, too, actively trying to pick out any young male who seemed to be deliberately keeping to himself. Shouldn't be many of those on the pier tonight, he thought; a couple of likely candidates over by the payphones, though.

"If you hurt them, I'll just leave," Ryan said hotly, "and I'll drop this tape off at the news on my way home."

"You know, I don't believe you," said the mean bastard, almost airily. "I think it's time to test that resolve."

"I'm warning you—" Ryan began, when suddenly he felt a hand grab hold of the back of his hood and rip it down off his head.

TWENTY

"I can't believe you!" Chloe shouted hotly. "Where have you been?"

"Chloe—" he tried but she kept talking over him.

"Do you know how long I waited for those T-shirts? Didn't I tell you it was important?"

"Look, it's not what you think," he said, taking hold of her arms and trying to lead her off to some place where they wouldn't attract quite so much attention. "I can explain, but not right now—"

"No, don't touch me!" She slapped his hands away, outraged, and raised her voice even louder. "You know, I called your cell, like, ten times! Why'd you do that to me, Ryan? Just to hurt me?"

"No, I—" he glared at a small group of people who were standing a few feet away and watching with undisguised interest.

"Was that your way of getting back at me for breaking up with you?" she demanded, which caused two or three of the onlookers to lean forward in obvious suspense.

"No, Chloe, listen to me!" Ryan grabbed her arms again and turned her away from the audience as he looked directly into her angry face, trying to make her understand that he was in the middle of something serious. "Listen, you've got to get out of here."

As Chloe started to answer, the air was filled with multiple blasts from the concert pyrotechnics which didn't quite drown out the delirious screams of approval from the audience.

The exploding pyrotechnics nearly knocked Mooney flat on his ass. What was it with these concerts and their goddamned fireworks, he thought dizzily? If the band didn't deafen you with the music, they hired some pyromaniacs to make sure they finished the job.

He moved further away from the edge of the cheering, screaming crowd and suddenly spotted the only two people who weren't, at that moment, looking at the stage and screaming their lungs out.

The kid hadn't been wearing that jacket earlier, but Mooney knew for certain it was him. He'd had the same freaked-out expression earlier as he did now while that girl was yelling at him. He yanked Tanner's arm hard and pointed.

"There!" he said. "That's him!"

"Chloe, listen to me!" Ryan begged. "It isn't safe here, people are after me!"

He tried to shoo her away but she wasn't about to let him get rid of her so easily. "What's going on with you?" she asked, her eyes narrowing suspiciously. "Are you drunk?"

Before he could even attempt to answer that one, he felt heavy hands close around his shoulders and a man's voice on his left said, "I've been looking for you, kid."

There was a thunder of tribal-sounding drums from the stage that Ryan thought could have been his heart and his brain blowing up in tandem. He tried to pull away and run but the guy was like some kind of octopus, countering every move Ryan made almost before he could think of it.

"Let go of me!" he yelled, realizing they'd found him. The motherfuckers had found him and that meant he was screwed, the show was over, lights out, thank you, Los Angeles and good night. "Sonofabitch, let me go!"

"Hey, what's going on here?" Chloe wanted to know, her voice high and frightened now.

"Would you relax—" grunted the guy who was all over him, pushing something into his face. A badge.

"Ryan!" Chloe's shock seemed to come off her in waves. "What did you do?"

She would have to ask him that right now, Ryan thought, struggling as hard as he could. But to no avail.

Dimitri kept scanning the crowd in spite of the fact that he was beginning to think the whole operation was pretty hopeless. On the other hand, it was better than just hanging around waiting for some ax to fall one way or another.

Abruptly, there was a crackle from his walkie-talkie and he heard Tanner's voice. "Found him. By the backstage entrance. Get down here. Now."

Dimitri was on the move before Tanner had finished saying the last word.

Thank God Mooney wasn't all by himself, Tanner thought, watching him grapple with the kid like they were a couple of rejects from the junior high school wrestling team.

"Jesus, kid, calm down!" Mooney said for what had to be the fiftieth time. The kid still wasn't paying attention. Abruptly, he managed to twist free and gave Mooney a hard shove that sent him hard into the pier railing. The way Mooney howled with pain and grabbed his neck, Tanner couldn't decide whether he felt feel sorry for the poor schlub or just embarrassed that he had to be there.

As the kid turned around to haul ass, Tanner stepped into him and drew his gun in one smooth motion. The kid stopped dead on the spot and Tanner could tell by the way his eyes were practically bugging out of his head that he knew exactly what was digging hard into his ribs without having to be told, or warned.

"Keep your friggin' mouth shut," Tanner said, speaking softly, almost gently, "or everybody dies. Everybody."

He was pleased to note that the kid didn't even breathe.

"We're here to help you," Mooney was saying as he got to his feet and brushed himself off, completely oblivious to the true nature of the situation. "That's what I was trying to tell you."

Tanner thought that was actually pretty funny, Mooney telling the kid they were here to help. Yeah, kid, we're from the city government and we're here to help you. The kid didn't crack a smile or give any sign that he had actually heard a thing the poor schlub had said. Tanner gave him a nearly imperceptible nod to let him know that he was doing exactly the right thing to avoid acquiring an unpleasant hole in the middle of his body. He raised his walkie-talkie and whispered into it quickly without looking away from the kid's frightened face.

"I've got the kid," said a voice on the walkie-talkie in the van.

Jessica raised her head sharply; the one called Deason didn't notice her moving. But then he probably figured there wasn't anything to be worried about any more now that they had grabbed Ryan.

Now it really was over, for all of them. They were all as good as dead. For all she knew, Ryan was already dead. But if this really was the end of the line, she had no intention of making it easy for them.

Careful to move so that she didn't make a sound, Jessica shifted position and dropped her shoulders as low as she could. She bent forward so that she could begin the process of working her cuffed wrists little by little down over her behind to her thighs.

Back in college, she'd done this trick a thousand times for the amusement of her friends. Usually, this would happen some hours into some informal evening activity involving a few drinks, quite a few, actually, which had served to enhance her youthful agility. But, she thought the old fight-or-flight response would no doubt be a more than adequate replacement for an absurd number of tequila shooters.

Ricky then caught her eye. The look on his terrified face said it all, louder than a scream. Don't, Mom! Don't!

She shook her head slightly and made a show of looking away, hoping he would get the idea. If he didn't stop staring at her like that, the thug sitting in the front seat was going to notice everything had gotten a little quiet and tense back here and decide that maybe he had better investigate. If he saw her like this, he would know right away what she was up to and that would be the end of it, and them. And if she didn't do it, that would be the end of them anyway.

I'm sorry, baby, she thought, for what felt like the millionth time in the last few hours. I'm sorry, baby, but we're all out of options and all out of time.

"Mooney, buddy." Tanner wrapped an arm around his shoulders roughly and squeezed until he felt the schlub start to resist. "You're not looking so good."

He held on tightly until he could feel Mooney actually had to fight for breath. Then he finally let the schlub pull himself loose. It took a major effort to keep from laughing out loud as Mooney backed away holding his neck. The schlub was practically staggering now.

"I'm okay," he said, giving Tanner a funny look.

Tanner thought he sounded kind of sulky. "Nah, I'm gonna have someone take you over to the hospital and get looked at," he said, pretending to look around before beckoning to Deason. "Moon, this is Detective Dimitri from CID. Dimitri, Mooney needs to get to the hospital right away. Can you take him?"

"Oh, yeah. Sure thing." Dimitri's mouth twitched slightly. Tanner could tell that he was having a hard time believing this was the same person who could not only survive a shootout with Bayback but kill her as well. He'd have to fill Dimitri in on Bob Mooney, deadeye schlub.

Just as Dimitri was reaching for him, Mooney turned back to the kid and clapped a reassuring hand on his shoulder. He had completely failed to notice that the kid was still petrified.

"Everything's gonna be okay now, kid," Mooney told him, and then nodded to Dimitri, who gave Tanner another incredulous look as he led the schlub away.

Yeah, everything sure is going to okay now, kid, Tanner said silently. He took an iron grip on the kid's upper arm and marched him off in the opposite direction.

"Wait a minute!" shouted a female voice so filled with outrage that Tanner couldn't help stopping to look back in some alarm.

She was very pretty, classic California blonde, all good hair and perfect tan skin and at the moment staring hard at the kid, of all people. Jesus, Tanner thought, her with him? There was no fucking justice.

"Who is she?" he asked the kid, squeezing his arm tighter.

"How the hell should I know?" the kid yelled, sounding furious all of a sudden. "I've never seen her before in my life!"

"What?!" she said, all but squeaking, obviously infuriated and surprised.

Tanner shrugged, deciding that whoever she was didn't matter and he could forget about her for the time being. He kept going, shoving the kid along half a step in front of him.

"Hey!" the girl called after them. "What just happened here?"

Nothing just happened here, Chloe, Ryan thought as the sharp-dressed detective from the videotape moved him forcibly through the crowd. Just my life coming to an end, but other than that, nothing really. Nothing at all.

Certainly nobody else thought anything was happening. Nobody would be able to see that the guy marching him along had a gun in his ribs.

Nobody would think there were anything especially strange about two guys even as mismatched as they were sticking close to each other as they walked along the pier. Hell, nobody would have looked twice if the detective had been wearing a diaper and he'd been decked out in a prom dress.

Or a whale costume, he added silently, catching sight of Chad. Good old Moby Chad was still surfing the concert crowd and obviously having the time of his young life. Which, Ryan thought miserably, would be a hell of a longer than his own.

Where did I go wrong?

"Hey, Ry!"

He turned his head sharply. Against all odds, good old Chad had actually seen him. Even more miraculously, the bastard marching him down the pier apparently hadn't heard Chad calling to him.

"Hey, Ryan!" Chad was struggling to get down from the eager hands passing him along overhead but wasn't having any luck. The costume was too clumsy. No help there—that whale was beached, Ryan thought glumly.

The detective gave him a hard prod with the gun and picked up the pace, practically trotting him past the amusement park tents and into the empty area behind them close to the edge of the pier.

As they drew closer to the rail, a man suddenly stepped out from behind a pile of packing crates and watched them approach with his arms folded. Ryan didn't have to wonder who he was.

* * *

Greer took a great deal of satisfaction in seeing how pale the kid's face was with fright. About time the little prick got smart enough to be scared, he thought, strolling over to meet him and Tanner before they got all the way to the railing. About time for a number of things, he thought and treated the kid to a head butt by way of saying hello.

The kid went down on his knees like the sack of shit he was, which gave Greer even more satisfaction.

"God, that felt good," he said, looking down at him. "I've been wanting to do that all day."

Before the kid could do more than groan, Greer bent down and ripped out his ear bud. Then he frisked him down quickly, finding the video camera right away. About time too. He stood up and decided to discourage the kid from doing likewise with a hard kick to the chest.

The sound of the little shit head sucking air while he lay on his side was real music, Greer thought, not the crap they were playing right now to save the frigging bay. He opened the LCD screen on the camera and found the play button.

Before he did anything else, Greer decided, he was going to watch this motherfucker all the way through, every goddamned second. This fucking piece of expensive electronic shit had fucked everything up bad enough to kill somebody—and not some worthless scumbag drug dealer but one of their own. Bayback was lying on a slab because some asshole had to be a good citizen and some other asshole, the asshole lying on the pier in front of him, had to be a fucking hero. But this was where it all came to a fucking end, right fucking here and now.

Holding the camera in both hands, Greer raised it high over his head and, with every ounce of strength he had, slammed it down on the pier. The smash of it shattering into a million pieces was also some pretty goddamned good music, he thought, kicking the fragments around until he found the videotape cassette sitting cracked and broken in the wreckage with a loose loop of the tape exposed.

It was a genuine pleasure to grind it under his shoe, grind it and grind it until there wasn't a piece of it left that was half the size of a postage stamp. Grind the tape into shreds and grind the shreds into nothing, and then kick all the tiny little nothings and shreds and pieces into the gaps between the boards on the pier, and watch them vanish into the salt water below.

"That it?" Tanner asked him calmly.

"Yeah." Greer nodded. "That's it."

Tanner smiled and raised his walkie-talkie to his mouth.

Mooney would never have thought someone like Dimitri would have any interest in skin care, and yet he'd actually asked him about moisturizers for men. Hell, he wouldn't have thought Dimitri would have even known a moisturizer from an exfoliant. He hadn't known himself until Marilyn had educated him.

Nothing wrong with that, though. And he seemed like a pretty okay guy. Maybe he should ask Marilyn to put together a sample basket for him, as a thank you for taking him to the hospital. Except now that he thought about it, he felt kind of bad about just walking off the case and leaving the kid to tell his story all over again to people he didn't even know.

"Hey, Dimitri," he said as he followed him through an alley next to the carousel building, "you know, really, I feel okay now, I really do. I'd like to go back there and make sure everything gets wrapped up—"

"No, no, no," Dimitri said, talking over him. "We've got to get you to a doctor right—"

The end of the sentence was drowned out by a loud squawk from the walkie-talkie, followed by Tanner's voice.

"All right, we got what we need. Get rid of the Martins."

There was a long, frozen moment where Mooney could only stare at Dimitri, who was staring back at him.

Then Dimitri went for his gun.

TWENTY-ONE

"Get rid of the Martins."

Jessica had known it was coming. She had been waiting for it and she knew the moose in the front seat of the van had been waiting for it, too. The moment the voice came out of the walkie-talkie, he went for his silenced gun, and Jessica went for him.

She was no longer quite as limber these days as she had been back in the last year of her teens and the beginning of her twenties. But she had done her best to stay in shape and maintain her natural athleticism as well as her agility. This, combined with the will to do what she had to do to keep her family alive made it possible for her to reprise her best party piece—sliding her bound hands from behind her back to up front by passing her lower body through the hoop of her arms.

Not that it had been an easy thing to accomplish in the cramped space of the van. It hadn't been easy at all, nowhere near it, and certainly not painless, either. At one point, she thought she would end up not only dislocating both her shoulders but literally ripping her arms right off her body. But against the strong, complaining ache she could feel lingering in her joints was the cheerful honey-drip of Miz Peach's voice echoing in her memory: Oooh, gal, you're gonna feel that tomorrow for sure but don't worry, you'll get over it.

Good old Miz Peach—right again as always, even though she couldn't be there to appreciate it in person. Having a tomorrow to ache in appealed to her far more than the best painkiller she could have laid her hands on; getting things to shake out that way, however, would be down to her determination. She was just going to have to be ready to jump on the moment when it came and if it hurt, she would just have to suck it up. Just like back in her old gymnastic competition days.

And here it was.

Get rid of the Martins.

As long as she was still breathing, Jessica thought fiercely, that was going to be a hell of a lot easier said than done.

Before the big bastard even had a chance to lean forward in the seat, she threw her aching arms around his neck from behind and hauled back with all her weight and every bit of strength she could muster.

Her immediate advantage, of course, was the element of surprise. While the son of a bitch was gasping and choking and fighting for air, his brutal little brain would be going in circles, chasing its own tail, thinking that what was happening to him was impossible.

As his body tried to heave itself out of the driver's seat, Jessica braced her knees against the back and pulled even harder.

The man's thick fingers scrabbled at the metal squeezing his windpipe but for the moment she had him secure; he couldn't have slipped a scrap of paper under the cuffs. Hurry up and pass out, you bastard, Jessica screamed at him silently. Pass out or drop dead!

But he kept flailing and flailing, refusing to stop and then she noticed that he had somehow managed to get hold of the gun. He wasn't merely flailing his arms around, he was trying to point the thing at her so he could shoot her. She felt a white-hot surge of fury. She was strangling him and instead of dying or even just losing consciousness, the son of a bitch was still intent on murdering them all.

Crying out from the increasing pain in her shoulders Jessica dug her knees into the back of the driver's seat and pulled for all she was worth, as if she were straining to drag him through the upholstery and out the other side.

All at once, there was a strange noise that was a bit like a muffled blast and the air in the van was filled with the stink of gunpowder strong enough to make Jessica's eyes water.

The gun had gone off.

Thank you, Los Angeles and good night, Greer thought as he and Tanner took aim at the kid lying on the pier.

This was definitely a most satisfying end to what had been an exceptionally shitty day. Now they would be able to work the drug racket and get rich for a change and if that just happened to make the mean streets of LA a little bit safer for those who didn't sport gang colors, well, hey now, how about that—a genuine win-win situation all the way around. And no more stupid goddamned interruptions.

Getting the gangbangers off the streets, cutting off a substantial amount of criminal income and channeling it into the pockets of guys who really needed it. Guys who deserved something extra for putting their asses at risk every day—what was wrong with that?

Besides, all that money would end up going back into legal circulation, which in the long run would benefit all those self-righteous, ungrateful taxpayers.

Not that any of them would know the difference one way or the other now that Craig Martin's fucking tape had been destroyed. Nobody was going to miss the gangbangers that he and the guys had disposed of. Hell, no one would even miss this piece of shit after he and Tanner—

"Dude!"

Greer looked over his shoulder and felt his jaw drop. What the fuck was that guy supposed to be? Some kind of giant foam rubber dildo?

It was at least a full second before he realized he was looking at an idiot wearing a whale costume. Moby fucking dickhead. Jesus Christ, was it the same one? Or, God help him, were there two idiots running around like that?

Moby fucking dickhead's face showing in the circular cutout of the costume seemed to go a little on the pale side then as he finally noticed the guns. He began to back away, taking tiny rapid steps because of his stupid outfit.

"Oh, wow. Never mind," he said. "Dude."

Never mind. Dude. Right. A dumb-ass running up the Santa Monica pier like a geisha and wearing a whale suit. Greer traded looks with Tanner and then they turned around again to finish the kid off.

He was gone.

The little shit head shouldn't even have been able to walk!

Horrified, Greer looked around and caught sight of the kid's jacket as he sprinted away and disappeared behind a pile of packing cases and equipment.

The carousel music was driving Mooney almost as mad as the idea that yet another detective he had only just met wanted to shoot him. Jesus Christ, he had already been through this once today, why the hell was it happening again? One minute he was just this okay guy who wanted to talk skin care regimes and the next, he was a homicidal maniac. Had the whole world gone completely dog shit? Or had somebody forgotten to mention that this was "National Shoot Bob Mooney Day?"

The guy took hold of the front of his shirt and swung him around, slamming him full length into the carousel housing. Mooney felt the shock pass through his already throbbing neck up into his head, where it seemed to rattle every filling in his mouth.

Even angrier now, he ignored the sensation of his eyes bouncing in their sockets and drove his stiffened fingers straight into the guy's chest, hitting the spot just under his breastbone. The guy—Dimmy? Dietrich? Christ, Mooney couldn't even remember his name now—whoever he was, he was pretty beefy and well padded all over but not so much that it gave him any extra protection. As he staggered back, Mooney kicked his legs out from under him and then dropped down on top of him, straddling his chest.

Mooney started to ask the guy what the hell he was doing but the detective reached up and gave his wounded neck a vicious squeeze.

The agony was literally blinding. For a moment, Mooney saw nothing, not even the backs of his clenched eyelids and the wordless, roaring scream seemed to come up from an inner depth he would not have associated with himself.

There was as much anger in it as pain. But when Mooney's vision cleared, he felt nothing but anger, a white-hot outrage at these bent, corrupt, dishonest cops who were so willing to kill one of their own. The bastards had forced him to kill a fellow officer. It was their fault that he had had to take a woman's life before she could take his and now they were trying to swat him like he was a goddamned fly.

"You're gonna shoot me?" Mooney bellowed furiously as he started banging the guy's head against the pavement. "You're gonna shoot me?"

Then he realized the guy actually wasn't going to shoot him or anyone else because he was now completely limp underneath him. Breathless and still furious, Mooney let go of the guy's hair and, with an enormous amount of effort, pushed himself to his feet.

Guess you're not gonna shoot me after all, douche-bag. Or whatever your name is.

No doubt everyone in the entire screaming, cheering audience of funk-metal fans would have killed to be backstage at an Incubus concert, Ryan thought as he made his way quickly through the obstacle course of trunks and cables and packing cases.

But not him, not good old Ryan Hewitt—he was backstage already and he was about to be killed.

If Chloe could have seen him now, he told himself bitterly, she would probably have had a lot to say about how he never had been able to do anything right. With any luck, that wasn't quite true—he hoped to God that the mean bastards had forgotten all about Chloe, especially now that they were chasing him. And as long as they were chasing him, they wouldn't get a chance to consider getting rid of Chloe as well.

Or Chad.

God, good old Chad. Good old incredible, amazing Moby Chad, a walking, life-saving miracle of timing in a dumb-ass rubber whale costume. If he actually did live through this, he'd give good old Chad his cellphone as a present all wrapped up with a bow along with a month's worth of free calls.

Ryan reached the railing then and looked back. The two mean bastards were coming after him fast, grinning like the jacked-up psycho killers they were. Because they thought they had him trapped.

Well, he was about to show them in no uncertain terms that they thought wrong.

Making sure that the waterproof pocket containing his cellphone was securely sealed, Ryan climbed up on the railing and threw himself into the Pacific Ocean.

Ryan had once read that the word "pacific" was related to peaceful or gentle. If that was really the case, then he was pretty sure that the person who had chosen that name for this particular ocean must have been a poor swimmer with a sarcastic streak a mile wide.

Someone an awful lot like himself.

The last coherent thought he had for a while was that perhaps this really hadn't been such a good idea after all. Then he was too busy fighting the powerful currents pulling at him from several different directions at once.

He had thought that this fall wouldn't be nearly as hard on him as the last one. The height he had jumped from was nowhere near six stories and he had been under the mistaken impression that water would be a lot easier than a trash dumpster to land in. A fat lot he knew about it. The water's surface wasn't soft—hitting it stung like a slap.

Below the surface it became a serious struggle for his life. His clothes had turned into horribly cumbersome, enormous swathes of cloth that dragged heavily on his arms and legs, hindering his movements. His lungs were burning and his lips were burning even more where the mean bastard had punched him. Every scratch and scrape on his body was on fire and the water was pushing him in every direction except up to where the air was.

Suddenly, he heard a strange unpleasant noise and something small zoomed down through the water near him. It was followed by another and then two more in rapid succession and he finally realized that the mean bastards were shooting into the water at him.

The salt water stung his eyes badly as he looked around for the pier's support pilings. In spite of the waterlogged clothes dragging at his arms and legs, he kept stroking as hard as he could, trying to make for an area that looked darker to him than where he was. He was unsure now whether the darkness was real. Perhaps it was the way things looked to someone who was drowning.

His chest went from burning agony to completely unbearable. At any moment, he was going to lose all control of his lungs and they would breathe in whatever was available—air or water, and he could do nothing about it.

Abruptly he felt a shockingly cool wind on his outstretched hands. Then his face broke the surface and he heard himself make a loud, sobbing noise as his lungs inflated with such force that they seemed to be trying to break out of his torso.

His lungs were still swelling on the intake when he felt the water lift him to a startling height and hurl him backwards. Tide coming in, said a small, strangely disconnected voice in his mind.

Then, impact.

Later on—much, much later, or possibly two seconds later, he was in too much shock to tell—he had an utterly detailed sense of how each of his internal organs had actually remained in motion after his body smashed into the piling. That feeling of internal impact was quite distinct from the outer one and the two seemed to fight each other for dominance of his pain threshold.

But before he could begin to get his mind around the overwhelming pain and nausea, the water took hold of him again, dragged him away and sent him into another piling.

And then another.

Pass out, you bastard, pass out! Jessica commanded silently as she kept on pulling and pulling and pulling the handcuffs against the man's throat. She might have said it aloud in a fury of frustration and effort but she had no breath for anything except trying to immobilize this man so he wouldn't shoot them.

Immobilize? Or kill?

Yes, all right, then: kill, she thought, sobbing from the pain of what she was doing as well as the agony of her tortured shoulders. When necessary, no other way out, then, yes. Kill.

Oh, right, of course. After all, she already had, hadn't she? That had almost slipped her mind. Exactly how she could have overlooked the memory of something so—

Jessica shoved the thought away and reached deeper into herself, beyond her awareness of Jessica as mother to the more instinctive mother as protector and found the will to pull even harder. The protector instinct had not so much awakened as it had ignited, and it was burning now in every part of her.

Body, soul, and mind, she was now the mother, the mother grizzly bear that would not permit any living creature to breach the eye-line between herself and her cubs, who in the defense of her young made sure nothing could move or even breathe to threaten them.

Except bear cubs didn't cry over what their mother had to do.

She became aware that Ricky had been watching her all along, sobbing with terror and heartbreak at the brutality of his mother's life-and-death struggle with this man, at having to see his mother's ferocity even for the sake of saving his life. In all of his eleven years, she had never raised a hand to him, had barely raised her voice except to laugh or shout happy birthday or call him in from the backyard.

As far as Ricky was concerned, whenever his mother got physical, it involved nice, safe, normal kinds of things—aerobics, gardening, dancing to old records in the living room with his father. His mother's hands stroked, held, comforted and if they ever struggled with anything, it was usually the stubborn lid on a jar of dill pickles or cocktail sausages. And she would usually end up giving them to his father and asking him to open them for her. Because her hands just weren't up to it.

But now it turned out that her hands were even stronger than that. She was stronger than that. And not just strong but mean. Mean enough to keep this man from killing them, so she had to be meaner than a killer. And that was a whole lot meaner than anyone or anything that Ricky had ever imagined.

Jessica felt a renewed surge of anger inside of her for everything these men had put her son through, and for forcing him to see what a human being was capable of. Not just any human being, but his own mother. She gave herself over to that anger without reserve, and it fuelled her strength.

"Son, look at me!" Craig yelled suddenly, rattling his handcuffs on the bar to get his attention. "Ricky, keep your eyes on me!"

Yes, Craig, that's it! You've got to be the one to shield him! Jessica felt like howling with relief.

Ricky's heartbroken sobs began to subside a little as he obeyed his father. When this was over, Jessica promised herself that she would make sure every day for the rest of their lives that Craig understood what an incredibly wise and inspired father he was—

Suddenly, a big, thick-fingered hand clamped onto her hair and began pulling hard. She tried to wriggle away but changing position would have meant easing up on the man's throat and she just couldn't, she absolutely could not do that. Not even if he tore her hair out by the roots and took her scalp with it.

The big man yanked her head forward sharply and she screamed as she went face first into the back of the seat. Before she could take another breath, he did it again, except this time she hit the back of his head instead of the seat and she screamed again, louder.

And then he did it again, jerking his head back so that he was actually head-butting her from behind.

Blind and dizzy with pain, she was screaming now at herself, at the pain in her face, and in her arms and her hands, in her muscles and tendons and bones. She was screaming at them not to hurt, not to weaken, not to loosen, not to fail.

If there was even a miniscule amount of justice in the world, Tanner said to himself as he skirted the waterline underneath the pier with his gun in hand, the incoming tide would have bashed the kid's brains out on the pilings. There was no irony in his thoughts, only impatience and a fed-up determination to bring the whole situation to a fast and irrevocable end.

Of all the things he had been involved in over the years, good, bad, gray or indifferent, he had never seen anything get so fucking out of hand. Not to this degree. They had all gone into it knowing that things could and would get tricky on them and they would have to deal with all kinds of trouble. They had been expecting to find themselves in a world of mega-hurt. Every single one of them was experienced enough to know that there was going to be an awful lot of bad shit in their collective future, and things weren't always going to turn out how they'd have liked.

But all that was supposed to apply to the gangbangers they were ripping off. There weren't supposed to be any Brentwood housewives or pier bums; this had nothing to do with them or with anyone else who came under the heading of John Q Public. Not even the John Qs who enjoyed a little recreational drug use of the less-than-legal variety. It didn't affect them one-way or the other; they would never know the difference.

Because there was no difference, as far as they were concerned. The only difference was that the money all the John Qs paid for their guilty pleasures would now supplement the obscenely meager incomes of civil servants who really deserved it. And if anybody paused to give that any serious thought, they would have seen that that was one hell of a lot better place for their happy little dollars to go. Why would they want to pour even more money into the obscenely bloated fortunes of psychopaths who were equally comfortable with the idea of selling the John Qs something to smoke, or just smoking them, period?

Tanner stopped to scan an area of the shore several feet above where the tide was coming in. It was shadowy under the pier and the day wasn't getting any brighter. Were those footprints? He squinted.

Yeah, they were, and although it was a pretty sure thing that a whole lot of people came down here to run around above the water line for a wide variety of unsavory reasons, he knew he was looking at only one set. Only one person had been running around under the pier in the very recent past. In the last few minutes. Tanner was disappointed that the kid hadn't gotten his brains bashed out on the pier supports, but knowing where he'd gone was some compensation. He grabbed his walkie-talkie.

"The kid's in the boathouse under the pier," he said into it. "Everyone copy that?"

If everybody did, nobody said so. Tanner felt a flare of impatience.

"Deason? Dimitri?" He waited; still no answer. "I could use some help over here." Lazy-assed fuckers, he fumed.

"Son of a bitch," Mooney groaned, looking at what's-his-name who was well and truly out cold.

Dimitri, he remembered suddenly for no apparent reason; the guy's name was Dimitri and he belonged to that small but utterly mystifying group of law enforcement officers who, for some reason, were united by their fanatical determination that Bob Mooney had to die today.

Well, Bob Mooney begged to differ. Bob Mooney had decided that he didn't have to die, today or any other day, and he didn't have to do anything else he didn't feel like, either. Because, goddamn it, Bob Mooney was his own man. Maybe a little bit giddy from loss of blood at the moment, he thought, leaning against the wall as he waited for the world to steady, but just give him a couple of days to recover and he would be good as new.

Although he wasn't too sure if his neck would ever be the same. Christ, but it hurt like a bastard. Ever since the stuff that the paramedic had numbed him up with had worn off, the pain had been getting steadily worse, and the punishment he had been taking hadn't helped. It seemed like the first thing everybody did was go straight for the place where he had been shot. Even people who weren't supposed to be trying to punch him out or kill him seemed to home in on his neck. Now the wound hurt a hell of a lot more than when he had actually gotten shot. And anything that hurt as bad as this did was going to look real gross for a real long time after it healed.

Hey, then it was a good thing for him that he just happened to run his own day spa, he thought as another wave of giddiness passed through him.

He would be able to sign himself up for some kind of treatment. Marilyn had a whole lot of stuff she said was good for all sorts of things—acne pits, stretch marks, surgical scarring, any kind of blemish there was. Now that he was thinking of it, he could remember her telling him something about how vitamin E oil was supposed to be good for minimizing scars. Of course, a gunshot wound was not exactly what anyone would think of as a minor blemish. He doubted that it was what the manufacturers had had in mind when they had been designing all that classy packaging for their expensive potions. He had to be realistic about what to expect—there was really only so much that vitamin E oil could do.

Like there was only so much he could do, Mooney thought, but that might well turn out to be one freakin' hell of a lot more than anyone had expected he could do.

With an effort, he pushed off from where he had been leaning and put himself in motion again, handcuffing the still-unconscious Dimitri to a nearby pipe. In spite of the fact that his neck was killing him and he kept going all goofy from loss of blood, he just had to see this situation, whatever it was, all the way through to the end.

And while he was at it, he also wanted to know why all of these would-be Mooney killers were cops. And how was this kid with the cellphone connected, and did that connection have anything to do with why the kid had decided to become a one man crime wave?

"The kid's in the boathouse under the pier." Tanner's voice on the walkie-talkie again. "Everyone copy that? Dimitri? Deason? I could use some help over here."

No, don't get up, Mooney told the unconscious Dimitri silently, I'll handle this one.

He picked up the walkie-talkie and the gun and went in search of the boathouse under the pier.

DORY STORAGE HOUSE said the sign over the door of the shabby structure. The set of footprints he had been following led inside, through the jimmied door left partially open.

Tanner double-checked to make sure that the safety on his gun was off before he slipped inside as quickly and quietly as he could. Although he really didn't think he had a whole lot to worry about when it came to making too much noise—he couldn't hear anything except the roar of the incoming tide. Nor could he see very much—there wasn't a whole lot of light down here, but that was all right, too. His eyes were gradually becoming accustomed to the murk.

He could now make out an incredible array of nautical stuff all over the place. The place was like a giant maritime junk drawer. Boats of various sizes were stacked in piles of various heights, either upside-down or nested right side up. The one on top was filled with oars and ropes and all kinds of weird equipment and crap people used on boats, for who the hell knew what reason.

Maybe just to keep all the weird equipment makers from going out of business.

Tanner's gaze traveled over the bright orange life jackets and the plastic seat cushions that doubled as flotation devices dangling from a multitude of hooks on all the pilings. A shadow flickered at the edge of his vision; he turned to look but saw nothing more than an array of rowing shells suspended from the rafters along the far wall.

There was definitely no shortage of places for the kid to hide in here, he thought. But it was a hell of a lot harder to make yourself disappear without a trace when you were dripping wet and the kid probably didn't realize that. He wasn't a gangster, after all, just a dumb-ass little pier bum. An amateur. Tanner grinned to himself. This was going to come to an end right here and now.

"Last chance, kid," he called. "If you just come out, I'll make it easy."

He waited, listening carefully for anything other than the rhythm of the surf. That kid had some pair of grapefruits on him for an amateur, he really did. But how long would he be able to last, knowing as he crouched somewhere in the shadows that he was being hunted by a man who was going to kill him, before his nerve finally broke? Tanner wondered. Most assholes who weren't amateurs couldn't go much more than thirty seconds before they lost it.

"Okay, then," he added as he began to make his way through the shadowy boathouse. In a minute or two, the little shit wouldn't be able to stop himself from poking his head up; he was just going to have to look and try to see what Tanner was doing, if he was actually leaving. Because the suspense would kill him if he didn't. Even though he knew full well that Tanner would kill him if he did.

Tanner moved silently around a piling, paused to survey the shadows carefully and decided to check out a large boat propped up on its side. But just as he started to head toward it, he spotted something bright sticking out from under a smaller rowboat that lay upside-down several feet away from him.

Christ, it was the kid's fucking jacket. Tanner could have laughed out loud. This was rich—a kid with big balls and no brains. What a shame.

He moved silently over to it and waited a second or two, just in case the kid realized he was near and decided he'd try making a break for it. But nothing happened.

Fuck this shit and fuck him, Tanner thought. He wasn't playing games, he was bringing this to a final, fucking end just like he had promised himself he would. Right here and right now.

He emptied his gun into the hull, watching the splinters fly.

In the aftermath of the flurry of blasts, the boathouse was as hushed as a church, even with the sound of the roaring ocean. There were no whimpers, no sobs, no groans, no gasps. Instant final, fucking end; he must have made it easy for the kid after all.

"Shoulda stayed at home this morning, kid," Tanner said, squatting down to flip the ruined hull over.

Only the jacket lay on the floor at his feet.

The sight banged through him like an electric current, jerking him to his feet. But before he could make another move, a voice suddenly spoke up behind him.

"I was about to say the same to you."

TWENTY-TWO

As he swung the short board with all his might directly into the guy's butt-ugly face, Ryan felt the impact run from his palms all the way up past his elbows and into his shoulders with a force that shocked the hell out of him.

He was probably going to have bruises on the heels of his hands for days, he thought, and he was going to hear it from his shoulder tendons as well. But then, his shoulder tendons were already pretty mad at him for all the abuse he had put them through. When you worked someone over, it apparently came with its own built-in payback. But damn, he had never imagined hitting someone could feel so freakin' good.

Of course, up until today he had never imagined he would fire a handgun in a store to get a salesperson's attention, even if he had fantasized about doing to a take-a-number dispenser exactly what he had done. Actually shooting one shaped like a smiley-face was one of the few crimes he had committed today that he absolutely could not bring himself to regret. All he could do now was hope that no one would think to ask him how remorseful he felt about that specific act during the sentencing phase of his trial. Assuming he lived to see his own prosecution, that was.

In any case, he hadn't thought anything could be nearly as satisfying to him personally as seeing that fucking smiley-face and its numbered tickets explode into smiley chunks. But as he swung the short board at the man again, he had to admit that getting to spring a surprise like this on the son of a bitching motherfucker definitely trumped everything else he'd done today, legal or illegal.

And when the guy staggered sideways and still didn't go down, the elation Ryan felt at knowing he was going to have to hit him again jumped from an all-time peak to an even greater level that bordered on life changing.

That first whack in the head, you bastard, that was for me, for what you did just now, Ryan thought fiercely. That second one I just laid on you, that one was for Jessica and her family and this one—

The force of the third blow sent the guy staggering backwards into a stack of rowboats.

This one's for deciding to be a gangbanger instead of a cop. Breathless from effort now, Ryan waited to see if the bastard was finally, finally going to fall. For a moment, it seemed as though he would. He wavered as he held himself up on the rowboats. But then he pushed off and stumbled several more steps backwards, his thick arms pin-wheeling as he fought to keep his balance.

Goddamn, but this sure was one tough mean bastard, Ryan thought, watching as the guy stood with his feet wide apart and tried to steady himself. Three hard shots with a hunk of fiberglass, blood pouring out of his head like a gory river and the guy was still looking around for him.

Next time he got trapped in a boathouse with a crooked cop, he would pick up a fucking anchor, Ryan thought as the mean bastard somehow managed to find him in the shadows and staggered forward, coming straight at him with his arms outstretched, like something out of a monster movie. Ryan reared back and then swung, letting go with everything he had.

And this one's for all of the above.

The bastard teetered on one foot for what seemed like an eternity until gravity finally won and he went down with a very final-sounding thud.

Ryan's breath rushed out and he sagged with relief, almost falling to his knees. If he had really had to wallop the guy several more times, he would probably have knocked himself out as well.

And then incredibly, the man groaned and rolled over onto his back. Oh, Christ, was he actually going to try to get up again?

No, Ryan thought. No way, no freakin' way. This was getting way too freakin' scary. He stood over the bastard and raised the short board high over his head, preparing to deliver a heavy dose of discouragement.

Abruptly there were two fast explosions. Ryan felt the board jerk in his hands; then there were fragments of fiberglass and foam raining down all around him. He looked up to see that he was now holding nothing more than two small pieces of jagged scrap in either hand.

"Do you have any idea," said a familiar and very unpleasant voice from the doorway, "how much trouble you've caused me today?"

Ryan lowered his arms and dropped what was left of the short board as the mean bastard came toward him through the shadowy boathouse. His legs had turned into mere sticks, and not very steady ones at that. Totally unsuitable for anything that involved any kind of movement. Like, say, running for his life.

Which was just as well, seeing as how there was nowhere to go.

There was nowhere these mean bastards couldn't follow him, apparently, no place where they didn't have some kind of help, nowhere they couldn't do exactly what they wanted, and to anyone they wanted to do it to. There was no place in the world where things didn't work just the way they wanted.

He came to a stop in front of Ryan and put the gun barrel directly against his forehead. The metal was still hot. Ryan closed his eyes, wondering in some distant part of his mind whether he would hear the shot.

His jaw spontaneously combusted with a ferocious, searing pain, filling his head with incoherent light and sound as he reeled backwards. Eventually, he stopped when his back met something hard, but flashbulbs were still going off in his brain and his ears were both ringing and buzzing. He had no idea whether the impact he had felt was actually the floor or a piling that he had staggered into or just his senses going haywire.

A rough hand took hold of the front of his shirt. "Who are you?"

Automatically, Ryan started to say something but he felt another sharp burst of pain in the lower half of his face, followed by a terrible pulling sensation. Suddenly all the muscles and tendons in his jaw seemed to be in the wrong positions and were struggling to right themselves. Spears of pain went all the way up to his temples and he barely felt himself fetch up against a nested stack of boats.

"How did you get involved?"

His jaw gave a silent *pop!* and the pain diminished enough to let his mind as well as his eyes snap back into focus. The oar was in his hands even as he saw it lying in the top boat on the stack that he was hanging on to, and it felt good and solid in his grip, like a club.

"I just answered my phone," he said and whirled on the mean bastard, swinging for his head.

Ryan's primal urge for mayhem cut off as if a switch had been flipped and his eyes widened in horror. The son of a bitch had actually caught the oar in mid-swing. He was standing there holding it up in one hand, grinning like this was exactly what he had hoped that Ryan would do.

In the next moment, he jerked it out of Ryan's grasp, twisted it around and broke it in two. As he tossed the pieces away, he lunged forward and chaos erupted in Ryan's skull again. His whole head was wrapped in pain, originating from the white-hot spot on his forehead where the mean bastard had head-butted him. Twice.

When his vision cleared again, he found himself clinging to a piling, trying to stay on his feet. The evil bastard seemed to find this highly entertaining.

"Pathetic," he said, shaking his head. "The bitch has more fight than you." Pause. "Well... she had."

This time, the explosion Ryan felt came from deep inside himself. Jessica must have gone down fighting, he thought as new rage quickened his heartbeat. Jessica would have gone down fighting for sure. She would have hurt somebody before it was over, and she would have hurt them bad.

He would now finish what she had started. Either that or he would go down fighting as hard as Jessica Martin had. If she could, he could.

Over the rattle and clang of Craig fighting to free himself from the bar he was handcuffed to, and the hideous choking gasps of the man she was strangling, Jessica could only hear the discordant groaning of metal as it bent and the sound of her own effortful breathing.

Her son seemed to have gone quiet, for which she was immensely grateful. She could only hope that he still had his gaze locked on his father, because she was at the limit of her capabilities. There was nothing she could do except pull until this man stopped struggling, until the unspeakable gasping and choking noises came to an end along with his life.

Otherwise, he would do the same to her and Ricky and Craig. She had no choice and only this one chance and the man was still struggling. God, how could he still be fighting her? Why wouldn't he quit, why wouldn't he pass out?

With a sob of effort and frustration, she threw both her legs over the back of the chair and hauled away with all her weight. The man in the seat in front of her kept gasping and fighting, but she thought she could feel that his movements were becoming less vigorous now, his arms weren't flailing around quite so much.

Weaken, damn you, weaken, she told him silently. Behind her, the sound of metal bending grew louder and more piercing.

Ryan immediately launched himself at the mean bastard without really thinking of what he was doing.

He didn't stop to wonder if the guy was playing him somehow so that he was actually lunging headfirst into some kind of trap. Nor was there any thought of what he wanted to do, or at least not thought as coherent mental activity. He had become a creature whose function came down to the intent that drove his instinct. His fists were up and ready to inflict as much damage as possible.

"That's better!" The bastard braced himself, started to raise his own fists. "Come on!"

The last word wasn't quite out of his mouth when Ryan's fist connected.

The blow hurt like a son of a bitch—more of that same old built-in payback. The nerves in his hand twanged like guitar strings pulled taut and his knuckles stung. But the look on the guy's face as he staggered back more than made up for it.

Surprise, surprise, asshole—it's not gonna be as easy to take me out as you thought. Ryan advanced on him, unconsciously adopting a classic aggressive boxing posture and keeping his fists up to protect his face. Maybe it's not even gonna be possible.

Ryan swung again and felt a fierce, animal joy when he connected and sent the son of a bitch staggering and stumbling several clumsy steps further backwards.

Jessica wasn't sure how long she had kept pulling before she realized that the man in the driver's seat had stopped struggling.

Even then, she was afraid to stop, afraid that as soon as she eased up on the pressure, he would suddenly bounce back even stronger than before and overpower her. And yet if he had finally, *finally*, finally passed out, then she *had* to let go. Because in spite of everything, she did not want to kill him.

At the same time, she didn't want to take any chances, either. Her family had to be completely safe, and if that meant this man had to die, then that was the way it would be.

It crossed Ryan's mind in a distant, detached way that if he ended up breaking a few of his own bones while punching this asshole's face in, he really didn't mind.

After all, there were some things in this life that you had to fight for literally. You had to put up or shut up, you couldn't just talk the talk; you had to walk the walk, and then keep on walking. You had to go all the way. But that meant you would have to take as much of what you gave out—more if necessary. But no matter what, you hung in and you kept fighting, and if some mean bastard told you to lay down and die because it was all over, you kept on swinging anyway. Nothing was over until you stopped.

Not to mention the fact that he was having a hell of a great time showing this son of a bitch that he had seriously underestimated what a guy like him was capable of when he was really up against it. And he really was showing him in a very serious way. He was hot, man, he was on fire. The last thing this son of a bitch must have been expecting was that Ryan would have that kind of juice in him. A couple more punches and the bastard was going to go down, he thought gleefully, and when he did, it was going to be real fucking sweet. He had a fast mental flash of himself actually putting the guy's own handcuffs on him as he said, citizen's arrest!

He swung on him with a hard right but suddenly felt his fist stop short in mid-air, before it could connect with the guy's face.

Ryan blinked; the guy had caught his hand like it was a sacrificial fly in the bottom of the ninth, the same way he had done with the oar, and now he was squeezing it.

The bastard's mouth stretched in an ugly, flat smile. "All right, kid," he said and squeezed Ryan's hand until he couldn't help letting out a sharp cry of pain. "That'll do."

Little by little, Jessica relaxed her arms, ready to yank back the moment she felt any resistance from the man in the front seat. But nothing happened. He was completely limp.

Quickly, she searched his pockets and came up with the key to the handcuffs, unlocking herself first, and then Ricky, who threw himself into her arms with a joyful cry before she could do the same for Craig.

Ryan was still trying to register what the guy had said to him when his jaw burst into a furious fire of agony again.

As he started to fall backwards, something as hard and dense as a brick smashed into his midsection as if it were trying to go through him. A giant bullet, he thought crazily and gave an involuntary bellow as his breath rushed out.

There was another explosive frenzy of pain in his head, followed by a wave of darkness and vertigo. The rest of the world vanished as it engulfed him. For some timeless interval what was left of his senses told him that everything in the boathouse had just been a delirious, dying man's dream. He was actually still caught in the incoming tide and getting his brains bashed out under the pier.

Then he found himself looking up at the motherfucker; he was standing over him, no, towering over him with that same ugly flat smile.

That'll do.

Ryan took a breath just to see if he still could; it turned into a pain-filled gasp. The noise obviously sounded like happiness to the mean bastard—the look on his face said it pleased him like nothing else could have.

"Y-you," Ryan managed finally, grimacing in pain as well as at the nauseating heavy-salt taste of blood filling his mouth. "You let me hit you?"

"Of course," the bastard said. He spat a fat gob of blood and phlegm just to the right of Ryan's head, then dragged the back of hand across his mouth. "You attacked me, and I killed you in self-defense."

A flash of panic jolted every nerve in Ryan's body and shut his mind down completely. It was only pure reflex made him open his mouth to scream. Just as he did, the bastard stepped forward and put his foot squarely on Ryan's neck, pressing down until he was absolutely sure that Ryan couldn't possibly move.

Then he drew his gun and took aim at Ryan's head.

"That's enough!" shouted a new voice from the doorway.

TWENTY-THREE

The sight of some strange guy standing there just inside the boathouse and pointing a .38 at him in a two-handed aim made no sense at all to Greer.

If anyone were supposed to be there with him just then, it would have been Deason. Deason would have been coming to help him out after getting rid of that asshole who'd put a cap in Bayback's ass and sent her to the morgue.

Except it was a little too soon for Deason to be back already, he thought. But not for Dimitri. By now, Dimitri would have put a bullet in the brain of each pain in the ass Martin family member, bringing that troublesome matter to a permanent end, case closed. Thank you, Los Angeles and good night.

Instead, he was looking at someone else entirely, and the guy just didn't belong. Who the fucking fuck was he, and what the fucking fuck did he think he was doing? Other than bleeding from the neck while he held a gun on him, that was.

It was all so confusing that he had pretty much forgotten about the kid on the floor, who suddenly came to frantic life under his foot. "Help me!" he yelled, his voice pitched high with pain and desperate fear. "Help me, he's a dirty cop—"

Greer immediately increased the amount of weight he was putting on the kid's neck, enjoying the way his voice cut off with a harsh gagging noise. Even if the sound was barely audible over the combined roar of the still incoming tide and the steadily rising wail of police sirens—

Wait a minute, Greer thought suddenly. Police sirens? It was way too soon for those—

"Let him up," said the guy with the .38 tensely. "Now."

Greer could damn near feel the way his gun was sighted on the spot right between his eyebrows. This had to be that asshole desk sergeant out of West Side, the cop Tanner had told him about, the one who just out of the blue went over to the Martin house and blew away Bayback.

He felt a white hot flash of fury. No way was this West Side asshole gonna get out of this alive, Greer told himself silently, channeling his swelling rage into controlled intent.

"He attacked my partner," he said in a careful, professional voice. "Then he tried to kill me—"

"I said, let him up!" the guy barked. "And I said now!"

Greer's rage threatened to soar past the threshold of rational thought and into the zone of no return. He stepped even harder on the kid's neck, enjoying the sensation of his flesh giving under the pressure.

"You're gonna believe this lying piece of shit over a cop?" he demanded.

"Doesn't matter what I believe," said the asshole desk sergeant in the doorway. "What's important is that you believe that I will put a .38 slug in your skull if you don't let the kid up right now."

Experience told Greer that he could believe every word that came out of this West Side asshole's mouth. With great reluctance, he eased off the kid's neck, hesitated, and then had to force himself to remove his foot altogether.

Immediately, the kid half-rolled, half-scrambled away from him, gasping and hacking as he rubbed his throat.

Greer gazed steadily into the cop's eyes while he tracked the kid's movements in his peripheral vision, knowing the other man was doing the same. Sooner or later, this West Side asshole was going to give in to the urge to look at the kid, take just a quick glance at him and see if he was all right, and the moment he looked away, Greer was going to take his ass down.

The kid suddenly found his voice, what there was of it. "He kidnapped Jessica Martin and her family!" he rasped. He tried to say something else but was overwhelmed by a fit of coughing.

Now, Greer thought and got ready to take him.

But the cop's gaze didn't waver, not even when his finger tightened on the trigger.

"Hands in the air," he ordered.

Greer's jaw dropped, sending a sharp pain through his head; he barely noticed. "What?" he asked incredulously.

"You heard me! Do it now!" the cop roared at him, still not looking away.

Shit—the son of a bitch just wasn't going to fuck up. Since when did they have any uniformed cops who were that good at West Side? Greer lowered his weapon slowly and set it down on top of a nearby crate. Goddamn it, he just hadn't been able to catch a single break all day and now he was royally and terminally fucked.

But then the guy told him to turn around.

Greer had to force himself not to grin until he had turned his back to the guy completely. Turn around. What a classic fucking mistake. Killing Bayback had to have been one hell of a fluke after all.

As soon as he heard the sound of the cop's footsteps coming toward him, he took aim at the light overhead and shot it out, plunging the warehouse into almost total darkness.

Despite his raw, tortured throat, Ryan couldn't help crying out in anger and alarm.

A good part of it was that he had known exactly what the bastard had been about to do—he had seen it on him just as plainly as if the guy had been wearing a fucking neon sign: Attention: I WILL BOOK, FUCK YOU VERY MUCH. Why it hadn't been just as plain to the other cop was a complete mystery.

Maybe I just know him better because I've spent more time with him, Ryan thought; he could feel nervous laughter silently bubbling up inside him again. He fell back as the cop from the police station rushed past to go after the bastard, at the same time reaching out with the vague idea that he had to stop him.

He heard two muffled shots then and splinters exploded from a piling bare inches from the cop's head. The cop ducked and fired back in the general direction of the shots before joining Ryan behind a rack of rowboats.

"We gotta get out of here," he whispered. "Stay with me."

No shit? Ryan wanted to answer, but his throat hurt too much. Just as well—this was a good guy, after all, he had just saved Ryan's life. Why give him a hard time? He simply nodded just as a chunk of rowboat blew up right in front of his face.

The cop pulled him back then suddenly yanked him up into a crouching run. He was firing his gun into the darkness while he kept a hard, painful grip on Ryan's arm with his free hand.

Abruptly, the cop was dragging him several feet to the nearest piling, where he forced him to get down as close to the floor as possible. He motioned for him to hug the base and keep quiet. Ryan barely had time to obey before the man yanked him up again and dragged him along to the next piling.

With a sudden burst of relief, Ryan understood that the cop was moving them in the general direction of the exit; he could see that they were now barely thirty feet away from it and he could hardly stand it. If the cop hadn't still had a hold on his arm like "The Totally Unbreakable Iron Claw of Death," Ryan didn't think he would have been able to keep himself from giving in to panic and just making a break for it. Which no doubt would have gotten his panicky ass thoroughly killed.

Ryan made himself stay low, trying to be ready to move quickly to the next piling so the cop wouldn't have to drag him. But several seconds measured by the terrified thumping of his heart went by and they stayed where they were. Uneasy, Ryan looked up at the cop, trying to see his face. He really hoped like hell that the guy hadn't picked this moment to choke. Not when they were so close to the fucking exit.

The cop met his gaze and let go of his arm just long enough to put his finger to his lips before he resumed cutting off the circulation to Ryan's hand. He was listening, Ryan realized finally; he was listening for the sound of the mean bastard moving around. Though how the cop could hear anything between the noise from the ocean and the aftermath of his un-silenced gun was a complete mystery to him. Ryan's own ears were ringing like gongs.

More seconds marched passed marked by the hard beat in his chest and still, the cop didn't show any sign that he was going to move. Ryan began to wonder if he knew what the hell he was listening for. What the hell did he think he was going to hear—the mean bastard yelling ally, ally, out and free, or just his favorite Incubus song?

Even as the thought ran through Ryan's mind, however, he became aware that underneath the ocean and the distant concert, he could hear something else, something that might have been soft sounds of another person moving around somewhere in the boathouse.

Jesus Christ, he realized suddenly—the bastard was actually stalking them in the dark.

Ryan was starting to poke his head up a little higher in an effort to hear better when the cop jerked him to his feet and hustled him quickly to another piling. They waited behind it for a fraction of a second and then the cop yanked him quickly along to another.

Ryan now saw with a great deal of dismay that they weren't getting any closer to the exit—if anything, they were starting to move further away. He tried to move up beside the cop but the man pushed him back with an impatient shake of his head.

Ryan waited a heartbeat or two and then straightened up slightly, pressing his back hard against the piling. Now he couldn't hear anything, no matter how hard he listened. The son of a bitch couldn't be gone, he thought, frustrated—aside from the fact that he couldn't have sneaked out the door without their seeing. There was no way the mean bastard would have taken off without killing them first.

So what the hell was going on? Was the bastard levitating now, or what?

Ryan pulled the arm the cop was holding toward himself so that the cop would have to lean toward him. "Where is he?" he whispered.

The cop winced. "I can't tell—"

Ryan barely had time to hear the next muffled shot before his calf exploded.

It was at least another second before he screamed.

In spite of the pain and shock overwhelming him at the time, Ryan was very clear about what had happened, and he knew that he would be for the rest of his life, no matter how long—or short—that might turn out to be. There had been no time between the sound of the shot and when he saw a sloppy red burst of his own blood and flesh erupt from his calf, spraying up and out.

If he had imagined that he had ever felt anything that he might have called pain, this was not it.

This was not something as mere and trivial as the sensation he had routinely referred to as pain; this was something else altogether. This was far beyond anything he could have imagined, let alone anything he had actually experienced. This was years of unbearable torture and suffering contained in a single projectile for delivery in one efficient, timesaving dose.

His leg felt as if it had been simultaneously burned, frozen, sandblasted, shredded, and smashed with a sledgehammer. His bones seemed to be screaming, so much so that he was barely aware of the cop dragging him across the floor to a darker, more sheltered area.

The man pried Ryan's hands away from the wound for a fast look before pressing them quickly back into place and motioning for him to maintain direct pressure, lying on his back if he could.

"It's okay," Ryan panted, squeezing his leg tighter against himself. "Really. It is. It's okay." He looked around but the door was no longer in sight.

"Stay down," the cop told him in a whisper, putting a restraining hand on his chest. "I'll draw him off." He waited for a moment to make sure Ryan wouldn't try to get up and then moved out quickly, disappearing around the stern of a rowboat that had seen better days.

Great, Ryan thought; he was supposed to lie on the floor behind a low budget shipwreck in dry-dock and not to bleed to death before either help arrived or the heavy finished him off. He dragged himself along the floor and part way around the rowboat, hoping he could see something.

Ryan spotted the cop between a piling and a barrel of oars, holding a cellphone radio close to his mouth and whispering into it. Abruptly, two more silenced rounds whispered dangerously close to him, the first one grazing the piling and the second one taking out some of the oars.

The cop dropped the phone, waited a moment and then started to move forward. There was another of those muffled blasts and Ryan saw a puff of dirt and wood splinters erupt at the point where the cop's foot would have been a second later.

The cop drew back. Ryan watched him as he surveyed his immediate surroundings, trying to decide which way to move. Except by the time he figured it out, Ryan thought with growing horror, the mean bastard would already be in position for a clear shot. Because somehow he knew where the cop was, whereas neither the cop nor Ryan knew where he was—

Unbidden, the image of his Bluetooth cell bloomed in his inner eye and with it, the answer.

He let go of his leg, took out the phone and half-whistled, half-hissed to get the cop's attention.

The cop looked at him sharply. He then saw the phone in Ryan's hand and his eyes widened with instant understanding. He gave an emphatic nod.

Got you, you bastard, Ryan thought and pressed for last-number redial.

The ringing only lasted for a couple of seconds before the cop was on his feet, blasting away. But that was long enough for Ryan to know that it came from somewhere on his right, from a spot closer than he had expected, much closer. So much closer that he wondered if he should count himself lucky not to have gotten a bullet in his head instead of an idea.

And then again, maybe not.

The ringing cut off sharply, as if the son of a bitch had simply shut the goddamned thing off.

Holding his breath, Ryan stared into the silent shadows. If we're dead after all, I swear I'm gonna find some way to get that sucker from the afterlife, Ryan's mind was babbling absurdly. I'm gonna haunt every fucking house he ever lives in, I swear to God. I'll haunt his car, I'll haunt his fucking shoes and socks, I'll haunt—

There was a noise from the shadows, that might have been a footstep and all thought in Ryan's mind ceased.

Silence for some unmeasured eternity, and then suddenly the bastard stepped forward out of the shadows.

For some reason, Ryan saw the bullet hole in the hand holding the remains of the telephone receiver before he saw the rest of the bullet holes running across the mean bastard's chest.

It was only a fraction of a second later that the man hit the floor but Ryan's memory of how he looked and how he fell, was burned into his mind with as much detail as if the heavy had been frozen there for hours.

Twenty-two years, Mooney thought, staring at the body on the boathouse floor with revulsion. Twenty-two years and that's what you get.

"Jessica. I have to—"

The kid's voice snapped Mooney back to reality. He turned to see that in spite of the gunshot to his leg, the kid was actually pushing himself to his feet.

"Hey, kid, wait!" Mooney yelled, but it was already too late. The kid was half-limping, half-loping out of the warehouse with a speed that should have been impossible. Mooney stared after him, shaking his head. Jesus, you just couldn't talk sense to someone in the middle of an adrenalin rush. You didn't have a hope in hell of making them listen. But boy, was the kid going to feel it when it wore off. And tomorrow he'd be hurting like he had never hurt before.

He turned back to look at the guy on the floor. Seemed pretty dead, all right, but he kept his gun trained on him anyway as he went to pick up his cellphone. With any luck, he thought as he hit speed-dial, this was the absolute, no fooling, totally *last* National Kill Bob Mooney Day ever.

"This is Sergeant Mooney, LAPD. I need paramedics at my location. We've got an officer down…"

TWENTY-FOUR

That Ricky would finally break down after all he had been through today was hardly surprising, Jessica thought as she held her son tightly in her arms, rocking him back and forth the way she had back when he was a baby. This had been an ordeal that would have reduced most adults to a gibbering, quivering mess that they wouldn't recover from for months, if not longer.

Her son had been a very, very brave boy, far and away above and beyond the call of duty for someone his age. Right now, she wanted more than anything to free Craig and get them all out of the back of this van that had very nearly been their tomb. But Ricky had her in such a death grip while he sobbed his little heart out that she literally couldn't move. She couldn't even stretch one arm out far enough to pass the key to the handcuffs over to Craig so he could free himself and she really felt bad about that. Craig had not exactly been on a picnic today himself. But all she could do was look in silent apology at her husband's poor swollen, bruised and battered face.

And, of course, Craig only smiled back at her as much as his poor injured face would allow and nodded to let her know that it was all right. He could wait and he didn't mind waiting now that there was no immediate threat to them. Taking care of their son and making sure he was all right always came first, always had and always would.

Seeing the love in him made her choke up all over again. Considering that she had been crying almost non-stop all day and tears were still leaking steadily from her eyes and running down her cheeks, the idea of her feeling choked up over anything at all probably should have funny. But at least now these were tears of joy and relief.

It seemed like hours before Jessica felt Ricky's sobs finally begin to lessen in force. Probably due more to exhaustion than anything else, she thought as she continued to rock him. Somebody's goin' to sleep good tonight—another one of Miz Peach's characteristic pronouncements. Somebody's goin' to sleep good tonight, but ooohh, child, you gonna feel that tomorrow for sure! She winced, suddenly aware that the ache in her shoulders was definitely becoming more intense. She was going to have to move soon regardless of how Ricky was doing or they were going to lock up altogether on her.

Fortunately, her son was feeling more cooperative now and she managed to get him to sit up and let her crawl over to where Craig was still cuffed to the back door. She was shaking so badly that he had to use his free hand to help her. But he wasn't much steadier than she was and it took several tries before they got the tiny little key into the hole.

Craig then had both arms around her and Ricky and they were all hugging and crying. Craig was saying something about how it was about time they got out of this van and rejoined the world of the living while Ricky was begging them to take him home. Jessica was too overwhelmed to say anything at all. Her own feelings, her family's, the sound of their voices, Ricky gasping and starting to sob again—the sheer noise filled her head and overwhelmed her. She was dimly aware that there was some kind of concert going on somewhere outside, something funky and metal at the same time, and a whole lot of people screaming and cheering, but all that was so far away it might as well not have been real. Nothing outside of the three of them, right there and right now, was real.

Taking all of that into consideration, it was a miracle that she heard the sound of someone moving around in the front of the van at all. It wasn't very loud, not compared to the noise of three people in the midst of hysterical relief at having escaped death. Much later on when Jessica looked back on it, she thought that she actually hadn't heard the man moving around so much as she had felt him, felt his pain, his anger, and his rage, felt his pure murderous intent barely a fraction of a second before he sat up, let out that ragged, throat-torturing roar, and pointed the gun at them.

No matter how often she looked back on that exact, precise moment, it never ceased to amaze her that it hadn't felt like it had lasted forever. There really hadn't been enough time for her to blame herself, to think that she shouldn't have sat for so long with Ricky, that she should have concentrated on getting them all out of there first even if it meant pushing her son away from her with enough force to knock him senseless, just so she could unlock Craig's handcuffs and they could all escape.

All that and more could have flashed through her mind in almost no time at all. But that would have been almost no time. This had been no time, period, full stop; zero, zippo, nothing, nihil, nadda. The man sat up pointing the gun at them and the driver's side window imploded.

She knew that some people might have argued with her choice of words, insisting that the window had exploded, not imploded. As a science teacher, Jessica knew the difference as well as she knew that dihydrogen monoxide was water, not poison and one hundred per cent humidity was fog not rain. In this case, she was sticking with imploded simply because it was the first word that had occurred to her and, as it had been her final near-death—or near-getting-murdered—experience, she felt entitled.

As quickly as it all happened, it seemed to Jessica that she saw the whole thing in perfect detail, every fragment of glass that hit him as well as the ones that missed, flying past him or just spraying in all directions. And then the way he turned his head just at the right moment so that the fist coming through the shattered window smashed him squarely in the center of his face.

The man hadn't not even had time to fall down again before the door flew open and he was forcibly dragged out of the front seat by someone that Jessica couldn't see clearly but that she knew had to be—could only be—Ryan.

He had never hurt so much in so many places in his entire life. But as Ryan dragged the motherfucker out of the van by the front of his shirt (and a lot of chest hair, judging from the feel), it just didn't seem terribly relevant.

In Ryan's view, the only thing relevant to this moment was that he deliver the most thorough and extensive beating this son of a bitch had ever experienced in his entire crooked, dirty, sleazy life.

Until today, he had never hit anyone. He had never even thought seriously about hitting anyone, not even good old Chad and Chloe, of course, was non-violence all the way. Old-school displays of testosterone didn't impress her and he didn't want to imagine what she would think if she saw him right now. But Chloe had not had the day he had just had. Then there was the matter of what this mean bastard had done to Jessica and her family. If Chloe knew about that, she might want to take a few swings at the guy himself, and maybe so would a lot of other people.

In which case, Ryan thought as he connected with a right cross that sent the guy staggering backwards to slam into the side of the van, they would all just have to get in line and wait their turn. Right now, this son of a bitch belonged only to him.

He was vaguely aware that he must have broken more than one bone in his hand when he had smashed his fist through the window. He hadn't stopped to think when he'd done that. There hadn't been time. He had seen the guy sit up and point the gun and it was only too clear that the bastard would have pulled the trigger before Ryan could yell stop! So instead, he had just acted on instinct, something that apparently involved a lot of momentum.

It wasn't until he bent the mean bastard over and drove a knee into his midsection that Ryan remembered he had actually been shot. The shock of seeing the wound as he flexed his leg was so strong that it was almost like being shot again. He shoved the meaby to the ground and stepped back unsteadily. His leg almost gave out under him but he managed to keep himself upright. The pain that he had been only distantly aware of suddenly began to assert itself. He felt as if every part of his body had suddenly decided to have an argument as to what hurt most.

Ryan limped over to the van so he could lean against it. The white-hot rage that had filled his head like a fever and put him into overdrive was dissipating now as quickly as it had come over him, leaving him limp, woozy and barely able to stand.

Then, all at once, he saw her standing near the rear of the van, where the door was hanging open. She looked as if someone had worked her over again since his last quick sight of her in the passenger-side window. And now that he thought of it, that last quick sight of her had also been his first quick sight of her. How weird. For all intents and purposes, he had just devoted an entire day to her and this was only the second time he had ever laid eyes on her.

She took a tentative step toward him. "Ryan?" she asked softly.

His awareness of pain damped down a little again as he smiled at her. "Jessica."

"Jessica."

His voice echoed in her head, saying her name. She couldn't move, couldn't speak, couldn't do anything at all except stare. What I've put him through, she thought, a storm of emotions roiling inside of her. What I've put him through.

But he was looking at her with a gentleness that reminded her very much of Craig and, to a certain extent, Ricky, probably because he was so young. So young to be so heroic.

A moment later, she was hugging him, trying to find the right words to thank him, and then just breaking down as she felt his arms go around her. One hand patted her hair gently.

"It's nice to meet you," he said after a moment.

It's nice to meet you, too, she tried to say, but the words simply wouldn't come.

Looking at the gunshot wound in his leg still made Ryan extremely queasy, but at least it didn't hurt anywhere near as much since the paramedic had given him the injection.

There had been two injections, actually—one that she'd said was for the leg and one she had told him would help him with that seriously freaked-out feeling. Ryan had thought it was pretty cool that she had known he was seriously freaked-out.

And she had sure known what she was doing, too. He was still a long way from all right but he sure felt a lot better now. He felt so much better that he almost didn't mind sitting in the back of the ambulance watching her tend to his leg.

Of course, it could have been worse, Ryan thought. He could have been shot in the neck, like the poor cop sitting next to him and getting worked on. Bob Mooney, that was his name. Ryan knew he was going to remember that name for the rest of his life. He would forget his own name before he would ever forget Bob Mooney. What a guy—man, he was tough. He'd been running around for God knew how long after getting shot in the neck, then beat down one of those mean bastards when he'd tried to kill him, and still had enough left to save both their lives in a dark boathouse.

And to top it all off, he told the paramedics they should give him only one injection, just to numb the area where they had to put the stitches. Because he was still on duty and he had to wrap the case up. Ryan was in awe; the guy probably ate iron bars for breakfast.

Shivering a little, Ryan pulled the blanket around his shoulders a little bit tighter. Damn, he just couldn't shake this chill for some reason, maybe because he was so tired. When the paramedics finally finished with his leg, he was going to turn off his cellphone, climb into bed and sleep for a week. In jammies, the kind with the feet in them. Wrapped in an electric blanket.

The more he thought about that, the better it sounded. He turned to look at Chloe who was standing on his other side and clutching his hand between both of hers. Especially he probably wouldn't be alone.

"This is bullshit, Mooney!"

With a sigh, Mooney looked up to see Jack Tanner between two uniformed officers who were escorting him toward some waiting squad cars so he could join the rest of Jessica Martin's kidnappers. All but two, he reminded himself, feeling a bit queasy all of a sudden; the two that he had killed.

"I'm telling you, I'm being set up!" Tanner yelled, forcing the uniforms to stop in front of him while he was having his neck worked on. It was the second time today he'd had to talk to Tanner with an open wound in his neck. Mooney hoped it wasn't the start of a trend. "Come on, Moon. Just ask Jessica Martin! She's never seen me before!"

Mooney winced, reacting both to Tanner and to whatever the paramedic was doing to him.

"And him—" Tanner went on, gesturing at Ryan Hewitt with his cuffed hands, "I was just trying to bring the kid in for questioning when he attacked me! For no reason! Come on, Mooney, you know me—"

Mooney took a deep, uncomfortable breath and tried to think, but his mind seemed to have quit for the day. What with all the blood he'd lost, the beating he'd taken and the shock of having to kill two people in one day, he probably wasn't thinking straight. If a good cop had to spend a night or even a couple of hours locked up with all the rest of the lowlifes, not to mention the gangbangers and the skinheads they had rounded up just because he was too fucked up to know his ass from a hole in the ground—oh, man, talk about unforgivable. Not to mention the fact that jail was an extremely dangerous place for a cop on the wrong side of the bars. If he put Tanner in and it was a wrong call, he might wake up tomorrow and find himself responsible for three deaths.

"Hey," said the kid sitting next to him. Mooney turned to see him holding out a Bluetooth cellphone. "Sorry to interrupt but have you seen these new phones? The new functions are amazing."

Mooney blinked at him. Was the kid delirious? Or was he himself imagining the kid wanted to chat about cellphones?

"Like downloading video files, for example," the kid went on, showing him the screen above the keypad.

"Don't listen to this punk!" Tanner called out angrily.

The kid ignored him and handed Mooney the phone. "They destroyed the original recording," he said, pointing to the play button, "but only after I made a copy of it."

Mooney hesitated, looking at the kid questioningly. The kid nodded at him and he pressed play.

It was amazing, Ryan thought, watching Bob Mooney's face grow hard and cold as the truth unfolded on the little screen. The video had lost no detail in visual quality when he had transferred it from the camera. Let's hear it for technology. Technology is our friend.

"There is no drug war," he said as the video came to an end and the cop looked up. "It's just these dirty cops killing off dealers for their money and drugs."

"Mooney, Goddamn it!" yelled the cop angrily, trying to shake off the uniformed officers still holding his arms. "You can't believe this shit!"

Bob Mooney looked down at the phone again and then glared at the detective. "Jack, I ever tell you how much I hate dirty cops?" he asked in a soft but dangerous tone.

"Are the chemicals from your beauty salon warping your brain, Mooney?" the other man demanded.

Ryan actually felt the cop's entire body tense, like a wire pulled taut. "It's a day spa, you fuck." Still glaring, he turned the phone around and showed the detective the video, which had begun to play again.

The blood drained out of the detective's face so quickly that Ryan was sure he was going to faint. But his knees only buckled a little as the uniformed officers marched him away. Ryan couldn't help grinning with satisfaction as he stared after him. He turned to say something to Bob Mooney but the cop was getting up and telling the paramedic that he had to go make sure a certain sleazeball was locked securely in the back of a police cruiser before it drove off.

Then his gaze fell on the Martins: Jessica, Ricky, and Craig, just as they were being ushered into another patrol car. Going home at last. Ryan felt his throat begin to tighten. Whatever else happened to him in the future, he thought, he would be able to say with complete certainty that he had done at least one good thing for someone else. That there was one whole day when he had actually been somebody's hero.

Then, as if she had somehow caught the flavor of what he was thinking, Jessica turned and looked directly at him. He smiled and gave her a small nod, expecting her to smile back and then get into the patrol car, followed by her husband who was holding their obviously exhausted son in his arms. Instead, she slipped out from behind the open car door and came over to him.

For a moment, she only stood there looking at him with a fondness that made him feel both proud of himself and embarrassed all at once.

"Are you all right?" she said finally.

Suddenly lost for words, Ryan nodded. He looked over at Craig Martin by the police car with their son in his arms looking as limp as a rag doll, sound asleep. Craig Martin smiled at him with the same fondness that Ryan had seen in Jessica's face and mouthed "thank you."

"You saved our lives," Jessica said and reached over to put a gentle hand on his arm. "Thank you, Ryan." She hesitated, pressing her lips together. "I don't know how I could ever repay you for today."

"I do," Ryan said and broke into a big grin. "No matter what you do or where you go, for the rest of your life, don't ever call me again."

She burst into surprisingly hearty laughter and Ryan laughed with her, getting up so he could give her a hug. All at once he understood that they were linked to each other in a way that they would never share with anyone else. That even though they would lead very different lives in very separate ways, what they were to each other was something no one else could ever match.

She then pulled away from him and went back to her husband and son. Ryan felt Chloe slip her arm around him. They both watched as the Martins hugged each other again before getting into the patrol car.

"You made quite an impression on her, you know," Chloe said, her face smiling and serious at the same time. It was an expression Ryan had seen before, a very special Chloe kind of look; one that he had once been afraid he would never see again.

"Just her?" he asked.

Her smile widened and to his supreme delight, she leaned in to kiss him. But just as her lips were about to touch his, her cellphone rang.

Ryan stared in disbelief as Chloe automatically went to answer it. Before she could get it up to her ear, he plucked it out of her hand and tossed it over his shoulder. Her eyes widened in surprise but then he was kissing her and, from the way she kissed him back, he could tell the subject of phone calls was closed.

Somewhere a world away, a roar of appreciation went up from the concert audience as the band played the last crashing funk-metal chord of their closing number.

"Thank you Los Angeles, and good night!"

Even if he had felt like talking, Ryan thought, still happily lost in Chloe's embrace, the only thing he'd have had to say to that was, "You're welcome."

ABOUT THE AUTHOR

Pat Cadigan, acclaimed by the London Guardian as "The Queen of Cyberpunk," is the author of the novels *Mindplayers*, *Synners*, *Fools*, *Tea from an Empty Cup*, and *Dervish Is Digital*, as well as three short story collections, *Patterns*, *Home By The Sea*, and *Dirty Work*, the nonfiction books, *The Making of Lost In Space* and *The Resurrection of the Mummy*, a young adult novel called *Avatars*, and the media tie-in novel *Lost In Space: Promised Land*.

Since that time her Hugo and Nebula Award-nominated short stories have appeared in such magazines as *Omni*, *The Magazine of Fantasy and Science Fiction*, and Asimov's *Science Fiction Magazine*, as well as numerous anthologies. Her short story *Angel* won the Locus Award in 1988 and her first collection, *Patterns*, won the Locus Award in 1990. To date, she is the first and only writer to have won the Arthur C Clarke Award twice, in 1992 for *Synners* and in 1995 for *Fools*. Cadigan has also written for Black Flame with *Twilight Zone #2: Upgrade/Sensuous Cindy*.

TALES FROM THE TWILIGHT ZONE

ISBN 1-84416-130-7   £6.99 / $7.99

Memphis
A dying man finds himself back in Memphis on the day before Martin Luther King Jr's assassination. Has he been offered a second chance?

The Pool Guy
A pool cleaner finds himself haunted by dreams of his own death, but just what does the VirtuaCorp dream clinic have to do with it?

WWW.BLACKFLAME.COM
TOUGH FICTION FOR A TOUGH PLANET

TALES FROM THE TWILIGHT ZONE

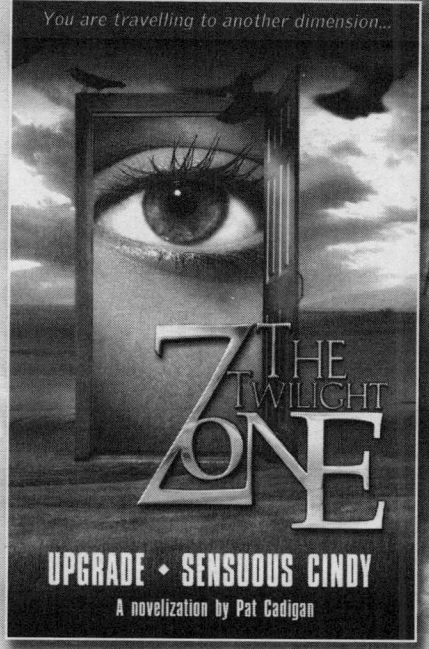

ISBN 1-84416-131-5   £6.99 / $7.99

Upgrade
A harassed mother escapes the mayhem of her home life by fantasizing about the ideal family, but then she wakes up to find her old family has been replaced!

Sensuous Cindy
Ben starts to enjoy the delights of a hot new virtual reality program called Sensuous Cindy. But it isn't really cheating when it's with a computer, is it?

WWW.BLACKFLAME.COM
TOUGH FICTION FOR A TOUGH PLANET

ISBN 1-84416-060-2 £6.99 / $7.99

One of the most terrifying stories in cinematic history is retold in its blood-soaked glory. Read the gruesome truth about what happened in Travis County, Texas when the notorious killer known as 'Leatherface' embarked on his infamous killing spree wielding a deadly chainsaw!

WHAT YOU KNOW ABOUT FEAR DOESN'T EVEN COME CLOSE!

WWW.BLACKFLAME.COM
TOUGH FICTION FOR A TOUGH PLANET

THE BLACK LIBRARY

LET THE GALAXY BURN!

THE AMBASSADOR

DAN ABNETT

IRON HANDS
JONATHAN GREEN

—ENOR

Storming carnage and mayhem from the war-torn far future and a grim world of magic and sweeping battle!

Available from all good bookstores!

For the latest news, free downloadable chapters and loads more, visit
www.blacklibrary.com

READ TILL YOU BLEED

NEWS, ARTICLES, FREE DOWNLOADS,
NOVEL EXTRACTS, ONLINE STORE, PREVIEWS AND MORE...

WWW.BLACKFLAME.COM
TOUGH FICTION FOR A TOUGH PLANET